THE OTHER HALF OF ME

THE OTHER HALF OF ME

MORGAN MCCARTHY

headline
review

First published in Great Britain in 2012 by
HEADLINE PUBLISHING GROUP

1

Cataloguing in Publication Data is available from the British Library

ISBN (HB) 978 0 7553 8873 8
ISBN (TPB) 978 0 7553 8874 5

Typeset in Dante MT by Palimpsest Book Production Limited,
Falkirk, Stirlingshire

Printed and bound in Great Britain by
Clays Ltd, St Ives plc

Headline's policy is to use papers that are natural, renewable
and recyclable products and made from wood grown in sustainable forests.
The logging and manufacturing processes are expected to conform to
the environmental regulations of the country of origin.

HEADLINE PUBLISHING GROUP
An Hachette UK Company
338 Euston Road
London NW1 3BH

www.headline.co.uk
www.hachette.co.uk

For Cian.

ACKNOWLEDGEMENTS

Thanks to Nicole, Diane and Sue for advice, support, and what must have seemed like endless rereads. Thanks to Richard for paper and ink, and to Cian for putting a (half-finished) roof over a struggling writer's head. Thanks to Penny, for having us to stay and introducing us to Carmarthenshire. Thanks to the team at Conville and Walsh: to David Llewelyn for his initial recommendation, and Jo Unwin for all her hard work and good advice. Thanks to Millicent Bennett for her insightful analysis. And many thanks to Leah Woodburn and everyone at Headline for all the work and support that goes into every stage of publication.

2008

It doesn't take long to divide an old life from a new life – a few minutes, not even that. One quick, unfair blow, and you find yourself looking back across the uncrossable, to a place that can't ever be reached again, despite the fact that you were there – brushing your teeth or reading a paper or wondering where you left your umbrella – just a moment ago. But that's over, the kind, old life, and you have to go out into the unknown, unbalanced world, where everything important is wrong. People vanish, the scenery changes. Things you loved become meaningless, and meaningless things stay that way.

Since this happened to me last November, one of the worst things has been the swap between the hemispheres of asleep and awake. I used to shake myself out of my dreams with relief; I would rush into the day and not look back. But now I start to wake up from a dream of my old life, in the uneasy, empty twilight of the morning, and I think *no* all over again, with the same force as the *no* on the telephone that day, standing in the arctic blank of the hotel room, gripping the receiver with my locked-up fingers, as if that could stop her disappearing.

This morning I turn away from it, diving down after my dream, which sinks like a coin falling through dark water, giving a faint flash (sun on glass, a voice) as it turns. The more I try to remember it, the more I wake up, until I am just in bed – lying angrily in the bed, drawing my eyelids open like stiff shutters, onto my new life. The brown walls and carpet of my rented room, the grey light seeping in at the window, the framed picture of a miscellaneous khaki countryside. Then my situation comes back to me; filing in one piece at a time. *I am in England. I am alone.* Trailing along at the end of the queue – a little late, but reliable as always – is the guilt. It settles in with its familiar weight, humming like a faulty appliance. *I was wrong.*

There is a knocking at the door, which must have been what woke me up, knocked my precious dream out of my head. The only person who comes to my door is my landlord, Mr Ramsey. He tends to visit early, which spoils my routine of sleeping for as long as I can, in order to skip as much of the day as possible.

'Mr Anthony?' he calls finally. I imagine him plucking at his cuffs, wondering if I have committed suicide in the night, and how much this might cost him in unpaid rent, paperwork and cleaning bills. 'Are you awake?'

When I go to the door I am startled to see that he has applied an unconvincing smile to his face, like a false moustache, and is holding out a flowered teacup along with the usual Sunday papers.

'Good *morning*, Mr Anthony, I took the liberty of making you tea. I have been meaning to check that your rooms are perfectly satisfactory – no problems, Mr Anthony?'

I look at him uncertainly. Mr Ramsey usually reminds me of a scarecrow, or a Bonfire Night guy – something sagging and stuffed, with his lumpen Argyle jumper and old trousers, creased jowls, curlicues of grey hair. Now something has shaken and patted him into shape; he looks almost lively, watching me intently as I take my tea and papers.

'No, everything is fine,' I say, taking a step back to signal an end to the conversation. But he persists, standing in the doorway saying 'It's a pity about the weather,' rambling through his insights into the weather, the Met Office, the myth of climate change, and back to the weather again, before finally running out of unrequited small talk and retreating back along the brown landing, giving me one last curious look, and vanishing through his beige door.

I sit back down on the edge of my bed, confused, and pick up the paper. A broadsheet now can last me three hours. I used to churn through the newspapers in ten minutes each morning, picking out paragraphs on architectural commissions or awards, but these days I have an excess of time to fill. It wells up, it swells sluggishly, like dough. I read everything: twins joined at the head, who will probably die, nurses in care homes killing the patients, wars in the Middle East. Then, amidst the assorted misfortunes of the world, my own face appears.

It was a picture taken just after I graduated from Cambridge; there was a party, a hired photographer. The day comes back to me: the rain in the morning – even though the sun had come out by the afternoon, we were all sinking into the grass – the awkwardly social lecturers. After the picture I turned to a girl whose name I can't even remember. She kissed me on the mouth, I spilled her champagne.

It hasn't been long since that day, but I find it hard to see myself in this boy. He looks straight into the lens, wearing a pale shirt, his face pared down and exposed, giving nothing away.

The photograph is actually incomplete; Theo was originally standing next to me. I can see what looks like a fault, a fringe of light in the corner to my left – her hair, just visible after the crop. I try to fill in her face, assemble her features, but I can only capture each one in isolation. Narrowed, vagrant eyes, hopeful smile. When we were young she always used to resist having her picture taken; her face in the albums is usually in flight, a blur of heightened colour, mouth downturned. As a result, there was only one framed picture at Evendon of the two of us as children. Theo's face was uncertain, caught briefly in the moment before she moved. She wore a dress like layers of whipped cream, patent-leather shoes. Our mother, Alicia, had always dressed her in those insipid whites and pinks, as if to neutralise her, but the effect was never quite right. Theo's hair was too yellow, her eyes too bright a blue, her lashes too black, like an old photograph where the colour has been added with dyes. In her doll clothes she looked stagey, made-up, like a child star.

In this picture I looked nothing like Theo. My eyes, combed-down hair and eyebrows were almost black. Only a year older than her, I resembled a small forty-year-old, standing stolidly in a grey suit with a little tie, frowning in the flash, in which my face became simple, blocks of light and dark.

I don't go over the print. The headline is enough for me – 'Anthony Heir Missing'. I suppose this explains the obsequious tea-offering of Ramsey, which is unlikely to make him rich. Even if the scale on the surface is ignored, its murky depths do not tempt investigation.

I'll have to move now, away from recognition, the touch of eyes on me, like creeping searchlights. I had felt a sort of safety here. The only other lodgers are two faded old ladies, and a family on a long weekend, who look increasingly puzzled and more subdued as each day brings greater awareness that the 'Sunny Seafront' bed and breakfast is not the charming find of their brochure. The women have a harmless, gentle interest in me; the family ignore me. Yet I felt we had something in common, sitting opposite each other in the breakfast room with its lace tablecloths and antiquated hostess trolley, the light thickened and discoloured like stagnant water; all of us bruised in one way or another, let down by our expectations.

e⌐

I go to the window and look out over the grey sea, where a thin strip of sun has fought its way out from behind the clouds. The sight of it brings the morning's dream back, clear and piercing. I was at Evendon, in the drawing room on a summer afternoon, the doors onto the terrace opened to let in the facing sun, a small procession of petals blown in across the polished squares of light. Outside, I could see Theo and Sebastian sitting on the steps, playing cards. (Sebastian had once tried to teach Theo poker, but she could never learn to bluff: her eyebrows shot up, she giggled, spoke too deliberately.) As if the doorway were a train window, the view beyond it shifted, sped up, stopped. In the next moment of stillness I saw Maria. She was standing with the beach behind her; she was smiling. I could almost smell her perfume in the movement of air off the sea.

Those thoughts are better left forgotten, I know. I haven't thought about Maria since I came here. Remembering her now brings a strange feeling, of old desire, unfamiliar with disuse. I feel the longing I had for her like trying to remember music, a strain here and there, a flute note, touches of sweetness. I try to imagine what she might say to me now, what she would do if she were in my position – but I can't. I used to think I understood her, but I didn't, not at all.

eↄ

Later, I think about Eve. She was absent from the dream, but then her absence always was a stark space, forcing the eye to notice it. What would she say, if she found me here? *I expected better of you, Jonathan.* I see myself as she would see me, the grandson of Eve Anthony, mouldering in damp brown anonymity, in undignified grief.

Eve, standing – as she always seems to now – within the confines of a film reel, asks me: *What good can the past do the living?* She has her arms folded; her dark mouth glitters under the lights of photography, which swirl and condense around her like sparks.

But I have nowhere else to go, I tell her. Eve has nothing to say to this. She blinks her glossy black eyes, hardening like tar. She shrugs.

PART ONE

1988

e⁓

. . . so we beat on, boats against the current,
borne back ceaselessly into the past.
F. Scott Fitzgerald, *The Great Gatsby*

ONE

When I look back for a place to start, I always think of the same day – a day that didn't seem unusual at the time, but was necessary to what came next. It is the last day of a backwards trajectory: I arrive at it as if tracing a thrown ball back through the air to the spot where the thrower stood. At the time, of course, you don't know that a ball was thrown. You hear the glass smash, then you rush to the window and look out, trying to see the culprit.

This particular day begins with a summer morning; the lawn burning green, the new, nectared sunlight. I was nearly eight years old, sitting on the grass next to a patch of earth, having uprooted some irises to clear room for a castle made out of Lego blocks. I could see the top of Theo's head through the remaining flowers. She was picking up ladybirds and snails and putting them lovingly into a toy pram, keeping up a gentle monologue of chatter and song that – unusually – didn't seem to need my participation, and which I had mainly tuned out.

Behind us the house sat indistinctly, the sun dazzling off its many windows, too bright to look at without squinting. Evendon, built sometime in the gloomy fifteenth century and embellished in the ambitious nineteeth by a slightly insane ancestor, was nothing like the other manors in Carmarthenshire, pale and genteel and homogenous. It was grey – all different darknesses of grey – steeply slate-roofed, with crow-stepped gables, pale cornerstones, black and white facings on the eaves, arched windows with white brick edging. It resembled an Escher palace for a witch, baroque and severe, sometimes beautiful, sometimes absurd – overly grand – standing out like a hallucination in the tame planes of the garden. Even to us there was something odd about it.

At this early time in the morning Evendon held only two people, both of whom were still asleep. The first was our mother, Alicia. She didn't like us much. That is not to say that she disliked us; she just didn't seem to have enough energy to feel one way or the other. The second was our nanny, Miss Black, who genuinely disliked us.

The rest of the house's inhabitants would arrive as the morning went on: Mrs Wynne Jones the housekeeper, Mrs Williams the cook, then the temporary maids and gardeners whose names were never in currency long enough to be remembered. It was in these people that the hurry and noise of Evendon was contained; they took it home with them in the evening and brought it back in the morning, and so for the moment everything was still, as if no one was in the house at all. Theo and I, on our hill with the silent house on one side and only the end of the rising grass and a strip of distant sea on the other, could have been all alone at the top of the world.

Theo broke off from singing to her collection of insects and called, 'Jonathan?'

Her face floated up over the flowers, one hand waving. Her nose was already red from the morning sun.

'Jonathan?' she asked. 'Do you think bees get hot? With all their fur?'

By the time I realised she was holding up a bee for me to see it had twisted, fizzing with outrage, and stung her. She stared at me for a moment, her mouth fallen open and her finger pointing as if she were in the middle of a speech. Then she clutched her hand and started to cry.

I tugged Theo back to the house to find Alicia, who had woken up and was now sitting in the shade in the drawing room reading a magazine. Her blonde hair was almost colourless in the sudden dim, her eyes like raindrops, cool and vague. She looked at us with languid surprise when we ran in, Theo gulping and gasping nearly silently, holding her hand out like something in flames.

'What on earth are you two doing?' Alicia asked.

'Theo got stung by a bee,' I explained. Theo held up her finger and Alicia peered unwillingly at it.

'Oh dear . . . Miss Black!' she called. 'Miss Black! How awful.'

Miss Black failed to appear, but in the kitchen we discovered the newly arrived Mrs Williams, who was in the process of transferring lasagne from its supermarket packaging into a baking dish. She jumped when she saw us and put her hand over her heart.

'You two are going to kill me one of these days,' she said. 'Not a word to your ma about this now. Though I don't know how people expect me to do everything. Think I'm bloody Superwoman or something. I've got problems of my own, I have.' She paused and noticed Theo's distress. 'What's up with you, lovey?'

Theo held her hand out again and Mrs Williams looked at it

with satisfaction, as if she had previously warned us to watch out for bees and was now vindicated. This expression of hers was a familiar one: worn at nearly every household mishap.

'*That*,' she said, 'is a bad sting. What we need for that is lemon juice. Or vinegar. It neutrifies the sting.'

We followed her to the fridge, where she found some lemon vinaigrette and doused the finger with it until Theo stopped gasping, and screamed.

'Is that wasps, then?' said Mrs Williams. 'I don't remember what it is for bees.'

When Theo's finger was rinsed and plastered and her sobs had subsided, we hung around the kitchen while Mrs Williams lit a cigarette. She had a lighter in the shape of a matador, which she told us her son Gareth had brought her from a holiday. She let us click its feet to make flames come out of the top of its head, and gave us some of her extra-strong mints. Then she sat back and put her feet on a stool and puffed speculatively. Mrs Williams was around fifty, a short, round woman with bright yellow hair, which was frazzled and acrylic-looking. She had indeterminate numbers of children and other relatives, who she would tell us about in the same way as she discussed the characters in soap operas, so that it was impossible to tell which were real and which fictional. 'Whatever you say about Gareth, he's good to his ma,' she said now. 'It were those . . . those *solicitors* that were the problem.'

Theo was sitting at the counter, her face tightly crimped.

'Does your finger still hurt?' I asked.

Theo shook her head, then started crying again. 'Why was that bee angry with me?'

'It wasn't angry with *you*,' I said, carefully, aware that if I told

Theo that she'd frightened the bee she'd be even more upset and I'd have to play by myself.

'Was it angry because it was hot?' Theo asked. 'Because of its fur?'

'Yes,' I said. 'I suppose so. Do you want to go back outside now?'

Theo cried even harder. 'That poor bee,' she sobbed. 'Why does it have so much fur?'

I considered telling her that the bee would be dead now anyway after losing its sting, but thought better of it. 'Do you want to go back outside and play?' I asked again.

'You two better play inside now, with that sunburn,' Mrs Williams said to Theo, smoke rising around her face as if she were some kind of ancient oracle. 'And you – keep an eye on your sister. Letting her get herself stung!'

This was so unfair that I decided not to answer, a punishment that went unnoticed by Mrs Williams, who had already switched the television onto her favourite show and was soaking up its fractious noises, her head tilted to one side like a canary. 'Don't tell me *she's* the murderer!' she exclaimed.

'Come on, Theo. We can play in the library,' I said, helping myself to another mint.

As we left, Mrs Williams said, 'Families ought to look out for each other,' though whether this was intended for me or the television, I really couldn't say.

e⌒

In the library at Evendon, where Theo and I piled books to make leathery castles or pushed at the shelves to find the magical one that would revolve us into a black and secret corridor, our ancestors could be found. They had once gazed majestically over the staircase, but in a past act of irreverence someone (Eve) had demoted them to the library, where there wasn't quite enough space, and so the walls were crammed with paintings of the dead Bennetts, with the longest-dead beginning at the door and my great-grandparents tailing off into a corner.

Miss Black had shown us the pictures of our great-grandfather George and his wife Louisa Bennett. She told us that George was a famous archaeologist, who had discovered Mayan temples in the rainforests of Honduras and was buried at Westminster Abbey. 'Only very important people are buried there,' she said, managing to imply that George's greatest achievement had been his admittance to London's most exclusive soil. Similarly, the only thing Miss Black could remember Louisa doing was dying, before she was even thirty. 'She was a very ill woman,' she said, with disapproval.

Louisa Bennett looked vaguely guilty in her picture; perhaps for being ill. She was sitting very straight but looked cautious, unsure of her right to canvas. Next to her, George stood with one hand resting on a jewelled skull. He had a block-shaped face with a moustache, and small, square blue eyes. He looked impatient.

Sometimes Mrs Williams would tell us different stories about our family. There was the story of how George's father Sir James Bennett spent all the family money, drinking and drinking until his parents died of disappointment, before dying himself, drunk, falling off a horse he had been jumping over a fence for a bet. But – she added – the thing about Sir James was his kind heart. He didn't think he was too good to sit and talk to the locals at the pub, something George would never have done. Then there was the story about Louisa being nothing more than the daughter of someone who made pencils ('Married her for her money, see'). She explained to me that George made all the family's money back and more ('more money than was right') but that the same bad luck got him in the end.

'It was that staircase out there,' Mrs Williams said, inclining her head in the direction of the marble-floored entrance hall with its twin pillars and the curling staircase that divided in two, like the mouth of a giant long-petrified snake, stone teeth and forked stone tongue. 'Now one day – don't you go telling your sister this and upsetting her – one day, he must have tripped when he was going down it, and that was it, he went cartwheeling all the way down. There's no stopping. You only stop when you get to the bottom. And what do you think happened to your great-grandfather then?'

'What happened?'

Mrs Williams paused and lit her cigarette. She knew how to draw a story out when she wanted to.

'He was *dead*, that's what,' she said. 'They found him dead at the bottom of the stairs.'

The most beautiful of the family portraits was separated from the Bennetts in the library, because it was the only image of a living person: Sir James's granddaughter, George and Louisa Bennett's daughter, Alicia's mother, and our grandmother. Eve Anthony.

Her picture hung in the dining room, gazing down at the table with watchful benevolence, as lovely as Snow White with her black hair and pale skin, her eyes tapering to points like arrow-heads. Her dress was such a bright, wounded red that even though I had grown up under the picture, I always glanced up at the unexpected colour when I went into the room.

Eve owned Evendon, though neither Theo nor I, who had lived here as long as we could remember, had ever met her. She had inherited the estate after her father died, but had left for America instead, and it was more than twenty years before she came back, after her second marriage had ended. She found the house filled with mice and mildew, said Miss Black; almost everything had to be thrown away, the woodworm-mazed floorboards burned, the damp plaster scourged from the walls. All that was left was a floor-less, windowless house, like a skeleton. Then she waved her wand of money at it and turned into a palace, filled with chimerical treasure. She decorated the morning room in red silk, with Turkish carpets and two carved Great Dane-sized elephants from India (given to Eve back in the seventies by an infatuated rajah), gilded with real gold. The chandelier-hung drawing room was cream, filled with bowls of lilies and roses, ivory damask fauteuils perched in gatherings like doves. She lined the disused library with shelves of glassed-over books, put the long walnut table and its stately guard of chairs into the dining room.

Then, only a few years later, she left again, called back to America by the siren song of international business, leaving her rooms locked until the day when she would be back. No one seemed to have much faith in this day. Miss Black said it wasn't likely Eve would want to live in the middle of Wales. (She said 'middle of Wales' in the same way as Mrs Williams said 'high-flyin'.' 'Too high-flyin', Mrs Anthony is, to come back here.')

What we knew of Eve, living as we did in her ghostly footprint, was all second-hand. We were told that she was a famous tycoon now but had been a politician in America a long time ago. Miss Black showed us television footage of a speech she gave: Eve – she was US Representative Eve Nicholson then – standing on a platform in crackling, slightly off colours, her hair set into doll-like waves. It was her portrait brought to life; we watched entranced. The recording turned her motions stately; talking, then waving from her platform, across the stiffness of time. Her voice preserved in amber, round and smooth. We were not told much about what she actually *did*; it was the standing on the platform that was supposed to be significant. Miss Black said that Eve led the way for women who came after her.

'Are there a lot of women like that now?' I asked.

'It's not the numbers that are important so much as the . . . principle.' said Miss Black.

Eve had also appeared on television in her most recent incarnation: Eve Anthony, the philanthropist and hotel magnate. The significance of these titles, and of her company, Charis, was lost on me. We saw her on the news cutting a ribbon outside a large building, wearing a white suit. Except for her hair, which was in a cohesive curl to her shoulders, she looked the same as in the earlier film. Her eyes dipped and rose seriously as she said to the camera, 'Yes, I have a personal love of restoring the past; of bringing something back that might otherwise be abandoned.'

Then there were the Eves we saw every day: the misty debutante Eve Bennett framed in the drawing room in her full-skirted cream dress, Eve Nicholson in a pale blue hat and pearls in the morning room, the Eve Anthony Theo found in a magazine, with her blazing smile, standing with another, less beautiful woman wearing a crown. I couldn't feel like this person was my grandmother. She reminded me more of Theo's paper dolls with their cut-out wardrobes, endlessly dressed and re-dressed. She too was multiple, always two-dimensional, always with the same face, the dark irises, the red and white mouth. When Theo was younger, she regarded Eve as a creature of fairy tale, a sparkling Tooth Fairy ('Can Eve fly?' she asked. 'Can she vanish?') and I wasn't sure that she even believed in her now. But then, the more Eves I saw, the harder it was to believe in her – not because she didn't seem real; it was that she was *too* real, more real than anything else.

e~

Later in the day I judged – correctly – that Mrs Williams would have forgotten that she had told us not to play outside, so we went back out into the hot, still afternoon, moving out of sight of the windows and wandering beyond the long reaches of the gardens into the arches and gullies of the woods, where we unearthed various fascinating relics: a child's wheelbarrow turned over in the tall ferns and completely covered in rust, an evening glove, a dead crow, a pair of scissors, all nearly vanished in the undergrowth.

The greatest discovery came at the end of the day. Our explorations had brought us to the beginning of a paved path that led from the grass into what appeared to be impenetrable ferns and trees. We fetched sticks and shears and cleared our way into the woods, kicking at the roots and weeds that laced the regular stones. As we got further in, the light of the sun faded, breaking through the willows and birch only in a haze flaring around the leaves, becoming cool and distant.

'Where are we going?' Theo asked from behind me.

'We're just following the path,' I told her. 'To see where it goes.'

'Maybe we'll end up in heaven,' Theo said. (She had heard the Lord's Prayer recently, and was not to be persuaded that heaven was not a tangible place, something that could easily be found just up the road, near Laugharne or St Clears – except with less rain perhaps, and more chocolate.)

After a protracted struggle through the flail and scratch of the briars, tripping on tree roots and drunken paving stones, we broke free from the trees into a clearing at the edge of a large expanse of water. The pool was oddly radiant with the green and silver light, covered in water lilies, underneath which small, murky fish could be seen. Around it there were ruins: the stone-paved path visible under the nettles, a marble nymph on a pedestal, leaning morosely to one side, ivy wrapped around her pale neck. It was a strange place, long ago choked off from the gardens, hushed under the pressure of abandonment.

'Does somebody live here?' Theo asked me, touching the nymph's frozen hair cautiously.

'No,' I said, without confidence.

'This isn't heaven, is it?'

'No.'

We tried to walk around to the far side of the pool to see

where it ended, but the way was blocked by nettles and brambles. Then we tried and failed to catch the fish, lying on our stomachs and sneaking our hands through the water, until the light turned evening-coloured and mosquitoes massed ominously above us. Green-stained and disappointed, we tried to find the original path through the trees back to the house, but as the light had faded, the scenery had reshaped itself, so that what had once been a clearing was now a willow tree, what had been a willow was a cluster of ferns, and where there had been a cluster of ferns was only darkness.

'Are we lost?' Theo asked. I tucked away my own uncertainty and said, 'Don't be stupid. It's this way.'

I plunged into a corridor between the trees and found myself on a steep, wrong path, Theo following silently, so that all we could hear was the whining sally of mosquitoes, the crackle of the undergrowth, our own worried breathing. The track sent us upwards, blocked our way, twisted us back and around, then finally relented and dropped us down, where we found ourselves back in familiar land, on the old stone paving of the original path.

'I told you we weren't lost,' I said, pompous with relief. 'Here's the path. Here's the yellow ivy, and the missing paving stone, and the old oak. Just like I remembered.'

Theo gazed around with admiration. 'You *are* clever, Jonathan.' She jumped from paving stone to paving stone, arms out, ending at the oak with a cry of delight. 'Did you write that for us? A secret message?'

'What?'

She pointed at the tree, where – deeply, scoring through the cracks and gullies of its crocodilian skin – someone had carved a heart. It was old and its lines were grey and vague with lichen, but the letters laid out inside were still readable. MC. AA.

'What does it mean?' Theo said, touching it.

'I didn't do that,' I said, wondering at it. 'It must have been our parents.' I ran my finger around the border of the heart. It occurred to me that this abandoned graffiti, something our father probably forgot about almost as soon as he had finished it, was the only real thing we had left of him.

Our father – Michael Caplin – had left the week after Theo was born and only a year after I was born. Miss Black, who had never met him, said that he went to Australia, where he died in a car accident. Nobody talked about him; he was missing from even the wide-ranging, richly populated gossip of Mrs Williams. Whatever I asked Alicia about him, her answer was always the same; she frowned and said she couldn't remember, and after a while I stopped asking. There were no photographs of him; no groom standing next to a flowery-haired Alicia, no new dad holding a bottle or nappy with game bafflement. Some kind of tornado had destroyed this early time, flinging out nothing salvageable. After the tornado hit there was no Eve and no father. Eve was back in America, being a business tycoon and philanthropist; our father – MC – had been carried away for good.

e

When we emerged from the trees, disentangling ourselves from the last of the brambles, the sky had become a dark, deep blue, with a glowing paleness streaking up from the horizon. A few lanterns were lit, the stones of the terrace glowing and shivering in their faulty luminescence. The lawns we passed were a strange green, waved like a sea blown with the wind off the trees, which carried in it the heavy sweetness of the roses.

I had thought that we might be in trouble, but it was as if some time dilation had occurred in the house, and Alicia and Miss Black were just as we had left them hours before. The arrival of the Sunday newspapers, read and then dropped, had turned the gold parlour at the back of the house into a wasteland of scattered pages like dead birds; the two women themselves were draped, nearly motionless, on the sofas.

'We found the secret lake,' Theo announced.

'A lake?' Alicia said, glancing up. 'A lake or a pond?'

'A large pond,' I said.

'Oh, a large pond.' She thought for a moment. 'No . . . I don't think there's anything like that here.'

'A small lake, then.'

'I've never seen a small lake,' said Alicia, turning to Miss Black. 'Have you?'

'I hope you're not making up stories again,' Miss Black said to us.

Miss Black was young and plump like a gingerbread figure, with her thick plait and little raisin eyes, but if she was gingerbread she was cold and uncooked; her fullness was not comforting. She never smiled at us, only at Alicia, who she liked to talk to. They would discuss Alicia's friends' love affairs and marriages in scientific, bored voices, as if they themselves had transcended such things.

Mrs Williams came in at that moment with the tea, as if she

had just appeared and had not, in fact, been hovering behind the door eavesdropping, and said, 'I know that pool. It's not safe, that place. That's where Eve fell in years and years ago, when she was little. Wandering about by herself, see. Had to be rescued by a gardener.' She put Miss Black's tea down so it spilled down the side of the cup. (In her opinion – she had told us in the kitchen – Miss Black should get her own bloody tea.)

'So anyway,' said Miss Black, 'you two should stay away from that pool.' She put on a strict voice for the benefit of Alicia, who had stopped listening and had picked up her magazine again.

'Didn't you write in the tree, Mama?' Theo asked. 'Did you and Daddy' – this 'Daddy' was a new addition to her vocabulary, and had an experimental feel – 'write in the tree?'

'What on earth are you talking about?' Alicia asked, quicker than usual, so that Miss Black looked up at her with surprise.

'*Daddy*,' Theo repeated. 'His name is in the tree. And your name.'

There was a short pause, then Alicia frowned and said, 'You aren't making any sense at all, Theodora. You two should go and play somewhere else. Quietly.'

Theo was reddening with hurt, so I took her arm and tugged her out of the room. 'Come on. There wasn't much point talking to *them* about it anyway.'

'What do you think of alligator, Alicia?' Miss Black asked, behind us.

'Vulgar,' said Alicia.

We went to the pool every day after that, though we never managed to catch any of the fish. I liked it there, the odd, foggy personality of the water, the unknown depth of it, the broken-backed trees. Then the initialled tree, like a marker, or the lamp post of *The Lion, the Witch and the Wardrobe*, showing the way to the open door. It seemed suitable – nicely unsettling – that the place had the story of a near-drowning, of *Eve*'s near-drowning. Like the marble staircase that our great-grandfather George fell down, these places of death and almost-death brought our missing antecedents nearer to us, even if it was just as ghosts, haunting their former home. I didn't tell Theo this thought, however – it being the kind of thing that upset her.

Towards the end of the summer our Uncle Alex came to visit. It was the first time we had seen him in a few years. Alex was Alicia's older brother and was a doctor of something at a university. I didn't realise that not all doctors practised medicine, and when I found out before his visit that he would not be bringing a stethoscope, my disappointment was sour and intense. I was slightly suspicious of the doctorate itself, and felt Alex might be something of a fraud.

Mrs Williams was of a similar mind. 'Sociology,' she said to Mrs Wynne Jones. 'What's sociology when it's at home?'

'It's *actually* a science,' said Mrs Wynne Jones. 'My Jane is studying it for A level.'

'Well, it sounds like a silly sort of science to me,' Mrs Williams said conclusively. (She had told me and Theo more than once that Mrs Wynne Jones was a stuck-up cow – and for no reason, because her husband only worked at the petrol station.)

The age difference between Alex and Alicia was only a couple of years, but Alex, with grey staining his hair and frown lines barring his forehead, seemed much older. His eyes were a worn china blue behind his glasses, his skin the off-white colour of clay, as if he were a recently unearthed artefact, only just exposed to the light. He greeted me and Theo diffidently, as if unsure of how to handle us, looking between us and Alicia as if she might explain us better, but Alicia only murmured something about the weather being tiresome, and that Alex really needn't have come all the way down to Wales from Oxford – which I thought was a pretty pointless thing to say, seeing as he was already here.

I felt not quite affection but a sort of gentle pity for Alex, his frangible ceramic body and his awkwardness with us, as if we weren't children but something more important, more worrying. It was a strange moment, then, when his eyes were reluctantly towed into contact with mine, and I realised that he had been avoiding looking at us not out of awkwardness, but because he felt pity too – and I was confused, because I had no idea what he could pity us for.

After the initial small talk of arrival, Alex and Alicia didn't seem to have much to say to each other. They just occupied the same rooms, cooling the air with their pale eyes and making occasional comments such as 'The rain seems slightly less heavy today,' until the night arrived and Theo and I were sent gratefully away.

At the time it used to be one of mine and Theo's games to pretend to go to bed, then sneak out of our rooms later and camp in one of the house's hiding places: under a spare bed, under the dining table. (Really, it wasn't much of a game, as Miss Black never noticed we weren't in bed, but we didn't know this yet and our camping was delicious with the fear of being found.) That night we had dragged our pillows and bedclothes down to the morning room, and made ourselves a nest behind one of the sofas.

Theo fell asleep first, and I was half asleep myself when Alex and Alicia walked in and turned the lights on. I contracted, in a panic, but they didn't see me and sat down at the other side of the room. Alicia was saying something I couldn't hear, to which Alex said, 'She *will* come back.'

I slowly extended my head out from behind the arm of the sofa to see my mother refilling her glass from the decanter, not answering.

'What are you going to do when she does? Just keep on pretending that nothing happened?'

There was a pause, and then Alicia said, 'I don't understand what you mean.'

'Bullshit.'

'Please don't use that language.'

'Fine. We don't have to discuss it. Business as usual. I don't know how you stand it, that's all. How you remember what to lie about. Where, so to speak, all the *bodies* are—'

Alicia put her glass down with a sharp noise, and Alex stopped speaking. There was a while of silence, after which Alicia sighed and picked up the glass again. It was hard to tell from the sigh whether she was angry, or sad, or tired. They were quiet for a long time, then Alex continued more gently, 'Remember when we were young, in that big house in California. Remember the maid? Leonie? I'd love to know where she is now. She always used to sing us that song . . . you used to dance to it . . . how did it go?'

Alicia shrugged and sipped her drink. She looked very beautiful in the light suspended from the chandeliers, the dusk coming in at the window; her eyes lowered so the lashes formed shadows on her cheeks. The ice chimed against the side of her glass.

'I'm afraid I can't remember any of the maids,' she said.

e

I tried not to fall asleep, in case Alex and Alicia said something to explain what Alicia might lie about, or what bodies might be hidden, or whether Eve was the person who might come back, but they didn't, and I couldn't help myself. I rested my head on the cushions and my thoughts folded in on themselves like cake mixture, heavy and soft, unformed shapes.

I carried on thinking about Eve, who I was familiar with only in the past or future tense; the ways everyone spoke about her. The only place she didn't exist was the aimless present, where we all lived under the sense of her absence, dried out and husked by Evendon's silence, the feeling that something important was missing. Because it wasn't just Eve, it was all of the lost people of Evendon: our great-grandfather George, in the corridors of the ruined temple with his flashlight; our father, carving his initials carefully into a tree. Eve was the one who had known them, heading a pantheon of characters more vivid than Alicia, who wouldn't answer anything, and Alex, who looked at me with pity.

I wondered what would happen to Evendon if Eve came back, but sleepiness was obscuring her image, switching it in and out of focus. Eve in her painting like Snow White, holding an apple, Eve standing on her podium like a statue, in the moment before she began to speak, Eve turning and smiling, the professional shimmer of her teeth in the camera's – in my own – unblinking eye.

Alex went back home the next morning, with an abrupt kiss on the cheek for Alicia, who accepted the contact with her usual mild distaste, and an uncertain ruffle of the head for Theo and me. After the door closed, the three of us stood in the hall for a silent moment before Alicia turned and went back up to bed.

'Uncle Alex doesn't like it here,' Theo said.

'Of course he does.' I was defensive of Evendon. 'He wouldn't visit if he didn't.'

'But he only comes once a year. And no one else visits us.' Theo spun on the marble with her arms out, hair flying. 'We visit other people. Like for birthday parties. But we don't have our own birthday parties.'

She said all this matter-of-factly, inexperienced in the art of resentment. But I was older and further along; I silently hopscotched the next steps. People didn't come to Evendon because Alicia didn't want them to come. Eve never came. Therefore, this was likely to be Alicia's fault.

That afternoon I went to find Alicia, who was having her usual rest in her room. I knew we weren't meant to disturb her at these times, but I also knew that no one had ever specifically told us this, so I pushed the door a little way open and slid along it and into the room like an eel. The curtains were closed, but they were white, like the walls and the sheets on the bed, so the room was filled with a dull, pale shade, like clotted light. Alicia was lying on her bed on top of the sheets, her eyes open. She was wearing an oyster-coloured dress and a string of pearls, almost the same colour as her skin, as if she were herself a pearl in a shell. She rested her head on one hand to avoid disturbing her hair, and turned it to look at me. Her eyes were slow and distant.

'What are you doing in here?' she asked without altering her tone, so that it sounded as if she wasn't actually asking a question.

'When is Eve going to visit us?' I asked.

There was a pause, before the dreamy dissipation of Alicia's gaze abruptly clarified, like dust blown off a glass surface.

'Have you spoken to her? Did she call here?' she demanded.

'No . . .' I was surprised by the change in her, her bare eyes still fixed on me. 'I was just wondering.'

Alicia turned her head away so that she was looking at the ceiling. 'Good,' she said, and said something to herself I couldn't hear.

As I hadn't actually been sent away, and Alicia seemed in an odd, reactive mood, I lingered by the bed. The room itself was nearly empty; no photographs, no pictures, no stray clothes or shoes to indicate that a woman might inhabit this space. The only personal objects in the room aside from the two of us were a carafe, a glass of water by the bed and a paper packet that I read sideways: Valium. Diazepam.

I looked again at Alicia. Usually I would have heard one of her standard three responses now: I can't remember. I have a headache. I don't understand what you are talking about. But she just lay there, eyes pointing upwards.

'You don't want her back,' I said.

Alicia laughed, a dry, white rustle, and said without looking at me, 'I don't decide anything. It isn't up to me. She does what she wants to do. She wouldn't care whether I wanted her here or not.'

Then the spell that had been on her broke – with a blink – and she was herself again. She looked at me as if I had only just arrived.

'I have a headache,' she said, with cold tiredness, and waved me away. 'Shut the door quietly after you.'

TWO

In September, Theo and I went back to pre-prep, a small school a half-hour drive away. Each morning the weather out of the car window became cooler and greyer, until most days the window itself would be covered in rain. We saw the familiar hills of Carmarthenshire through a lens of water, thinner, wiped of colour.

I liked school; it was a warm circle of brightness, stuck together with glue and Sellotape, a perfect papier-mâché globe. I had formed a ruling partnership of this tiny world with the small-headed and noisy Charlie Tremayne; we directed ball games in the playground and deconstructed the props of our lessons: potato clocks, plastic skeletons. Charlie's marks suffered for our bad behaviour; mine did not.

I didn't see Theo very much at school, partly because we weren't in the same classes, partly because I had banned her from bothering me and my friends. At lunch she sat with a table of girls from her year, whispering and giggling just like the others, indistinguishable aside from her hair, a little dazzle of blonde. Despite my school rules, I'd often feel her watching me hopefully, waiting for me to turn around so she could wave, her smile full-blown like a white sail, excited just to have been noticed.

ℰ

After Christmas, Charlie Tremayne came to stay with us. His own parents were going to Antigua and his nanny had apparently insisted on taking two weeks off over the holidays. 'How awful,' Alicia sighed on the telephone to Anne Tremayne. Our own Miss Black had no such demanding social life and arrived back promptly on Boxing Day, so Alicia was unruffled about the prospect of another child in the house. 'It won't be any trouble,' she said to Miss Black.

Charlie Tremayne, the playground hero, didn't translate so well at Evendon. He was too shrill, too effortful. I found myself looking forward to the end of his visit.

'Have you two seen any horror films yet?' he asked us. 'I saw one at the cinema last week. It was about zombies.'

'You're too young,' I said, to stop him telling Theo about it.

'They let me in anyway,' Charlie said. He had also told us that a week ago he caught a cobra in his garden. 'I let it go,' he added.

Finally I offered to take him to the secret pool, where I hoped to enjoy the necessary silence of fishing. We hadn't been since the summer, mainly because Theo didn't want to, and after making her go with me a few times (when she would sit, uneasily, and wait for us to leave), I had given up.

'Oh no, let's not,' she said now. 'Mrs Williams says it's haunted.'

'But no one drowned there. You shouldn't have told her we went back there. She's just trying to put us off.'

'*Please*, Jonathan,' Theo said. 'It's night-time . . . it's scary. Let's not.'

We looked outside, where the gardens had almost vanished

into the darkly drawn-down evening and the horizon shone a fiery white edge at the rim of the hill. The view was suddenly unfamiliar, as inky and cold as the bottom of the sea.

'I don't mind doing something else,' said Charlie.

'Scared?' I said, hitting him on the arm.

'Don't be stupid,' he snapped, shoving me in the back as I opened the door and led us out, Theo trailing miserably behind. 'You don't have to come,' I said to her, but she only shook her head, because no matter how much she hated what I was doing, to not be able to follow me was the worse option. As we crossed the terrace I looked through the windows into the bright morning room. Miss Black was facing away from us and Alicia was falling asleep, her hand sagging around her glass. Neither of them noticed us go. The thin air had the tang of frost in it; the winter evening furled over us, a thick clouded dark. The grass tugged wetly at our shoes as we got closer to the beginning of the trees.

'If I saw a ghost I'd punch its head off,' Charlie said. '*Baff.*' He mimed a punch, then stuck his hands in his pockets and started whistling. I didn't know how to whistle, though I had tried, and the sound – high and hostile – irritated me.

We got to the trees and forced our way through the ferns to the alleyway of willows, the dark, pewtery tunnel lit by faint patches of evening light, like a subterranean goblin path. We looked for the initialled oak but it was too dark to find it, and Charlie wasn't interested anyway ('Sounds stupid'). When we reached the pool it was glimmering and quiet, reflecting the dark sky like an old, spotted mirror. It seemed different now that the summer had withdrawn, taking all its light and friendliness back. There was something damp and burdensome in the air, catching at our skin. When we stood still, we could hear water moving slowly, the sodden, prickling sound of the moss.

'So . . . this is our pool,' I said uncertainly.

'What if the ghost comes out?' Theo asked, holding onto the sleeve of my jumper. 'What if it doesn't want us here?' I shook her hand off.

'There's no ghost, Theo. Shut up.'

'We'll see its face through the trees.' Theo pointed to where the darkness was thickest on the far side of the water, so dark it was only a heavy emptiness, the virulent colour of a bruise. We all stopped talking to listen to the low creaks and scuffles of the leaves and branches shifting in the dispirited wind. The dim light rose and fell in pieces above us. Theo looked around nervily until Charlie caught the unease and started doing the same. I made a scornful 'pfff' sound, which was promptly gulped up by the dark.

'We'll see it looking around . . . staring with its enormous ghost eyes – looking for us,' she continued. 'And then it'll see us . . . and it will reach out with its horrid claws, because it's hungry, and it's angry . . . and then – it will float right out and *get* us.'

This pronouncement was rewarded with a loud cracking noise in the trees behind us, and we all jumped.

'The ghost!' Charlie yelped, turned, and ran. Theo followed him, wailing. I sauntered after them at first, then, looking behind me, I scurried out too, until we all got to the edge of the trees and ran as fast as we could down the hill, sliding and tripping and starting to laugh. Evendon, reassuringly, was just below us, its windows coloured with interior light, and we ran towards it.

Charlie and I, energised, chased along the grass and gave Red

Indian howls, leaping and shoving each other. Theo hung back until I stopped and waited for her.

'Cheer up.' I buffeted her shoulder and ran around her in circles, until her smile uncertainly hovered, unfolded, and finally was restored to full beam. But she said later, reflectively, 'That scary person nearly got us.'

'What is it – a ghost or a person?'

'A ghost person. A dead person. We shouldn't go back there.'

After that night Theo refused to go anywhere near the pool. It was the first time she'd been prepared to separate herself from me – a shadow pulling her feet free – but if I went without her, it was with the guilty knowledge that she would be at home; not playing by herself, but waiting at the window for me to come back. And though I didn't like to admit it, the pool wasn't so much fun alone, muffled with the cold quiet of winter, broken only by the occasional flurry of wind through the dry remanants of leaves, hissing and sudden, so that in the end I abandoned the whole thing – pool and fish and tree and ruins – and didn't go again.

❧

After Christmas something changed in Alicia, as if an oddity had appeared in her tranquil glassiness, a chip only seen from certain angles. She still read the same magazines, but she frowned at them, or stared at a page for a long time, and I could tell she wasn't reading. Sometimes she was snappish; she asked Mrs Williams why her food was burnt or undercooked, rather than just leaving it on the plate as she used to. Her face was not so still as it once was; there was a drawn-up energy about her, puckering and fraught, disturbing her smooth forehead.

I took it upon myself to encourage this developing fault in my mother. I cut all the heads off her roses, which she didn't appear to notice, though Miss Black did, and I got no pocket money for a week. Then I set one of her hats floating in the bath with a crew of Action Men. Alicia said to Miss Black, 'I don't understand how children can be so destructive,' and lowered her eyebrows vaguely when she saw me over the next few days. For this I went without pocket money for another two weeks, though Theo spent all her own money buying me sweets. But I was encouraged by the response. Through all this I had no clear purpose; I didn't know why I wanted to heighten the pressure – to provoke a raised voice, even a slap.

My *pièce de résistance* was to dress an obedient Theo in Alicia's silk scarf, gloves and white fur coat, take her to the steepest slope of the garden, and roll her down it. She vanished in a white blur, like a dandelion head, and hit the mud at the bottom with force. Then I escorted her back to the house, Theo dripping and high-spirited, and me quiet, with the adrenalin-tasting anticipation of rage to come.

Things after that didn't go as planned. Miss Black gasped when she saw us; overawed by the gravity of the crime, she took us straight to Alicia, who was napping in the morning room. Her lower lip had dropped slightly ajar; a magazine lolled out of her hands. When Miss Black said, 'Excuse me, Alicia?' she woke up suddenly, her mouth snapping back into line.

'Is there a problem?' she said to Miss Black, who explained what we'd done, holding out one of the sullied gloves like a dead pet. Alicia frowned at it. She turned away and looked out of the window for a while, as if she had asked a question and was waiting for the window to answer. She didn't look at me or Theo.

'I wasn't sure what to do . . .' Miss Black said eventually.

'Just keep them out of my rooms,' Alicia replied. 'Isn't that why you're here?' The sound of her voice was peculiar – not angry, not anything. Just an echo, on a blank wall.

Miss Black was surprised by the reprimand; I heard her crying in her room later that night. Neither Theo nor I got any pocket money for a month as punishment, to pay for the cleaning bill. I told Theo that this was the reason we had to behave better from now on, which was a lie. Really it was the thought of Alicia saying 'keep them out of my rooms'; the stillness of her voice, the pale ellipse of her face like an empty bowl, turned away from the small Jonathan, waiting wrong and unwanted.

'Sorry, Jonathan,' Theo said, as if it were all her fault.

e~

It wasn't long after my campaign of provocation that I was woken up by what I thought – propelled upwards to consciousness – was a shout. The early light through the parting of the curtain was milky and grey; I squinted at it and wondered slowly what the noise had been. Then there was another shout, from below, and the sound of more than one person crossing the loud marble of the entrance hall. I got out of bed, my legs still uncertain from sleep, and went downstairs, where two of the young gardeners were standing near the foot of the stairs, with turned-down shocked faces, hands hanging forgotten like gloves. Rhys, my favourite, usually said, 'All right, boss?' when he saw me. But that morning they both looked at me with an odd, almost frightened evasiveness.

'Miss Black,' I called with relief, seeing her standing with the telephone. 'What's happening?'

She didn't hear me; she was saying, 'Near Llansteffan. It's empty. I don't know.'

She kept looking up at the open door of the gold parlour, and so I slipped around her and went inside.

At first I almost laughed, because it was only Alicia, sitting on the sofa with her eyes closed. She had fallen asleep there several times before. Then I noticed that her hair was all over her shoulders; it looked wrong, unravelled. She was sagging so her head tilted forward, and her mouth was slightly open. I stared at her face, which was greyish, unclear, as if she were underwater.

One of the gardeners rushed in behind me and carried me back out. He was saying something I couldn't quite understand. Then there were sirens, and the noise of wheels on the gravel like the crunching of broken glass. I sat on the front steps and watched the ambulance drive away, thinking not of my mother's shape inside it, surrounded by so much haste and clamour, but of her drooping on the sofa, slack and white and drowned.

Theo's bedroom was at the back of the house, and she was a heavy – almost inanimate – sleeper. She didn't appear while the various denizens of the house were wheeling through it, cut loose and flapping with tragedy, drinking whisky (Mrs Williams) and discussing the moments of the morning until they lost all human resonance and become an inane sequence, repeated continually.

'And then John saw her through the window . . . and then he fetched Rhys . . . and then they knocked on the window . . .'

There was a stillness in my ears, as if the air inside them was very dense. I sat on the floor and let the sound of them talking vanish into the cold, crystallised air, compressed into silence.

Finally the hospital telephoned and Miss Black came over and told me that I mustn't worry about my mother; that she was absolutely fine and had gone away to have a short rest, and that she'd be back before I knew it. She was almost affectionate with relief and gave my hand a squeeze.

'Don't tell Theo what happened,' she said. 'She may not understand.'

I didn't understand either, but I didn't say anything. Mrs Wynne Jones stood nearby with a pitying smile that was nonetheless a smile, as if she knew that something bad had happened but felt that it was deserved. She was a tall woman, with rigid pewter hair; there was something implacable about her. She folded her arms across her chest, and shook her head.

'Are you phoning Mrs Anthony?' everyone asked Miss Black in the days that followed. By which they meant *Eve*. Miss Black looked nervous at the idea of this. Almost a week later I still wasn't sure whether she had called Eve or not. She often sat in the study on the telephone, but when I went past I could hear her saying things like 'I don't know if I could get a better salary,' which meant she was talking to her mother.

Theo certainly understood something of the atmosphere in the house. After she got up that morning she sat in her pink flowered pyjamas, shadowy-eyed and quiet, while I explained that Alicia had gone on holiday.

'Where?' asked Theo.

'Er . . . Spain,' I said. 'The Costa del Sol.' This was where Mrs Williams's relatives went.

'Oh,' said Theo, thinking for a moment. Then her face was illuminated, like an opening flower, and she gave her trusting smile. 'That's where oranges come from. I like Spain.'

೧

A week after Alicia's removal, I was in the kitchen making breakfast. Mrs Williams wasn't there (her working hours having slipped and sagged like Dali's clocks in the absence of Alicia) and the empty kitchen looked very cold, vast and white, like a laboratory or a hospital. This changed when she got in, jaunty in her pink coat and yellow hair, took an ashtray out of the cutlery drawer and put the kettle on.

'What are you up to? Hiding?' she said when she saw me. 'If anyone asks, I got here at eight, all right?'

'Can I have this?' I asked, holding up a tub of hundreds and thousands.

'Help yourself. It's not like I'll bother making a cake, I suppose.'

Mrs Wynne Jones arrived at this point and bade Mrs Williams a cheery good morning. They seemed to have called a truce on disapproving of each other, in order to gossip about Alicia, which they began doing as soon as I had left the kitchen. I sat outside with my hundreds and thousands to listen.

'They said after she had Theo,' Mrs Williams said, 'she didn't *speak* for three days. Post-natal depression.' I couldn't imagine Alicia – our porcelain and silk mother – with a distended stomach, moving effortfully like the other pregnant women I had seen. Perhaps that was what was wrong with her; she couldn't imagine it either. The way she looked at us with a faint surprise – curiosity, even – that we should be her children.

'No wonder he left,' Mrs Williams continued, more quietly.

'What did they tell the little one about Alicia?' Mrs Wynne Jones asked.

'Holiday.'

'Does she believe it?'

'Theodora . . . well, you know. She's not all there, in *my* opinion. And it's not surprising.'

'Eve should come back,' Mrs Wynne Jones said.

'She *should*,' said Mrs Williams, 'but whether she will or not . . .'

'You're the expert, I suppose,' Mrs Wynne Jones said coolly.

Mrs Williams was immune to sarcasm. 'She won't come back,' she pronounced. 'Not in a million years.'

I made a face in the direction of the kitchen. I pictured Eve, a flickering black and white figure, with her glowing smile, arriving like Snow White in a cinematic, blinding vision. She would fly in on her own plane and land on the lawn, she would tell us how glad she was to see us, she would dish out extravagant presents and cakes, and Mrs Williams and Mrs Wynne Jones would be proved wrong, wrong, wrong.

Around this time I went through a phase of watching a lot of television. Not for the programmes themselves – it was the adverts I liked best. Theo would sing loudly along to most of the jingles she knew until she recognised the opening images of a particular laundry detergent commercial and had to rush behind the sofa to block her ears. She used to run upstairs when someone came to the house, in case it was the Whiter Than White man coming to get her.

My favourites were for supermarkets or food. They usually featured a mother and at least two children, in coloured T-shirts and jeans. They smiled at each other with absorption or conducted good-humoured arguments, eating their pre-packaged food with loud noises of approval.

At night I lay in bed and imagined I was in an advert. I followed my mother – not Alicia, but a woman in a pink jumper and neat jeans – as she wheeled a trolley around the supermarket, packed food into striped bags. I sat with my brothers and sisters around a table, while our mother set out a dish of roast potatoes, a glossy joint of beef, luminous green peas. Before I got to the gravy, I fell asleep. The door from the kitchen opened – it was Alicia after all, bringing in the gravy. Her hair was loose over her shoulders again, dusty blonde, like spiderwebs. She was wavering; focusing on me, she drifted towards me. I was frightened, but I couldn't get up. I could feel my mouth moving like somebody else's mouth. Then she was not holding gravy any more, but a big silver covered dish, like a gleaming, robot breast. She placed it in front of me, the lid came up – and there was nothing.

Nearly two weeks after Alicia's removal (time for me was measured by this date, like BC, AD: before Alicia was driven off in the ambulance; after Alicia was driven off in the ambulance), I was lying on the floor of the morning room stacking dominoes to make a fort. It was a warmish day, but I didn't feel much like playing outside. The wintry sun drifted in through the open window, showing the dust rising off the cream damask of the sofa and the drapes at the window; it rested on the vase of Alicia's roses still standing on the side table. The roses were drying out like crêpe paper, shedding petals, but no one had noticed or thrown them away.

Theo danced in, making exaggerated sweeps around the room, toes pointed, singing, 'When will I be famous?'

'Sssh,' I said. I was balancing the blocks to make a gateway at the front, which threatened to collapse.

'Eve's famous, isn't she?' Theo said. 'But I don't want to be famous. I don't *want* my picture in the paper.'

'Then you can't be a ballerina, can you?' I said. This was Theo's latest ambition.

'I'll be an artist.'

'Artists are famous too.'

Theo was silent for a moment. Then she started singing again, turned a clumsy pirouette, and jerked the rug with her foot. The fort was rubble.

'Leave me alone, can't you?' I said, and she backed out, mouth sagging, eyes flooding.

I put the domino pieces back in their box. I didn't believe Eve was going to come to Evendon, not now. After the first days, when she had been invoked like a genie, over and over, or like Bloody Mary summoned in the mirror, I thought she would have to come back. But no one mentioned her any more, and they didn't talk about Alicia either.

I wondered when Alicia would come home; what she might be like when she did. The idea that she might come home and be different was too strange to imagine. Yesterday Theo had said, 'Maybe when Alicia comes back from holiday she'll be happy,' but I couldn't answer. For if Alicia wasn't happy, did that mean she was sad? I didn't think so, not even in her irritable phase. She never laughed, but she never cried either. She emerged from her room each morning at nearly midday, scented, hair pinned up; lit and polished for display. After that she read magazines, cut roses, answered the occasional invitation (*I must regretfully decline*) and called for drinks. Then she went to bed. Happy or sad were not concepts that could be applied to her; she simply didn't occupy the same emotional space as the rest of us.

Theo had never really understood that. When she was very young, she used to follow Alicia around the house, reaching out to touch her legs, or her hands, until Alicia noticed and waved her away. They both looked baffled, not comprehending the other. Eventually Theo stopped following Alicia, and started following me instead.

Sometimes it's hard being the one who is followed. With nothing to follow yourself – no one looking back, to beckon you on. No one up ahead.

e∽

On the exact month's anniversary of Alicia's exit, we sat in the kitchen with Mrs Williams and Mrs Wynne Jones, eating our lunch. The domestic rule – of sorts – we once had was now wholly broken down, and we insisted on having our meals in the kitchen, where we could watch the television and add mayonnaise to everything.

Mrs Wynne Jones was leaning against the fridge with her woolly arms folded, saying, 'So, no chance of an appeal?'

'He's a good boy,' said Mrs Williams. 'It was that judge who was the problem.'

Mrs Wynne Jones gave her a tight smile. 'I'm sure.'

Mrs Williams was not above making a face behind Mrs Wynne Jones's back, which she did then.

Theo had discarded her sandwich and was pouring herself some cornflakes with chocolate sauce on, saying to Mrs Williams, 'My mother's gone to Spain and she'll bring us back some oranges.'

'Is that so?' Mrs Williams said, raising her eyebrows over Theo's head.

'We're going to have a cactus,' said Theo.

'Nasty prickly things, cactuses,' said Mrs Williams. Theo, not listening, started eating her cornflakes, humming a tune from a television show.

'Just like her mother, see,' Mrs Williams murmured to Mrs Wynne Jones, tapping the side of her head.

I stared viciously at their two backs, which were heavy and final, like their voices. They had the power of summary, of sentencing. Compared to Mrs Williams and Mrs Wynne Jones our family were weightless; they could blow us away, just by talking about us.

'I hate you,' I said to Mrs Williams, rattling my chair back and leaving with noisy dignity. I closed the door to my room and drew pictures of her trapped under a landslide, or on fire, aware that Theo would be waiting outside my room. When I went out, she was sitting on the window seat of the landing with the sash wide open, looking down at the curve of the drive where it disappeared into the trees. She often sat this way, with her head poking out to rest on the sill, the glass hanging over her like a guillotine. She shifted and put her head on my shoulder when I sat down next to her.

'Why did you shout at Mrs Williams?' she asked reproachfully.

'She said . . .' I hesitated. 'She's stupid.'

'Oh.' Theo considered this. 'Okay.'

We sat in silence and looked out of the window at the bend in the road where Alicia was last seen.

'What will we do if Alicia doesn't come back?' Theo asked. I glanced at her, checking for incipient tears, but it seemed the question was a practical one.

'We could do whatever we wanted,' I said. 'We could sack Miss Black and Mrs Williams and Mrs Wynne Jones and live all by ourselves.'

'Could we make meringue?'

'Yes, and trifle.'

'Could we make a water slide on the stairs?'

'Definitely.'

'And get a trampoline? And then we could jump up to our bedrooms on the trampoline and slide down on the water slide and we wouldn't have to use the stairs ever again.'

'Yes, and we could get a dog,' I said. 'Two dogs. And a horse.'

'And an *owl*,' Theo cried. We sat for a moment, shoulder to shoulder, gazing out not onto the empty drive but on our rainbowed dream selves, sailing down our water slide, hands full of trifle. I was starting to hope that, like our father, Alicia wouldn't ever come back.

THREE

The silence at Evendon was a distinctive one: lethargic, torpid and heavy with the expiration of many years, the gradual cooling of time. It was thickest in the vaulted entrance hall, with its two great columns (looted from Greece by a dead Bennett) and marble floor like an Arctic sea. I think we were all used to it; it was just another of those things that we breathed in so often we stopped noticing. Like the lack of Eve, the lack of our father, the lack of Alicia. The ambulances that came for Alicia rattled the silence briefly, but then they went away and it settled back cold and white, not to be disturbed until nearly two months later, in March.

The first sign that something unusual was happening was the sound of the engines of several cars outside. Then the engines stopped and doors started opening. Theo and I ran into the hall and stood to listen to what sounded like dozens of different voices, the hungry crackling of the gravel. I remember in particular the laugh just outside, that fluid, clear sound. I don't think I had ever heard any of the adults laugh like that before. Theo and I could only stare at the doors, as Miss Black hurried in after us awkwardly.

'What on earth – what's going on?' she asked us.

Mrs Williams, who never moved so fast as when she sniffed incipient drama, appeared close behind her.

'It's *Eve*,' she said. 'Did you call her, then?'

'No!' Miss Black said, as there came the sound of a key connecting with a lock, the scratch and clunk. 'I meant to . . . but . . .' And then the doors were opened and the silence shivered and tore and scurried to the corners of the house away from the clamour and colour of the people, anonymous in the initial blinding slice of light, fanning out into the hall.

The first person I made out was Alicia, who walked in wearing a peach jacket and pearls, and then stood looking bored, as if she had been there all day. Her skin had an unreal sheen; her irises were diluted as if water had got into them, her pupils large and dark. Despite her appearance of fragility there was something flatly unapproachable in her face, and even Theo, hovering and uncertain behind me, didn't move towards her. We stood still and watched instead. All around Alicia were people I had never seen before, carrying large leather suitcases and hatboxes, tripping over each other. The last person to walk through the door was different – carrying nothing, moving decisively and quickly – a woman with hair like black birds' wings, white skin, a red suit.

It was Eve – it had to be – smiling as if she was enjoying the effects of some huge joke she had planned. Her eyes ticked off the activity around her, made a sharp swoop of familiarity over the hall, then alighted on me.

'Jonathan!' she said, and looked behind me. 'And this is Theo! It's Eve – come back to stay.' Her voice on the television, while lovely, had been as small and distant as if it really were trapped in a box. Here in our ears it was unusually substantial; not loud, but smoothly cohesive, rolling like mercury.

Theo gazed at her, visibly frightened, and then at Alicia, who appeared to notice us for the first time. 'Hello, you two,' she said, the same way we recited our responses in school assemblies. She handed her coat to one of the unfamiliar people, gave a vague wave in our direction as she walked past, up the stairs, then we heard the sound of her door closing.

Eve frowned for a moment, then retrieved her humorous air and dipped down on her knee to shake our hands. After the surprise of first seeing her, I could see that she was not as tall as I had thought – not even as tall as Alicia. She had a compact slenderness that looked almost unyielding; her legs next to me were hard, smooth with silk. It was her eyes that made her so striking – her eyes or her mouth, or possibly something else. I tried not to stare at her.

'Your mother is very tired after travelling, I'm afraid. Let's get all this unpacked, and then we can sit down in peace and talk,' she said to us, winking, then stood up to direct the people holding cases and boxes, who departed one by one until only Theo and I were left in the hall.

'Is that really Eve?' Theo whispered.

'Who else do you think it would be?' I said.

'She brought Mama back from Spain,' Theo said, thinking. 'So it must be her.'

‹͜›

That night we stayed up in the morning room with Eve. I sat next to her. Theo had tucked herself into a nest of cushions on the floor in front of the fire, hands wound together, the light moving over her face. The colours of the fire extended beyond her, lapping up the carpet, becoming hundreds of flames in the window panes, falling just short of Alicia, who sat across the room, her gaze lost somewhere in the middle distance.

'Did you see Grandad Sam in America?' I asked Eve (she had already told us not to call her Grandma, or Grandmother, but it was apparently all right for Sam). Sam wasn't actually our grandfather; he was Eve's second husband at one time, though not now. We hadn't seen him since we visited LA as babies: there was a photograph of Theo crawling around a flat, kidney shape of blue; the glare of the sun, her white frilly hat. Every year at Christmas Sam sent us rocking horses, sleds, a remote-control miniature Porsche – which famously toppled Mrs Wynne Jones – a diamond necklace that Theo lost, an air rifle that Miss Black confiscated.

'I did indeed. He sends his love.'

'Is he coming back too?' Theo asked.

'No, darling. I'm afraid not.' Eve smiled after she said this and Theo smiled too, looking confused.

'So . . .' Eve said, 'I want to know how everything has been here . . . Alicia of course has no idea.' (Alicia appeared not to hear this.) 'Have you both been doing well at school?'

Eve was the first person, aside from teachers, who seemed genuinely interested in my high marks. She smiled and patted my hand with her fingers, which were cool and firm as if gloved. Hand-pats were all we had had from Eve so far; no embracing, and her lips didn't touch our skin when she kissed us, as if we were adults. But she paid us a serious kind of attention, which we hadn't experienced before. I was exasperated to see Theo contracting under her scrutiny, like a prodded shellfish. I didn't want Eve to lose interest in us.

Eve told us the story of how she first came to England. 'I

was born in America, but my father always preferred the UK. He disapproved of New York – he thought it was crass. We sailed back here right after my mother died, when I was a little girl.'

'To Evendon?' I asked.

'Oh no.' Eve twirled her wine in her hands. 'We moved to a house in Mayfair, even though the Blitz had only just ended. My grandfather James lived here – he was stuck here really. He couldn't afford London by then. Besides, the two of them didn't exactly get along.'

'Why didn't they get along?' Theo asked.

'Who knows?' Eve said, raising her hands. 'My father didn't get along with a lot of people. He was a . . . disapproving type of man.'

Eve hated London back then, she said.

'It was nothing like the city it is today. It was so dark! It smelled of rubble, and poverty. In America there was chocolate; we had fruit. But in England those things were scarce even in the best houses. And the people were unfriendly. I saw none of the famous wartime spirit; they all hid under their black umbrellas and scuttled around the pavements like pigeons. Even in the summer it rained . . , and the winters . . . there was the thick fog. You couldn't see further than a few feet in front of you, because of the chemicals in the air.'

'From the bombs?' I asked.

Eve laughed. 'No, from the coal London ate up every day. It was just pollution. We came to Evendon a couple of years later, after James died. I remember arriving and being shocked by the greenness and the beauty of it all. I had only seen London up until that day, and New York before that. It seemed as if when I closed my eyes at night everything was still green. And so quiet. I couldn't sleep the first few nights because I was used to the noise of people and traffic and music, all night.'

'Poor Eve,' said Theo.

'Oh, it happens to everyone who goes from the city to the countryside. It was the same when I came back here in the late seventies. I remember Alicia and Alex being horrified. They were teenagers at that time. Alicia in particular was quite devastated to be away from her LA friends' parties.'

Theo and I looked dubiously at Alicia, who we could tell – by the barest shift of an eyelid, the lowered angle of her neck – had fallen asleep.

'Anyway, I suppose it will be the same when I try to go to sleep tonight . . . I have to get used to the peace and quiet again.' She looked around the room with satisfaction, while I thought that what seemed like silence to Eve was, to me, lighter and brighter than the silence of before, as if she had brought the secret of the people and traffic and music with her.

'Why have you been away for so long?' I asked.

Eve lifted her eyebrows exaggeratedly. 'Business! I've been very busy for the last few years. I would have much rather been here, of course. But I left not long after your mother moved back in, with the two of you. You were only tiny then, but I knew the three of you would look after Evendon until I got back.'

Theo looked confused. 'How long are you staying this time?'

'Oh!' Eve smiled, 'Well, darling, this time I'm back for good.'

Evendon changed after Eve came back. For example, Mrs Williams started going outside to smoke. She also abandoned her habit of eating pieces of whatever she was cooking, and the one of taking home 'leftover' chickens or steaks in carrier bags. Mrs Wynne Jones too was a more frequent presence, supervising a tribe of black-clothed maids. The house itself became brighter, more present, and I realised that a layer of dust had been lifted off it like a veil, the thin film of grey on the windows wiped away. The dining table became reflective, the silver radiant. The drapes were lighter, clean as milk. The winter light, no longer barred, dived in and burst from the polished floors, the serpentine-edged rosewood, the oyster faces of the clocks. Evendon had emerged from its sleep, its subdued state of waiting; vivid and delighted, it glittered like Eve herself. It was like a piano that only she could play, calling up its eerie music.

Alicia was lost in the new Evendon; she seemed dimmer, paler – though of all of us she was the only one who had not changed her behaviour. Her hair was back in its perpetual chignon; the clocks could still be set by her afternoon gin and tonics, from which she took careful, brittle-lipped sips, as though at a Dorchester luncheon. Eve didn't pay much attention to her, and so no one else did either. I had almost forgotten about the time I had spent trying to make her angry.

Miss Black, like the dust, was an early casualty of Eve's reappearance. One afternoon when we got back from playing on the fences that bordered the estate, Theo's dress torn and my shoes be-cowpatted, we saw Eve standing on the terrace watching us.

'Where have you two been?' she asked pleasantly.

'In the fields,' Theo said, before I was able to reply. 'We saw some black and white cows.'

'And where is Miss Black?'

Neither of us knew.

A few days later Eve said, 'I think you two are old enough not to need a nanny,' and that was the end of Miss Black. The day she left was odd, rather than sad, though Theo cried. Miss Black, disconcertingly, tried to hug us. (She was upset, I think, by Alicia's dispassionately murmured goodbye.) When she leant in I could smell her perfume, a thin, glassy scent.

Theo mourned Miss Black for nearly a month after her departure, for no reason I could think of other than the parting hug.

'There's no need to be sad,' Eve told her. 'You can always write to Miss Black, if you miss her.'

'But what if she dies?' Theo asked. To which there was no answer.

In another change, parties returned to Evendon, involving teams of precise black and white people like monochrome Christmas elves, assembling something astonishing. When their work was finished the gardens were lit with hundreds of lanterns, and ice sculptures of naiads presided mournfully over the circulating waiters, clustered champagne flutes, jazz pianists, the towers of flowers with their petals luminescent in the weaving, heaving light.

Before the parties began, Theo and I would sit with Eve while she got ready. She'd unlock a safe in the wall and draw out diamonds, pearls and opals. The boxes of treasure made her playful: 'Look at this, Theo,' she said, holding up a ruby pendant, glimmering and liquid like a rabbit heart. 'Remember, a woman should never have to buy her own jewellery.'

We were meant to go to bed long before guests started to arrive, but we couldn't sleep, drawn out to the landing by the noise of the people, the floor writhing with their reflections, heating the air floating in through the French windows and loading it with perfume and cigar smoke. The music rose fitfully up to us as we watched, stunned and unblinking, through the banisters at the top of the stairs. Once we sneaked under the dining table and settled down with a tray of canapés to watch people's legs. The women's feet were more interesting than their black-shoed partners, with their enamelled toenails, shoes decorated with feathers and crystals and flowers, and once a silver lizard, its eyes made of purple stones. The sounds of the party swung over our heads: pieces of conversations I didn't understand:

I'm telling him it's over for good unless he ends it with her. They aren't having sex – he told me so.

What the public don't know won't hurt them.

She looked like a whore.

What we need is to sell the whole lot off. The insurance alone is crippling.

'What's a whore?' Theo whispered.

'I think it's a kind of animal,' I said, scraping the gleaming black beads off the top of a canapé before eating it.

Finally Eve's voice came close and hummed overhead, distinct from the others.

'Oh, we can solve that,' she said, replying to a question I didn't hear, and then she was gone.

The most exciting event of the night happened very late, Theo curled up asleep next to me with parsley stuck to her cheek. A woman in a shiny green dress threw her glass onto the floor and shouted something at a man. She was carried out of the front doors by two other people through a rising silence, raging and twisting like a snake, until the door shut and everyone turned back around and started talking again.

e→

The next day we sat at breakfast with Eve. I was trying not to yawn, while Theo ate croissants and orange juice with vivacious zeal, telling Eve about how she'd dreamed she had a party too but didn't have any insurance.

'Mmm,' Eve said, smiling at her as she opened the *Financial Times*.

'Why doesn't Uncle Alex come to parties?' Theo asked. We hadn't seen him since Eve's return.

'Oh, they're not his sort of thing,' Eve said.

'Aren't they fun?'

'Of course they are! But you can't make people have fun.' Eve sighed. 'What your Uncle Alex doesn't understand is how to be sociable . . . how to meet people who could be important to him.'

Eve's parties were always purposeful. There was always a *someone* she had intended to come, tempting them within her reach, offering alcohol and celebrities. 'Then get them with the business stuff,' she told us cheerfully.

'What's business stuff?' Theo asked.

'Well, for me it's hotels. But it's different for everybody. Some people's business is money. Other people might make jam, or drill for oil, or anything really.'

'What is Mrs Williams's business?' Theo asked, as the lady herself appeared at the breakfast table with a plate of burnt bacon.

'Making delicious food,' Mrs Williams replied shamelessly.

'I want to build houses,' I informed Eve.

'Oh yes, you could be a builder,' Mrs Williams interrupted. 'Fit right in on a building site, you would!'

As Mrs Williams exited, laughing, Eve looked at us both thoughtfully. Then she said, 'Hold on,' and went out, coming back with a large photograph album.

'Look at this.' She opened the album to show us a black and white image of a beautiful girl with waved hair like a stiff little hat. She wore a coat with a fur collar; patent shoes tipped her narrow legs. 'I was eighteen,' she said.

'When will I be eighteen?' asked Theo.

'In a much better year than I was, darling. It was 1955, and people weren't very happy at that time. I remember one day I was coming out of a theatre in London after seeing a new Coward play. It was raining and I wasn't looking where I was going, and I collided with another girl. She had a cheap coat and no umbrella, a shop girl perhaps, walking quickly. Of course I apologised to her.

'She said to me, "What have *you* got to be sorry about?" and walked off before I could say anything else. I think all she saw when she looked at me was an empty fur, a pair of floating pearl earrings.

'But I *did* have something to be sorry about. I was a woman too. I was tiny and pointless. We used to call the twentieth century the great engine of change – we said it a lot. Or the men did. Women weren't meant to be engine drivers.' Eve gave a small smile, which quickly cooled, as if she were thinking about something else.

'Where to?' Theo asked, interested. 'Where were they driving the engine?'

'Oh, it's a figure of speech. Anyway, that day I decided that I wasn't going to be held back by the men any more. And for you two – things are different now, but there are still people who will try to hold you back. If you want to build houses, Jonathan, you must build houses. And Theo, if you want to . . . whatever you want to do – don't let anybody stop you either.'

'I want to drive a red and yellow train to Africa,' Theo said, sliding down from her chair to stamp and wheel a tribal dance around the table.

'Do you now!' Eve said, and laughed, going back to her newspaper.

Afterwards I said to Theo, 'You act like such a baby sometimes.' Then when she looked at me with uncomprehending hurt I had to apologise. (Sometimes – just once – I would have welcomed a fight with her. Name-calling, hair-pulling; a more even distribution of guilt.)

The new, unexpected shape of our family made me happy, but it wasn't without its worries. I felt more responsible, as if I were its custodian, guarding the harmony that had descended, keeping things the same. One of my worries was that there were certain things about Theo that Eve, unfamiliar with the quirks and crinkles of her personality, might find odd – or worse, might not like.

Around that time, Theo was 'experiencing some challenges' in school, according to the letters and phone calls from her teachers. The most recent challenge was her horror about learning how to tell the time. She had asked the teacher what the time was counting down to.

'Nothing,' said the teacher. 'It just carries on.'

'How do you know it's doing that?' Theo asked.

'Things get older and older,' the teacher replied. 'Like you. Every year you'll grow bigger and bigger, until you're a grown-up.'

'That's horrible,' Theo protested. 'It's not true.'

Eve had stood with the telephone in the morning room murmuring to the teacher, her smooth head held straight and unmoving, one hand tapping an irregular percussion against her leg. Theo overheard the conversation and said to me later, 'Eve thinks I'm a strange child.'

'You must've heard her wrong,' I said.

But I saw that Eve had developed a certain expression when she was thinking about Theo. It appeared for the first time when she told us the story of the ant and the grasshopper and Theo cried. She couldn't understand why the ant wouldn't help the grasshopper at the end. (For my part, I was on the ant's side. The grasshopper irritated me, with his refusal to prepare for cold, for the simple hostility of the winter.) Then there was the day Theo watched the Wicked Witch of the East die under the house and couldn't sleep for a week. The expression appeared again every time Eve had to tell her that there were no ghosts, no fairies, no lion in the wardrobe. Eve's mouth would lengthen, her eyebrows turn questioning, and I thought it was because she was trying to work Theo out. I suppose I was worried about what she might decide, when she finally came to a conclusion.

ℰ⌒

Summer came around again, and on the days when Eve wasn't at home Theo and I would cross the border between Evendon and Wales and wander up and down the quiet hills, to the surrounding villages or farms. One day we walked to Carmarthen, where the stone ramparts and battlements of the former castle could be tracked around the narrow roads. We found a chocolate shop, where sated flies dawdled under the glass counter, and admired the cakes until we were asked to leave. In the high street we were mostly ignored, gently buffeted by shopping bags and pushchairs. At first Theo said, 'Hello,' and smiled at people as we passed, but mostly they looked back at us without replying. They were not exactly unfriendly; but very few of them said hello back, and eventually I told her to stop.

On another day we walked down to the beach at Llansteffan. It took us almost an hour in the solid sun, but we didn't mind; we were dizzy with the smell of it, the glimpses of the sea through the gaps in the hedgerow, the sky like a purer distillation of the blue water. Most of the way we walked a thin lane lined with trees, keeping back from the occasional cars that went by. The barred gaps in the light that slid over the car windows alternately revealed and veiled their puzzled inhabitants, looking at Theo with her pink straw hat and bucket and spade, smiling and waving at them, me with a rolled-up blanket over my shoulder, two dwarf tourists.

Llansteffan was small, a few streets of tiny houses painted in jaunty pastels, with balconies and palm-like trees in the gardens and an air of the carnival about them. On the cliff above the village there was a ruined castle, peering down at us with its one-eyed window, a bright blue eye like Theo's. We laid out our blanket near the rocks at the edge of the bay and started building a sandcastle. I went to the sea to get water, wading into the slow thinning of the tide, sliding over the flat cream sand into a moving glass pane. When I got back, Theo was watching a man and a woman with a small child, holding its hands as it wobbled in the shallow water.

'Why didn't we see our father before he died?' she asked me.

This startled me. Our father was something that hadn't been talked about in a while. When Eve first came back I had thought she might tell us more about him – the mysterious Michael Caplin – beginning and ending in his Antipodean car crash. But she was as vague about him as Alicia always was; she even gave me the same blink, the same repressive frown, when I asked what he was like. I caught the sense of unease, and didn't mention my father again.

It bothered me now that Theo had asked about him; I imagined her bringing it up at home, in the same way that she asked fat women if there was a baby in their tummy – and if so, how many – or asked why there were dark people on television but none at our house. I felt that the new life of Evendon – the happiness of Evendon – was delicate, a balance of things that were said and not said. I didn't want Theo disturbing it with one of her sudden, unwelcome wonderings. So I said, 'I don't know, and you shouldn't go on about him all the time. He's dead. You're not meant to talk about dead people because it upsets everyone. Didn't you know that?'

'We talk about other dead people . . .' Theo said, but she ran down into a murmur, gave up, and started filling her bucket with sand again.

'You have to get the sand packed in,' I told her, more kindly. 'Or the towers will collapse.'

As we piled sand I noticed two boys watching us from a slight distance. Eventually, with tentative nonchalance, they approached us.

'Can we help?' one of them asked, in a heavy Welsh accent.

'Hurrah,' Theo cried, before I could say no. I would have preferred to be left alone, but the boys had a larger bucket, and for a while we built together in silence.

'Nice tower,' I said to one of them.

'Your moat's good,' he said, nodding at it shyly. 'Are you here on holiday?'

'We live here,' Theo said, then added proudly, 'We walked down to the beach by ourselves.'

'But you're English,' the other boy said. 'You talk like English people.'

Just then an older girl arrived awkward-footed across the sand, haughty in her flowered bikini. She took the boys by their arms and pulled them off, saying, 'Come on now, come *on*.' We couldn't hear the rest of what she said, but the boys didn't come back. They sat in the distance, building a new sandcastle of their own.

'I don't understand,' Theo said. 'Why are they over there?'

I didn't exactly understand either, but I knew dismissal when

I saw it. 'Because they're idiots,' I said. 'We don't want to play with them.'

'Don't we?' asked Theo.

'No.' We carried on, ignoring the spade the two boys had left, until one ran over to get it. I didn't look at him, but Theo jumped up. 'Please come back and help,' she said.

The boy shook his head, hard-mouthed. 'We're not playing with *you*,' he said. 'You think you're better than us.'

'No, I don't,' Theo said, distressed.

'Yes, you do,' the boy said. 'My sister says so.' He picked up his spade; Theo caught hold of the end of it to stop him going, and then he jerked it and she fell backwards onto the sand. When she landed, tears spilled out of her eyes with surprise.

I jumped up and hit him, hard, just missing his nose. We stared at each other for a moment, bewildered. Then his face became shapeless and he turned around and ran, crying jerkily, tripping on the sand.

❧

This incident on the beach continued to bother Theo long after I had forgotten about it. It was a few weeks later when she asked me, 'Do people like us?'

'No,' I said. I had begun to understand how the locals – as Alicia called them – saw us. They were disapproving, like Mrs Wynne Jones; I knew that the tiny pastel houses of the beach, crowded together like penny sweets, squeezed us out. I didn't particularly care about this: I did not want admittance.

'Why?' Theo asked.

'Because we have more money than them.' (This was some-thing Eve had told me.)

'I don't,' Theo said promptly. 'I spent all my money yesterday.'

'No,' I said. 'Eve's money. It's sort of our money too.'

I didn't pass on the information to Theo – who was left looking confused – that we would have this money when Eve died. It was not a possibility I really believed in anyway: the death of Eve. Death was something that might happen to Alicia; she was already its familiar, its wraithly inmate. But Eve was more present and alive than anybody I knew, her colours brighter, her edges more clearly defined. Eve was like the people in commercials – a magni-fied, amplified kind of real. Too real to just disappear.

'I don't want money,' Theo said. 'I'll give it to the people who don't like us, and then we'll all be happy.'

'Where would you live if you didn't have any money?' I asked her. 'What would you eat?'

'I'll live with you,' Theo said, leaning her head on my arm and smiling at me. 'And we can eat pizza.'

FOUR

I think my favourite times back then were the summer evenings, with the French windows open onto the cool blue-green of the garden, its edges appearing to vanish into the black glittering sea. In the red morning room the lamps would be glowing; the papers under Eve's hands shone as she moved them. This was her reading time, she said: newspapers, contracts, letters disembowelled with a jewelled knife, paper-clipped press cuttings.

'Why don't you read stories?' Theo asked her once.

'I have enough stories of my own,' Eve said.

I preferred Eve's stories, when she chose to tell them, to the pirates and firemen of my own neglected books. Her life as she told it was defined by a series of events – big bangs and revelations. These moments fell easily into conversation: at times there would be an anecdote, over dinner; other times she would feel prompted to tell a longer story in the evening, sitting perfectly still except for one hand gesturing, gliding in the air like a conductor's baton. If she was in the mood, she'd tell us about how Senator This drank too much, or how Prince That's children weren't really his own. Eve said it was all right for us to hear these things because we had to know how the world worked. Infidelity and addiction; she was educating us.

The stories Eve told best were the ones about herself. But she rarely offered them; she had to be pressed into it, cajoled and entreated. In this way we heard about why she left England ('It's really not that interesting . . . but if you insist'), when some American friends of hers were having dinner with us.

'Well, I left to go back to my mother's family in New York when I was eighteen, after my father died,' she said. 'It wasn't just because of grief – though that was part of it – but because it hadn't been long since the Second World War had ended, and at that time it just seemed America had more to offer.'

'Was England very badly affected?' asked one of the guests.

'Of course. The English were rebuilding after the Blitz while the Americans were dancing to "Rock Around the Clock". Everyone was poorer here – even the rich. The great houses of the aristocracy were being sold one by one. There were backslides for women too. During the war, some women I knew had their own Tiger Moth planes, and one of my friends' aunts drove a canal boat for the River Emergency Service. But these freedoms were withdrawn when the men came back. Our world had contracted again. I was a debutante, but I felt I was at the beginning of nothing at all. Missing my coming-out ball seemed like an escape. I had no reason to suppose that things would be much better for women in America, but at least they weren't getting worse. And money was being made, people were hopeful. America – right then – seemed a place for success, rather than remembrance.'

'So brave of you to go alone,' one woman murmured.

Eve laughed. 'I didn't feel brave! That was the first time I travelled on a plane. When we took off, I was frightened I might die – I could hardly breathe. Then when I finally opened my eyes I saw the stewardesses bringing around the tea. They looked like soldiers in their rigid little hats. Their hands didn't even quaver. I admired them terribly. That was the moment I made my own plan. I decided I'd go to university – be the first woman in my family to do it – and then I'd become something important in America. It was an awful plan really – I had no idea *how* I'd do it, but I was confident I could. I suppose that's the beauty of being young.'

'I wonder if your father felt something similar going off into the jungle,' one guest said. 'You obviously inherited the desire for adventure.'

'I suppose I did,' Eve said, with a mouth smile, above which her eyes remained cool.

After the events of the following day, I wondered whether it was this story – Eve's story – that had done it. She had invoked the paternal dead, stirred up the missing past, and wrong things were made to resurface.

The day itself, a Sunday, was not particularly unusual. Eve was at home but spent most of the time in the room she had turned into an office. Alicia sat on the terrace with gardening gloves, a wide-brimmed hat and a glass on a small table next to her, getting up every now and again to make feints towards the rose bushes. Theo was at a school friend's birthday party, and I was left aimless. My favourite toys – the remote-controlled car, the tin soldiers, the battered football – didn't inspire me. I found a magnifying glass and some dry sticks and tried unsuccessfully to build a fire out of Alicia's sight, near the open window of Eve's office. The day was hot, but an unsettled wind blew from the sea and pulled the drapes of Eve's window out towards me, then back, like a ship's sail. It carried the electric bell of a telephone with it, then the ringing ended, and I heard Eve's voice quite clearly. I had overheard her speaking on the phone before without paying much attention, but her tone now made me pause and listen.

'When did he arrive?' she said, without saying hello. The sail billowed in again and I couldn't hear for a moment. Then it blew back and Eve was saying, 'Where else would he be going?'

There was a pause, and I stood up just under the window trying to hear better. Then Eve's voice said, right above me, 'Just send some people over,' and I heard for the first time that she was angry.

 ℮ 

Eventually the windy day blew the sun out like a light, leaving the house shimmering in the cool vagaries of the evening. There was another telephone call; Theo's birthday party had run on late and the car Eve had sent for her was still waiting, far away at a zoo in England.

Listening at the foot of the stairs, I felt an increasing misery that Theo was not back. The shadows growing on the floor like a tide bothered me, and I didn't want to go to sleep. I went to join Alicia in the gold sitting room, with the idea that if I stayed quiet enough I would evade being sent upstairs.

Alicia was watching an old film, her face greyed in its dusky projections, her eyes beginning to close. The people on the screen were fuzzed, obscured by a great weight of time as they moved towards each other. I was uninterested by the ending, the crackling edges of the black and white lips and teeth, but I stared sleeplessly anyway, feeling anything was better than going up to bed and shutting my eyes against the darkness outside, the new security men I had noticed occasionally passing the window. I knew that for some reason, we were under siege.

I felt worse when Eve came in and snapped, 'What rubbish are you watching, Alicia?' She didn't usually comment on anything my mother did, and Alicia woke up and looked at her with serene surprise.

'I don't know,' she said.

Eve looked at me next.

'Jonathan! Shouldn't you be in bed?' she said. 'Come on, I'll go with you.'

As we walked up the stairs, she took my hand in her own cool hand, and smiled at me with something more like her usual sangfroid.

'Wanted to stay up tonight, did you?' she said teasingly.

'Why are there security men here?' I asked.

'Oh, darling, you mustn't be worried about that. There have been some burglaries nearby and so I thought for a few nights we should have a couple of men about, just to act as a deterrent. Of course, we have cameras and alarms, so it's not as if anybody could just . . . *get in*, anyway . . .' She trailed off, then laughed and squeezed my hand when we got to the top of the stairs. 'We're perfectly secure. Now, off you go to bed.'

As she turned there came the sudden, deep chime of the doorbell, rolling up like a cold bronze wave, hitting Eve and me. For a moment we looked at each other blankly, shocked. Then she blinked and said, 'Goodness – it must be Theo. I'd almost forgotten her!'

Theo was brought in asleep by the driver, her mouth open. She always slept like this, as if she had slipped into an unfathomable coma. Her hair was wound around her neck, plastered to her flushed pink cheek. In her blue party dress she was a surprising patch of colour in the pewter lake of the hall.

'Follow me,' Eve said to the driver, who carried Theo upstairs. I lingered to look at the front doors, which were promptly closed by the navy shape of one of the security men. Then I ran up after them.

As soon as Eve had gone I went into Theo's room, where she was snoring in her bed, and shook her. She gasped and sat up with a shocked splutter as if resuscitated from drowning, then looked at me with delight.

'Jonathan!' she cried. 'I missed you.'

'How was the zoo?' I asked, half watching her bedroom door, from which a line of light stretched across the black void of the floor, crossing toys and clothes like a laser. The house was silent.

'It was fun,' Theo whispered happily. 'And I got a hat, but I lost it, but I made a plan, to get a zoo when we grow up, and I can feed the animals, and we can live at the zoo, in a house, with flamingos in the garden, and you can have a pet lion.'

'The lion would eat the flamingos,' I said, trying to listen for sounds outside.

'We could get a crocodile to protect them from the lion,' Theo said reasonably. 'I don't want them all to live in cages. I was sad when I saw the lion in the cage.'

Talking to Theo, I understood why I had come to wake her up; it was this normality I wanted, the sunny atmosphere she had retained from her day out, the sparkling traces of birthday cake and paper hats. But she was frowning now, her smile gone, as if the pressure of the house had descended on her too.

'It's hot in here,' she said suddenly.

It was hot. All the windows in the house had been closed earlier, despite the high July temperature. I went to her window and quietly opened it, leaning out for a moment. The cool air swept over my damp face. Theo's room overlooked the gardens, which were empty, faintly patterned by the gold-coloured light from within the house. The only sounds from outside were the susurrations of the trees and the sea, and an owl far away, calling out with no answer.

Theo had fallen asleep again on the bed behind me, eyelids flickering. I pulled the sheets over her, hesitated, then climbed in next to her, and finally slept.

*

I remember being woken up by the thick, obscure sound of voices, in the room below me. The room was dark; the sky outside showed no signs of the morning. The voices moved up and down rapidly, loud with unhappiness, before travelling out of my hearing again. After a while of waiting – head lifted, still and tense with the effort of listening – for them to come back, I let myself sink back into the bed.

Then I heard someone crying outside. It was a quiet noise, rising to the open window. It sounded like it could have been my mother, except Alicia did not cry. I got out of bed, my muffled head dreamlike and unsteady, and went to the window, where I stood on a chair to look out onto the terrace. I saw my mother, standing alone in a long shadow. I realised that the shadow, long, thin, rippling like a dark stream of water, must belong to someone else, standing in the French windows below, just out of my sight. There was a glitter on the flagstones of the terrace, from a smashed glass. I could see Alicia's face clearly, broken up like a reflection on water. Her pale skin was barred with the black lines of her dissolved eye make-up.

Then my mother put her hands to her face, and the shadow was joined by other shadows, until it shook and grew into a monstrous, many-limbed thing, drawing gradually away from her. As it did so I heard a shout, a man's voice breaking up into an elemental cry, its sense lost. It could have been 'Don't do this,' or equally it could have been 'I knew this,' or 'You Judas,' or 'Who's this?' Then the shadows were gone. Alicia said something through her hands that I couldn't make out, in a voice I had never heard before, full of different things.

Then Eve walked out onto the terrace. Unlike Alicia, who stood unsteadily, Eve was quick and decisive. She stood near Alicia, and spoke as if she wasn't really talking to Alicia but to herself, and in turn Alicia didn't look at her. 'I suppose this should have been foreseen,' Eve said. Her voice – as always – was so distinct that it rose right up to my window with all its intonation intact, sharp and incensed. 'We obviously haven't been clear enough.' She turned to Alicia now, impatiently. 'For God's sake, there's no need to cry. It's over. Nothing happened.'

At this point I was frightened by the sound of my door opening, and jumped back from the window, forgetting I was standing on a chair. A security guard put his head around the door, saw me lying on the floor and came in frowning.

'What are you up to then, Jonny?' he asked.

'My name's not Jonny,' I said, getting up and holding my bruised elbow angrily.

We both looked at the open window, and then the security guard went over and closed it. Theo made a snoring sound from the bed.

'Let's not wake your sister up, shall we?' he said with the same uncomfortable heartiness. 'Where's your room?'

After that there was not much I could do except allow myself to be led to my bedroom and suffer the security guard to sit with me until I 'dropped off', as he put it.

'Seems a burglar's got into the grounds,' he said cheerfully, 'but we caught him. He didn't get anywhere near the house.'

'I thought someone was in the house,' I said.

'Nope. Just us security guards. The police will be here soon, so you get some sleep.'

His face was opaque; his mouth moved seamlessly. I realised there was no point asking him what the burglar had shouted to my mother, or why Eve hadn't been clear enough, because his mouth would have that covered too. Adults talked, and talked, I thought. They talked over everything, and eventually flattened it all into their own shapes. I could not compete with that.

e~

When I woke up it was sunny and there was no security guard in the room. There wasn't even an indentation on the sofa he had occupied by the window. But my elbow had a bruise on it, and when

I sat up my stomach rolled itself up like a snail, slippery with unease.

The stairs and hall were quiet when I came down, but I followed the sounds of china to the breakfast room, where Eve, Theo and Alicia were sitting. Eve was pouring some coffee, holding back the sleeve of her silk robe like a geisha. Alicia was reading a magazine on the sofa and ignored my entrance, as if it were any other morning. Theo, who was nibbling the edge of a piece of toast abstractedly, cried in lieu of a welcome, 'There's no more jam!'

I couldn't make sense of what she had said at first; it was a call from another place, from before last night. It was as if the previous night had been a dream; the newspapers, the toast, the coffee, the sun floating in the fresh air rising off the damp grass outside all said so. I looked out of the open French windows for the smashed glass. It wasn't there.

'Good morning darling,' Eve said, smiling. 'You look a little tired. Mark said you were up and about when he came to check on you. Did you sleep badly?'

'I slept okay,' I said.

'May I get down?' Theo asked. 'I'm going to ask Mrs Williams if I can make some jam.'

'Of course you may,' Eve said.

When Theo had gone she put down her cup and said, 'Now, Jonathan, we thought it best not to tell Theo about the intruder yesterday. Everything's fine now' – I looked across at Alicia, but her eyes did not miss a beat in their glide across the page '– and it's probably better not to worry her. You know how sensitive she is.'

After breakfast I went into the kitchen, where everything was the same as usual. Theo was sitting on a chair putting strawberries alternately into a bowl, and then into her mouth. Mrs Williams was picking up some fallen sliced tomatoes off the floor. She huffed on them.

'Blows the germs away,' she explained, laying the slices on top of a quiche, then changed tack. 'You two don't know how lucky you are. I had some bad news this morning. Peri-modontal gum disease, whatever that is. Doesn't sound like a disease if you ask me. They make half of it up, those dentists. That's how they afford those cars. You two stay away from that business.' She looked at us accusingly.

'I won't be a dentist,' Theo said, tipping golden syrup into the bowl of strawberries. 'I'm going to be a cook, and I'm going to feed poor people in developing countries.'

'Feed them with your jam, eh? They won't thank you for that,' said Mrs Williams, laughing. 'Will they, Jonathan?'

'No,' I agreed, not really listening. I sat down at the table and ate some strawberries as I put my thoughts together. I didn't understand what had happened last night, but it was over now, and I wasn't going to question the strange luck that had made everything go back to exactly the way it was – with a snap of its fingers and a brilliant smile; sweeping the night back like a curtain to reveal Evendon as it should be – Theo with strawberry round her mouth, the sun on the table, Mrs Williams taking her cigarettes out of her bag. Nothing missing, and everything in its place.

Only one thing really changed after that day – the day of the bad dream, as I preferred to think of it. Theo, who had always slept so soundly, lost her powers of torpor. The next night she crept into my room, sobbing; I woke up to find my face wet with her tears, her hand gripping mine, hot and pulpy with fever.

'Whats wrong?' I sat up hurriedly, thinking of the burglar. 'Is there someone in the house?'

'It's the ghost,' Theo cried. 'It crawled in and it's under the bed.'

I lay back with exasperated relief.

'Theo! You worried me. There's no ghost. It's just a dream.'

'It wants to come back,' she said. 'It wants to come back but it can't.'

I lay there for a moment, my nerves still irritated and scratchy, my brain stupid with sleep, before I noticed that she was shivering. Her eyes were marked underneath with grey moth-wings and her skin was clammily white.

'You can stay in here tonight if you want,' I offered, moved. I put my arm around her. 'Ghosts aren't allowed in my room.'

'Poor ghost,' said Theo, and closed her eyes. I sat still, unwilling to disturb her, until she breathed more regularly, and I thought she was asleep. Then she said in an indistinct and anxious mumble, 'Look after me.'

'I will,' I said.

'Promise?'

'I promise.'

Then, quickly and easily, she fell asleep.

I couldn't sleep. I remember lying awake for a long time. The sky was so clear it seemed like the stars were inside the window; the air on my face kept my eyes open. Theo was on her back with her mouth open, her hair silvery in the faint light, rising up in curls around her face, her eyelids serenely blank, like shells. She murmured in her sleep, without making sense; a low, unintelligible hum, the music of my uncomfortable night.

e

For months after that Theo would go to bed obediently, if Eve was around, and allow her light to be turned off. But in the morning I would find her on the floor of my room, or next to me in bed, wrapped in her blanket as if it was a chrysalis, my hand or even just a corner of my sheet pulled over to hold to her cheek. Some nights she would roll herself in my sheet as well as her own; when I tried to wrestle it back she would cling inside it like a baby monkey, still asleep.

Theo's night fears exasperated Eve, who said I should lock my door until she learned to sleep alone. But I couldn't do it. I knew that Theo needed me, more than another person might ever need me: she was less resilient, less easily fixed.

'Do you remember your nightmares?' I asked her once.

'I think so,' she said, and her mouth drooped.

I tried to remember my dreams, but I couldn't. Night for me was a closed eye, a blank space; I was nowhere inside it.

2008

It's almost three o'clock when I look up from the newspaper brought by Mr Ramsey, which I have long stopped reading. On the surface of the full cup of tea next to me separated milk drifts like broken ice, reminding me that I ought to go out and buy something to drink. Something to eat, too. I have to make an effort to remember these things – the normal motions of life, that for me keep seizing, like old gears.

As I leave the house, I bump into the family from below issuing out of the door into a people carrier. They look delighted now that they are going home; they wave at me in an excess of high spirits. Then they all whirl off, the woman turning to speak to her husband, the boy with his face pressed in a comic. Their happiness circles in the car; self-contained, tenacious as rubber. I wonder what my happiness would be like if I could have another chance at it. I can't imagine it being so clean and bright: there would be something murky about it, something dull and slow and wounded.

On the seafront I see a chip shop and head towards it, walking faster when a half-hearted rain begins. Two teenage girls go by, wearing short skirts. Their English legs are whipped red and white in the wind; they walk like hurried storks, gawky in their high heels, drinking from bottles. One looks at me, and after they pass they giggle. The sound floats back, an odd, soft note amid the rush of the sea and the shriek of gulls.

For me the smell of chips has only ever associated itself with one place: the little hut next to Llansteffan beach, where the chips were served in small trays, with fat little two-pronged wooden forks, to be eaten with the sun dimming behind us in the evening, looking over the bluish sand. Here there is no beach; the concrete road turns sharply into boat masts, staking the opaque, steel-grey water. The wind gusting off the ocean smells cold and raw, like oysters, colliding queasily with the warm, oily air of the chip shop. Its interior is tiled like a lavatory, lit with a fluorescent blue cod wearing an improbable smile. A fat woman stands behind the counter like a warning, her dyed blonde hair greenish in the light.

'You want salt and vinegar?' she asks me shortly, then wraps the food without waiting for an answer. I take my chips, my warm can of cola, my parcel with its bleeding spots of grease, and before I can thank her, she is calling to the next person.

℮

When I finish the chips I realise they are wrapped in the same newspaper article that surprised me this morning. My younger face smirks up at me, reflective with oil. Anthony Heir Missing. I wonder how my missingness was decided. I'm not missing – I'm gone. Furthermore, I told everyone I was going. When I read the article properly, I see that my mother, with 'tears in her eyes', has confided to a journalist that she does not know where I am.

I call her using my new mobile phone, the number of which I have not given to anybody except Mr Crace. I don't want anybody to contact me now, not after the first grim weeks. Who sends a text message to convey condolences? I wouldn't have thought such people existed, but it seems they do, and it seems they are my friends.

'Jonathan?' Alicia says when she answers, but her tone is hard to interpret. 'Where are you?'

'I said I'd be away for a while. I told you. I'm not missing. Did you talk to the papers about me?'

'No, of course not.'

'There's a quote from you.'

'Oh, I don't know what I said . . . I was distraught.'

'Yes, it says that here too – "I'm distraught," Alicia Anthony told us.'

'I didn't expect to have to deal with the press.' Now I recognise the tone: petulance. 'You've left me to deal with them alone.'

'You're not alone. You have plenty of people around you.'

'Only staff. The cook gets everything wrong, the maids . . . oh, they may as well not be here.'

'Alicia, you'll have to work that out for yourself. I was only calling to let you know I'm all right.' Then I lie: 'This phone has no battery left, I can't talk much longer,' and I hang up.

⁊

I don't put the phone down, which has warmed in my hand, as if waking from hibernation. The screen displays no voicemail messages but I check it anyway, in the hope that the call from

Mr Crace has become hidden somehow, fallen victim to one of the unknowable and obscure rules by which the phone is guided.

There is no call, which is partly a relief, because I don't know what will happen when I hear from him. What I might find out, whether I would rather not know. But on the other side of that relief is the practical awareness that it would be better for me to be summoned somewhere else, to leave Southampton. It was probably a mistake to drive until I reached the sea, drawn to the edge of it, to watch it as it breathes in and out, giving its changeable sighs and cries, telling me that it can hold me if I want it to: envelop me, turn me into a tiny speck, a blink. Facts would fall away from me like dried mud: Jonathan Anthony: architect, heir, brother, grandson. I would forget she is dead, and I would be nothing at all, hopeless and free.

PART TWO

2000

The Feet, mechanical, go round –
Of Ground, or Air, or Ought –
A Wooden way
Regardless grown,
A Quartz contentment, like a stone –

Emily Dickinson,
'After great pain . . .'

FIVE

At the end of my first year at Cambridge, I drove back to Wales with the motorway sloughing either side of me in the summer rain, trying to focus on its grey width rather than my own hangover. The car's motion was rocking my brain in a sickening wallow; my eyes were stiff and reluctant in their bearings. I was surviving by watching the road and thinking no thoughts, not listening to my passengers' busy reconstruction of the previous night, not imagining the time it would take to get back to Evendon, the hours stretching out ahead of me.

'So, did you sleep with that girl last night?' Sebastian asked me.

'Yeah,' I said, trying to avoid the people carrier that had bumbled blindly into my path like a stag beetle. I mouthed a half-hearted fuck-off to the children in the back, who turned and waved.

'Any good?' asked Felix. He was wearing a policeman's hat and had his arm around Caroline Tyler, a third year famous for her beauty and her humourlessness. Caroline's lovely head rested enervated on Felix's shoulder, her eyes lost behind large sunglasses. She hadn't spoken so far during the journey, though her hand moved occasionally to forestall Felix's, which he was attempting to ease onto her breast.

'I suppose so,' I said.

'You can't remember her name,' Sebastian said slyly.

I had worked hard during the past year at remembering names: Foster, Gaudí, Lloyd Wright. Atria, mansard, cantilever. Louvre, Casa Botines, Guggenheim Bilbao. In all these stacked, solid names there wasn't much room for female names – temporary names, drunk names, lacy and insubstantial in the dark, slipping into bed, hanging around lecture-room doorways, signing off text messages.

'Yes, I can,' I lied.

'What is it then?'

'Shut up.'

Sebastian laughed and peered around at Charlie, who was slumped like a bankrupt financier on the other side of Caroline. 'I can't believe Charlie's face. It's green. Look! Have you ever seen that colour on a human *face*?'

'Sick,' Charlie mumbled.

'I think he is actually going to be sick,' Felix informed me.

'Christ,' I switched on the indicator. 'Hold on, Charlie. I'll pull over.'

Caroline shrieked. 'Too late,' Felix said, laughing. 'Oh dear.'

We pulled into a service station, opened the doors, and made Charlie stand in the rain, which swept over him in sheets, flattening his hair against his forehead. He swayed slightly and wiped at his shirt front disconsolately.

'So, let's not change the subject,' Felix said to me. 'You were super smooth last night. It was like watching Casanova.'

'Whereas the most we had to look forward to was being raped in prison,' Sebastian said, opening a can of cola and spilling it down himself.

I had come home from the party at nine in the morning, without having slept, and was just getting into bed for a nap when the phone rang and I had to go to the police station to collect Felix and Sebastian. They'd spent the night there after stealing a ladder they had found near a building site on their way home. Apparently a police car passed them at four in the morning carrying it between them, and they thought it would be funny to pretend they were burglars. They were so convincing that the police refused to believe they were students, and took them back to the station.

'I should have left you there,' I said.

Sebastian whispered to Felix, 'Jonathan's grumpy.'

I squinted out of the rain-sluiced window: the traffic ahead appeared to be slowing to a halt. Charlie was still retching on the grass verge. I effortfully assembled my few pieces of the girl from last night. Dark hair with a fringe. A short polka-dotted dress, which at the time had reminded me of Minnie Mouse. Her mouth had the bitter, dusty taste of cigarettes; her breasts were surprisingly heavy for her narrow body. She had fallen asleep afterwards in the unknown person's bedroom, and I had gone back to the party.

'Laura Chamberlain,' I said with triumph. 'She's studying architecture. She's in our seminars, Felix.'

'Oh yeah, I slept with her last term,' Felix said. 'She was a dirty bitch.'

'I wish I could remember,' I said, resting my head on the steering wheel. Tiredness moved into my vision like a crowd of grey birds, wheeling and scattering. 'Someone go and tell Charlie he can come back now.'

Several hours later, Felix and Caroline had been deposited at his parents' house in London (Felix giving a quick thumbs-up behind her back), Charlie had been dropped off in Aberthin, and the rain had started to ease off, becoming a light, comprehensive mist that clouded the windows of the car.

'Never heard of it getting less rainy in Wales,' Sebastian said. He was energised with his fourth cola and concertinaed in his seat to gaze up at the hills rising either side of the motorway.

'It's not the usual way,' I said. 'Now that it's too late, you may as well know it was a mistake to come and stay with me.'

'Better than spending the holidays with my family,' Sebastian said, grimacing. 'My mother wanted me to go to LA. But I have this weird feeling that LA is where I'm going to die . . . Hey, when does Theo get back?'

'She's home already,' I said. 'She's left several messages every day asking when we're coming.'

'Did she ask about me?'

Sebastian had been visibly in love with Theo since she first visited the flat we shared in halls. His initial eager attentiveness had settled – as the months passed without her noticing it – into an unhappily poignant attentiveness, which none of us ever mentioned: tactful and cheery as hospice nurses.

'Sure,' I said kindly, unable to remember whether this was true.

I wondered how Theo, who was also spending the summer at Evendon after finishing her A levels, would be when we got back. The last time I saw her she had brought me a cross-eyed stray dog she thought could live with me, and before that she had forgotten what time I was collecting her from her own student flat and slept in, and I had to throw my shoes at her window to wake her up.

Theo and I were still as unalike as when we were children; back when I looked like a stolid little businessman and she was made of glass and feathers, fiery and weightless. 'That's your sister?' people said when they met us; they thought we were joking. We shared a family outline – Eve's template – but it was coloured in differently. I was dark-haired, Theo was bright-haired. My eyes were opaque, hers as sheer and ingenuous as a gas flame. I followed familiar laws and rules: sow and reap, action and reaction, inspiration and perspiration. Whereas Theo – Theo's motives were a mystery, even to herself.

When we finally turned the car up the drive to Evendon Sebastian had fallen asleep, lulled by the slurring rain and the gentle clamour of empty cans rolling at his feet. His head – with its tired lower eyelids, hair collapsed in various directions – had the sudden rumpled simplicity of a child's. I was grateful to be left in silence just then; I had the familiar vision of the trees in the curving road to myself, the peculiar radiance of the light. Then Evendon itself moved gradually into view, its dark roof slick in the wet, all its windows as white as the sky.

I was surprised to see several unfamiliar cars and vans around the drive, all of them black, none of them occupied, their sides blankly reflective in the rain. I turned off the engine and opened my door into a wide quiet; the sound of birds, the drowsy tap of water on the car roof. The trees were very still, the house expressionless. A flat note hummed in the hall of my chest like a wrong-footed conductor. I glanced at Sebastian, still sleeping, and back at the house. Then I heard Theo cry out, 'Jonathan!'

She was sitting on the front steps nearly hidden behind one of the vans, a small shape under a large golfing umbrella, a pale spray of curls, swinging her bare feet. Waving energetically, she stood up and began picking her way across the gravelled drive.

'Wait, Theo!' I called. She ignored me, hopped and winced over to us, then clung to my arm until I dropped a suitcase on my foot. Sebastian yawned and unrolled himself from the other door.

'Oh Jonathan, I thought you were one of *them*,' she said into my shoulder. 'Hello, Sebastian!'

'What's going on?' Sebastian said with disbelief. 'Is this your house? Are we in the middle of a wood? How barbaric. It's like the Brothers Grimm. I'm going to be pushed into an oven by a witch, aren't I, all because I didn't want to go to LA to drink pomegranate cocktails and watch my mother flirt with her yoga guru.'

'What's going on?' I asked. 'Who's here?'

'Lots of people,' Theo said darkly. 'That's why I came outside. They're making a documentary about Charis.'

'I hadn't heard about this,' I said, relieved, though I couldn't have said why I had been worried in the first place. We carried the cases into the house, stepping over a mass of cables that lay across the doorway, and entered the hard white heights of the hall, which lifted our suddenly small voices up above our heads. The hall, filled with its motionless light, was as deserted as the front of the house, so we followed the path of the cables like a puzzle, Theo treading warily behind us.

Finally in the drawing room we found Eve in the centre of a tableau like the Botticelli Venus, surrounded by people, a titanic arrangement of flowers perching on a pillar behind her, a silver umbrella reflecting light onto the cool oval of her face, cables converging around her feet like snakes, a furred boom mic hanging above her head. Someone turned and made a hushing signal to us, so we stood in the doorway and watched Eve speaking to the camera.

'I always saw my youth as being shaped by three unfair deaths,' she said, in her distinctive accent, not quite English, not American, not flatly transatlantic. It was, it occurred to me now, a voice particularly for television, full and golden and liquid. 'After my mother's death in 1943, my father George decided to move to England. Then, after his death in 1955, I went back to New York. I suppose my father and I shared that instinct, to leave home after a devastating loss. Finally, in 1969, my husband Freddie died. We had been holidaying in Cape Cod with some friends, the Bressards, and Sam Anthony. I'll never forget the conversation we had that morning, trying to decide whether to take the boat out. The Bressards were the most experienced sailors and we almost didn't go out because they were ill. But it was such a beautiful sunny morning that Freddie convinced us to go. The boom knocked him overboard; it knocked him unconscious. Neither Sam nor I could swim well – I had a broken wrist at the time from a silly fall – and we just couldn't reach him, he sank so fast. That was the last I ever saw of him, his shape in the water, falling away from me. The divers were sent down afterwards but he was never found.' She paused, drawing her face away from the camera briefly. The crew were silent, before she resumed: 'I think that was the hardest thing.

'So there I was at thirty-two, with two young children, at a funeral with an empty casket. Beyond my own personal grief, it seemed a symbol of Freddie's career – something left unfinished, a space that should not be empty. That was the day I decided to go from the world of charity work into the world of politics. And the first, as I found out, was certainly not good preparation for the second.' She laughed wryly.

'And cut,' said one of the men standing near her, wearing sunglasses and a gilet. 'Nice.'

The gilet and Eve gave each other the thumbs-up, then someone came and put a towel around her shoulders and solicitously dusted her face with a brush.

It had been almost a year since I had seen Eve, who had been away the last time I was back, but she hadn't changed. Her hair was as black as her eyes, which looked newly painted, a clear demarcation between the ink of her iris and its porcelain setting. The skin of her face was still lucent, still moving smoothly over the symmetrical bones, where it should have loosened into powdery sags and creases. Her beauty was not something still and passive – it had its own peculiar power, forcing the people around her to scurry and trip, irresistibly turning their heads around in her direction, catching and recapturing their eyes. She looked over, noticing us, and winked.

'Hello, darling. I'll be half an hour,' she said. 'And this must be Sebastian! So sorry you have to arrive to such chaos.' Sebastian became shy for the first time and murmured something, before a producer began trying to recapture Eve's attention. She smiled at us as if to say *what a bore this is!* then gave her consideration to the question of whether having a soundbite from the Prince of Wales might work, or whether it would be seen as stuffy.

e

The camera crew were gone a week later, which Mrs Williams was very sorry about, as she had been in the habit of drinking tea and smoking in the herb garden with the production assistants and gossiping about various celebrities. Mrs Wynne Jones, in contrast, had maintained a dignified disdain for the whole thing, though it was to be noted that her hair was now in a Thatcherish curl, and her straight lips had become a fanciful salmon-tinted bow.

Several of Eve's famous friends had been enlisted to show off their dentistry and tell amusing stories – which they did with professional ease ('She was absolutely ruthless at musical chairs, as I recall') – but our family, for the most part, did not appear in the documentary. Alicia had agreed to sit on the terrace in a low-cut dress and say that Eve was not only a great mother, but an inspiration ('Very tiring,' she said about this experience). The director had in fact developed something of a crush on Alicia, and in the final documentary she was shown juxtaposed with her roses like some airy flower spirit. They omitted her snapping at Mrs Wynne Jones and the time when, moving with stilted grace, she tripped on one of the electrical leads. It was also suggested that Theo – wearing make-up and an outfit chosen by a stylist – stand laughing with me in the garden for a 'family moment'.

'That face should *not* be wasted,' the director protested, but Theo tipped the face obstinately down, and shook her head.

My Uncle Alex was the only one of the family not asked to participate, possibly because of concerns over damage to his academic credibility, possibly because he and Eve were in the midst of some unspecified disagreement. He had not visited at Christmas for the past few years, and no one had heard from him – or, indeed, asked about him. I didn't really care whether he visited or not. Alex was hard to talk to; his alternating silences and outbursts made him difficult company. Worse, he reheated the old, cold tensions of Evendon, moving sluggish as glaciers between Eve and Alicia, until they simmered into fractious flurries of raised eyebrows and tightened lips. Even Theo, patron saint of the lost and afflicted, didn't question Alex's absence. 'Uncle Alex is just so . . . cross,' was all she could think of to say about him.

e

Eve herself, despite her air of tolerant amusement during filming, took the documentary seriously and had insisted on final approval.

'I wouldn't have dreamed of it otherwise,' she said to me. 'Good God! It would be like throwing myself to the lions. Never, ever let somebody else edit you.'

'Why did you do it anyway?' I asked. I had been a little hurt not to have been told about it; I was used to considering myself 'in the know' about Eve's various projects.

'Partly to prevent an unauthorised version. It's only a matter of time before something like that comes out. They've done poor Betty Ford. If I died tomorrow there would be a *Secret Life of Eve*

Anthony within a month. And then, partly because this thing will be perfect publicity. It seems people want something personal from corporations now. No one ever expected to feel like they were a part of Aristotle Onassis's life. People just bought things that they believed would work. But if the public needs to see me pouring tea or laying pipes, if they want to empathise with me, then so be it.'

'*Did* you have a secret life?' I asked her.

'A secret life!' Eve started to laugh. 'Darling, I didn't have the time.'

SIX

A few days after we arrived, the ever-hovering rain was burned out of the sky by the late July sun, and Theo, Sebastian and I walked down the hill to the beach at Llansteffan, lagging in the heavy gold heat of the afternoon. The pattern of leaves under my feet barely shifted; the drifts of wind from the sea were exhausted, the water itself flat in the distance.

'If you had to write the story of your life, what would you call it?' Sebastian asked us. He had been smoking weed since nine o'clock. 'I'd call mine *Underprepared.*'

Theo thought hard and loud for the next ten minutes but was unable to come up with an idea.

'I'll do yours for you,' Sebastian offered. 'It should be something confusing, like you. How about *Pyjama Owl Riddles.*'

'I love it!' Theo cried. 'Do Jonathan's.'

'I don't want one,' I said. 'He'll only put a pun in it.'

'It should be about architecture,' Theo said.

'*The Remorseless Rise of Jonathan Anthony,*' Sebastian announced. 'Subheading: *The Storey So Far* – storey as in building storey, obviously.'

'Awful.'

'Let's get ice cream,' Theo said. 'The shop's on this corner.'

'Good idea.' Sebastian nudged me. 'Interesting views you've got round here.'

I looked up, not understanding, then saw a girl further along the road, standing in the bowl of shade under a tree. She was not immediately striking – thin, brunette, her face turned slightly away – but as I got closer I could see that she wasn't just the standard pretty girl around town. There was an excitement in realising that, like tapping away in a mine and seeing something unexpected: the beginnings of a fierce brightness. I stared at her with the possessiveness of the frontier man; her almond skin and thoughtful mouth, the white dress resting against the steep heights of her thighs. Her hair lifted and fell as the coastal wind picked up, dividing into streamers that ran down her back. She looked up as we passed – her eyes a brief, gold colour under the lashes, like the glint of a tossed coin – but it was only a routine glance, not allowing itself to be held.

'She looked nice,' Theo said once we were past.

'Nice!' was all Sebastian could say, with an incredulous laugh.

Theo went into the shop while Sebastian and I waited outside in the sun. I looked back at the girl stealthily, partly to check that she was still there. There was no one else in the empty road, spare and bright in the sun; no bus stop, telephone box, idling car, or anything else to tie her to her surroundings. And her beauty was so unlikely, almost absurd. She was like a person in front of a blue screen, a complete and dissociated image, set against the background but not of it. I looked back at her again – wanting the look to be sensed, to make her turn around – but she was gazing towards the sea, and didn't notice.

Sebastian, who had been watching me, laughed. 'Look, I'm

going to go in the shop and get some water,' he said. 'Then she can approach you and suggest some sort of sexual adventure. That kind of thing always happens to you.'

He exited, leaving the girl and me alone outside for a moment that shivered and stretched into a tense, infinitely promising blank space. I straightened my back, took my hands out of my pockets, wondered briefly how my introductory smile would look to her – lecherous possibly, or worse, nervous – and then a dark-haired boy came out of the shop and walked away, taking the girl with him. I frowned at their backs until Sebastian and Theo came out.

'I'm upset,' Sebastian complained. 'Theo and I have made an enemy and all we did was ask for ice creams.'

'That's just how Mrs Edwards is,' I said.

Mrs Edwards, the shop's proprietor, could usually be found sitting toadlike in the dim, crowded depths behind her counter, staring unblinkingly at the flies circling her ceiling. She would address even Welsh customers perfunctorily, but if she overheard the accent of an English tourist or expat she wouldn't speak at all, silently handing over her wares: the soft, white-laced chocolate, the obsolete fizzy drinks with their faded labels.

'A lot of the older Welsh people are like that with us,' I explained. 'Though they aren't usually so obvious about it.'

'She smiled at me once,' Theo told us.

For Theo had – not completely or without difficulty – charmed our neighbours. She had picked up fragments of Welsh and with it addressed shopkeepers, farmers, passers-by, most of whom only spoke English. She bought things from Carmarthen market and remembered everybody's name. Sooner or later people ended up liking her, asking after her, making excuses for her, with the half-enthralled, half-confused expression that characterised all Theo's fans.

'Did you talk to that girl?' Sebastian asked me. I shook my head.

'Maria,' said Theo. 'She's called Maria Dumas.'

'How do you know?' I asked.

'I spoke to her brother in the shop – Nick. They've come to live here, they have a house on Castle Hill. Do you know that house?'

'Her brother?'

'Anyway, I said that they should come over this week. I told Nick he didn't have to worry, because the cameras are gone now.'

'Oh Theo . . .' I said, but was too pleased to add anything other than, 'That must have confused him.'

℮⌐

At the beach Theo ran off to swim, quickly becoming indistinguishable from the dark arms and heads of the other sea-goers, scattered in the luminous water. We lay on the flat cream sand under the blue blaze of the sky, Sebastian, sandy-fingered, rolling another joint. We were half dozing when Theo came running back up the beach, stumbling occasionally as she trod on other people's beach towels and buckets.

'Jonathan! Sebastian! I almost got swept out,' she said breathlessly, throwing herself down on the towel. 'But I shouted for help and I got rescued.'

'Swept out?' I sat up. 'Why did you go out so far? Who rescued you?'

'Another man who was swimming,' Theo said. 'He looked like a *dad*, with a hairy stomach, and a bald spot.'

'A bald spot on his stomach?' enquired Sebastian.

'No, on his head. He said I ought to be careful next time.' She smiled reflectively. 'That's the kind of dad I'd like – stern but nice.'

'He was right. You shouldn't swim out so far,' I said.

'I wasn't swimming, I was floating,' Theo explained. 'I didn't notice how far I'd drifted out.'

'Then pay more attention to where you're going,' I snapped, and she contracted, winding her fingers through her hair.

Theo's lack of survival skills bothered me. She had never learned when to say no to strangers, when to look both ways. When I lectured her about the various things she did – accepting lifts from people she had met the same day, walking alone at night – she would just smile and nod at me, leaving the house like a balloon heading gaily into the broad, cold sky.

'Look,' she said now, forgetting to be shamefaced. She pointed up at the hill. 'That's the house I told you about . . . where Maria and Nick live. I remember that house from when we were little, because you can see it from the edge of Evendon too. I always used to wonder who lived in it. Isn't that funny!'

'I suppose it is,' I said, squinting up to where the small house sat on the highest point of the hill, like a white tooth, a white mint, isolated in the blue.

℮

Theo, Sebastian and I watched the final cut of the documentary after it was sent to Eve, drinking in my room from a decanter lifted earlier that day and shushing Theo when her attention slid off in random directions. On screen a camera was sweeping up a New York street, taking in some strategically placed beggars before rolling its gaze up the facade of a grand hotel. The voiceover sonorously explained that after Eve's retirement from politics and her marriage to the film studio head Sam Anthony, she had spent a day at a homeless shelter in New York run by a charity of which she was a board member.

The camera returned to Eve in close-up, her face vivid with its own contrasts, sharply edged. She said: 'I stayed that night at the Waldorf after spending the day talking to people who for one reason or another had found themselves dispossessed, owning nothing. Going back to my suite with its champagne glasses and silk wallpaper made for an uncomfortable night. I thought then that people like me, enjoying a good night's sleep, could help less fortunate people to get a night free of fear and cold.'

The voiceover came back, along with footage of Eve standing in front of various grand hotels and homeless shelters, cutting ribbon after ribbon. 'Eve founded Charis Hotels in 1977,' it explained. 'A large cut of the profit from each hotel is used to fund a nearby homeless shelter, soup kitchen or free health clinic. It was an innovative venture, at a time when big business had little thought of social conscience. At first the hotels were located in upscale areas of New York and other cities; then, during the eighties, Charis expanded to Europe, Australia and Canada, even Mumbai. In a 2006 poll of business leaders, it was voted one of the most highly regarded global brands.'

The on-screen Eve changed from a woman smiling alongside Mother Teresa, swimming forward in time to a nearly identical woman smiling in front of her flower arrangement. 'It's not to my credit that Charis has grown so astonishingly,' she said. 'It is down to the conscience of everyday people: tourists, lovers, businessmen and -women. People have an enormous well of compassion for other people. All I did was tap into it.'

'It's us!' Theo cried, as a helicopter view of Evendon and the surrounding hills appeared on the screen, accompanied by the voiceover: 'When Eve Anthony returned to the UK in 1979, she took on the task of renovating her family estate, Evendon, and its architecturally significant house, which had fallen into disrepair following the death of her father.'

Eve's face returned, more serious this time. 'Evendon was my childhood home, but for a long time after my father's death – which happened at the house itself – I couldn't face going back there. Later, after my divorce, I decided it was time to revisit Evendon, even if it meant facing painful memories. In fact, the restoration was a very cathartic process. Most of the furnishings I remembered were in such bad shape that they had to be stripped out. I was upset at first, but then I felt it was better to start again. To make the house my own.' She smiled seraphically. 'I think my father would have liked that.

'Not long after I had finished Evendon,' she continued, 'I was speaking to a distant relative of mine, Lavinia Thorne, who couldn't afford to live at her own estate any longer but couldn't sell to the National Trust as it didn't meet their criteria. I offered to buy it, renovate it and operate it as part of Charis, as a hotel supporting a charity. Lavinia and I chose a charity very dear to her heart, the local animal rescue. That's how Charis Heritage began. Letters came flooding in from acquaintances or extended family, asking if I wouldn't mind "doing something" with their own houses, most of which were falling apart or burdened by running costs. Overseas I had mainly bought commercial sites in city centres, but Charis Heritage had two functions, not only supporting charities, but preserving our precious architectural history.'

The documentary then began following the redevelopment of Charis Heritage's latest acquisition, a seventeenth-century manor in Buckinghamshire. Eve appeared briefly in a hard hat, apparently supervising the implantation of new central heating, the rising bricks of a spa in the grounds. She chatted pleasantly with a plumber, who was rather too chirpy and cockney to ring true.

'Whose house is that?' Theo asked, looking up from her doodle on the cover of one of my textbooks.

'I don't know,' I said. I was never entirely sure what the rehomed upper classes made of Charis, run by one of their own, always ready with its chequebook when the electricity bills swallowed the legacy or when a will revealed a money pit. The former owners did not appear in the documentary, to see their human traces dusted away: the furniture carried out, the fingerprints covered over by fresh paint, the hotel room numbers nailed onto bedroom doors.

'Eve looks incredible,' Sebastian said. 'She's not exactly like a granny, is she?' We watched the on-screen Eve crossing a lawn, her legs scissoring sharply in a red dress. 'My grandmother just watches television or complains to newspapers. She wears cardigans. And she looks old.'

'She sounds nice,' Theo said.

'Well, she always has cake, I suppose,' Sebastian said. 'But

Eve . . . do you think she would adopt me? Then I'd have someone to look up to. It might even give me some purpose in life.'

e⁓

I didn't forget Maria Dumas as the days passed. I noticed dark-haired girls who had some resemblance to her – a brown arm, a smoothly executed gesture, a shapely mouth under sunglasses – but when I caught up to them, always hopeful, they never had more than that one piece of her. I knew sensibly that there was a window of a week or two in which she might appear at Evendon, before the introduction would time out. This scratched at my nerves in a way I wasn't familiar with – a vague stress, like the feeling of having forgotten something but not knowing what.

Theo, Sebastian and I drifted through August like sinking stones, settling into a Sunday that was unbreathably hot. I'd been preparing a structure for a presentation during the last few days, in the cool paper dark of the library with only the dead Bennetts for company, and when I finished that afternoon and went outside I was surprised by the sudden pressure of the sun, the garden floating like strange water, its green stretch transfigured by the haze of light.

Eve was away in London, so Mrs Williams was in the herb garden sending lazy plumes of smoke into the still sky, and most of the maids had gone to the beach. Alicia was sitting on the terrace under a large white parasol, in a large hat and large opaque sunglasses, steeped in *Vogue*.

I squinted out over the lawn, where Theo and Sebastian were lying in the grass under a pear tree, playing cards. Theo was wearing a yellow sundress; her legs and arms androgynously slender and straight – almost a young boy's limbs – marooned in the fierce light. I was about to join them when I was interrupted by Mrs Wynne Jones, emerging at her usual swift pace onto the terrace, magnificently unencumbered by the heat in her self-imposed uniform of black cardigan, black tights and wool skirt. Not for her the polyester dresses sported by Mrs Williams, lone bra strap lolling from brightly flowered sleeve.

'Jonathan, Theo,' she called. 'There are visitors here for you.' And before I could possibly be prepared for it, Maria and her brother were shown out into the garden, blinking their leonine eyes as they crossed the line from interior to sun.

'Hurrah!' Theo shouted, rushing up to kiss them. In the round of naming, the compliments and counter-compliments, my introduction to Maria was brief and flurried.

'I knew you would come to visit,' Theo cried. 'Didn't I, Jonathan? Jonathan never believes me. But I liked you both, and when you like someone, I think there is a ninety-nine per cent chance they must like you back. Or it would just be *unreasonable*.'

Nick shaded his eyes and gave Theo an uncertain look. 'Well, we would have come sooner except we weren't sure where Evendon was. Then it turned out everybody knew where it was.'

'Really?' Theo said, delighted. 'I wonder why more people don't visit us.'

There was a brief pause.

'Maybe because you're at the top of a hill,' Nick said diplomatically.

'So you've moved here?' I said to Maria, who was standing

next to me. I had been trying to look at as much of her as I could before she noticed. The slope of her cheek, the blazing white of her shirt peeling out from her tanned skin, the symmetry of her well-shaped fingers. I examined her eyes now under their massed lashes, like a Victorian scientist trying to discover the secret of their electricity.

'From Bath,' she said. 'Our mother's divorcing our father.'

'Oh,' I said, 'I'm sorry.'

Maria looked at me for a moment, then she smiled.

'Don't worry, we're not traumatised. Not much.'

'It's Maria's fault anyway,' Nick said, with an irritated laugh. 'She persuaded our mother to leave. I just went along with it. I had no idea we'd be moving so far.'

Theo gazed at him with deep sympathy.

'Our father doesn't live with us any more either,' she said.

'If he's anything like ours then you're lucky,' Nick said. 'Where's yours?'

'Everyone thinks he's dead,' Theo explained, 'because nobody wants him back. But *I* do.'

'Right,' said Nick, looking puzzled.

'He *is* dead,' I said. I had no idea what she was talking about, and could only send her a severe frown, which she didn't notice.

'Let's all have a drink,' Sebastian said hastily.

I was relieved to see that Alicia had gone inside to avoid social exertion, taking her glass with her. I had never brought a girl to Evendon before and the arrival of Maria was a new kind of pressure: one I wasn't exactly enjoying, with my determined smile, my tapping fingers. But she was sitting down now – talking and laughing – and I made an effort to relax myself and join in.

Nick was talking about a girl called Emily he had left in Bath. 'She's beautiful. I told her I wouldn't be away long if I can help it, so she's waiting for me. I'm going to visit her every weekend.'

'Won't she come here?' Maria asked.

Nick gave a surprised cry. 'She's used to the best of everything, Maria. I can't ask her to stay here.'

'Nick thinks anywhere you can't buy a mojito within a hundred yards may as well be the North Pole,' Maria said, laughing. 'But I like it here. I always wanted to live next to the sea. And you could take her to the beach, Nick.'

'Emily doesn't like sand,' Nick said shortly.

'I had a cat called Emily once,' Theo said. 'Well, she wasn't really my cat. I don't know whose cat she was—'

'So are you at university, Maria?' I interrupted.

'Just finished my first year,' she said. 'I'm studying psychology in Paris. How about you?'

'Architecture,' I said. 'In the same year as you. I'm at Cambridge – so is Sebastian. He's studying philosophy.'

'It's hilarious,' Sebastian confirmed.

Nick was a year younger than Maria but he wasn't starting university this autumn, and he wasn't working. 'I'll do *something*,' he explained. 'I just want to make sure it's not going to be a waste of time.'

After several jugs of Pimm's, I was feeling pleased with the way the afternoon was going. Maria was telling Sebastian a joke, eating cucumber and apple with her fingers, while Nick's look of restless disapproval had eased into something like a smile. I leaned back and poured myself another drink.

'I just had an idea,' said Sebastian. 'Theo was telling me about this creepy secret pool hidden in the woods. Apparently a ghost lives there. We could look for the pool.'

'Why not,' Nick said. 'Let's go on a ghost hunt.'

'I don't want to go there,' Theo interrupted, startling him.

'There's no ghost,' I said. 'Our grandmother almost drowned there a long time ago. But as she's still alive, I'm not sure why she'd haunt the pool. That's without getting into whether there is such a thing as ghosts.'

'I don't like it there anyway,' Theo said obstinately.

I watched in resignation: the flushed face and distressed lower lip of Theo, the surprise of the others. Theo had never lost her childhood talent for unexpected conversation stoppers; collapsing various hopeful moments of mine like so many tugged kites. There was the time she managed to let slip to one girl that I was also dating her friend. The time I brought a holidaymaker home one night to be met by Theo sobbing over a dead mole: my date – drunkenly shocked by the tears, the animal blood, or the unexpected memento mori – insisting I call her a taxi back to her Tenby hotel.

I glanced at Maria now, but she only raised her eyebrows and said, 'This isn't Scooby-Doo, Nick. Anyway, it's too hot for ghosts. Why don't we just have another drink?' And she turned to Theo, talking to her until Theo's smile wavered back into place, icecream white and sunny, and the conversation was set back on its tracks.

When Maria and Nick left in the late afternoon we took them back through the house, which had become a deep lake of shade, cool and silent after the blaze and hum of the gardens. Maria stopped when she noticed the painting of Eve in the dining room.

'That's Eve Anthony, isn't it?' she asked. 'Are you related to her?' We all looked up at the picture with a collective superstitiousness, as if it might suddenly open its mouth and answer.

'She's our grandmother. She's in London at the moment.'

'How strange! I remember studying her for modern history,' Maria said. 'You know, I never quite thought of her as a real person. And that means your great-grandfather is George Bennett?'

'Yes, but we never knew him. I don't think Eve even knew him that well. I came home once from school and brought her a tracing I'd done, of a famous mosaic mask he'd discovered. When I showed it to her she said, "Very nice, darling, but what is it?"' Maria and Nick laughed.

I remembered what Eve had said after I explained the mask to her – 'So George Bennett lingers on in the school textbooks, does he?' – her smile fixed to her mouth, as if she'd forgotten to take it off. Since then I'd noticed she only ever spoke of her father in the vaguest terms: he was always in another country, obscured by jungle and crumbling stones, or glimpsed at the end of a long, long dinner table. It seemed as if George for Eve was like a story she had heard and was passing on, rather than a person she had known.

'Quite a weighty family history,' Maria murmured.

'I saw a trailer for a programme about that hotel company on television the other day,' Nick said. 'Are you two next in line to run the business?'

'Oh no.' Theo shuddered. 'I want to work in a shelter for monkeys.'

'You won't win Miss World with that,' said Sebastian. 'Why not battered women?'

'Monkeys are less complicated.'

I said, 'Well, I'm going to be an architect,' though the idea of working with Eve had occurred to me before. Sometimes I wondered if Eve herself had thought of this. The way she would ask me what I was working on, looking through my sketches and notes with a quick, professional hand. 'So how much would this kind of thing cost?' she would ask. 'How many floors does it have?' and then she would nod, as if my answers were exactly what she'd hoped to hear.

'What sort of things will you design?' Maria asked.

'Something . . . significant,' I said. 'Something that people will remember me for.'

'Jonathan's incredibly dedicated,' Sebastian said, a mocking overlay in his voice, and Maria glanced at me sidelong, then looked away.

After they left I sat outside in the early evening sun and remembered the way Maria had looked at me, with the edges of the smile she wore earlier – polite and shadowy – lying dormant in the corners of her mouth. As if she had thought of something, but decided to keep it to herself.

SEVEN

Unexpectedly, Eve knew about Maria and Nick Dumas – or their mother, anyway – down to the date they arrived in Llansteffan. Not through local gossip, for Eve did not chase and scatter pieces of information in the usual way; I never saw her conducting anything that could be described as a 'chat'. Rather, the knowledge of the workings of others seeped through to her silently and completely, as if she had known it all along.

'What a waste,' she said. 'A sad story. Dumas is their mother Nathalie's maiden name; she was married to Sir John Bankbridge, who as it happens I knew years ago. A well-respected man, perhaps rather a hard husband.' She didn't elaborate. 'It seems she didn't take any of the money, nothing. That may be appropriate for her, but what about the children? She has incapacitated them. It's a good job their education is almost over. She works as a proofreader now or something.'

'The Bankbridge family?' asked Alicia, who paid attention to conversations like someone tuning a radio, hovering for a moment on a sound that interested her; in this case the word 'Sir'. 'Where are they living?'

'The cottage on Castle Hill,' I said.

'Oh yes. That tiny place,' she said, with a sigh that was either expressive of the inexplicable cruelty of fate, or disapproval of Nathalie Dumas and her cramped living arrangements.

e⌒

After a few weeks of Sebastian staying with us, his mother called from LA to tell him she was flying back at the weekend.

'I've got to get back to London before she arrives and finds out I put her dogs into kennels,' he told us.

'Don't go.' Theo looked stricken.

'I'm back in Wales next week,' he said. 'For Charlie's party, remember? Our party really, since it was us that organised it. It's going to be the party of the year. Everyone will have sex. Even me. Even Charlie. God help *that* girl.'

At the end of pre-prep I had bidden a cheery farewell to Charlie Tremayne, who went to Harrow, only to encounter him again at Cambridge, where he assumed our friendship would pick up where it left off. The unshakeability of this conviction of his had seen him become a concrete, basic figure in our group, oblivious to the bafflement he caused in my newer, shinier friends, spending a surprising amount of time with us considering nobody ever phoned him. I wouldn't have said I liked Charlie – his childhood boastfulness had congealed into a lumpy self-satisfaction and a disapproval of anything he considered 'weird' (a wide and murky category that encompassed everything from cocktails to people who didn't like fox-hunting) – but I didn't find him objectionable enough to actively oust him. Sebastian despised him.

'Maybe we could get Victor to come to the party,' I suggested.

Sebastian smiled but didn't take up the joke. Victor was a long-running theme of Sebastian's. Outraged that Charlie had got into Cambridge without any evidence of intelligence, Sebastian insisted that his place had been bought at the expense of a young and bright black kid from Hackney. He had named this kid Victor, and was fond of regaling Charlie with extended monologues on Victor's life, dwelling on the crushing of his hopes of higher education, the late nights he was forced to work at the supermarket, his dedication to his sick grandmother, and so on. Charlie remained stolidly unmoved by this, dismissing Sebastian's riffs as the mumbo-jumbo of a philosophy student: philosophy being categorised by him at his most charitable as 'weird', and at worst, as somehow analogous to mental illness.

'He told a good joke the other day,' I said, trying to provoke Sebastian, to revive our game and prod him and Theo out of the melancholy that had sagged down over them both that afternoon.

'He gets his jokes from the TV,' Sebastian snapped, annoyed rather than amused. 'And he can't even get them right. He takes a good joke and just shits all over it.'

'I don't want you to go,' Theo repeated, and Sebastian coughed, frowned, and rubbed his wilful hair, waiting until she turned away before sitting back and gazing at her with baffled longing. I felt sorry for him, but then I couldn't help but feel a little impatient – scornful, even – because it had been months now, and how long was he really going to waste his time?

Later I went to Theo's bedroom, where she was sitting cross-legged on the floor, sketching out a picture. She painted and drew with facility – not with industry or commitment, but with a shrugging deftness; her pictures inspired and dropped in a day. I leaned in the doorway and looked around. Theo's room was a manifestation of her inner life, every idea or impulse trackable across its messy landscape. Sequins affixed to the Lalique lamp, stickers covering the walnut four-poster, the unmistakable darkness of a wine stain on the oriental rug. Her paintings were propped against walls covered in a Warholesque découpage of cut-out images from magazines; a hippyish throw was draped over the curtain rail, where it suffused the room with a dark pinkish light. Clothes, shoes and teacups littered the floor. I noticed a missing cricket jumper of mine hanging over the back of a chair and picked it up.

'What are you drawing?' I asked.

'It's going to be Sebastian,' Theo explained. 'As a goodbye present.'

'You like him a lot, don't you?' I said, wondering for the first time if Sebastian's hopeful romance with Theo wasn't entirely one-sided.

'He's my best friend,' Theo said sadly.

'Oh.' I tried to think of something appropriate to say and settled for what I felt was a comforting silence.

'I know – why don't the three of us get a flat together?' Theo cried, startling me. 'In London! I could live there in the week while I'm at college, and you and Sebastian could come to stay in the holidays. We'd have so much more fun in London than coming back here every summer.'

'But Alicia would miss us terribly,' I said facetiously.

'She won't miss us,' Theo said earnestly. 'She doesn't love us. Not really. Nor does Eve.'

I wasn't sure how to reply to this. The idea of love for or from Alicia was just blankly inappropriate. Loving her would be like cherishing an old piece of Christmas wrapping paper, without remembering the present it had once contained, and whether or not you had liked it. But while I couldn't explain it to Theo, I felt I understood Eve. Though she might not love us in a traditional, sentimental way, doling out indiscriminate kisses and embraces, I knew there was something reliable in her presence, something fixed and defined and more important than love, with its faulty batteries; the dim, uncertain showiness of love.

I was driving back from the off-licence later that day, bottles chattering merrily in the back of the car, when I saw Maria up ahead. She was wearing large sunglasses and a loose dress, and her hair was pulled back, but I recognised the arrangement of her limbs, their easy angles. The road was too narrow and hedge-bound to pull over, so I stopped next to her and waved. She leaned down to the window.

'Fancy meeting you here!'

'Would you like a lift?' I asked.

'Oh, no, don't worry . . . I'm going home, it's not in your way,' she said.

'Get in,' I opened the passenger door, motioning at the empty road behind us. 'You're holding up the traffic.'

Maria arrived in the car with a faint, sweet draught of sun lotion.

'I've just been at the beach,' she told me. 'I'm going to cover your car in sand.'

'It's already full of empty cans and sweet wrappers,' I said. 'A little sand won't hurt.'

'I'm so glad to meet you here actually,' she said. 'It's not that I can't scale the hill – I've done it before, and I'm sure I can do it again. But I hadn't packed any provisions, and there's always the danger of running out of energy before the top, in which case I'd just have to lie there and hope someone finds me . . . Oh! Look at the sheep!'

I had to stop for the flock of sheep being herded languidly across the road by a farmer, who nodded to us reprovingly as if we were in his way and not the other way round. We sat and watched as the sheep kept coming, banging and barging together, cushioned by their soft wrapping, with a despondent clamour that made Maria laugh.

'You won't be so delighted to see them after a few more weeks here,' I warned.

'You're probably right. Anyway – speaking of here, you have to give me some tips on places to go. What pubs are the nicest? And restaurants?'

'I don't tend to go to pubs around here,' I said. 'In fact, I'm not sure I'm the best person to give advice.'

'Really?' she said, as the last sheep trotted past and I started the engine again. 'What about your friends in the area? Where do you go?'

'I don't know anyone in the area,' I said.

She laughed, then realised I wasn't joking.

'Well, maybe Nick and I came at the right time,' she said.

'I think so.' I tried to catch her eye so she felt the compliment, but she was looking at the road, swinging out around a bend as the sea vanished and reappeared over the wall.

'It's funny,' she said. 'You and Nick feel the same about this place, and he's only been here for a few days.'

'I don't mean to sound as if I hate it here,' I said. 'I suppose everyone gets bored of their home. Nick's just ahead of the game.'

'But when you leave for a while and come back, sometimes you realise what a place might mean to you,' Maria replied.

'Like going to university?'

'No, that's not really leaving. I mean, when you're a grown-up,' she said, smiling.

'I used to think I would know I was a grown-up when I could have a pocketful of change and not know how much I had,' I said. 'Instead of calculating how to spend my allowance to the penny.'

'I used to think I'd be a grown-up when I could buy my own biscuits, and not have to wait for them to be offered. And when I wouldn't have scabs on my knees.'

I glanced at her knees, smooth and brown as hazelnuts with their light sugaring of sand, my eyes leaping along her legs – the rumpled patterns of her short dress, her hand resting loosely on her thigh – before I remembered to look away.

'This is my turning,' she said, looking amused.

When I dropped her at the house we agreed we'd all meet up later in the week ('I'd love to see your sister again,' she said, warmly. 'I'd like to see Nick too,' I said, insincerely) and she got out of the car before I could make a show of opening her door for her. She looked back once over her shoulder, with her usual ambiguous smile, then waved, before she went into the house and closed the door, and I went back to Evendon flustered and driving too fast, causing a group of teenagers crossing the road to scatter and shout at me as I passed, in accompaniment to the clashing of all the bottles of wine.

e⌇

When I got home Theo was asleep on the terrace, snoring softly in the low sun, and Sebastian was sitting nearby, reading through a book from his course literature and making notes.

'It can't be that bad, can it?' I said, opening the wine and pouring a tumbler for us each.

Sebastian looked at me curiously. 'You look smug,' he said. 'What happened while you were out?'

'I just went to the shop,' I said. 'I saw Maria, actually. Gave her a lift home.'

'Oh, I see,' Sebastian said, putting his book down. 'And how was that?'

'Maria seems nice,' I said. 'Not sure about her brother. But she's okay.'

Sebastian started to laugh. 'Maria Dumas . . . well, yes, I suppose you could say she's *okay*. Maybe if you'd just landed on earth and she was the first girl you saw and you hadn't had a chance to compare her to anyone else and find out she's about ten times more beautiful.'

'Do you think she has a boyfriend?' I asked. 'I can't tell.'

'Does this mean she hasn't made it clear she wants to sleep

with you yet? I've never seen that before. I'm curious about the effect it might have.' Sebastian inspected me with interest. 'You might have some sort of breakdown,' he warned.

'I don't know why I asked,' I said.

'Maybe you'll actually have to put in some effort for the first time in your life,' Sebastian continued.

'Unfair.'

'Is it? Okay, I'm going to run through a list of romantic gestures. Stop me when I name something you've actually done. Bought a girl flowers. Bought a girl . . . anything. Celebrated Valentine's Day. Invited a girl to dinner. Written a poem for a girl—'

'Oh, come on,' I interrupted. 'Nobody does that. Except for you.'

'Which makes it even more unfair! I write poems and try to think about people's feelings. You're forgetful and dismissive and women can't get enough of it.'

'Maybe you should think about changing your approach,' I say, amused. 'Listen – women say they want poems and flowers, but in practice that's bullshit. They like the thrill of the chase more than we do. They see someone who isn't that interested in them, and they try to change their mind. And the better-looking the girl is, the more effort she makes, because she can't handle being ignored.'

'How depressing,' Sebastian sighed.

'Not everyone's like that,' I added. 'But a lot of girls are, and they're the ones I end up with. I'm not interested in them – beyond the obvious – and that's fine because they're not that interested in me. Not really.'

'I don't think Maria's like that,' Sebastian said. 'She's not the type.'

'What makes you think I just want to sleep with her?' I said loftily. 'I might want a relationship,' which made Sebastian laugh so much he woke Theo up.

I understood why Sebastian didn't believe me. Girls, girls – I'd had a few, since I was fifteen shucking off my virginity in someone's parents' bed to a girl I never saw again. All I remembered of that was the brief heat and the dark, the smell of vanilla and alcohol on her skin, the plastic-feeling lace of her bra. Afterwards I didn't feel happiness exactly, more an easing of stress, like walking out of an exam. Since that time I had got a lot better at sex, but not much better at lingering afterward. The lazy calm of the bed made me uncomfortable. I tried not to go back to girls I'd slept with before; the better I knew someone, the more I felt the weight of expectation, the pressure of history.

I'd never had this kind of *want* before; I'd never cared if a girl said yes or no to me – and I very rarely had to ask. I'd never experienced this sternness of memory, its attention to detail. I could remember the topography of her legs – a mole above one knee, the pale brown turning paler at her thigh – I knew the precise copper colour of her eyes, the length of her fingers. But I didn't know what she thought of me. When I said something serious, she laughed. When she smiled, her smile could mean anything. I didn't like the uncertainty, so I decided I'd invite her to the beach tomorrow night. We could all go, in fact: I sensed that rushing things would be a mistake. I'd take the Grandmother's Footsteps approach – softly, softly, but always moving forward.

When I called Maria's house the next day Nick answered and was so enthusiastic about the idea that I smirked as I hung up. I could imagine the boredom, the solid green Welsh isolation that must be pressing in on the two of them, turning even their mobile calls into a fuzz of blank blips and impenetrable hissing. Whether or not in their real lives they would have come to the beach, here there was no other choice.

Theo and Sebastian had bought some discontinued Romanian wine from the supermarket, delightedly urging me to guess at its price. The wine turned out to be as thin and sour as it was cheap, so we took it in turns to hold our noses and drink it as we walked down to the beach. The sky was a rose colour, the sun setting slowly, dreamily. The road, constellated with leaf shadows, still gave off the heat of the day. Near the trees the gathering midges made their batty circles around our heads, forcing us to talk with our mouths half closed, like gangsters.

'So who's going to Charlie's party?' I asked Sebastian.

'Antonia said she would come,' Theo said.

'Who is that?' I asked, trying to remember the faces of Theo's friends. Theo's eccentricity had strangely never alienated her from the hard core of popular girls at her schools. When she was little, a set of pretty, well-behaved girls would invite her to their houses to dress up their Barbies and practise dance steps. Later at boarding school, she was friends with the same kind of girls, and they would dress each other up and go out to dance. Theo was half cosseted by them, half admired. They thought she was quirky, but not *weird*, and they quoted the bizarre things she said. In this way she had ended up with a group of fluorinated, glamorous females whom my friends would try to pick off during the holidays, with varying degrees of success.

'My friend from sixth form. Anty's really *nice*,' Theo said. 'She's nice to everyone but she makes her boyfriends miserable. Not on purpose. One of them had to go to a mental institution. Another one had to take anxiety pills. And another one moved to Australia because he said she'd murdered his soul. He used to stand outside her window and shout it and she'd ask us to go out and tell him to go away.'

'Poor old Antonia,' said Sebastian gaily. He had made his way through a second bottle of the wine and every so often would tilt and plough into the hedgerow before setting himself back on course, his shoulders covered in small leaves and pollen.

'Let's ask Nick and Maria to the party,' I said. 'The more the merrier, right?'

Nick, when we met him, was as pleased about the party as he had been about the beach.

'Anything to get out of this shithole,' he said rattily.

We had built a fire, which wavered and bloomed in the exhaling sea, stretching our black shadows out across the sand like blowing laundry. The earlier pink of the sky had seeped below the horizon, pressed down by a dark, serious blue. It was late, and Maria was not here.

'So, does Maria like Llansteffan?' I asked Nick. I was hoping he might explain why he had arrived alone, but he seemed to take it for granted that his presence was the top billing of the evening and that we would be indifferent to who else might or might not show up.

'Who knows,' he said. 'She says she does, but she's probably pretending. She's worried about our mother – she doesn't want her to feel guilty for moving us here. I think she *ought* to feel guilty.'

'Where's Maria?' Theo asked.

'I don't know,' Nick said. 'She didn't come home this afternoon. Probably with David.'

'David?' I asked.

'She met him in a car park earlier today.'

'A car park?' I repeated.

'The supermarket car park,' Nick explained. 'Our mother dropped a shopping bag and he helped her pick it up or something. It was a boring story.'

I thought it was a ridiculous story. The supermarket, the car park, the unfairness of it all. I wasn't able to prevent Maria being preyed upon in the romantic confusion of torn plastic, rolling apples, burst eggs. I tried to remember the employees of the local store, but couldn't think of a single fluorescent-lit face from which to pick an enemy.

'What does he do at the supermarket?' I asked sourly.

'He doesn't work there,' Nick said with amusement. 'He works at a school near here. Children with learning difficulties or something.'

'Ahh,' Theo cried. 'So he's *kind*.'

I grimaced, which wasn't noticed, and thought again how unfair the whole thing was. Apparently I was just as bad as Sebastian, with his hopes carefully constructed out of tissue paper and glitter. But at least I hadn't given away how I felt; I could quietly dismantle my attraction without anyone – especially Maria – feeling sorry for me, or laughing about it. That was something.

EIGHT

In late August Theo got her A-level results, a set of murky letters with the exception of an A in art. Eve put them up on her office wall next to my prim row of certificates. Theo and I stood and looked at the frames. 'I'm glad one of us is good at this stuff,' she said thoughtfully. 'The important stuff.'

'You could have got better results if you'd worked harder,' I reproved her. Throughout school Eve had made phone calls and allowances were made for Theo, but there was a limit to what influence could achieve at her sixth form. She had read all the books in English lit, but her essays were inconsistent if they appeared at all, her teachers said. Her French was 'appalling', and her sociology tutor said she had assumed Theo was a mistake on the timetable, because she'd never seen her. Theo said she hadn't realised she was meant to be studying sociology either.

'Sorry, Jonathan,' Theo said.

'Don't apologise! Anyway, at least Fairchild is accepting you.'

Eve wasn't exactly pleased that Theo was going to art college, but she approved of Theo's freedom, in principle, to make such a choice. She remarked later, cheered, that it might always lead her into advertising.

'How much the world has changed!' she said warmly at a

dinner to celebrate the results. 'I would have been laughed at if I said I wanted to go to art college. Husbands were all we heard about – you weren't considered a woman if you didn't have one. It was like an education in itself . . . a stage one had to go through.

'I remember at the end of university back in America, talking to a friend about the results we wanted. We'd both been scoring the highest essay marks, and I always thought we were in a sort of friendly competition. I said to her, "We both ought to win a prize this year." She looked at me, obviously surprised, and said, "Oh Eve, there's more to life than marks. I'm getting *married* this year. I don't care about graduation." And then I realised we had never been in any kind of competition; we weren't even playing the same game.'

She paused and looked reflective, then smiled at Theo. 'You can do whatever you want in life.'

Theo was always uncomfortable around Eve. She behaved as if Eve were a teacher about to ask a difficult maths question – becoming quiet and small so as not to attract attention to herself. She gave a coerced smile now, twisting her napkin in her fingers.

'Anyway, I always look forward to seeing what you'll both achieve,' Eve continued. 'You can *change* things. Take something, change it, then no one can forget you. Isn't it simple? That's all success is.'

'Okay,' Theo said uncertainly. She reached for her wine glass but her vague fingers slid on the wet stem and the glass arced gracefully down onto the table, where it smashed. The sound startled all of us; Eve drew back slightly in her chair, Theo gasped, even Alicia – gently bowed with alcohol, her eyes resting on her own glass coiled into her hand – blinked and looked up.

I knew the glass was irreplaceable: it was Victorian, made from slender crystal and gold-leafed around its rim. We all stared at its bright pieces on the table, like a broken phoenix egg, and then at Eve.

'Sorry, Eve,' Theo said.

'Don't worry,' Eve said lightly. 'We have an even set of four now, I suppose.'

'Why were there only five, anyway?' Theo asked. 'Don't glasses come in even sets? What happened to the sixth one?'

Eve frowned, not as if she were trying to remember, but as if she were annoyed somehow by the question. She didn't reply immediately and that, along with the scattered light in the remains on the table, raised some old nausea in me, some unknown fright, like a slow chill from a door previously left open and forgotten. I stared at the fragments, unable to identify what it was about them that had disturbed me. Then Eve said, 'Oh, I only ever had five. The sixth is . . . lost in history.'

'That's sad,' Theo said, struck by this thought.

'Indeed,' Alicia said, making us all look at her, not just because her contribution was unexpected, but for the sarcasm of its delivery – her voice well shaped and lucid, and in that moment sounding exactly like Eve's.

I had decided I wouldn't contact Maria – less from a reluctance to interrupt the flowering of her supermarket car-park romance than from not wanting her to doubt the deeply casual nature of my feelings towards her – but after finding myself with nothing to do but sit for several of Theo's subsequently discarded portraits, I called her to ask if she and Nick wanted to play tennis with us. Maria, her voice easy and sleek on the telephone, explained that Nick was in Bath visiting Emily, but she could bring David along to make up a four. I agreed pleasantly and hung up, pulling a face in the hall mirror.

Maria arrived looking pornographically innocent in blazing white shorts and halterneck against the dreamlike green blur of the grass. The darkness of her ponytail swung over her shoulder like a whip. David, following on behind, was a suntanned athlete with well-structured arms, khaki shorts, wooden beads hinting at surfing prowess. I longed for him to be transformed into the original David, the pale shop manager in his flammable suit.

Nick had already reported that David was involved with an environmental campaign group to prevent some bypass mowing its way through an ancient forest, that he enjoyed running, and had just saved to buy his own house by the beach. His father worked at a garage and his uncle ran one of the two pubs in Llansteffan. He was well liked locally and had taken the Dumas family to the market to show them the best places to buy fresh food. In his spare time he volunteered at the local hospice. It was difficult to dislike him, but I thought it was to my credit that I succeeded.

David was predictably capable with a racquet and Maria had a languorously moving trick of always reaching shots, but I had been playing all summer. Despite Theo forgetting to watch the ball, then looking at it with surprise as it dawdled past her, we beat them two sets to one.

'Well done, good game,' David called, loping genially up to the net and grasping my hand.

'Jonathan's been practising against the machine,' Theo said proudly.

'Be quiet,' I muttered.

Not long after the game David excused himself to head a scout meeting or escort some old ladies to church or something, and Maria, Theo and I sat talking under the pear trees, where the sun had become a haze of blond, hay-scented stillness.

'Look at that bumble bee,' Theo said, pointing at a bee making its way across the grass, clambering and tumbling over the long green blades. She laughed. 'How lazy! Why doesn't it just fly?'

Maria leaned over the bee. 'It's either old, or cold, or tired. Look' – she pointed at its wings – 'if they have ragged wings it means they're old and will probably die.'

'Oh!' Theo said, dismayed.

'But these wings are okay. And it's not cold today. So basically, this bee has worked too much and exhausted itself.'

'I know the feeling,' I said. 'Though you might need to explain it to Theo.'

Theo, not to be distracted, asked, 'So is it going to be okay?'

'It needs some honey,' Maria said. 'Or sugar water. Have you got any?'

As Theo hurried away across the lawn I turned to Maria. 'That was well handled. I thought you were going to tell her it was a no-hoper. Right, I'll get rid of that bee and we'll tell her it recovered and flew off.'

'No – it really is fine,' Maria said. 'Wait and see. Theo's sensitive about this sort of thing, is she?'

'About any sort of thing,' I said. 'She's impossible to live with. If a newspaper has a headline about some tragedy, I have to put it in the bin face down, in case she's confronted with Five Dead After Car Bomb, or whatever, and then she'll be upset.'

'It's lovely that you're protective of her,' Maria said, looking at me from under the shade of her hand. Beneath the dark that hid her eyes, her mouth was lit up in the sun, a classical cyma curve.

'I suppose so,' I said.

'I got it!' Theo came running back out of the house, holding a jar of honey above her head like the Olympic flame, dropping down beside us excitedly and examining the now unmoving bee. 'What do we do now? Is it too late?'

Maria took the honey, spooned out a small amount onto a leaf, then – as we watched solemn and silent – slid the leaf towards the bee, which shivered, stirred, and unfurled its proboscis into the honey.

'It's drinking!' Theo said. She looked at Maria with the pure and devoted admiration of a Renaissance Nativity painting, the sunlight sliding in through the tree branches and enfolding them both where they knelt.

'Maria, patron saint of bumblebees,' I said lightly, a little moved myself.

After the bee had consumed an improbable amount of honey and flown off, Theo fell asleep in the long grass, the lurid straw hat she had bought at the beach slipping forward over her eyes. Maria sipped her lemonade. 'What a stunning day,' she said.

'Thanks so much for inviting us,' as if it had been her and David I had originally asked.

'Well, David's great,' I said, stiff-mouthed.

'He is, isn't he?' she said. 'I think he was a little reserved about coming here. Perhaps that isn't the word. A bit shy. I think people here have a perception of your family as different to them – rather aloof, I suppose. But I told him that really you were nothing like that.'

I smiled vaguely, picturing what Alicia would say if I told her we had been playing tennis with the son of a local mechanic.

'Anyway,' she continued, 'I meant to ask you earlier. David is playing football this weekend and one of his team can't make it. He wanted to ask you but wasn't sure if you'd be interested. Nick's playing too.'

Without a prepared excuse, I said, 'Sure, I'll do it.'

'Perfect. I'll tell him to call you. Hey, remember in the car when you said you don't have friends in the area? Now it's just one new friend after another.'

'Maria, I don't want you to think that I'm some sort of misanthrope,' I began.

'I didn't think that for a second.'

We smiled at each other, then she looked away, and then there was a moment of hesitation in which she didn't look back up at me, but gazed at the grass, as Theo slept on and the wind faded, leaving the air blue and tangible, enclosing us. I waited, and then she sat up and her politeness was back and impermeable as ever, like a fresh sheet of paper.

'You know, I think we've been so incredibly lucky,' she said. 'Coming here where I – if I'm honest – thought I wouldn't know anyone and would be lonely and miserable – and then finding you two, and David, and us all being friends . . .' She smiled in summation. 'It just couldn't be nicer.'

ℯ⌒

I had assumed Mrs Williams had been on holiday for the past week, as I hadn't seen her around the house and the food at Evendon had noticeably improved. There was a firming up of vegetables, a softening of meat. Gone were the impenetrable plutonic lumps of potato, the quiches like bogs of mulchy yellow with their weary salads. Then Theo came running up to my room, out of breath and distressed.

'Oh Jonathan, she's fired her, she's gone.'

'Who fired who? Who's gone?'

'Eve! And Mrs Williams!'

'Well, that was long overdue. Didn't you ever eat her food? When she made any, that is. She was always smoking in the kitchen, and she just watched that Welsh soap all day.'

'I used to watch it with her.' Theo sniffled. 'She gave me cigarettes.'

'Is that why you're so upset?' I said. 'I'll get you some cigarettes if it will cheer you up.'

'She needs the money! Her cat has to have an operation and her daughter's husband has run off and left her, and now her daughter's turning to drink. They could lose the house! She said it seems like God only helps the rich.' Theo recited this as passionately as if she were Mrs Williams herself. 'And we're rich, aren't we? So we should help her.'

'I'm sure Mrs Williams will be paid for a few months, while she gets another job.'

'She says she doesn't know where on earth she's going to find a job now,' Theo said, with all the faint reproach she was capable of. 'I'm going to visit her.'

‿

While Theo was visiting Mrs Williams, I found myself spending more and more time playing football, tennis – even going fishing. The reason for this was that David invited me to do these things, and I couldn't seem to say no. It wasn't that I had started to like him, though he remained no less likeable. I did it to find out the extent of the problem: David being the problem. I would talk to him and wait with patience for him to say 'we'. He confided that he wasn't really sure how Maria felt about him. That they had not slept together yet. He thought maybe she was uncertain about the relationship; that she was holding something back. I listened with satisfaction.

I didn't think my outings with David were good for me; they made me a little more deceitful, a little less kind. Beside him I saw the hazy form of Maria; on his skin lingered the touch of hers. I even felt like giving him a shove sometimes, as if his arms still rested around her. I wasn't proud of it – the compulsion to draw him out – but at the same time, I wasn't prepared to stop.

I suppose I got what I deserved in the end, reeling in my line to find not the silvery solidity of a fish, but a previously abandoned piece of rubbish – a rotting shoe, a tin can – brought to light instead. We had been talking about David's father, who was apparently good and caring and kind and hard-working and generally represented everything that could be hoped for in a father. I was trying not to appear bored, but he misinterpreted my expression and flushed.

'Uh – sorry. That was tactless.'

'No, it's fine,' I said. 'Really. I *can* hear about other fathers without bursting into tears. Mine died a long time ago.'

'But I should have remembered . . . the divorce and everything . . .' I watched the distress spread across his genial, evenly featured face. 'I forgot about that.'

'No worries,' I said, shrugging, and we went back to fishing. But I had seen that brief look on his face, before his embarrassment, an expression I hadn't seen since Uncle Alex visited when we were children: the unmistakable flush of pity, and I felt my own discomfort at this unwanted connection, the bare vivid sting of it, the mutual exposure.

I remembered that David had not always been Maria's boyfriend and my convenient friend; before that he was simply a local, and he was still a local. Now, I didn't believe the people of Carmarthen and Llansteffan actively hated me, but there is a lot of ground between hatred and affection and they were scattered across it, a grey no-man's-land of mild dislike. They laughed about me, discussed and added new technicolour to my life and my family history, or simply watched me with the amused interest of spectators at the zoo every time I came down from the hill. There was nothing I could do that wouldn't seem wrong to them: evidence of difference – or worse, of a degrading attempt to *not* be different. When I took my dated hatchback to the garage the mechanic hooted at it ('Can't you afford something better than this?'), but when I used Eve's car, armoured in its aggressive black gloss, I could feel the hostility sizzling off the street like a panto-mime hiss. While an exception had been made for Theo – who could no more be called snooty and distant than could a puppy – these thwarted epithets were flung enthusiastically at me. I was nothing more than a spoilt rich kid. My reserve was arrogance, my politeness was condescension. For my part, I refused to make any effort to overturn the unfair verdict and dismissed the locals as small-minded sheep-fuckers. And so the distance grew.

Now when David, who I had casually made use of, brought up my parents' divorce, I realised that he was on the other side of the iron curtain between Evendon and the locals, subject to who knows what propaganda and misinformation – and that, finally, was what put an end to our fishing trips.

℮

The day before Charlie's party, Theo and I were sitting by the reservoir that bordered Evendon's land, the swans floating past motionlessly, eyeing us. It was cooler here under the Nordic green of the trees, stretching their images across the silver bowl of the lake, broken and remade by the air skirling over the water's surface. I cut through a drift of Theo's cigarette smoke with my finger, disrupting its curly filigree.

'Why are you smoking roll-ups anyway?' I asked her. 'You're not an art student yet.'

'I don't have much allowance left this month.'

'But you haven't bought anything.'

'I gave it to Oxfam.'

I frowned. Theo was always falling victim to the fluorescent-coated charitable young people lying in wait on Carmarthen high street, the black and white television commercials and their intoned digits, the drunks slumped in their doorways. I fully expected her visits to Mrs Williams to end with the house being repossessed and Theo inviting the whole family to stay with us – Mrs Williams, alcoholic daughter, criminal sons, unwell cat. The daughter could be good company for Alicia, so long as she minded her Ps and Qs.

'Anyway, I wanted to show you something,' Theo said, searching through her bag. 'Oh dear . . . where did it go?'

I watched as various items were unearthed and placed on the grass like exhibits from an archaeological dig: one striped glove, an acorn, a pack of cigarettes ("Oh, I do have some left!"), a religious pamphlet she must have been handed on the street showing people of various colours dancing in a field under a rainbow, a diamond bracelet belonging to Alicia, a mouth organ, a magpie feather, and finally, a photograph, which she pushed enthusiastically at me.

The photograph was of a bride and groom, gradually establishing themselves as Alicia and a man who had to be my father, under a storm of confetti. This young Alicia was fuller, her hair in a round thick wave rolling back from her plum-shaped cheeks. She held her bouquet as if she was half-frightened of it; she looked gathered up, excited. There was nothing about her expression to identify her as my mother. Her broad skirt frothed whitely against my father's black-suited legs, hiding them, so he appeared to be floating. The uneven sunlight had hit my father's face so that his eyes were just dark patches, his blond hair glowing. His resemblance to Theo was apparent despite this – he even had the same way of looking into the camera: head turned down slightly, defensively, but then that wide, hopeful smile.

'Where did you find this?' I asked, running my finger over it.

'It was in an album in the library, just inside the back cover. I spent a whole day looking through every single album and that's the only picture I found of him. I don't think anyone meant to keep it.'

'Maybe not,' I said. 'Alicia's always been a bit weird about the subject. I don't think she ever got over the divorce, or something.'

'Well, that's what I have to tell you about,' Theo said, eyes lit with sudden fever. 'I showed the photo to Mrs Williams and she said I'd better keep that picture to myself because my dad wasn't so popular around here. I said, what did she mean? And she said that Eve and my dad didn't like each other at all, and best not to say any more about it.'

'You can bet if she did know any more about it she would have told you all the gossip,' I said, amused.

'She thinks she was sacked because Eve found out that she told me about Eve not liking our father. She says Mrs Wynne Jones probably told Eve what she said because she wanted to get rid of Mrs Williams, and then Eve sacked her.'

My good humour dissipating, I snapped, 'She has no place to say that – to imply that Eve would sack her unfairly. She got sacked for being a shit cook. Anyway, it's hardly going to be top secret that Eve didn't like the man who divorced her daughter. That crazy old hag is just trying to stir up trouble. You should stop visiting her.'

Theo looked down and fiddled with her cigarette.

'Oh, no,' I said. 'Please don't tell me you believe this rubbish.'

'Well, I went home and I looked on the internet,' Theo said, rushing along, not meeting my eye, as if expecting to be stopped. 'And I looked up all our names and everything and I found the wedding announcement with Alicia Anthony and Michael Caplin and there was a piece in a magazine, but I couldn't find one single thing that said our father – *our* Michael Caplin – was dead, and I was thinking about what Mrs Williams said, that no one liked him – and they must *really* not like him because there are no photos of him, and Eve doesn't even let us talk about him – and I was thinking maybe what if he wasn't really dead, that it was just a mistake in Australia, and nobody checked it because they hated him and they were just relieved he was gone and didn't want him back.'

She finished, running out of breath, and looked at me with her mouth open, eyes earnest and bright.

Baffled and disquieted, I managed a 'Theo – that's absolutely ridiculous,' and watched as her agitated, hopeful face sank downwards, like a deflating balloon.

'But sometimes people make mistakes about deaths,' she said in a little voice. 'And the internet . . .'

'Why would his death be reported online?' I said, trying to sound patient. 'It's Eve that's famous, not the rest of us. Even if it was reported, Michael Caplin is a pretty common name to search for, and it was years ago. You've been looking for a needle in a haystack. And now you've created a conspiracy theory around the needle's disappearance.'

'You think I'm silly,' Theo murmured. She stared at her

cigarette, which had burned down to a long strip of ash in the grass.

'No, I think you wish our father wasn't dead.' I touched her arm gently. 'But it's not fair to believe that Eve would sack someone for no good reason.' Then, trying to lighten her depression, 'You remember Mrs Williams's overboiled carrots, right? Trying to pick them up with your fork?'

Theo giggled. 'They were like ghost carrots.'

'All you could hear at dinner was the ping, ping of everyone stabbing at their carrots.'

'Maybe I shouldn't visit Mrs Williams any more,' Theo said later. 'She is a bit . . . negative. And her daughter's husband has come back. I don't think he likes me being there. He called me "Fucking Lady Bountiful".'

'I think it's best to let her go,' I said. 'What did Eve say the other day? "Lost in history." Let Mrs Williams be lost in history.'

I didn't mention this conversation to Eve. I almost did, because I thought she'd find it funny, but then I realised that it didn't reflect very well on Theo, and it would be unfair to draw unnecessary attention to her strange theories. Not only that, the attempt to shoehorn our long-gone father back into the present day, into our living family, was almost ungrateful to Eve, who had been an unexpected and welcome parent to us – a ready-made role model parachuted serendipitously into our dim and borderless childhood.

I also found it hard to understand that Theo could have felt the absence of our father so sharply that she had begun to believe he *could* be alive. But then, Theo had always picked up on odd things to cherish and keep hold of: our father had obviously taken on some significance in her imagination. Whereas I couldn't imagine him at all. MC, the wandering artist, gone up in smoke in Australia. He was not real to me; he was a character from an Arabic fairy tale, exiled from court to the fierce, bare desert, to meet his tragic end. The more I thought about him, the more outlandish he became.

NINE

The day of Charlie's party arrived, along with the end of the summer. In a week I would be back in Cambridge, with Sebastian and Felix. Maria would be in France. Theo would be in London. Nick, responding to family pressure, had gone through clearing and would be going to St Andrews to study economics. 'That's got to get me some money,' he said.

My car had broken down so Eve lent us her car and driver to get to Aberthin. The Tremaynes, having lived uneventfully at Aberthin House since one of them slept with Henry V in the fifteenth century, were a dull family, grand with the weight of their feudal responsibilities (which, after so many years of social change, were now wholly imaginary). Despite this fond sense of *noblesse oblige*, each summer Charlie's parents Leo and Anne Tremayne packed up and abandoned their indifferent Welsh subjects to spend a month in England. In their absence we had convinced Charlie to have the party.

I felt slightly guilty now at the number of people crowding the steps of the long white manor and revolving erratically past the windows, the noise clattering out into the fading summer night. In the venerable depths of the house the party crowed and capered, borne along in a rush of faces, a spillage of sounds.

There were paper hats on the skeletal deer heads, a pall of smoke hung over the Aubussons and the oak panelling, the steady, voluptuous bass of the music travelled through the stone floors. Charlie, who I skirted, already had the bemused and antagonised look of the host whose party is no longer under his control.

We found Nick first, in the kitchen, leaning his elbows on the top of the range and trying to light a cigar off a plate. 'Found a box of these,' he explained, offering them to us. 'I'll need to get a lift home with you, by the way. Maria's staying with a friend. She's breaking up with David, apparently. It was completely short notice, I had to get the train down from Bath. Emily was really annoyed about dropping me at the station. She's not a very experienced driver. She's terrible, really. Fuck knows how she passed her test.' He gave up and put down the cigar. 'Have you seen how many people are here? It's packed upstairs.'

'Is Maria all right?' I asked, hope unfolding inside me like a birthday card. 'Is she still coming tonight?'

'Who? Oh, yeah, she said she was. She's coming with her girlfriends.'

I stayed with Nick for a while – lying in wait, in the hope that Maria would call him when she arrived. Nick told me about the argument he and Emily were having, which was something to do with Nick not having answered his phone because of the reception on the train, and then Emily not answering her phone out of spite. We finished our beers, then some girls joined us and we began a bottle of whisky that was conveniently at hand.

In the meantime the night turned dreamy and obscure. The light vanished; one minute it was summery dusk, the next it was a dark blue heaviness, filling the windows with a quiet chill. The party ran on regardless, like a circus train, musical and violent. It seemed like I'd been wondering so long where Maria was that the question had become an underlying process in my body, like a heart pulsing or oxygen circling, silent and regular. Sebastian arrived and joined us, then Felix arrived, then Theo vanished, then we were all on a rug in the drawing room, smoking a joint. I saw Nick tipping out the last of the marijuana into a paper and said, 'That didn't last long.'

'It's three o'clock,' someone said. A slow fright came over me. Three o'clock. In six hours something mysterious had happened; when I wasn't looking, time had wheeled away and Maria had been taken with it. I had the strange feeling that I was dreaming. I thought Felix was next to me but he had been replaced by a girl I didn't recognise. I got to my feet, drunk but determined that I would not be tricked by clocks and musical chairs. I was going to find Maria.

I went from room to room, small rooms filled with smokers, cupboards of lovers, bedrooms of coke-sniffers, hallways of crying girls on their mobile phones. It was like a ridiculous puzzle, essentially unsolvable, because of course Maria wasn't here. I sat down on the stairs, drunk and miserable, and an unpleasant coldness settled over my shoulders and face. Like a stranger, I saw the dark-panelled hall clearly, the music deconstructed into its constituent noises, the smell of smoke cooling, stagnating. A boy stumbled past me, bouncing off one wall then the other. Muffled laughter came from the room in front of me, sounding as if it had passed through a great distance. I looked at it, surprised, and went over to the door, at the same time as Maria opened it and came out. She gave a startled exclamation, then recognised me.

'Jonathan! How funny, I was just wondering where you were.'

I glanced through the door and realised my mistake – this room was the drawing room. I had thought we were in there earlier but we had actually been in a smaller room at the front of the house. I had been the obscure one – not her – hidden at the edge of the party, easily missed.

'I was just trying to explain to someone who had invited us here,' Maria continued. 'I think everybody thought we might have just crashed the party.'

I saw in her enchantingly slow smile that she was at least half drunk: drunk enough to improve my chances, not so drunk that it would be unethical. I took in the wine glass she held, the bottle in her other hand, the top that left her back a clean brown sweep, nearly naked. Her eyes were darker, larger with make-up; her lips shone like the inner recesses of oyster shells.

'Let's sit down,' I said quickly. 'Come this way.'

With my new awareness of the geography of the party, I brought her to a back parlour and through French windows into the silence outside. The garden was covered in a light that, in the beginnings of the dawn, gave the impression of existing several hours later than the dark interior of the house. There was an empty terrace and a stone bench, beyond which the hills stretched far off into the dark clouds of the woods. The smudged charcoal of the sky was rising from the eastern horizon like smoke, to make room for a clear bluish purple. The light painted Maria's body in economical contrasts: her fawn throat, the dark slice between her breasts.

'I was looking for you too,' I said. I sat down and she joined me, not quite close enough to touch.

'Not very hard, surely? I arrived hours ago. In fact – I haven't seen you much recently at all. Were you only friendly before because I was new? Or were you just using me to get to David?' She spoke lightly but her smile was an artificial version of the original.

'What happened with him?' I asked.

'I'm going back to France . . . we thought it wouldn't work.'

'It *would* be very difficult,' I said sagely. 'Probably too difficult.'

'You sound like you have experience of this sort of thing,' Maria said.

'Well, sort of,' I said. 'At the end of sixth form. It was only a few months, though – it wasn't love or anything. It ended when we went to university.'

'How did you feel?'

'I was okay. I don't know how it went on so long, really – the longest I've been with someone. It was just a casual relationship.' I grew uncomfortable; to call it a relationship felt like overstating it. It was a *thing*, I supposed. I'd had a thing with her, which ended because she decided she wanted something more than a thing.

'Why do you think she went out with you?' Maria asked.

'I don't know.' I glanced at her, sensing that the emphasis of the conversation had swung out of my reach, but she was smiling and unreadable. 'It's just what you do when you're teenagers. Pairing off.' As I said it I remembered the past girlfriend, crying in a corridor at school after I told her that letters and weekend visits weren't really 'me'; the dutiful glare of her friend.

'Maybe she did it for the sex,' Maria said. I was startled to hear her say it, casual and without emphasis. Her mouth barely moved. 'You're good-looking. It's a hazard.'

'You're teasing me,' I said, relieved to begin a familiar exchange. 'You're the beautiful one.'

'Thanks.' She turned her face away, but even tipped down and shadowed, it was near to mine; I could see the curve of her cheek patterned by the heavy lashes, the corner of her mouth. I had moved closer to her and I could feel her bare arm through the sleeve of my shirt.

'Maria,' I ventured. 'You must know I really like you.'

She frowned, then said: 'How can you decide that?'

'What?'

'Am I a happy person?' she asked. I sat up straighter, beginning to feel unsure of myself.

'What do you mean? Aren't you happy?'

'What kind of temper do I have?'

'Maria—'

'Am I religious? Am I liberal or traditional? Am I for or against drugs? Nuclear power? What do I think about art, or music, or sport?'

'I don't know,' I said.

'Of course you don't,' Maria said. Then she laughed, and got up. 'And you don't really *like* me. You have . . . a favourable impression of me.'

'Isn't that enough?' I asked her, not understanding.

'It's enough for friends,' she said. 'And I want us to be friends. I'm not just saying that – I really do. But I have to go now. I'm sorry. Our taxi is arriving in a minute.'

I looked at her with what must have been an expression of injury or surprise, and she said again, 'I'm sorry,' brushing my arm with her hand. 'See you soon, okay?'

e⌒

After Maria left I think I passed out; when I woke up, the light was rising and my whole body had soaked up the cold torpor of the stone bench. I stood and saw a group of people lying on the lawn in the thin, early sun, singing 'Wonderwall'. Theo was among them, wearing a top hat. She noticed me and started waving.

Closed and spoilt by disappointment, I turned and went back inside, where I found the party was being energetically continued as if time, previously so hasty, had at last stopped. The house was almost exactly the same as when I left it; the same girl was crying on the stairs, the same couple were kissing against a window. I saw Felix sitting on a radiator in the hall, smiling indulgently while two girls who looked about fifteen tried to undo his shirt buttons.

'I need to talk to Felix now,' I said to them, and they both darkened and sulked away.

'That was unnecessary,' Felix said.

'I just saved you from prison. Come on, we'll find some other girls. Our own age.'

Felix half leaned on me as we walked, saying, 'Seb says you're in love. He showed me this girl, Maria. Oh! Maria. She's phenomenal, isn't she? I can see why you're in a bad mood now she's gone. Vanished into the night. What have I told you? Tits first. Then the rest. But you can't wait, can you, Jonathan.'

'You're hurting my head,' I said, contracting myself onto a

sofa in the darkest, noisiest room. The girls here were dancing like Balinese temple dancers to a lethargic hip-hop track. Their hair and weaving arms glimmered in the hot dusk of the curtained room, looking somehow unreal. In the air the pear-drop scent of hairspray and perfume circulated in the botanical fumes of tobacco and marijuana.

'Anyway,' Felix said, handing me a beer and opening one for himself, 'Maria looks . . . what's the word? Self-assured. That's not a good thing. What you need is someone a bit crazy, a bit insecure. Easier target. Or someone a bit . . . attention-seeking.' He paused thoughtfully, looking past me to where Theo had appeared with another girl.

'Jonathan! Felix!' Theo cried. 'This is Antonia.'

Antonia, the siren of Theo's sixth-form mythology, stood haloed in the stares from other partygoers, a small, bright dress rising over her legs in a red ferment, bottle of vodka swinging in her fingers, face and naked shoulders pale in the masked light. She had near-black hair, lifted back off her face, and tapering, heavy-lidded eyes, which she raised with a showgirl's panache, as if aware of their potency.

'Hello, Jonathan, hello, Felix,' she said, with mocking courtliness. 'Are you having a nice party?'

'Jesus Christ,' said Felix in my ear.

'Go for it,' I said, turning away, though there was something about her that jarred me, that prickled and stirred the hairs on my arms. Unsettled, I went to find myself another drink, and didn't go back. My head had Maria in it, her brown back and sympathetic smile, the coolness of the air in the garden. I wasn't up to Antonia; I couldn't raise the effort due to a girl of such stark sexiness. What was it she had done – made someone mad? That seemed plausible to me, and also good reason to avoid her. So I stayed away, made new friends in the drawing room, and ended up kissing a girl wearing a fake fur coat, though my heart wasn't in it. I was wondering where the evening went off its tracks, how I ended up tired, and baffled, unlatched like a vacillating gate, and not having a nice party at all.

e⌒

Later in the morning the car arrived for us. The house was gradually subsiding into inaction; the music throbbed on but the people had fallen one by one, as in an epic war film. Bodies lay on sofas, floors and under tables, unmoving in the fresh light. About fifteen people had formed a tight knot of survivors in the sitting room, Antonia charmingly presiding, her dress slunk up over the soft pale polish of her thighs, with Felix at her side, like the Prom King and Queen. As I skirted them and called goodbye, she looked up and smiled. Between the flush of her lips and cheeks her eyes glinted, her teeth. Then she turned away, back to the group.

I picked my way through the bottles scattered across the steps of the house with Nick, who was exhausted from the night-long continuation of his telephone argument with Emily – a dispute dropped and revived over and over – and was now mulishly silent. In the purring car interior he fell asleep, sagging like an older man. Theo, still top-hatted and with a monocle drawn on her face in biro, jumped into the car like the March Hare, crying, 'How funny!' to no one in particular, before putting her head on my shoulder and passing out.

I couldn't sleep. I was still sitting next to Maria, the promising closeness of her, wondering what had happened. I sat awake until the car climbed the hill to Evendon, past the trees, past the familiar kinks of the drive, turning the corner and seeing the first gold of the sun. It wreathed the front of the house, rising up the stone, soaking the lawn in light, turning all the windows of the house into flashing blue jewels. Once inside I went to bed, pulled the sheets up over my eyes to shut out the sun, and finally slept.

e⁓

When I woke up, it was with a sudden shock, at the wrong time. The blank night was staring at the window, my head hurt with a slumped, heavy exhaustion, my brain was wet clay. I moaned and tipped myself out of the bed. Then I heard Theo cry out, and realised she had called me already, and I had thought it was a dream.

'Jonathan!' she called again.

I stumbled around my dark room, pulling on clothes, and went to the window. I had no idea what time it was, and the eerie absence of temporal placement gave me the idea that somehow I was small again. I was reminded of something just out of the reach of my memory, only catching it in pieces, getting no more than a sense of it. The night there was a burglar, that was it – a burglar who had been active in the area. A security guard in my room. But that had to be wrong somehow, because I also remembered Alicia, her make-up bleeding down under her eyes, the light dividing the flagstones. The image brought an intense wrong feeling, and I had to force myself to open the window and put my head out.

Outside, the lawn was a swathe of black on which Theo appeared to float, pale as a moth, wearing her pyjamas. She was facing away from me, standing very still. I could hear her speaking to someone, then remembered that the house was empty – Eve was in London, making more money, Alicia was at a spa – and felt a dive of dread, an internal shiver.

'Theo,' I shouted. She didn't look up. I ran downstairs – stubbing my toe on the door as I went – and ran out of the softly swinging French windows into the cool air of the garden, the newly settled chill. Outside the steady light of the house the garden was formless – unresolved – as if submerged in dark water. What I could make out beyond Theo ended in inky hollows of foliage, seeping into the foggy edges of the trees.

Theo turned around to me, looking at me for a second as if she wasn't sure who I was. 'Did you see?' she said, then stopped and stared right over my shoulder. 'There he is,' she whispered urgently.

I swung round nervously, finding only the blank garden behind me.

'Who?'

I wondered if she was sleepwalking, but then she looked at me curiously, as if I ought to understand. Her eyes were pale, dusty-lidded; their colours translucent. Her mouth was loose and trembling; she looked as if she might fall, just softly fold up like a dropped handkerchief.

'Theo, there's nobody there.'

'It's hiding,' Theo said. 'The ghost wants to see us, but it can't. It's lost.'

'The ghost?' I said incredulously, but she continued to stare at me.

'Okay . . . let's just relax,' I said. 'You've obviously smoked too much weed. There aren't any ghosts. You must have seen a fox, or a shadow.'

'Why can't you see it?' she cried. Then she came forward and clung to me. 'Don't go, Jonathan.'

'I'm not going anywhere . . . it's okay.'

'You're going to university.'

'Well, you're going to London soon. And you can come to see me whenever you want.' There was silence. 'It's okay.' I repeated.

That night I sat with Theo in her room and – just the same as when we were children and she used to have nightmares – watched until her face relaxed and she moved murmurously into sleep. Then I went to my own room, where I lay uncomfortably until the morning, thinking about Theo's face, and ghosts, and the little girl who hadn't drowned after all, and the look Maria gave me as she left – half sympathetic, and half something else – and finally, without meaning to, the cream skin of Antonia, the smooth bridge of her shoulders, her naked smile.

e⸴

Before my return to Cambridge, as the summer cooled and thinned, I paid closer attention to Theo, but she was unclouded, excitable over going to London, and seemed to have forgotten her marijuana dream. I warned her not to smoke so much in future and left it at that.

Maria called at the house a few days after the party, but I was in Bristol at the time. To be more precise, I was with a platinum-headed girl who worked behind the bar of the club we had been to that night, planning how to extricate myself from her flat, the lilac sheets, the smell of cigarette smoke in her unlikely hair. I regretted it all when I got home and found I'd missed Maria, and I regretted it more when I drove over to Castle Hill House and saw her car wasn't there.

I rang at the door anyway, which was answered by her mother, Nathalie Dumas. I looked at her curiously: a small woman with worn, sunned skin and a paint splash on her nose.

'You must be Jonathan Anthony,' she said. 'This is a pleasure! Come in for coffee – oh . . . you probably prefer tea. I have run out of tea. We have fruit juice? Wine?'

'Coffee would be great.'

I followed her inside, looking around for items belonging to Maria that might indicate she was at home. Alicia was right – the house was small. The hallway was messy, the kitchen more so. A cake was in progress on the kitchen table, while in the corner a half-painted chair stood upside down on a pile of newspapers. Nathalie set about making coffee with inefficient vigour.

'Neither of my children are home today,' she said. 'Nick is in Bristol – with you, apparently.' (I knew where Nick was; at the barmaid's friend's house.) She looked around for the milk, couldn't find it, then forgot the drinks and sat down at the table to break eggs into a bowl. 'I don't want this mix to go off,' she explained. 'So you are Eve Anthony's grandson? You look like her. Both of you are very beautiful. She must be pleased you turned out so similar, eh?'

I laughed awkwardly and said I supposed so.

'So, Maria left this morning for France,' Nathalie continued. 'Ah, I'm sorry – this is sad for you, to come all the way here, and just miss her.'

'Oh, I thought I might be too late. I was just calling . . . on the off-chance. I wasn't really expecting . . .'

'Maria, she has always been a hard girl to track down,' Nathalie said. I nodded, drawing circles in the spilled sugar with a spoon, before realising what I was doing and putting the spoon back down, thinking that this was becoming a familiar sensation, this disappointment, blunt and painful and gritty in the teeth.

I had entered an unknown country with Maria – inviting her to Evendon, visiting her house, trying to interpret the things she said, things I had never done before. And, like any tourist, unfamiliar with the rules of a new land, I had misread the situation. All the things she had said about me not knowing her well enough; it was not a demand, it was a refusal. She was telling me she wasn't interested – I understood that now – and that was fine with me. Sitting here at her table with the real Maria in France, I found her easier to dismiss. I was already shaping the summer into a story for Felix: bored Jonathan, trapped in Wales, gets carried away chasing after the only attractive girl in the village, girl turns him down, ha ha, onto the next. Her loss.

e

The time before Theo left for London seemed to accelerate and merge, until finally she was in the car and being driven away, her small face in the window like an extinguished flame, her smile making her look like a child going to nursery school for the first time, waving frantically.

After that I was alone in the house. It would be a few days before Eve got back, and Alicia was still at the health spa. Every year or so she would go away for a while to the 'spa', a visit that could usually be predicted by the levels in the spirit decanters. After a few weeks she would return, looking brighter and paler, like a stained-glass martyr. This energy faded before long, sometimes not even outlasting the time her suitcases spent in the hallway before being carried away. The sight of these cases was always slightly unsettling to me, arousing the rinds of an old worry, a long-defunct worry, from a different time.

I wouldn't have said that I was lonely, exactly, but there could be something perturbing about Evendon when all its rooms were empty; when the sprinklers were turned off and the kitchen was shinily silent, and the gardeners and maids had left, their voices high and delighted as they wandered down the drive, because for them it was the end of a tedious day, and they were going home. I would walk outside, pushed out by the quietness of the house into the velvety garden, until it got dark and the mosquitoes bit me. Then I would sit in the gold parlour reading, accompanied by the television with the volume high; one night abandoning my Renzo Piano biography for a French film about a mysterious young woman, who I masturbated over briefly and unsatisfactorily before I went to bed. This didn't stop me dreaming about Maria, lying on a sheet of grass wearing nothing but her tennis skirt, laughing and saying, 'You don't really *like* me.'

I spent a day wandering, unmoored, round Llansteffan, sitting on the wall overlooking the empty beach, blurred with rain and the rising spray of the tide, feeling like I was haunting this familiar place, that I had already left. A group of boys crossed the road not far from me, listing aimlessly like boats in a squall, smoking ostentatiously. They fell silent as they passed, and then, 'Twll din,' said one in a low voice, and they laughed. I tried not to smile, feeling absurdly touched that they chose Welsh for the insult; not intending me to understand.

By the final day of my alone time I found myself wishing not only that Theo or Eve would come back, but for Alicia's company, or even that of Mrs Williams. I half considered going into Carmarthen, where Mrs Williams could often be found in the small café, holding forth with her usual passion on the unfairness of the legal system, the NHS, Tesco, her daughter's husband, Muslims, and the multitude of other wrongdoers who had purposely or accidentally crossed her. I was putting my shoes on when I realised how strange I had become, and spent the day finishing the Piano book instead.

Finally Eve came back, from whatever she had been doing in London. She arrived at night in a black suit and a glaze of money, glowing with mysterious victories. I went to greet her with relief, catching her before she had even taken off her coat.

'Congratulate me, Jonathan,' she said, kissing my cheek. 'I've just pulled off something fantastic. These barracks I've been chasing – I got them. You should look at the drawings with me. Would that interest you?'

'Definitely,' I said. 'I missed you.'

She looked surprised, then smiled. 'Well, I've missed you too. Has anything happened here? Oh of course – Theo's at college now. I almost spoke to somebody I know there' – by which she meant someone on the board – 'but I decided against it. I know your sister can be . . . dreamy . . . but I think she'll really *commit* to this course. I can almost picture myself at a gallery now pretending that I understand what her paintings mean.' She smiled. 'Theo would make such a beautiful artist. Infinitely more market-able than that Emin woman.'

'Nothing else has been happening here,' I said. 'I was bored.'

'Let's have some champagne,' Eve said. 'Where's Alicia? Drying out still? Probably for the best.'

When the glasses were brought she raised her own. 'Not to the barracks, darling. To you.'

'To anything in particular?'

'No, just you. I've been telling everyone about you, and how proud I am of you.'

She smiled, her eyes starry with immediacy, and I raised my glass back to her.

ー

Eve once said that people who are truly successful see their work as the most important thing, which causes trouble for the people who love them. I asked her what she chose as her most important thing – love or work. Eve said she'd known many great romances, and they had all ended. Love is changeable, but it is selfish, she said, love consumes you. Elizabeth I got it right. She looked for more permanence. Then she laughed, and said, 'I'm joking, of course,' but I could see she meant it.

I remembered this conversation later that night, long past midnight and after several glasses of champagne. I was standing at a spot quite a distance from the house, where the roll of the lawn plateaued then dropped, beginning the wooded slope down to the lake. From this place I could see all Llansteffan in a scattering of sparks, the lighter shadow of the beach, the black hills – and a small white house with its windows lit, on the edge of a sea that was invisible in the darkness, becoming only a darker place on the horizon, a line of absence.

2008

On the first of June, summer arrives promptly in Southampton, the light from the blinding sky hitting the room with force. The air is cool when I open the window: it will take a long time for the heat to reach into the tarmac roads of the town, the cold steel-coloured sea, impassive as concrete. But the birds clamour frantically; they know the people are coming – the yacht-owners, the sailors, the restless locals.

When I hear my new phone ring for the first time I am startled by the unfamiliar sound – a harsh bell clanging in the corner – before I realise it is Mr Crace. A small and economical man, Mr Crace spoke to me for only half an hour when we first met, and he concludes our business with the same brevity. His interest lies less in the personal than in admin; once he has given me an address, told me that copies of all relevant documentation will be forwarded to me, and established his preferred method of payment, he wishes me all the best with the neutral intonation of a speech synthesizer. 'I'm sorry,' he adds, communicating no sympathy. 'Goodbye, Mr Anthony.'

I put the phone down and sit on the bed, looking out at the wavering perimeter of the sea, its blurred horizon. I have reached the limit of the land, pushed back and back, until I stand at the brink of the water, like a man walking the plank. I always thought walking the plank was a strange concept. Why give the condemned man the illusion of choice – to step into the water and drown, or be killed anyway by the pirates? I don't understand why the pirates wouldn't simply tip him in. Perhaps it comes down to guilt. The man on the plank is at one remove from the murderer; he is giving the appearance of free will, which makes the whole thing easier to bear, for the pirates. Either that or it comes down to cruelty: drawing out the moment, the big joke.

I have read a lot about drowning. That to prevent shallow-water blackout, divers are warned not to take deep breaths before entering the water, because it can override the internal mechanism that demands the body breathe, so that the diver holds their breath for too long and passes out below the surface. A drowning person who opens their mouth and chokes on water will actually survive for several minutes longer than this diver. It's a warning for people who don't want to drown, and good advice for people who do. The man walking the plank would be better off breathing deeply, tricking his body so that he might be allowed to slip, denuded of oxygen, into a new state, a beatific calm, as spacious as a sky without clouds, as still as a densely snowed morning – a place that, in its airless splendour, must seem a lot like heaven.

I look at the sea again, refocusing, and try to remember what I was originally thinking about. The phone call. Mr Crace's dry wicker voice. The address, written on a piece of paper, lying in my lap.

The travel agency in town is decorated in yellow and grey, the drab palette of the airport. One wall is lined with brochures showing electric-blue skies, palm trees, white boats and mountains. The other wall consists of a curving desk hemming a row of blank-faced employees in red polyester. The gulf between fantasy and reality has never seemed quite so stark.

'Hello!' says the nearest girl perkily. I sit down opposite her and realise she is much older than I first thought; a woman with a lot of make-up, false hair, false nails. She smiles. 'Can I help you?'

'Thank you,' I say. 'I need a single ticket to New York. To fly as soon as possible.'

It takes me half an hour to convince the woman that I do not want a hotel, or a hire car, or holiday insurance. Finally she stares at me with uncertain dislike filtering through her melded lashes and informs me that the next available flight leaves tomorrow morning.

'Would you like to minimise your queuing time?'

'No, thank you.'

'Extra legroom? For just ten pounds each way, you can enjoy a position with no seats in front of you.'

'No, thank you. Just a basic single flight.'

'You don't want a return?' she repeats, but the fight has gone out of her, and she shrugs and books me a flight to JFK airport.

When I get home, I tell Mr Ramsey that I will be leaving tomorrow, and give him a cheque for two weeks' board in advance. I watch him deliberate. The offer is generous, but he looks as if he might try for more. He knows I have plenty to spare, after all, and it would be fair enough to conclude that I am a little cracked. In the end he settles for a reproachful 'Well, it's been a pleasure to have you here, sir' ('sir' is a recent addition) and goes back to his room. He always blends in perfectly: mulch trousers, a new jumper the colour of soil. The top of his head alone stands out, floating along the dark brown corridor like a pale flying saucer.

I pack my uninsured possessions into my case. Trousers, shirts, socks. Blue, grey, brown. Toothbrush, razor, soap. Any one of these things could belong to anybody. It would almost be appropriate if the suitcase and its contents were to be lost in transit; I imagine a plane crash, my suitcase floating out to sea, ready to baffle police with its cheerful anonymity.

❧

Later I lie in bed, hoping to be spared my dreams. I never know whether I will dream of something I miss – with the sting at the end when I wake up – or whether it will just be a straightforward bad dream. Tonight it's the latter. I wander through the usual routine: passing through rooms I do not recognise, trying to find my own. I hear voices, but cannot track down their owners. I dream of Eve, looking down at the top of her head, gleaming black and impervious. Finally I am in my bedroom at Evendon, listening to a woman crying.

Theo was marked down for an essay once after she misquoted the *Macbeth* line 'The night is long that never finds the day.' She wrote 'The night is young' instead, and argued over the correction: if it didn't say 'young', it should have. I understand what she meant now. It is the day that ages the night; without days the nights can have no past, no memory; they lose their menace. A young night without guilt. I can see the appeal.

When I wake up, it is five a.m. The light in the morning is narrow and bare and strips all the traces of sleep out of me, so I do something I have been delaying and write a letter to Alicia to tell her about my 'trip'. *Dear Alicia, I think it would be beneficial for me to take a short break abroad. I don't know exactly where I am going or how long I will be . . .* By the time it gets to her I will have left the country. This is a cowardice, but such a small one that I can't bring myself to worry about it – an endearing little cowardice, really, in comparison with the great, dark cowardices of the past.

e~

On the crowded train to the airport I attempt to get to my carriage without stumbling or abruptly sitting down in people's laps. The train's windows are not protected from the sunlight; passengers fan themselves and repeat 'It's *so* hot,' in the way that English people always do.

I notice the people around me; certain things stand out. A teenage girl's black eye, an old man with a missing arm, a woman reading something and wiping her nose surreptitiously, trying not to cry. A young man sits in a suit too big for him around the shoulders. His eyes are skittish, landing on mine and lifting away just as quickly; he looks like a child, spidery and unsure.

In another seat there is a carer with a small woman, who from time to time emits a high-pitched, soft wailing. She has a bird face, nose pointing to the floor, eyes looking up at odd angles.

Her stare fixes on me; she says suddenly, 'N-guh,' pointing away from me, at nothing specific. 'N-*guh*.' It is a question – I know that – but I do not know how to answer. I can only look back at her. The woman next to her looks up from her book. 'Quiet now,' she says.

PART THREE

2005

When I come to think of it, she was out of my sight most of the time . . .

Ford Madox Ford, *The Good Soldier*

TEN

The next five years of university passed quickly – not so much a progression of time as a suspension from the usual rules of living. I went to lectures and the library in the day and from there to the bars and parties; work and drink the two disciplines between which every drop of time was wrung out. During my two years of professional practice at the offices of Maher and Wade, I moved in with Felix in Kensington and continued the same routine: doing my work, getting in late, getting up early. ('We're really *living*,' I said to Eve.)

But then sometimes late at night I found myself watching my friends laughing, stumbling, making their fuddled overtures – the same things that I did – and I wondered if I had missed something. I didn't seem to feel the same enthusiasm that they did. Dressing, drinking, finding a girl, going to bed, opening my eyes into the shrill morning. Repeat. My heart wasn't in it.

It was the work I really loved – though love wasn't quite the right word. It was more than that; it was an absorption, a different state of existence outside which everything else was less coloured, less immediate, less natural. When I came back to Cambridge for my final year in 2005 I was impatient to be qualified. I wanted to shrug it all off – glib Maher, lazy Wade, my tired lecturers – like a school tie. I wanted to *do* something. I understood this need in myself as a cumulative presence; the acquirement and hardening of my ideas, my ambitions, until finally they could become steel, concrete, glass.

When the Christmas holiday came I packed my books and laptop into carrier bags to take back to Evendon, with Theo huddled in a blanket watching from my three-legged sofa. Felix, Sebastian and I shared a large and empty old flat in the city centre, which had white walls, tall oriel windows, and ceilings so high that our footsteps on the dulled wooden floors sounded like the knocking of a Victorian seance. The great boiler, which used to clang and boom ominously in its own room, had died quietly a few nights ago, and a preternatural chill hung in the flat like a white fog, sugaring the inside of the windows with frost.

'Don't you have a suitcase?' Theo asked me, after one of my bags burst open, showering the floor with paper.

'I lent it to you,' I said shortly. 'And you lost it.'

'Oh. Sorry.' She pulled the blanket up to her chin and peered over it reflectively. 'I *did* think that you were the type of person to own a suitcase.'

Theo had quit art college in her final year. She and the course didn't really 'get along', as she put it, by which we understood that Theo wasn't turning up. Eve had convinced her to take a few extra A levels at college with the intention of applying to university in future ('Perhaps it will settle her mind'), and Theo had been working at these intermittently for the past couple of years. She still lived with her Fairchild friends in Shoreditch, a group that always seemed larger than it was because its members changed their appearance so often. They customised everything, cutting up their vintage clothes, tattooing their necks and feet, dyeing their hair platinum blonde or black. Theo had never coloured her hair but they said approvingly that it looked fake anyway, and they loved what they thought was her ironic way of dressing.

'Hello, all,' Felix called, arriving arm in arm with Sebastian, both of them plastic-antlered and drunk. 'Cheer up, Jonathan, it's Christmas! Let's carol.' They started noisily singing a Christmas song, and dancing around the room. Theo struggled delightedly out of her blanket and was picked up by Felix and twirled around. (At one time I had been concerned that Felix – constrained by friendship but compelled by his own prey drive – might make a pass at Theo, but it never happened. 'She's good-looking,' he said once, 'but she's not really *like that*, is she?')

'Star of wonder, star of night,' they sang. 'Star with royal beauty bright,' before the song broke up into dissonant voices and they started arguing over the next verse.

'I'll look it up,' Sebastian said, studying his mobile phone. Sebastian had gone travelling for a year after he finished his philosophy degree, then took a masters in anthropology. He was currently studying for a PhD in South Asian Studies in an attempt to further delay his inevitable entry into the job market, which he envisaged as the swimming pool of his schooldays, a cold, chlorine-smelling turquoise vastness, his toes curling fearfully on the rim of it, shoulders shivering.

'Christ,' he said now. 'Listen to this – "Myrrh is mine, its bitter perfume, Breathes of life of gathering gloom, Sorrowing, sighing, bleeding, dying, Sealed in the stone-cold tomb".'

'Not a very merry Christmas present,' Felix said.

'What's myrrh?' Theo wondered.

'It's the main ingredient in Jonathan's aftershave,' Sebastian said. 'Seems to have that effect on women, anyway.' I ignored him; I was reading a note that had fallen out of my Pugin book, an old love note, undiscovered until now (*at times I glimpse the possibility of a deep connection with you* . . .). I vaguely remembered the author: a psychology student with ambiguous, whisky-coloured eyes, who had given up on our connection in the end. At the time I had been going through a phase of dating psychology students, but they turned out to be just the same as everyone else: hurried, worried, vibrating with effort. I didn't meet anyone like Maria.

I had seen her a few times over the years, the rare times when she was in the UK, the last being almost six months ago. We met for coffee in London, sitting on small hard chairs with a circle of marble between us. Her eyes contained all the light in the café, liquor colour, late-sun colour. I was aware she had been seeing someone, from what Nick said, a colleague named Olivier, but I didn't want to talk about him. Instead I found out that she had an apartment in a reasonably upmarket area of Paris, that she was working with a famous specialist in autism, that her mother had begun dating again. I went away knowing all the facts of her life and none of the substance, though I couldn't have said what was missing from what she told me. She was funny and interesting, as ever, but her conversation was like a glass wall going up between us.

I thought about her now, studying for her PhD in Paris. In my picture she was black and white and indistinct, in a café with coffee and cigarette smoke flavouring her mouth. She was laughing; jazz music played. An unwelcome shape appeared next to her, casual and prowling, a man – Olivier – his arm curling around her shoulder. I shrugged the image away, tilting my head; as if, after all these years, I might finally be able to tip her out of it.

e⌐

Theo and I arrived back to the worst of winter in Wales. I recognised the petulant billow and whip of the air; the wind that lies low, then bursts up with a well-timed shower of rain in the face, smashing umbrellas into foreheads and grabbing hats. The drive as we pulled up was husked around by the grey arms of the trees, under a hard, colourless sky, but Evendon's windows were bright, the rooms blazing like the heart of a fire; the Christmas tree in the hall, the chandeliers, the lustrous wood, the deep red of the drapes lit by the clusters of candles.

'Remember how Christmas was when we were little?' Theo said. 'Really little, before Eve came back.'

I thought of the afternoons once Mrs Williams and Mrs Wynne Jones had gone home, and Alicia had retreated to her rooms with a headache. Theo and I would sit on the sofa with all the wrapping paper around us, glittering like a festival, and watch the Queen's speech, and *The Snowman*, eating our chocolates. Theo was happiest at Christmas; it was as if her hair were brighter, her eyes bluer; the colour and the baubles and the lights kept her buoyant, invisibly working their magic.

'I remember,' I said, and she smiled at me.

I went to Eve's study before unpacking, pushing the door gently half open to see her talking on the telephone. She looked up and winked, so I went in, stretched out on her sofa and pretended to study the framed photographs on the wall behind me while listening to the conversation. I had done this since I was small, watching her talk, sitting unmoving except to make the occasional note.

'I need you to be more innovative when it comes to identifying opportunities,' she was saying. 'Remember what we did in Dublin? I'll speak to the developer and we'll make an offer . . . No, I'll deal with that side of things. I can't see that it will be a problem if we handle it properly.'

The longer I spent away from home, the more peculiar it was returning and seeing Eve in the flesh. University always made her seem unreal; there she was public currency, a picture in a magazine, a politics essay topic. I had even seen a poster in a friend's room of inspirational quotations, which included the 'blood of humanity' speech she made when Nixon accused of her of not being American enough (*It is the blood of humanity that flows through my veins. It does not mark me out as English or American, male or female, black or white. It marks me out as a human being – one who is determined to fight for all people, for the end of walls and wars, for trust and unity, for our children and our future*).

But then there never had been any simple division between the Eve sitting a few feet away and the world's Eve. I remembered going to a talk she gave for the UN, the way she walked onto the stage and stood there for a moment alone, absorbing the strange light, like the first visitor to the moon. She was so white and complete, hair glassy, more like a tiny Kokeshi doll than a human. Then she smiled, and started talking, as intimate and at home as if she were with us at Evendon, leaning over to tell a joke.

'Jonathan!' she said now, hanging up the receiver. 'What do you think of the UAE? Charis Dubai . . . Charis Abu Dhabi.'

'Really? That's fantastic. When?'

'Next summer. We already have the sites. It's about time really,' she said. 'I'll tell you all about it later. Where is Theo? Unpacking?'

'I think she went out to see the swans,' I said.

'The swans,' she repeated, as if unsure what swans might be. 'And how are her A levels going? I'd have thought she would breeze through them – she's already had a practise round, after all.'

'I didn't ask.'

'You know,' Eve said, tapping the pen she held on the side of her desk, as if it were a restless thing in her fingers, and she was trying to restrain it, 'I spent a lot of my political career promoting female rights; female freedom. My generation fought for these abstract principles, but now that the battle is over and the dust has settled, I try to get to know the women of subsequent genera- tions – my own descendants – and I find very little common ground. In practice I don't often understand women at all.' I wasn't sure what to say, but she didn't seem to expect a reply, adding more brightly: 'Well, we'll be having dinner in about an hour, so if you could find her before that time . . . ? Thank you, Jonathan.'

e⌒

Surprisingly, our Uncle Alex came for Christmas dinner. It had been a long time since we last saw him, something no one mentioned. My last contact – of sorts – with him was a few months ago; I had been startled by his voice on the radio, bursting erratically loud then quiet on the topic of free will in society, until I turned it off, unsettled.

Now he was sitting at the table next to Alicia and opposite Theo, silently looking over the division of the feast like someone from a much poorer country confronted for the first time with Western excess, and I could see for a moment what he saw: the vaguely obscene glisten of the meat, the hungry flare of the candles in their snaking candelabras, the icy clash of wine glasses, the heat rising off the bowls, the hectic glare of gold over it all, from the painted china, the baubles, the chandelier, the wreaths, and from Eve herself, sequin-scaled and queenly.

All Eve had said when Alex arrived about the blackout in relations was, 'Darling, how long has it been!' in a playfully rhetorical tone. Alex himself looked disconcerted, and asked if it had rained much lately.

'It's rained solidly for three weeks,' Alicia sighed, untruthfully.

'Oh,' Alex said, then was silent.

Looking at Alex I could almost have believed that stress and work had their own physical force, like a tide beating away at the wearable flesh of his face, abrading it down to the barest structure. (Alicia's skin, in contrast, had a peculiar smooth, set quality, like butter.) Academia had not been kind to him; aside from spoiling his looks, it had left him with an awkwardness of manner: sudden, faltering gestures, a habit of ducking eye contact. Eve, sitting perfectly still as usual, watched him now with interest and faint concern.

'So, what are you writing about at the moment?' she asked him. 'Haven't you published a book recently?'

'That does not preclude my writing another,' said Alex.

Eve lifted her hand to concede this. 'It always amazes me how you can sit for so long writing,' she said cheerfully. 'What is this one about?'

'It's a study of how the structures of religion and social morality have influenced the way we are governed and the way we live. I've made connections with the welfare state, the legal system, drug-taking, homelessness. Things that can be changed if our public consciousness becomes one of personal responsibility. Letting people live the way they want to, if you will.' Alex stopped, as if suddenly hearing the voluminous solitude of his voice over the table, and blinked out like a light bulb, murmuring, 'It has many aspects.'

'It sounds very interesting,' Eve said. 'Are these kind of books popular?'

'No.'

'Oh. But it will have an impact on . . . society?' She pronounced the word carefully, as if it were an unfamiliar language.

'Of course not.'

'Oh. I see.' Eve sipped her wine, looking at him over the rim with bright incomprehension. Alex frowned at the paper hat lying next to him. Only Theo, who had insisted on crackers, was wearing her hat. She had also collected all the jokes from the cracker carcasses.

'Why did the man get the sack from the orange juice factory?'

'I don't know,' I said.

'Because he couldn't concentrate.' She looked up and laughed. 'Like me!'

e⌒

After Christmas Nick and Nathalie Dumas came back from a visit to Maria in France, so the next day I drove over to their house, knowing shamefully that my hastiness as I slid along the snowy roads to Castle Hill was not for Nick's company. He and I were very different – sometimes I found him genuinely irritating – but still, he carried a faint impression of Maria; what she had said, what she had done, in the most recent past. From him I had her second-hand.

Nick had taken a year out before university and gone travelling with a friend. He had found travelling 'pretty boring' and come home after a month, starting a degree in management studies. He dropped out of this course after deciding it wasn't relevant and started another degree at Bristol University, in business this time. After an hour of conversation, I wondered why I had bothered visiting him. Looking for Maria in her brother was like looking at an eclipse in a bucket of water.

'I don't really want to be at Bristol,' he told me now. 'I'd rather be out earning some real money. As I'm not asking my father for anything.'

'Real money?' I asked.

'As in, lots of money. Emily's hardly going to be able to contribute much on a teacher's salary,' Nick explained.

I had met Emily a few times, a ringleted blonde with large, heavy breasts and a very slender body, as though she had been modelled by an adolescent Pygmalion. We had a short discussion on one occasion about how the sun gave her a rash, and another, longer talk about the surliness of sales assistants in Harvey Nichols. I had avoided a third conversation so far.

'It's okay when she's living with her family,' Nick continued, 'but I can't ask her to move in with me into some shitty one-bedroom flat.'

'It should not be important how big the flat is,' interrupted Nathalie, who was making coffee. 'Look at this place. We are happy here.'

'It's too small,' Nick said. 'I mean, good for you that you left et cetera, et cetera, but I don't want to live in this kind of house.'

'My ambitious son,' Nathalie said, with a laugh. She handed Nick his cup, which he accepted with an air of faint annoyance.

'Can you get some proper coffee?' he asked. 'This stuff is appalling.'

'Proper coffee!' Nathalie left the kitchen with dramatic emphasis.

'What's up with her?' Nick asked, rhetorically.

'Your mother's great,' I said. 'You're lucky to have her.'

Really I enjoyed Nathalie's company more than Nick's; there was something quick and attentive about her, always doing several things at once, as if the energy with which she had negotiated the difficulties of her former life had been loosed and could alight on anything. Nick had told me about their father once before. 'He's a shit,' he said. 'He was awful to my mother. None of us could ever please him.'

I waited for an hour with impatience before finally asking, 'So, what's going on with your sister?' as lightly as I could.

'Doing really well, I think,' Nick said. 'You know Maria.'

'Do I?' I murmured.

I had spoken to her on the phone to wish her Merry Christmas. I asked her in a mock-casual tone that made my throat contract to remember it if she was still seeing Olivier. She said she was. I added quickly that I was with someone too. 'Oh that's great,' she said. 'We should all meet up when I come back.' Her voice was pearly with politeness; smooth-surfaced, nothing to hang meaning onto.

I had an impulse to just ask her why she didn't want to be with me – what she wanted that I wasn't. But I couldn't do that, and so I said goodbye and hung up, and that was the last I had heard from her except for Nick, telling me she was doing really well, whatever that meant.

❧

Later that night Theo and I sat together on the terrace in the cold, as she tried and failed to light a cigarette. The wind would fall still for a moment, like a crouching dog, before it leapt again, whipping up the dark shapes of the sky and catching our clothes like torn paper. I accepted a cigarette from her, from a packet I had paid for. Theo had no money at this time of year – it was tramp season in Carmarthen and she had given her allowance away within the first few days of the holiday. When I walked through town it seemed as if there were an unkempt shape under every cash machine, raking in the proceeds of festive guilt. They all knew Theo and would call out to her, 'Hello, Theo, how's college going?'

There were lights on in Llansteffan below us; only a few, scattered like stars on a rugged sky, a glitter perched on the edge of the fluctuating darkness of the sea. Out of our sight was the single light of Castle Hill House, giving its lighthouse wink out to the night; a signal come loose from meaning, calling to no ships.

'Don't you feel odd, coming back here?' Theo asked me, most of her voice missing in the wind. Her mouth was small and grave.

'Of course not. Why would I?'

'I don't know,' she said, looking down. 'I just wondered.'

'You wonder some strange things,' I said, amused. We sat in silence for a while, with our black shadows side by side on the flagstones, surrounded by the flaming light of the windows behind. I stubbed out my cigarette once it was half burnt-down; I smoked a little only occasionally, to preserve the sensation of the nicotine, the faintly sickening buzz.

Despite what I had told Theo, I was already looking forward to going back to Cambridge. Eve had left for America the day before, and without her Evendon had a certain unease – not exactly a bad feeling, but a sense of time and place slipping and overlapping with the dim, penumbral past. Theo herself was a part of this; she encouraged the past, she called it up like a spirit. 'Remember when we used to build castles in the garden?' she would ask. 'Remember when we stole the cake from Mrs Williams, and dropped it?' 'Remember the musical box I had that played *The Nutcracker*, with the broken doll?' 'Remember the tree with the initials?'

I didn't like her habit of reminiscing, though I couldn't have said why. Childhood for me was distant and brightly coloured and strange, like a dream. It carried the overtones of fever, of helplessness. I would rather leave it as that dream, as something I had woken up from; unclenching my eyes and going gladly into the new, sensible light of the morning.

ELEVEN

When I got back to the Cambridge flat the heating was back on, Felix was nowhere to be found, and there was a girl asleep on the sofa in her underwear. When I woke her up she turned out to be articulate and pleasant, unlike some of Felix's female guests, who were screened only for appearance. We had a cup of tea together and she fixed our toaster so we could eat breakfast. About half an hour after she left, Felix came back with some carrier bags from the off-licence.

'The toaster's fixed,' I told him. 'Your friend mended it.'

'Did she leave her number?' Felix asked. 'The kettle needs fixing too. It gave me an electric shock yesterday. Anyway, I said we'd go to a New Year's Eve party in London tonight. Sebastian's going to a different party – some friend of Theo's. But her friends never have any decent drugs and I don't want my phone stolen, so I said we'd leave him to it. I guess New Year's Eve is his only chance of getting to first base with your sis.'

'He's wasting his time,' I said.

'That's what I told him. He's like something from the sixteenth century . . . courtly love. Poor bastard. He should come out with us and get laid. But will he listen?' Felix paused, frowning. 'I almost forgot to tell you – the party's at Chessie Turner's place. Are you and Chessie all right?'

'Fine, as far as I know,' I said. 'Why?'

'I know *you're* fine,' Felix said, laughing. 'Well, she invited us both, so I'm assuming she's over it.'

I tried to remember whether there had been any bad feeling between Chessie and me, following the week or so last year that we were sleeping together. She was the one who finished the affair; she explained that we wanted different things. It was a polite ending, a calm and civilised ending. Since then we had smiled at each other in passing, and I had thought we were friends.

Before the party Felix and I went to a bar, where we were joined by some girls Felix knew, who persuaded us to drink absinthe, lining up the virulent green glasses like a chemistry experiment. After several shots my drunkenness became piercing and strange, time whipped past, a girl kissed me, and I found myself holding the edge of the bar and her arm like an unsteady fawn, trying to sing along to a song I didn't recognise. 'Come on, come on, it's nearly twelve,' Felix was saying, agitated as Cinderella. 'The best girls will be taken.'

'Where's Maria?' I asked as we left.

'In France, Jonathan. In France.'

The party was being held in a few rooms of a terraced house in Camden; all of them choked with smoke and dark and moving bodies, like Newgate, the music heavy over the massed heads. We arrived as the clock was striking midnight and got mixed up in the general rush for kisses. Chessie was nowhere to be seen; another girl welcomed us and gave us a line of coke each. 'Happy New Year,' she said.

The coke sobered me; my head turned clear and crystalline, like a glass bowl. Light radiated through it, and sound; the noise of the party divided and became distinct as harp strings. One note I recognised – a low, persuasive laugh. When I turned around I saw Theo's one-time friend Antonia sitting on a sofa with two other girls, looking at me. She and Theo had drifted affectionately apart, the way friends do when they have no reason to dislike each other but nothing at all in common. She hadn't changed much in the years since I saw her last, the morning of Charlie's party; she still sat straight under the weight of everyone staring. Her hair was longer, curled at her shoulders like a doll's. She wore a corset top above which the pale top halves of her breasts rose, smooth as mascarpone.

'Why don't you sit down?' she said, so I did.

Antonia told me she had been in America working for a film company; now she worked at a PR firm in London, though this might have been the other way round. I tried to follow the conversation, but the clarity of the cocaine was slipping back gradually into an alcohol torpor, and the sharp, sweet perfume rising off her, the whiteness of her skin in the lower half of my vision, was distracting me.

'I have to go now,' she said eventually. 'I have to work tomorrow.'

'Oh.' I blinked at her.

'Don't be sad,' she said, starting to laugh. 'You can come back with me, if you like.'

I thought about Maria then, and my feelings for her, a longing and disappointment so close that it was hard to tell which followed the other, or even how to distinguish them. I wanted to duck away from it, fold into someone else, be overwhelmed.

'Yes, please,' I said.

In the taxi to her Fulham apartment my thoughts were suspended; she talked with a composure that I tried drunkenly to match. Finally, in her room, she turned all the lights on and stepped towards me. Her face was bleached by the sudden brightness, emphasising its flawlessness; she looked for a moment like an advertisement, holding my eye. The way we kissed was deliberate; artificial. Her fingers unpicked the buttons of my shirt without faltering.

'Let's not sleep at all,' she said.

I walked to the station the next morning with a new confusion with the world and – after the way she kissed me goodbye – an unreasonable erection. I couldn't concentrate on the street or the people I nearly walked into; I saw only one thing: her hair over the edge of the bed, the steep dip of her white back, my hand on her. The night had been oddly defined, like looking through a telescope and seeing everything in perfect detail; the distance of it was almost voyeuristic, a thrill. Being near and far at once; I turned it wonderingly in my mind as I walked.

e⌐

By the time I got back to Cambridge, the cold air and the first unpleasant needles of rain had sobered me, and I was feeling more like my usual self. The flat was empty; Felix and Sebastian presumably still lying unconscious on unknown beds, sofas or floors somewhere in London. I switched on the kettle, which gave me an electric shock, and made a cup of coffee. Then I read the papers, letting the tax and war wash over me, numbing the shocked nerve ends of last night, until I heard a shriek of crunching metal outside. I opened the window to see Theo in the street below, getting out of the driver's side of a Cadillac.

'Oh dear,' she said. 'Hello, Jonathan! Happy New Year!'

I went downstairs to inspect the damage; she had backed into a road sign, crushing it, and dented the bumper.

'This isn't mine,' she said. She looked thinner, which could have been the effect of the large man's cardigan she wore over a loose pair of jeans; the comparative frailty of her collarbone.

'No shit,' I said. 'Are you insured to drive it?'

'No – I've passed my test, though. Hurrah for me!'

'You still need insurance. And whose car is it anyway? Do they know you're driving it?'

'Oh, I'm looking after it while Louise is on holiday. Aren't you happy to see me?'

'Of course I am. You'd better come in,' I said. A small crowd had gathered morbidly around the remains of the road sign. 'That girl's someone famous, isn't she?' somebody said. 'She's that model, what's her name?'

Theo took two binbags full of clothes out of the car. 'I thought I'd stay with you for the weekend,' she said. 'Isn't Sebastian back yet? I got muddled with which party I was meant to be going to and we ended up in different places.'

Once we were inside I began to make tea, forgetting the kettle was broken, and got another electric shock. 'Shouldn't you be doing some work before your term starts again?' I asked her.

'Oh, I'm not really at college now. They asked me to leave. At the end of the autumn term. They said I wasn't doing enough work. I don't mind,' she said, fiddling with her unlit cigarette until it split and snowed tobacco onto the table.

'So what are you going to do now?'

'Just be useless,' said Theo sadly. 'It seems it's all I *can* do.'

'You'll have to get a job,' I said, annoyed. I disliked the suddenness of my morning transition from pleasant after-sex apathy to exasperated parent. Every time I felt like I could take my eye off Theo, she would do something unexpectedly stupid, like a toddler quietly feeding its toast into the DVD player.

'I could go to India with Sebastian,' Theo said now, hopefully. Sebastian was leaving in February to live in Kerala for a few months as part of his PhD. 'I'd like to go there. I could work in an elephant orphanage. Remember when we were little and we used to sit on the gold elephants in the morning room?'

'No, I don't.'

'Anyway, you have to help me think of what to say to Eve,' Theo continued. 'I don't think she'll like it, you know.'

At this point Sebastian arrived home and I was relieved not to have to think of an answer that wouldn't upset Theo, annoy Eve, or inconvenience myself. He and Theo began retracing the convoluted paths of the previous night like Hansel and Gretel in their twilight forest, excitedly following their breadcrumb trail of missed text messages and empty vodka bottles. I retreated to watch a TV programme I had recorded, a dramatisation of the life of Eve's father George Bennett, but it wasn't long before they followed me and started talking over it.

'Look at that moustache,' Sebastian said, as the actor playing

George sat thoughtfully in his claret-coloured study, gazing at a globe. 'Do you think it's fake?'

'It's a very grand moustache,' Theo mused.

'It looks like a broom. What did Eve say about this thing? Do you think she's watching it?'

'Her solicitors probably are,' I said.

(Eve, on the telephone, had said, 'We should be grateful that Geroge is a British hero and this is all we get.' She laughed, adding: 'If it seems like the media are intrusive now, imagine what they're like with their villains.')

A scene followed with George opening crate after crate in the black-and-white-tiled hall of his London house, withdrawing turquoise masks and stone stelae to the delight of a small girl kneeling rapt in the straw packing. The light struck her white face and for a moment she did look like a younger version of Eve, newer and softer, but with the same deliberate motion, a thought-out grace evidently common to both child actors and politicians.

'Imagine being there for that,' Sebastian marvelled, forgetting his humorous commentary.

'Sorry to break it to you, but Eve said that scene with the boxes being brought home would never have happened. He was very guarded about his work, apparently. Nobody was allowed near it.'

'The television is . . . lying?' Sebastian asked with mock horror.

After the drama ended, with a touching scene of the teenage Eve's speech at George's funeral, wrapped stiffly in so many layers of rigid black fabric that she resembled a sad Spanish doll, Sebastian shook his head.

'But now I'm not sure what to believe,' he said. 'Who knows what actually happened? Maybe he never died at all and really did find the Mayans' secret of eternal life. Or maybe Eve got fed up of him being selfish with his treasure and pushed him down the stairs.'

'Don't forget this is our grandmother,' I said reprovingly. 'These are real people.'

'In a way, Jonathan,' Sebastian said, with the solemn 'philosopher' face he liked to put on. 'Only in a way.'

e⌒

Eve arrived in Cambridge for a visit in February, appearing from the car in one familiar, quickly unfolding movement. 'You look well,' I told her. But under the white sky, the most searching light, she looked better than well – better than most of the students around us, with their alcohol-marked faces, their slept-on skin. For the first time I wondered, disloyally, whether she had had surgery.

'Let's go somewhere you usually go,' Eve said. 'Somewhere casual.' She looked around the small café I took her to with the obscure delight of a famous person slumming it, pronouncing: 'It's charming!'

Eve already knew about Theo leaving college: it turned out her intervention had been the only reason the college had kept Theo on so long. She hadn't heard about Theo's plan to go to India, which she had refused to drop. Sebastian had been teaching her Hindi ('*Namaste*, Jonathan!') and she had bought herself a sari from a charity shop.

'Which is silly,' I concluded, 'because why would anyone expect her to wear a sari anyway? They'd probably think she was taking the piss.'

'Theo does not have *drive*,' Eve said with finality, putting her teaspoon down like a gavel. 'She isn't a teenager any more. If she doesn't want to study, she'll have to find something else to do.'

There was a note in her voice I hadn't heard before; something I couldn't identify. I guessed Eve – like most people – was beginning to see Theo as idle, or lazy. But that wasn't quite right; it was almost that there was something missing in Theo, with her aversion to the linear, the cumulative. She blew and flitted like a feather, never landing for long, alternately enthused and dismayed. It was impossible to keep track of her.

'How's business?' I asked Eve, to change the subject.

'I'm going to Dubai next week to explore a few things,' Eve said. 'It all has to be absolutely perfect; there's no room for error when you open a hotel in such a crowded market. We need to organise some good media coverage.' She paused as the waitress passed us. 'We've had a few problems with competitors; there was an editorial in the *Emirates Times* about how Charis has been buying up sites in an underhand way. Some journalist essentially accused us of bribing a property developer to break its contract with another firm.'

'What are you going to do?' I asked.

'I'll deal with it,' Eve said, visibly enlivened. 'As far as accusations go, it's rather minor. I remember when I was investigated for tax fraud as a congresswoman; a team of accountants were virtually living at my house. I knew there was nothing they would find to discredit me. A few weeks before it all happened, Henry

Kissinger had called me. He was a good friend of mine, despite everything. A prudent, practical man. He didn't like Nixon particularly – Nixon was such an awful old anti-Semite. Henry warned me, "Nixon will get you." "No, he won't," I said. And he never did.'

'Do you miss it?' I asked her. 'Politics, I mean.'

'In a way. It was a ruthless time but also an exciting one. In the end I left politics not long after Nixon resigned. I suppose the fun went out of it a bit after that. But I'm not sorry I left. There was only so far, as a woman, that I could go. I knew it was time to take on something different. I was looking for that something when I had the idea to found Charis.' She smiled and leant forward, lowering her voice. 'Politics is only a theatre. You can look good in politics or you can make good in business. Since I switched, I've made much more money, I've become much more powerful, and – most importantly – I've been much more able to help those in need.'

℮⁓

After that meeting, Eve spoke to Theo over the telephone, laying out terms. She said she would not fund Theo's trip to India. She offered to pay the rent on a new London flat – if Theo would share with a friend's daughter, who happened to need a housemate. She added that she would look for a job for Theo, something not too demanding.

When Theo was younger Eve used to watch her with puzzlement, as if trying to work her out. But the way she spoke about her now was brisk and incurious, and the arrangements she made were for tidying purposes only: to fit Theo into a place in which she could be safely left.

Eve's disapproval of Theo bothered me, but Theo herself didn't perceive any change in Eve's attitude, acquiescing to her decision about the flat in the same way she had agreed that she ought to retake her A levels. 'I suppose I do need to earn some money,' she said. But she was unhappy about India.

'I'll probably never live in a temple now,' she said. 'That's what I want. A simple place, with a sacred cow to look after me.'

'Really,' was what I said, impatiently.

'It could be a sacred anything, I don't care,' she said, and looked away out of the grey window, winding her hair through her fingers.

e

Feeling faintly guilty about Theo's thwarted plans, even though I had – when I thought about it – done nothing wrong, I went to London to visit her the next week. We met at Oxford Circus and walked together to a restaurant in Soho to meet Felix. I disliked this part of London: the clatter of the thickly peopled streets, the demanding shop fascias blazing through the grey flicker of uncertain rain. I tucked my head down against it, as if weathering a storm. Theo was in a more-than-usually distractible mood, moving like a wren from one idea to the next, pointing and exclaiming as we walked, getting in everybody's way.

'You look nice,' I said, noticing the flower-print dress she was wearing. She looked at it with confusion.

'Oh! I picked it out of the washing because I was in a hurry. It must be Lucy's. I hope she doesn't mind.'

She stopped, startled again, as we passed a bookstore. In the window, on the cover of a large book, under the title *A Century of Style*, was Eve. The picture was black and white, though it took a moment to tell, being so similar to her actual colouring. Only the dark grey lips gave her away. Her eyes met ours; amused, slightly dismissive.

'It's like she's watching us,' Theo said, nearly whispering.

'Don't be silly,' I said, pulling her onwards. 'Come on, we're going to be late to meet Felix.'

Hurrying Theo that day turned out to be like gathering up a handful of ants. We made it down the road as slowly as if it were a church aisle, first stopping to pet a dog that had entranced her – then going to the cash machine, then stopping to speak to a man sitting untidily on a wall, encircled by several cans of lager, to whom Theo gave the money she'd withdrawn. ('That wasn't even a tramp,' I complained.) When we went back to the cash machine I took the money from her and put it in my own pocket – Theo submitting to this as if she were a child.

Delayed again by a 'hilarious' clock in a shop window, a small Japanese child with a balloon, and an unexpected purple flower growing out of a crack in a brick wall, when Theo finally stopped short, I didn't even look to see what had drawn her head around, sucked her breath out in a suprised 'Ah!' I just carried on, muttering, 'Theo, for Christ's sake, come on.'

'Jonathan – it's him.' She caught my arm hard, pointing across the road. 'That's *him*.'

In the sights of her pointing finger there were several teenagers, two older women, and what must have been the him: a man's back, walking away from us.

'Who?'

'Our father!' Theo cried, as if I ought to have known.

My first response was to stare harder at the man we were watching, as if there was some way of establishing through looking fixedly at the back of his blond head, his grey featureless jacket, whether this was indeed our dead father. Then I turned on her, exasperated. 'What the fuck, Theo? Not this again.'

'Come on!' She pulled my arm excitedly in the direction the man had taken. When I didn't move, she let go and started after him.

'Theo,' I called quietly, trying not to sound angry, but she didn't turn back. The people around me hadn't quite reached the point of stopping and watching us – the lovely girl and the angry-looking man, their brief tug of war – but the length of the looks had noticeably increased. Londoners, alert to possible soap opera in their midst, like hundreds of Mrs Williamses. I stood furiously and watched as the man turned away down a different street, Theo running behind. He was a fast walker, already substantially smaller: it seemed unlikely that she would catch up to him.

Rather than wait for her, I sent her a text and walked to the restaurant to meet Felix. He had been there for half an hour and had invited some girls at the neighbouring table to join us, so that when Theo finally trailed in, in high colour, breathless, eyes vivid with disappointment, I couldn't say anything to her in front of them. I waited until later, in the taxi, to say, 'What was that about?'

I had meant to sound neutral but the words crashed out instead like stone blocks falling, loud and harsh, and she jumped. 'I take it you didn't catch up with him?' I said, more quietly. She shook her head. 'What is this thing with our father, Theo?'

'I knew it was his face. From the picture,' she said. Then she turned her face down so far that her hair slid between us like a door closing.

A long, unhappy silence followed, in which I decided not to say anything else. I wondered if Theo's behaviour was actually fairly common, in psychological terms – the delayed grief of the loss that is never experienced. A known *type* of grief, something documented and taxonomic. That would be reassuring; to read that people who have never met a dead parent often imagine that parent's continued existence. But then, Theo wasn't comparable to other people. She never had been.

℮

After a week of waking up in the night thinking about Antonia, I wanted to see her again. First I checked with Felix whether he had slept with her at Charlie Tremayne's party. 'No – I don't know why she wouldn't,' he said, puzzled. 'I looked hot that night.' So I called and asked her out for a drink, and she said 'Why not?' in her voice that was like embers; soft, redolent of both sex and boredom. We went out a few times, to bars, and to restaurants, then after that we dispensed with the consumption and just went to each other's apartments, barely talking before we went to bed.

I got to know a little of her this way; I saw that despite her sociability she was often dismissive with others. She collected friends idly and forgot them, she laughed about men who she had broken up with or rejected, at the roses that appeared regularly at her door, the dropped phone calls, the tear-speckled letters.

She was pursued by romance – the daily shots of love – but she ignored it all.

I liked how casual she was with me, only tangentially involved with my life. She didn't eat with me, she didn't spend time with my friends, not even Theo. The greenish water of her eyes gave off the temperature of Icelandic hot springs, but really she was cool all the way through. The other men she had been with had been pained by it, but I understood her; I didn't want love either, I didn't want to be weighted with someone else's needs. Antonia would lie back on the bed and look at me with a smile of something like disinterest after we had slept together – and I always went back, finding myself at her apartment door in the afternoon, late at night, the earliest hours of the morning, already taking off my coat. She was usually dressed and decorated – in evening gowns, business suits – for whatever events were going on in her own life, events we never discussed.

There were times of course when I saw her in a less finished state: the rare mornings when she woke after me, looking confused, her face new, ready to firm and take shape. Without make-up her eyelids were touchingly naked, her mouth uncertain. Once I saw her in a face mask; she looked vulnerable, like a baby owl. I was intrigued by these glimpses of her, but then in another way it made me uncomfortable. I knew her better with the gold plate, the mascara, the lace and silk underwear, the brilliant hair.

℮

In the summer Felix and I qualified for the final professional practice exam. The first person I called was Eve, then Theo, who shouted excitedly into the phone that we should celebrate in London.

'Why not?' I said, so Felix and I met her in a Hoxton bar, a hot box of fog irradiated by tubes of glowing fluorescent colour, like a 1980s vision of an electronic dystopia. There were a few celebrities there I recognised, dancing with self-conscious skill, otherwise indistinguishable from the tousled clientele with their clinging jeans and eyeliner. Theo ran over from the bar, her pale arms and face lambent in the gloom, like Ophelia in the dark water.

'I got paid today,' she cried, handing us a bottle of champagne each. 'Congratulations!'

'How's the job going?' I asked. Theo had obediently become a 'creative assistant' to an advertising executive with the agency that handled the Charis account. After a couple of weeks she appeared to have forgotten about India and sent me a card with a picture of a London skyline on it. ('Dear Jonathan, I am having a hoot here. Hope you like these buildings. I have enclosed a pen from my company so you can write your reply with it. Then I can read your letter when I have nothing to do at work and it will be company business. All my love (that's true) Theo.')

'Oh, fine,' she said now. 'The office has grass indoors. Not real grass.'

'And your housemate? Do you get on?'

'Sort of . . . Lucy's very *focused*. She won't go out for drinks. I'm not allowed to smoke in the house and I have to be quiet so she can do her work. I didn't know why she'd live with me, but then I found out Eve is giving her extra money so we can live in South Kensington. So Lucy is staff really, or a paid spy maybe . . .'

She tailed off, as if someone had turned her volume down, and looked at me sidelong.

'So, I think I'm going to get a place in Westminster now I'm qualified,' I said, to change the subject.

'You'll be in London?' Theo asked. 'Oh! Why don't I live with you? Instead of Lucy.'

'Hardly fair on Lucy,' I said lightly, annoyed with myself for steering the conversation down an even more hazardous route. But Theo seemed to accept the reasoning of this and agreed that Lucy did not deserve to be cast out of her home so summarily. 'Maybe one day, when she moves out herself . . .' she said, to which I didn't reply.

By the end of the night I was trying to stay awake. Some friend of Theo's was sitting on my knee and talking piercingly about the art of the liminal. Felix had his hand innocuously up the skirt of another girl, who smiled enigmatically and sipped her drink. Theo had been away dancing for a while, and when she came back I noticed she was behaving strangely; talking faster, gesturing erratically. She stared around at the dance floor, her eyes strangely fixed, pupils open like umbrellas.

'I think we should call it a night,' I said to her.

'It's only three o'clock,' she said. She looked at her watch and giggled. 'Look at the hands! It's like twitching . . . Oh, but they're like spider legs . . . I don't like it.' Her mouth quivered with distress and she started trying to remove the watch. I took her arm.

'Come on, Theo. I'll take you home.'

'I'll catch you up,' Felix said when I told him we were leaving, waving with his free hand. I moved Theo through the crowds as she pried at her watch, and finally brought her out into the rainy night, the faint sadness of the collapsed heat of the day. She almost slipped on the damp glimmer of the paving stones, and again when getting into a taxi.

'Is she all right?' the driver asked, looking at us with hostility. Theo had curled herself into my arm and appeared to be asleep.

'She's fine.'

'Not going to throw up, is she?' he said. ''Cause I've cleaned up some of that already tonight. These girls . . . drinking too much. They just can't handle it.'

Theo's flat was dark and uninhabited when we got in. She stared at it as if it was an unfamiliar place, so I turned the lights on and shut the open windows that had allowed rain to blow in over the floor.

'I'll get you some water,' I said, but she refused to let go of me and started to cry. I stared down at her with concern. Theo was tenuously threaded together even when she was sober; in this loosened and frail state I just didn't know how to deal with her. I was in a leaky boat myself, unsteady and sick with drink, bailing out the waves of my own nausea.

'What have you taken?' I asked her, adopting the calm and capable manner of a TV doctor.

'Taken! Taken away,' she shouted. 'We have to stop them.'

'Well, whatever it is, you need to sleep it off,' I said, half carrying, half marching her to her room and tipping her onto the bed, where she lay looking confused. I drew her curtains and cleared a path through the towers of mugs, books, tissues and make-up on the table beside her bed before reaching my arm in and switching on the lamp. 'I'm going to get you some water.'

'Don't leave!' She struggled upright. Her face reminded me of the times when we were young and she would wake up from one of her dreams, sitting up half asleep, her hair sticking to her fiery cheek, eyes bowls of fright. It could have been the same girl but for the make-up trailing over her cheeks like writing, the scent of smoke rising from her rumpled clothes.

'Stay there. I'll be one minute. Look, I'll keep talking so you can still hear me . . .' I went into the kitchen, calling to her as I went – 'Just getting a glass . . . pouring the water . . . coming back now' – but when I got back into her room she had gone to sleep. I sat on the armchair in the corner, planning to watch over her for a while, before giving in almost immediately and passing out, letting my grip relax, my eyes, close, tumbling gently into the soft ocean.

TWELVE

At the beginning of autumn Maria came back for a few days. She was meeting her father in London at the Dorchester, then going to Llansteffan later that night, she told me on the phone.

'I can't come to Wales; I have a meeting I can't miss,' I said with dismay.

'Well, meet us for lunch, if you like,' she said. 'It's his birthday; the more the merrier. Though it won't be very merry, I'm afraid. Otherwise I could meet you for a quick drink before I catch my train?'

I wasn't giving up on this couple-like activity. 'The Dorchester it is,' I said firmly.

'Who was that on the phone?' asked Antonia, after I hung up.

'Maria Dumas . . . she's a friend of the family.'

'I remember her from a party, I think,' Antonia said. 'She was a nice girl – beautiful, actually.'

'I suppose,' I said casually. I was protective of my unrequited feeling for Maria, like a little Fabergé egg with nothing inside. I didn't want Antonia's ill will – which could be quite sudden and decisive – identifying this love. 'If you like that type of look.'

Antonia looked at me sharply. 'Don't be stupid,' she said. 'Everyone likes that type of look.'

ℰ

As I walked to meet Maria I wondered whether I would always do this for her – cancel all my afternoon appointments, get home to shower, put on a scarf (bought for me by Antonia) I thought she might like, rush out to the Dorchester. I couldn't help it. I couldn't help but want her, seeing her turn towards me, wrapped in a dove-coloured coat with her hair pinned up, looking even more collected than usual. I couldn't even identify what it was about her that made her seem so necessary: something in her centrality, her calmness; this mysterious thing she had that I didn't. But I sensed the value of it, like a thief in possession of a painting by an artist he doesn't recognise.

'You look serious today,' she murmured, as we waited for the table.

'Just thinking about work,' I said. 'Sorry.'

Maria's father, Sir John, was a good-looking man, but side by side there was little in his appearance to remind me of her. Perhaps if he had smiled there would have been a similarity; but all through lunch I never saw it happen. 'Eve Anthony's grandson,' he said when we met, as if I wasn't there and he was telling a friend about me.

After initial civilities, Sir John got down to what appeared to be his most serious occupation: complaining. He complained about his house, about his shares, he complained about the waiter, who he was rude to. He still kept a butler, probably for the purpose of complaining about him. He despised the government, the shadow cabinet, the general public, the foreigners. He was, however, pleasant to Maria, with an effort that was painful to watch, gazing at her with his heavy yellow eyes, though he couldn't help frowning when she said she planned to work with autistic children.

'What, as a nurse?' he said.

'No, as a psychologist. I'd like to have my own practice.'

'Well,' he said, and stared down into his cup. Maria didn't seem to expect anything more, smiling and changing the subject.

Before we left, he said to me, 'I remember your parents' wedding now. Alicia and Michael Caplin. He seemed solid enough at the time. There really was no way of knowing what a bad business it would be. I heard about the custody fiasco . . . though as I recall, nothing was mentioned in the press.' He paused, reflective, then added, 'I suppose credit is due to your grandmother for that. A very great lady.'

e⌒⌐

Afterwards we went to a bar I liked in Belgravia, where we could sit alone in a low-lit silk-lined booth, close and low-voiced over a small table. Maria refused wine, ordering tea instead.

'I'm sorry, that must have been unbelievably boring for you,' she said. 'I know it's selfish of me, but I am glad you came. It imposes limits on the conversation; he was a little more sociable than usual too, believe it or not.'

'Nick doesn't visit him?'

(I had been at Nick's new flat in Canary Wharf the previous week, which he had showed me proudly: 'It's crazy how much

they let you borrow if you can get self-cert. I see it as an invest-
ment – property prices are only going to rise around here. Emily's
going to move in soon, which should finally put a stop to all the
arguments we've had lately. And once I'm qualified, I'll get into
one of the big finance houses.')

'No. Which is fair enough, given the way our father's behaved
in the past. I'm guessing that's the reason anyway . . . Nick doesn't
really talk about it.'

I had heard too much from Nick on his family's various fail-
ings to entirely agree, but I said, 'I don't blame him. You have to
get on with things – you don't need to let family history affect
you. You just put it behind you.'

She rubbed her temples with her face tilted downwards, and
for a moment I couldn't see her expression.

'So, what's the important business meeting?' she said when
she looked up.

'Felix and I are starting our own firm,' I told her. 'Anthony
and Crosse. We hadn't really thought of going independent so
soon, but we've been given commissions already. I have to meet
Marcus Britton tomorrow to talk about a house he wants built.
He's the son of a film producer Eve knew.'

'That's a lucky opportunity,' Maria said.

'Well, not really. The architect he originally hired committed
suicide. He needed someone else in a hurry. I suppose it's an
honour that he would trust us, though. He said we could submit
any designs we thought might be post-modern enough to make
the *Times* property supplement.

'Anyway,' I added, 'I didn't know you wanted your own
practice. That's great.'

She looked at me with amusement.

'Why great?' she asked.

'Well, success can never be a bad thing,' I said, shrugging. The bar must have passed some invisible marker between day and evening, because the lights over us dimmed. The booth took on the interior glow of a rose, warmly shadowing our faces. She put her elbows on the table and leaned forward on them.

'How would you define success?' she asked.

I thought of Eve – of her world at the top floor of a tower, governed by the laws of profit and acquisition, moving up the gradings of fame like an earthly version of *Pilgrim's Progress*. Christian stripping back the past, attaining a state of corporate purity.

'Your name being known,' I said. 'Power . . . money.'

'Do you want to be powerful?'

'Well, in society some people will always end up with more power than others,' I said, trying to sound light. 'So why not me?'

Her smile was becoming more indecipherable. 'You are very much like Eve,' she said.

'I do get told that sometimes.'

She glanced away as the waiter approached, then asked, 'So . . . how's Theo?'

'Fine,' I said. Actually I had been avoiding Theo for the last couple of weeks, after the episode at the club. She had called several times, usually late at night, and left some strange messages, but I couldn't follow these monologues, interpret the smoke and hiss of her chemistry experiments. Yesterday I had absent-mindedly answered the phone when she rang, but the line was bad, and I could only make out the outlines of words, delivered in a buzzing clatter. The only thing I heard her say was something that sounded like 'take half, and lose half'. Then the connection blanked out, taking her voice with it.

'I'm glad she wasn't here today,' I said. 'God knows what she would have made of what your father said – about my parents.'

'I had no idea he even knew them,' Maria said. 'I'm sorry if he offended you.'

'No, not at all,' I said, and laughed. 'It was nothing. But Theo gets carried away – she reads too much into that sort of thing.'

'What happened? With your parents? You never mention it,' Maria said.

'There's nothing to say,' I said, not liking the direction of the conversation. I wanted to bring it back to the two of us, excluding everything else – fathers, sisters, Antonia, Olivier. 'They divorced, that's all. Then my father died.'

'You just put it behind you . . .' Maria said.

I realised, as the conversation eddied onwards, that her polite friendliness had returned – so polite it bordered on coolness – but late at night in my flat when I thought back over the evening, I couldn't tell how or when it had happened. The night ended as my time with her always did – a brief wave, a postcard smile, already far away.

e

I had trouble sleeping that night. In the early hours of the morning I got up and sat at the computer, half working, half browsing aimlessly, ending up typing Eve's name into a search engine and finding her entry in a newspaper feature on its Top Ten Female Politicians.

Eve Anthony was born in 1937, the daughter of another twentieth-century icon, the archaeologist George Bennett, and the American heiress Louisa Cleveland. She studied economics at Wellesley College before graduating and marrying the Democrat politician Freddie Nicholson, who had recently been elected to the House of Representatives. After Freddie Nicholson's death in a boating accident, Eve Nicholson was elected to the House of Representatives in 1969 to serve the rest of her late husband's term.

As a politician, Eve Nicholson became an early heroine for the rising number of women seeking greater personal and political empowerment in the 1970s. She gave a speech in which she urged women to find their voice and become 'more involved in the future of [their] country'. She said, 'When women were granted the vote, it was a hard fight. Now women are becoming politicised, it is a hard fight. The next hard fight will be for a woman to become president, and after that happens, people will look back and marvel that it was a fight at all.'

Eve Nicholson's popularity and her family's long-standing friendship with the Kennedys put her on an early master list of Nixon's enemies. She compounded this by attacking Nixon's actions in Vietnam in 1972. He had said early on that there was no greater title than that of peacekeeper; Nicholson retorted: 'He is a "peacekeeper" who bombed Laos and sent troops into Cambodia. And now he bombs Hanoi. It is dangerous to have a President who gets muddled about what is war and what is peace.' Eve Nicholson's entry on the list – subtitled 'screwing our political enemies' – read: 'High support. Get her on association with Sam Anthony or JFK.' The media seized on the physical disparity between the famously beautiful congresswoman and the gruff President, dubbing the pair 'Beauty and the Beast'.

Nixon's administration consequently attempted to unseat Nicholson on charges of tax fraud, which she successfully disproved. A subsequent break-in at her Manhattan house, in which several files and letters were stolen, was found to have been carried out by a Johnny Wymans, who had received payment from the Nixon aide Edward Delores. Nixon denied all knowledge of the affair and Delores was sacked. After this incident Nixon was forced to abandon his pursuit of Nicholson, who emerged from the political battling with public sympathy on her side. 'Truth wins out,' she said. 'I have always believed that.'

I shut the computer and went to bed. For some reason reading the article had made me feel more uneasy than before. I wasn't sure why I had looked it up – almost as an impulse to confirm something, as if to touch land after an unsettling sea journey, but it hadn't had the desired effect. It took a long time, the light between the blinds striping my face and the traffic noise rising outside, before I could finally sleep.

e⌁

After Theo's strange weeks, as I had begun to think of them, she seemed to go back to if not exactly normal, at least Theo-normal. We met for lunch a few times and she seemed happy; she was technically living with Lucy still, but spent most nights on the floors and sofas of her carousel of friends, each of whom she expected me to remember. ('Floss, I told you about her . . . she's got black hair and it used to be red – she's a DJ, she wants to make a CD of jazz and hip hop, she's really nice.')

I didn't ask about the strange weeks, and she didn't explain them. I put it down to the influence of some past friends, fallen out of rotation. Anoushka perhaps, who was in Thailand, fat Michael, tattoo-graffitied Carrie. Maybe Floss was a good influence after all; I felt a relieved swell of benevolence towards her.

Theo had lost her advertising job after she forgot to go to work for a week ('I really did think I'd asked if I could have a holiday,' she said, puzzled) and was working now at a London gallery, though she didn't seem to be there very often either. She spent a lot of her time at my apartment in Westminster.

'Why aren't you at work?' I asked her one afternoon, trying to sound trusting.

'Oh, I hate the underground, tunnelling around all the time. It makes me feel like an ant. And there's not so much for me to do at the gallery, really. They pretend there is, but usually I just do little things, like going to get them sandwiches.'

'That's not what you're paid for, is it?'

'I don't really know . . . that's the thing about these Eve-jobs. I don't go to any interviews or anything. I don't know what my job title is. Anyway,' she said, 'I don't mind dusting all that much.'

In the end I stopped questioning her when she arrived, and would just work at my desk while she piled cushions on the floor and lay on them to watch the cookery and gardening channels on television.

'Why do you like that rubbish?' I said, turning the volume down.

But I could see why she liked it. It reminded me of when I was very young and used to watch commercials instead of television shows. It was the bright cleanness of that world, the simplicity; where triumph could be found in a soufflé, or a flowering border. She watched it with absorption, her hair glowing backlit by the television screen, her eyes the colour and clarity of the Atlantic.

Antonia tended to come to my apartment at different times to Theo, though lately she was visiting less and arguing more; our nights together often devolving into an angry silence. I could feel her impatience with me hovering, as if she were waiting for a reason to fight, like a drunk knocking into somebody deliberately hard, pretending it was an accident. But I wasn't interested in arguing with her; I would walk away, or sit in silence, letting the bad feeling swirl over my turned-down head. The last time I saw her was when we went to a party together, where a woman discreetly gave me her number. When we got back to the apartment Antonia ignored me, and read a magazine rather than come to bed.

'What's wrong?' I said finally. 'I'm not going to call her.'

'You obviously encouraged her,' she said. 'Not that I particularly care. It's just unfair on the woman, that's all.'

'I'm sure she'll be fine.'

'Also, it looked ridiculous. You flirting with her. It's beneath you.'

'Forget about it,' I said shortly. I was starting to feel irritated;

her bad mood was blowing in on our uncomplicated night like a coating of dust and grit; I wanted to brush it off. 'Are you going to come to bed or not?'

She was silent for a while, looking at her closed hands in her lap and frowning as if they might suddenly open, and show something unexpected. I went to the kitchen and poured myself a glass of water, then brushed my teeth. When I went back into the sitting room Antonia stood up, took off her dress and came over to me, smiling.

Felix made a sympathetic wince when I told him about it. 'You and her – it's just sex?' he asked. 'Is that all she wants? Is that all you want?'

'It's always been that way. We've never even needed to discuss it.'

'Okay . . .' he said, raising his eyebrows. 'You must be pretty good in bed, that's all I can say.'

When it was working well, I liked my relationship with Antonia. I could enjoy her cinematic sexiness, her showy beauty, without having to fully engage with her life. I didn't wonder why she wasn't interested in love; I was grateful for it. I didn't have the time to be more involved; the hours left over at the end of the day after the meetings with clients, builders, engineers. More than that – I didn't feel capable of sustaining someone else's happiness, rolling it up the slope of the day, over and over, like Sisyphus. There were times now when I felt only partly functional, like the overused musical box we used to have when we were small, its *Nutcracker* prince turning round and round, then stopping, then turning again. I wondered what happened to the other figure, the little Clara. I vaguely recalled her being snapped off – an accident – after which she must have got lost.

e⌒

Sebastian came back from India at the start of the winter, after extending his trip for so long that when he told us he was coming home, no one believed him. Felix and I then had to rush to arrange a welcome-back party for him at a bar. Sebastian was hard to recognise: darker and stiller than before he left, short-haired as a greyhound. He ordered a lot of drinks and drank them efficiently; there was something almost serious about the way he set about it, the way he played his old self for us.

'If you had to make a TV series, what would it be about?' he asked us. It was the kind of question he had loved when he stayed with us over that summer, and I saw what he wanted, to recapture that heat and light, cup it in his hands like a match.

Theo clapped her hands. 'Animals that can sing.'

Sebastian said, 'I'd call mine *Salt and Pepper*. It'd be about Dr Jason Salt, a rural vet who is also a detective, and his assistant, Judy Pepper. It would be really gritty. At the end of the Christmas special, Judy dies. Caught in some farm machinery.'

'Can it have a singing pig in it?' Theo asked.

'Yes,' Sebastian said magnanimously. I had noticed that he treated Theo with the same half-teasing, half-wary deference as before, looking at her when she wasn't looking at him, moving to block someone who was about to stumble into her. Theo was oblivious to it, laughing and dancing in the silver bracelets and silk scarf he had bought her.

I was tired from work and went back to the apartment first, where I sat up with a coffee in the wan circle of a lamp, trying to decide whether to call Antonia. In the end I put the phone down and dropped into a concrete, unsatisfying sleep.

I was woken up at five by Sebastian calling me and knocking on my bedroom door. He was supporting Theo, who lolled in his arms as if asleep. The hair was damp around her face, her eyes only half visible under the drooping lids. Her skin was pale and slick, giving off an unhealthy radiation.

'I think Theo's taken too many pills,' he said. He looked frightened. 'She was talking earlier but now she's stopped.'

Theo looked up when he said this and made us both jump. Her fingers clutched around Sebastian's shoulders.

'We need to open the door!' she said, her voice high and compressed in the back of her throat. 'The door's shut. I can't hear them – what are they saying?'

'The door's open,' I said.

'No . . . that door,' she said, pointing at the blank wall impatiently. 'We have to watch the door. They're talking about the ghost.'

'You let her take them?' I said angrily to Sebastian. I was trying to get her to sit down on the sofa but she was resisting me; her body went rigid, girdered. I gave up and let her stand, eyeing the wall suspiciously.

'I didn't know! Her friends arrived. I didn't even know where she'd gone. But I've never seen anyone like this after a few pills. She must have taken something else – but that's all they said she had: pills and a bit of weed.'

'We should take her to the hospital,' I said.

'No!' Theo shouted. We must have woken up my neighbours; one banged on the wall, the same place Theo had been staring at. She cowered away from the noise.

'If we do, it'll get in the papers,' Sebastian pointed out.

'Yes.' I thought about Eve. 'Shit!'

'It's probably acid, and she'll calm down,' he suggested.

'What if she gets worse?'

'Then we should definitely take her to hospital.'

'I don't want to go to the hospital,' Theo moaned. 'I don't want to be taken away, I don't want to end up there. I can't shut my eyes.'

'Then you'd better calm down,' I said to her sharply.

The words seemed to have a sudden effect on her; she sat down and stopped talking. Sebastian brought her water and we made her stay sitting upright, watching the television, which she insisted on switching to the gardening channel. We all stayed up that way, watching a woman dashing about an uncanny, bluish lawn talking about bamboo, until the morning burned through the curtains and Theo started looking more lucid.

'It's half past nine. I'm going to bed,' I said, rubbing my eyes with my cold hands. I didn't know if I could even sleep now: I was left tired but alert, burning with an unearthly brightness.

'I'm sorry,' Theo said, starting to cry. 'I didn't mean to be any trouble.'

'I didn't say anything before, but you have to stop the drugs now, Theo.' I was stern. 'You can't handle them. You always go too far with everything. Promise me you won't do them any more.'

'I promise,' Theo said quickly. 'I promise.'

'Good,' I said, getting up. I left her with Sebastian, her black-ened cheek resting on his shoulder, his hand stroking her damp hair. I went to bed and lay there with my eyes closed, waiting for the slow fog of sleep to roll down over me, but as it drew in, my thoughts were someone else's thoughts – Theo's – fitting wrong like old clothes, uneasy and familiar. The last of these was a memory of the secret pool at Evendon, its water thick like heavy metal, shivering under the low night wind.

e⌐

After Theo and Sebastian left the next morning I couldn't concen-trate on the work I had to do, so I switched on the television and couldn't concentrate on that either. I wondered whether I should make myself a drink, but halfway to the off-licence to buy some-thing strong I was reminded of Alicia, and turned back. By the time I got back to the flat a crow-coloured dark had dropped unceremoniously over London, met by the yellow of the street lights, the white glare of the shops. I switched the lights on in my flat and was surprised how strange my hands looked: bluish pale, roaming restlessly over the computer keyboard when I tried to start my work.

What was the time in France? Maria would be at home now, in her apartment, making coffee, enjoying the lag time of Sunday. I hesitated, then called her.

'Jonathan, hi!' she exclaimed when she picked up. I could hear music in the background, people talking. Someone gave a short, harsh laugh, like a magpie call. 'This is a surprise. How are you?'

'Sorry – is this a bad time to call? Are you busy?' I asked.

'What? Oh no, no, it's fine.'

'I was just calling to ah . . . well, because I might be in Paris on business soon. That's why I was calling.'

'What business?' she asked, 'Are you designing something here? How exciting!'

'It's not definite yet – I won't tell you about it now, but I'll call back another time and, yes, hopefully if it works out then I can visit,' I said, trying to end the conversation before my lie became too complicated.

The noise on the end of the line dimmed, as if Maria had left the room. 'Jonathan, is something wrong?' she asked. 'You don't sound like your usual self.'

'No, nothing's wrong. I do have a cold.'

'Oh no, I'm sorry . . . Poor old you.'

There was a pause, and then she said, 'Well, let me know if you're coming to France, anyway. That would be lovely,' and we said goodbye and hung up, and I went back to staring at my work, and wondering if there was any way I could get a commission in France, and feeling worse – more dissatisfied – than before I had called her.

Eve, who had been in America for the past month, called to say she was home and to invite me and Theo back to Evendon for the weekend.

'Just family,' she said, by which I understood it would be the four of us. Alex's attendance at family events had ended abruptly after an argument with Eve earlier in the year. I had been there, sitting in the gold parlour with a dozing Alicia, overhearing Alex's raised voice, passing the door and ringing up into the heights of the hall, magnified like a choirboy's.

'No, you didn't,' he said angrily. 'Let's tell the truth for once!'

Eve's voice was too quiet to hear. There was a pause. Then Alex said, 'Yes. But it's because of you. And you're going to do the same to them.' The door slammed, and that was the last we saw of him for a while. Eve didn't mention him, and there was a general understanding that there would be no reconciliation this time. I didn't mention the argument, out of a vague feeling that it was better not to have Alex around anyway. I sensed in his shy rancour a kind of aggression; his resentment of Eve could do harm to our family, arranged like delicately balanced chess pieces, unmoving so long as nobody touched them, fixed in the strange, lovely peace of Evendon.

Theo and I drove to Wales late at night, so late that everyone would have gone to bed by the time we arrived. I was annoyed with Theo – I had arrived at her apartment to collect her and found her noisily asleep, with a cat's nose and whiskers drawn on her face in eyeliner and battlements of wine bottles surrounding her bed. In an ashtray next to her head a cigarette had become a strip of ash. I shook her awake and found some clothes for her to pack.

'Sorry, Jonathan,' she murmured, trying to focus on me. 'I had to go out last night. I had to say goodbye to Sebastian.'

Sebastian was going to India again to teach, which had upset Theo. She didn't understand why he had come home, stayed only for the weeks it took to finish his PhD, and promptly started making arrangements to leave again. She took it personally – trying to be a better friend, making him pictures and buying him little presents; as if Sebastian were a sort of errant pet that could be tamed with treats. But I could see it was Theo's friendship itself that pained him; he had to protect himself from England, the place where he wasn't loved.

'Maybe I could go with him,' she said hopefully once we were in the car. 'Maybe Eve will see it's not one of my "fads" this time and lend me the money. Or you could lend me the money?'

'Sorry, Theo, but I'm not getting into sub-prime lending. You owe me enough money already. Besides, you have a job here,' I said.

'Oh, I can't work at the gallery any more.'

'Why not?'

'They sort of sacked me. They said my sales style was "unusual" and they didn't like it that I didn't work all the time. But there really wasn't much for me to do, so some days I just went home. So they called Eve and said I couldn't stay. I guess she'll find me something else . . .' Theo fiddled thoughtfully with her cigarette lighter. 'I think it makes her happy when I'm doing something.'

'That's not really the point, Theo,' I said.

'The gallery was quite strange really,' Theo said. 'I asked them how they can decide how much art should cost. They said it costs as much as people are prepared to pay. Then someone came in to buy a painting and it didn't have a price on it, so I asked them what they were prepared to pay and I just charged them that. Then I got in trouble.'

I started to laugh.

'I think all art should be free anyway.' Theo said, leaning her head back and yawning. 'Don't you think that?'

'Sure,' I said. 'So long as we're not counting what I do as art.'

'Oh no,' she said, which made me smile, but her eyes had already closed. She slept for the rest of the journey, as the indistinct road slipped past us with its punctuation of lights, the signs counting down the stops, pasted against the darkness, the narrowing and narrowing of the motorway, until finally we were on the black track to Evendon, shrouded all round with trees.

The house was dark and silent when we went inside, with a single light burning at the entrance like a will-o'-the-wisp. I passed through the twin pillars and went up the stairs, feeling the cool air settle over me, the familiar scent of the house. I didn't turn any lights on; I could see my outline in the shivering light from the windows, my feet knew how many steps they needed to take. Both Theo and I walked to our bedrooms like somnambulists, re-entering the familiar tracks of our dreams.

℮↷

After lunch the next day I spent a few hours talking to Eve, while Theo went to the local pub with a couple of the maids.

'I'm not sure that's a good idea,' Eve said. 'They are employees, after all.'

'I told her that.'

Eve shook her head. 'It baffles me that your sister would want to go and sit in that place listening to local gossip.'

'Maybe she'll hear something about our family,' I joked, but she frowned. There was a pause. I was reminded obscurely of that day by the reservoir several years ago: Theo's faltering story about our father, the oystery, cold smell of the water. I had the same queasy, nervy feeling now, noticing my leg twitching, my fingers slipping on the handle of my teacup.

'Speaking of that,' I said, putting the cup down, 'I saw Maria's father a couple of months ago. He made a reference to Alicia's wedding.'

Eve looked surprised, her eyebrows drawing up like stage curtains, so that her eyes stood alone in full force, black on white in black. 'I had forgotten he was there,' she said lightly. 'What did he say?'

'He said something about it being a bad business.'

'Your father's death?'

'No . . . the marriage. He didn't know that he was dead.'

'How peculiar,' Eve said. She watched me curiously, eyebrows still hovering, as if to say, *well?*

'He mentioned a custody issue,' I said.

'Darling,' Eve said, 'your parents' marriage wasn't the happiest of unions. Do you really want to hear the details?'

There was something in her look of set calmness, her straightened mouth, that unsettled me, as if I were edging close to disapproval. I felt the cool boundary of it, like stepping into water; the first shock on the skin.

'Give me a precis,' I said.

Eve paused, then said, 'The marriage barely lasted a year. I'm sorry to say that Michael was a troubled man: depressed, angry, drinking too much. He never managed to emerge from his past, really. He was an adopted son and his parents had died. He met your mother at a bar when she was on holiday. I was concerned about his motivation, but he seemed pleasant and had a career of sorts as a photographer – and by then it had become clear that Alicia had no grand ideas of her own. They certainly were happy at first.'

'So what happened after that?' I asked.

Eve looked questioningly into her teacup, as if she were a gypsy deciphering its dregs. 'The divorce wasn't amicable. Your father tried to get full custody of you and Theo, accusing Alicia of not being a fit parent, in which I suppose he had a point, but then neither was he. He probably realised that in the end, which is why he dropped the suit. I made it clear that he could see you both at any time, but it seemed only full custody would satisfy him. After that he simply vanished. That was the last any of us heard from him, until the news of his death in Australia. An accident at a junction, apparently.'

'What a shit,' I said. 'He obviously just wanted the money for our care.'

'I'm sorry, Jonathan,' Eve said. 'I had wanted to spare you both these details. I don't know the whole story, of course. I don't want to jump to conclusions about money, although he would have stood to benefit financially . . .'

I nodded, already tired of the subject. My curiosity had sparked and died like an old lighter, half-heartedly tested. The nerviness had withdrawn from my legs and fingers, as if it had never been there at all. Hearing about my father was like hearing about a stranger; it had no more relevance to me than one of Mrs Williams's monologues.

'Oh,' I said. 'It all sounds rather . . . pointless.'

'In a very selfish way there has been a silver lining for me,'

Eve said. 'I was very busy politically when Alex and Alicia were growing up, and I was busy with the hotels when you and Theo were small. Your mother's "crisis"' – she pronounced it with the delicacy of a lady picking up a dead mouse – 'was of course terrible, but it finally brought me home. Once I was here and I got to know you two, I realised that I could play a role in your upbringing. It was my second chance at parenting, in a way.'

'Well, I'm glad we have you,' I said. She smiled at me, affectionate again, as if her magnetic field, previously dimmed, had returned to full power.

'I remember when I saw you in the hall for the first time, looking so solemn but at the same time calm and collected – even though you were only eight and your mother had been taken away. I saw myself in you – the way you had to learn self-sufficiency so early. And since then I've often marvelled at how alike we are.'

'That's a huge compliment to me,' I said, moved. 'Though I'm not sure I can do the comparison justice.'

'Rubbish,' Eve cried. Then, becoming serious again, she leant towards me, eyes moving over my face investigatively. 'Anyway, I'm sorry I don't have anything better to tell you about your father. I hope you won't dwell on it, though, Jonathan. I've never seen the point of brooding over one's "roots". It's really just a refusal to let go of what is gone. What good can the past do the living?'

'I feel the same,' I said quickly, and she smiled at me; but darkly, muffled like a finger pressed in damp velveted moss – it was only an indentation – there appeared the shape of the other question, which I didn't ask. What harm? What harm can the past do the living?

e⁓

I waited until evening for Theo to get back from the pub, sitting in the morning room half reading a paper, with the lamps shimmering around me and a scrabbling sound at the black window from some overhanging clematis. I kept sliding into a doze, then starting and glancing up at the tapping sound, before dozing again.

Finally I heard her crossing the marble of the hall, her footsteps small and echoing like a child in a goblin cave.

'Theo?' I called.

She peered around the door and then smiled with relief and came in. She smelled of alcohol and the after-odour of cigarettes, but her eyes were lucid, her face flushed with the cold. She sat next to me and put her head on my shoulder.

'Why are you still awake, Jonathan?'

'I was just reading the paper,' I said. 'Fun night?'

'It was the funnest,' she said, and repeated a joke the barman had told them, forgetting the punchline. 'Oh dear! I'll remember it in a minute.'

'I think I've heard it anyway.'

Theo sighed, already thinking of something else. 'Remember when we used to go to that secret pool?' she asked. 'And Mrs Williams told us it was haunted?'

'I guess that was a good way of stopping us playing there – scaring the shit out of you. She probably made the whole thing up about Eve falling in too.'

'No, I asked Eve about it and she did fall in,' Theo said. 'She said she couldn't remember it very well. She said she was probably playing some sort of game there – hide and seek, hiding from George. Then she slipped in and nearly drowned.'

'Maybe it's a good thing we stopped playing there,' I said, amused. 'Hooray for Mrs Williams after all.'

'Yes,' said Theo. 'I still don't like it. The trees are so dark down there. So close.'

I looked out of the window, where the gardens were vaguely visible. Elongated shadows stretched out from the dim shapes of trees over the lawns, as if the black towers of the sky had begun to crumble down, forming holes that swallow up the grass.

'Cheer up,' I said, noticing how sombre Theo had become, and patted her hair. I didn't know why she did this, always reaching for the wrong or absent past, defocusing in sudden reveries, to find herself back in her old bedroom, at a children's party in her white dress, under a dining table peering out at a theatre of legs. No wonder she couldn't concentrate.

'It's late,' I told her, standing up. 'We should get some sleep.'

But when I went to bed I found I couldn't shake off the greyness of her mood, the unsettlement. Her shiver clung to me, and I dreamed strange things. I remembered pieces of it like a sunk ship seen through dark water. The staircase in front of me, vanishing away under my feet. Phantom light, shining through the bedroom door, as if the rest of the house was awake. Maria's father's face, saying 'a bad business', his hands knotted and old around a small glass of port. I stared at the hands, which looked monstrous to me. Finally Eve was there, standing below me with her shadow pouring away from her on the flagstones.

I woke up sweating, with my sheets knotted around my legs like a kraken. I was clutching the pillow over my head and it took me a moment to realise what was on my face, and another moment to relax my arms and hands, to stop holding on so tightly.

When I slept again I dreamed of Maria, but it was not a nice dream. She was standing on the deck of a ship that was moving away from me. Her lips moved and she smiled, but there was no sound except the churn of water and the whipping of the air. She became bluish, cold and faint, and finally was lost in the haze between the sea and the sky, the vanishing point.

THIRTEEN

Over the winter months, while Christmas blared and bullied its glittering way around the shops and streets, Antonia grew cooler and quieter. Her wit, which had always been mocking, wasn't so subtle these days; she couldn't hide its metal, its jab of annoyance. Sometimes she didn't meet me, or would forget to call me. She flirted with other people in front of me, mouth set, implacable as a soldier. I remembered when we would spend hours in bed having sex, and afterwards she would tell me stories about people we knew, to make me laugh. I realised she had been happy then, incandescent and weightless, and that this had gone. I didn't know why things had changed. I hadn't changed, but it seemed her time with me had gradually weighted her down, turned her hard and still like sedimentary rock, a shape pressed under the seabed.

I didn't know what I felt about the prospect of us breaking up. The term *break-up* implied some sort of cohesion to begin with, a structure that could be demolished, and our relationship had never been structural. That's what I said to Felix, anyway. To myself I admitted that the concept of a break-up with Antonia – its finality – had a guilty allure; open like the sea, empty in the dark . . . and then the small light, high on the edge of the land. I wanted to see what Maria would say when she asked, 'How's your girlfriend?' and I could confide in a grave voice, 'Oh, we're not together any more.'

And yet, though I had expected it to happen for several weeks, during many arguments, the break-up itself when it came was unexpected, and oddly jarring. It happened at the end of an argument I thought was run-of-the-mill, having been lulled by our previous arguments into thinking I knew the shape of them by now. But then she said, with a jerk of her mouth:

'I'm seeing someone else, you know. I have been for a while.' She faced me tensely, looking uncertain and victorious.

I had guessed this but said, 'Oh,' not wanting to stir her into combat. I could see the end of us, new and glowing like molten glass; I wanted to take the heat away from it, allow it to cool and set, into its new form.

'Well, good luck to you both,' I said politely. 'I assume – as you're telling me – that you two are getting together.'

She took a step back. Her eyes, dark and wet, had no expression I had seen before. The light on them was trembling and angry. I was shocked by her tears, her lips, which had become brighter and redder, like crumpled poppy petals.

'How cold you are,' she said quietly, and began to say something else, then stopped. She turned her face away and walked out, and I stood with my hand on the door, until I realised that there was no point standing there, and went back inside.

The Britton house designed by me and Felix was entered for a RIBA award in 2007. The house was all in white, resembling a basic staircase when viewed from the side. At the front of the building another staircase ascended up a glass wall to a door that floated in the glass like an image from *Alice in Wonderland*. Britton had already broken his nose tripping over the threshold, but insisted he was delighted with it. 'I got a double spread. Look! *We* got a double spread. Well done, boys.'

I had just started work on a new project: a house made to look like a simple block of white stone, with a black roof tilted like a top hat. It was trimmed all around with a ribbon of window, below which the walls were black granite. I had designed it myself, aiming for a striking, discrete strictness of border. No element merged, nothing was compromised. (After seeing the plans the client had called it the Humbug House, a name that irritated me, especially when it caught on at my office.)

I had expected to find something to push against in my career, but I had slipped smoothly up to the top like a salmon, with a few lucky leaps. My name did not often appear in the press without the word Wunderkind attached to it. I worked hard without needing to think or motivate myself; the difficult thing was to stop working. When I said it to Eve she laughed and said *that* was my most valuable inheritance.

And yet . . . I didn't tell her about the bad days, the afternoons where I would be in my office and I would feel I was only half sitting at my desk, my hand only half moving. Sometimes I had the urge to call Theo and ask her what she thought of my designs, though I knew already she found them baffling. (I could picture her in my office, frowning, mouth loose, twisting her hair while she tried to think of something appropriate to say.)

I was finding it harder to concentrate on the future, which

had previously seemed so exciting: my work spearing the skyline, slicing the tired streets with chromeful purpose. I looked outside, where the clouds of London had hung a cool glaze over the city. I was worried there was a weakness in me, something that would stop me. Eve was here, fifty years ago, untarnished and intent, and now look, a Charis in Belgravia, a Charis in Bloomsbury, Marylebone, Soho. She looked at the disassociated greys outside and saw a city to win. I looked out and I saw rain over the sea, the stone of a broken nymph, the blink of a far-off window.

Sometimes I wondered about going away for a while, staying somewhere remote, though I wasn't sure how that would help. I didn't want to find myself – I already knew what myself was. I could be no one other than Jonathan Anthony, sitting in my London tower, working on greatness.

℮

During a weekend at Evendon (these family gatherings had become rarer, but I still drove myself and a reluctant Theo to Wales every few months), Eve was reading through the papers that she had brought to her at the breakfast table. While she was rustling through one – a tabloid – she stopped, frowned and opened it out. Her fingers moved reflexively across to her mobile phone, then put it down. Upside down across the table I could read the headline – New Light Shed On President's Murder – and see two pictures, one of Eve and Sam Anthony on their wedding day, and a large picture of Eve in a ballgown, talking to JFK.

Eve turned the page to finish the article – the remains of the frown still on her face – then flipped back and began to read it through again. I looked over at Theo but she was winding her hair in one hand and buttering toast with the other, and hadn't noticed the silence building next to her. Watching Theo, I noticed she had developed a habit of looking up suddenly, as if someone had said something, someone not even at the table but beyond it. A new tic for the collection. Alicia was staring off out of the window. I decided to pretend to read a supplement. None of us spoke to Eve, who closed the newspaper and sat still, appearing to be in impenetrable thought.

'Well,' she said after a few minutes, 'I'm terribly sorry, but I must rush off. I have a few appointments to reschedule.'

'Appointments,' said Theo suddenly. 'It sounds funny because it divides into "a" and "point" and "meant". Like, a point is meant. But what's the point? You could make a cracker joke out of it, maybe.'

'That's enough, Theo,' Eve snapped, picking up her phone and leaving the room. There was a brief silence. Theo looked confused. Alicia was still gazing out of the window. Just then I felt a black admiration for Alicia: she had managed over time to remove herself so completely from her body, there was something almost spiritual in her disappearance. When Eve spoke, she didn't even blink. She just looked out into the garden, her mermaid face pale and unearthly in the towering light.

As soon as Eve had left the house, her heels rapping the marble in the hall with the sharp sound of ice cracking, I reached across the table for the paper and found the same page.

. . . But under the glamour and charisma of the Democrat elite there lurked more than a few sordid secrets. No one looking at the beautiful

Eve Nicholson, newly married to the promising young politician Freddie Nicholson, laughing with the gentlemanly JFK in 1961, would have suspected that the two were having an explosive affair. Yet that is precisely what Johnny Wymans, imprisoned for stealing letters and documents from Eve Anthony's home and one of the only men to see these letters before they were confiscated by the FBI, has alleged.

'What are you reading?' Theo asked.
'Something bad.'
I scanned the rest.

Eve Anthony's career has always been driven by unusual coincidences and unlikely twists – damaging information on her political rivals had a habit of emerging at very convenient times. Some might say she was born under a lucky star – others might point at her long-time associate and eventual husband Sam Anthony. The head of the film studio SA, Sam Anthony not only had connections with prominent mafiosi but was one of the last people to see Marilyn Monroe before her mysterious death in 1962 . . . When Eve Nicholson left politics to move to Los Angeles in 1976 and marry Sam Anthony, their wedding was attended by celebrities including Frank Sinatra, Humphrey Bogart and Elizabeth Taylor, to name but a few. Less photo-friendly attendees included Paul Castellano and other members of the notorious Gambino crime family . . .

Among the allegations the article approached then shied coquettishly away from was that the Anthonys' marriage was a mutually beneficial sham, a structure intended only to protect their secrets. It hinted that Freddie Nicholson, as a friend of Sam's, might have wittingly or unwittingly become a target for a Mafia hit. Freddie's underwater bones being unavailable for comment, the article quoted Wymans heavily, photographing him at his shabby LA split-level house, a man like a worn-out old iguana, squinting defensively in the sun.

Theo picked up the paper after me and read it. 'Do you think Eve will be angry?' she asked.

ℯ~

Eve was angry. I didn't see much of her in the days following the article, but I saw the evidence of her movements: the sacking of the journalist, the legal action, the printed apology, the broadsheet editorial sighing at the standards of lower forms of publication. (Wymans himself was not heard from again and died not long after: he had sold the story to cover his medical bills, paying off a greedy disease that could not, finally, be satisfied with money.)

Sam himself called Evendon later that day, after Eve had left. I took the call.

'What a disgrace,' he said, a voluminous American voice yawling out of the telephone. 'What a load of bullshit. I know she can deal with this herself but I had ta call. What a disgrace.'

I wasn't sure what to say. 'Thank you.'

'Anyways, this gets me thinking. Why not come over for a visit? All of ya. Eve, the kids, the grandkids. Get the family together.'

I responded vaguely to this suggestion. Eve had explained their divorce to me: 'We realised we had become nothing more than friends. And we still are. Sam was always very good like that. A very civilised man.'

Civilised as Sam was, and friendly as the two were, I suspected that if Eve hadn't visited him since their divorce, she would be unlikely to visit now. But I was curious to see him for myself. Not because of the claims made about him in the article – which I had found almost disappointingly predictable – but because of an older fascination with him, the invisible sender of presents, the cigar-smoking tycoon I had pictured since I was little, a big Italian in a suit with a gold watch and a blonde on each arm. He was the only person in Eve's stories who still had an independent existence from those stories, and that made him interesting to me. And in a few weeks I was meant to be going to Los Angeles, to discuss the possibility of designing an office block for a US developer. I decided I'd visit Sam while I was there.

I told Eve about my trip, but she said she was too busy to join me. 'It's sweet of him, I suppose, but I can't just go out there on his whim, darling. In any case, I'm not sure it would be appropriate so soon after that muck-raking article. It might look as if we were plotting.' Alicia was at her spa, and I didn't know Alex's number. In any case, I didn't think either of them would have wanted to come with me. Alicia had no interest at all in Sam, which in itself wasn't unusual. Sometimes, however, I thought I detected a distinctive *will* in the lack of interest, as if the cool fog of her detachment had cleared, revealing the stone and ice of the mountain face beyond it.

Alex was more forthcoming and not so quellingly hostile as Alicia when it came to his one-time stepfather. In one of the rare times when he wasn't estranged from us, he had told me that he and Alicia barely knew Sam when they were young, being at boarding school for the majority of his and Eve's marriage. 'And besides, you have to understand that he was only our stepfather because we were part of the deal. Though he was kind enough. A shady character, doubtless, but a decent stepfather.' Alex and Sam hadn't kept in touch: 'What on earth would we talk about?' he asked rhetorically, with his hurried laugh. (When Alex laughed, it was always quickly, as if the sound was rushing to free itself, worried that it might be recaptured.)

I called Theo to invite her, but she couldn't come either. 'My new job won't let me,' she explained sadly.

'What is this job?' I asked, relieved to hear that she had one.

'Oh, putting numbers into a computer. It's okay. If I get them wrong, no one seems to notice. Sometimes I wonder if they've just made them up to give me something to do. Eve probably posts them sheets of numbers, and money to pay me. The numbers could be anything at all. But I get money, which I suppose is the point, so that my money becomes rent and food and clothes, and then my money becomes someone else's money and they buy more houses and food and clothes . . . They said I was practically part time and I'm not allowed to take any more holiday.'

'Okay,' I said, not really listening. 'I'll send your love.'

'Do you want to come to a protest tomorrow?' she asked. 'It's for human rights.'

'That sounds pretty vague.'

'Oh, well, I don't know exactly what it's about. But it's this Chinese company, I think, and they've been really mean to people in China, and now there's going to be a protest outside their offices here. All my friends are going.'

'Jesus Christ, not *that* protest,' I said. 'That's the firm that's going to be the tenant of this office block I'm hoping to design in America.'

'Oh no!' Theo cried. 'What are you going to do? Are you going to tell them you don't want them to be your tenant?'

'It doesn't work like that. I can't do that. Besides, nothing's been proven about what Tang Beijing has actually done.'

There was a silence on the other end of the phone, which I began to argue with. 'Listen, I'm not supporting this firm. I don't work for them. I don't deal with them directly. My link to them is probably more tenuous than most of the people who've bought things from the shops they own here. You've probably bought their products yourself! Your money has become their money.'

'Oh dear . . . So I ought to go to the protest, to make up for it,' Theo said uncertainly. 'Right?'

'No! These things always get out of hand. You should stay out of it.'

'But people should know you don't have a link to them . . .'

'Don't worry about me, Theo, for God's sake. Okay?'

'Okay,' Theo said, sounding confused.

*

The next evening I put on the news and there she was, standing in front of people rushing one way and then the other, like litter moved by an invisible tide of shouting and security alarms. Theo looked at the camera that homed shakily in on her face with a wondering wariness. Her eyes were larger than usual, the pupils fiery-dark. She had a peace sign drawn on her cheek and what appeared to be either blood or red paint on her arm. For a moment

I thought the broadcast was live until I realised the sky over her was the pale, luminous grey of the afternoon.

'Would you say this protest has been compromised by the criminal damage that has occurred?' a reporter shouted at her.

'Oh no,' I said. Images were relayed on the screen: broken windows, cowled teens, police like the palings of a dark blue fence, before Theo's face reappeared, hesitating. I could see a couple of her friends standing behind her, one of whom I recognised as her disorganised dealer, clown-haired, waving vacantly at the camera and mouthing something.

'I'm just trying to make up for the things I might have bought,' Theo shouted earnestly. 'It's a conspiracy. A conspiracy of *buying things.*'

'A conspiracy?' the reporter asked.

'It was only a CD,' Theo said. 'They wouldn't let me return it! Because they're using the money to kill people!'

The camera moved closer in to Theo's passionate face, as I covered my own face with my hands. She continued, 'You mustn't blame Jonathan for this! He doesn't have anything to do with it. He doesn't want a bad company in his office! He doesn't want to be in the conspiracy and neither do I . . .'

At this point everyone's attention was caught by a protester in the background pissing on a police car and Theo wandered off camera.

'They don't know it's me,' I said into my hands.

'Now back to the studio,' I heard from the television, the squeal and roar of the protest abruptly gone, as if someone had closed a window. I took my hands away. A woman in an electric-blue suit and the make-up of a prostitute and a man with tan-colour hair and a tan-colour face were now discussing the protest with the enjoyment of people granted a break from genuine atrocity and disaster. On the screen behind them a man was dancing naked in front of a wall of police shields.

'So that was Theo Anthony, the granddaughter of the hotel tycoon and former US politician Eve Anthony. She is of course referring to her brother, the architect Jonathan Anthony, whose firm is currently bidding for the contract to design Tang Tower in Los Angeles.'

'What are the implications of this?' the tanned character asked with mock perplexity.

'Without an official statement from Anthony and Crosse, we can only speculate—'

I switched the television off, allowing the silence to flood me, the relief of the dark screen, but the little knot of anger and fright in my stomach was untying itself, loose ends extending into my arms to my curled fingers, down my legs to my retracted toes. Then the phone rang and I burst out of the chair like a torsion spring.

'Jonathan?' Theo's voice sounded very tiny in the wide, blank background of the call. 'I'm at the police station. Can you come and get me?'

℮

Sam lived in a pink Spanish mansion with palms outside and a security guard on the gate who looked at me without taking off his mirrored sunglasses. It was hot there, hot and empty; the sky a blue burn above the scruffy, bare hills. A maid opened the door to show me into the sudden coolness; the great distance of glittering tiled floor. There was a white-carpeted staircase, white leather sofas and tall glass sculptures, then more palms, so the overall effect was of an ice palace that someone had tried to enliven with greenery.

When Sam came in I was surprised to see that he was in a wheelchair, though he was still tanned and fat as a seal. His almost bald head had the full sheen of a nut, his eyes were small and shinily opaque. He made an involuntary noise of effort when he reached up a hand for me to shake.

'How you doing?' Before I could reply he said, 'Just look at you. My good-looking grandson. You're tall, aren't you? Do the girls like you? Course they do. You got your grandmother's eyes. The only one who has, right?'

I had brought him photographs of the family and Sam inspected Theo with admiration. 'She's a pretty thing. You look after her. Not a safe world for women.'

'True,' I said, frowning at the photograph, remembering Theo coming out of the police station, emerging like a moth in a denim jacket, crushed in the building's brutalist concrete, her chemical shimmer worn away. She hadn't been charged with anything but was warned by a grimly avuncular policeman to take more care with the company she kept. She hadn't wanted to call me, either, but they thought it was better that she be taken home rather than let fly on the breeze, as if she were a little feather or parasol-topped dandelion seed, incapable of getting on a bus.

'I told you not to go,' I said when we were inside the car.

'I know, I just thought that maybe I could make things better, and—'

'What the hell did you take, anyway? I thought you were off drugs.'

'I didn't take anything.' Her eyes widened, as if surprised that I'd asked.

'Come on, Theo, I saw that loser dealer friend of yours behind you. And if you weren't taking anything, then what you said was just insane. It was nonsense. And you named me! Do you have any idea what the consequences of your celebrity guest appearance on the news will be?'

Theo bowed her head, and the dimmed blue light in her eyes quivered and spilled out. I was too angry to comfort her.

'So what was it – drugs or madness?' I demanded, but she just shook her head fiercely, and I couldn't say anything else: her lie had separated us, suspended darkly in the air. She was travelling down a path away from me and I couldn't follow; I just sat there inert while she sobbed, wiping her eyes with her coat sleeve, my own eyes full of dust and rubble.

Sam continued to flip through the rest of the photographs and ask about 'the family'. I wasn't sure how much he really wanted to hear about Eve, but ended up talking about her for too long anyway, trying to avoid mentioning Alex and Alicia, as I wasn't sure what to say about either of them. For his part Sam seemed puzzled by the very concept of Alex, and didn't ask much about him. 'Inna-lectual,' he said with a shrug that reminded me for the first time of Eve. He also didn't seem interested in discussing Alicia; I told him cheerily that she was enjoying her gardening and that watching films was another of her hobbies – as if trying to gloss over a difficult family member in the annual Christmas-card update – but he looked at me peculiarly when I said her name, as if searching for something in my face, and then dropped his eyes, expressionless, so that I had no idea whether he had found what he was looking for.

'I appreciate you coming out here to see me,' he said finally. 'You didn't have to be here, right?'

'Right,' I said. Following the media attention given to the protest, Anthony & Crosse had received a letter from the US developer to the effect that we would not be invited to participate in the tender process for the Tang Tower design. 'But we've got some other things we're working on instead, which I can't say too much about, naturally.'

'That's the spirit,' said Sam, as if my words were analogous to my spirit, and not something neat and insincere and devised only for ending conversations such as this one.

My work had become more difficult: formerly swift-moving, it kept hitching itself up, getting caught, needing unravelling. My personal assistant divorced her husband, and started making mistakes that I had to fix. She had also taken to crying quietly at her desk, and I felt incapable of speaking to her about her lack of professionalism. Then a major restaurant project in Germany that Felix and I were meant to be working on was shelved when the client was taken into custody for apparently having murdered his wife. Felix was working independently on some sustainable apartments and offered for me to join him, but it was a small project and seemed too much like deceleration.

Sam took me on a tour of the house, which was more of the same expensive whiteness. He seemed most at home in the large private cinema, where he showed me some of his studio's new films. In the dark warmth of the room and the obliging red plush of my chair I fought a jet-lagged doze; emerging unsure of how many films I had actually watched. I thought two – a spaceship with a large-breasted and feisty captain; a mummified pharaoh doing battle with blonde cheerleaders – but it could just as easily have been one, or three.

Sam did not talk much; he would comment briefly on the films and then look at me, as if hunting for something. 'That dress – with the lights – that cost three hundred thousand dollars. Caught on fire in the last take. Nearly had a lawsuit on our hands.'

He told me about his girlfriend; an inadequate, frilly word for the dignified forty-year-old who had been living with him for ten years. Marina came home while we were in the garden, waved, then disappeared, so that I only saw a slice of her good looks; a dark profile like a Roman matron.

'Yeah, we get on,' Sam said, watching her go. 'She don't speak much English. She could be a goddamn inna-lectual for all I know.' As he said this he peered at me suddenly, as if struck by the suspicion that I too might be an intellectual. 'We're happy,' he carried on. 'I ain't living with some up-and-coming actress. I want a bit of peace.'

While he talked I looked at the white hair at the sides of his smooth head, the reflections of his floor, the pool, so perfectly flat it looked painted onto the pink patio, a chemical blue like the sky, the colour of dead, polluted rivers. More palm trees, a rocky slope. Eve had looked out on this view once, slowly drifting and shivering in the rising heat.

In the morning, over bacon, pancakes and maple syrup, Sam asked, 'So how's that business of Eve's going? I don't hear from her much – she must be busy, right?' I told him about Charis, and he nodded along with me as I was talking. 'Nothing stops her, does it,' he said, with barely hidden delight. 'She don't need any help now. I did a lot for that woman. I would have done more.' He stabbed a piece of pancake at me, with severity. I felt uncomfortable.

'I think she managed to get that article set right quite quickly,' I said.

'That was a cheap shot, that piece of crap,' Sam said meditatively. 'These things make me laugh. There's one little bit of truth in there and the rest is just stretched and twisted and . . .' Running out of inspiration, he gestured a convoluted path in the air with his fork. 'That little bastard Wymans said what he had to say to get the money. Guess I can't blame him too much for that. That's what we all do, ain't it?'

'So you don't know who killed Marilyn Monroe?' I said lightly.

'Nope, and Eve wasn't fucking JFK neither. Excuse my language.'

'Where was the one little bit of truth?' I asked, becoming curious, encouraged by his genial waving of the fork.

'Well, we was friendly with gangsters. But that was Hollywood, and who the hell wasn't?'

'I thought the worst bit of it was about Freddie,' I said. 'The way he died was hard enough for you and Eve without lies being made up about it.'

Sam put his fork down with sudden and complete anger, dropping his affability like a napkin, like the last vestiges of civility. 'Yeah, that was the worst fucking bit of it all right. Making out that I was a friend of that rotten little bastard. That goddamn too-white WASP prince. I'm the one with the Mafia connections and he's just caught in the fucking crossfire.'

I could only stare at him, startled. 'I thought he *was* your friend?'

'I wouldn't have pissed on him if he was on fire. Matter of fact, I wouldn't have saved him from drowning. Freddie Nicholson' – he pronounced it grandly – 'was a woman-beater. Had to see Eve showing up with her bruises like she was just fucking clumsy or something. That woman never spilled a drink or tripped up in her life. She's not your clumsy bimbo type, right?'

'But – Eve wouldn't have . . . She never said anything like this to us,' I said. My voice sounded strange, harsh, like the bark of an animal. The pancake and syrup and bacon and coffee had collided poisonously in my stomach.

Sam's anger appeared to lose force. 'Yeah, well. They had kids together. Don't want them to think bad of their pa. Coulda affected her political career too.' His eyes moved off mine; he looked uncomfortable for the first time. He picked up his fork again as if wondering how it had been dropped. 'I didn't mean to say anything. I just can't stand to hear you – her grandson – talking about that bastard like he was a hero or something. Okay? Better forget I said anything.' Understanding this to be a command rather than a request, I nodded.

I spent the rest of the morning in a vaguely shocked state as Sam regaled me with Hollywood gossip, real-estate speculation and a list of which of his friends had died of cancer. The only reference he made to our conversation was just as I was leaving, the taxi dawdling outside, watched by the twin mirrors of the security guard.

'I was a good husband to her,' Sam said, gripping my hand hard. 'I would never have stopped treating her right.' Then I understood what was missing for him: it was the big love, now gone out of his life.

ℯ⸜

On the plane, a night flight, I lay awake and unsettled under the quiet yellow light, trying to think about what Sam had told me. I didn't think he was lying, which left two possible explanations. The first being that he had seen bruises on Eve, of a perfectly innocent nature, and assumed they were the marks of an abusive marriage because he was envious of Freddie and in love with Eve. After all, he hadn't said that Eve had actually confirmed his theory. The second explanation was that Freddie *had* hit Eve and she covered it up, in the time-honoured tradition of mistreated women, and continued to safeguard him after his death for the sake of Alex and Alicia's memories. Doing this must have cost something, required some strange and pure internal reserve to be tapped, like a clear underground river, and I found myself moved, imagining what she had done, without really believing it to be true. By the end of the flight I had settled on the first explanation, but the rill of unease still ran over me, tensing my skin as it went, pressing my eyes open.

Sam himself hadn't been what I expected – not at all. Not just the fact of his being in a wheelchair, which he had evaded discussing, but who he was, the composition of his soul, the metal workings so bare and strenuous. I couldn't see anything in him that Eve would love – I could only assume that he had been different back then, in some undefined way, but he didn't even give off a clue as to what that once-loved Sam might have been like. It was astonishing to me that they had ever been married.

I felt sorry for Sam because he seemed to be the only person who didn't see how unlikely his marriage to Eve was. But layered over this pity was another, less simple feeling. I had gone to see Sam as the sole survivor of Eve's stories; I wanted to marvel at his heroic autonomy. But – like Freddie Nicholson, George Bennett, my own father – it turned out Sam was nothing more than another part of the narrative, a chapter, an anecdote. He hadn't survived being in her story at all; he was beached like a ship in the hills, static and pointless. The story had moved on, and left him behind.

I closed my eyes and let the noise of the flight, the judder and growl, move over me, sanding away the flat blue pool, the flat blue sky, the great door closing on Sam in his wheelchair, waiting for Eve to come back for him.

e⌒

Not long after my visit to Sam, I ran into my Uncle Alex on the street in London. We both saw each other at the same time, realised conversation would be inevitable, and nodded awkwardly. It was odd how much he resembled Alicia these days; both of them were wasting, consumed, as they aged. Alicia like a pale, dry chrysalis, Alex like a fanatical monk.

'How are you?' I asked, wondering whether to make reference to the years that had passed without us meeting, or to adopt Eve's usual technique of pretending that hardly any time had elapsed.

Alex didn't seem to care either way. He was preoccupied with a recent problem: he had just read a colleague's criticism of his new book – apparently it was too personal, too fervid. I nodded sympathetically, while trying to work out what the book might have been about; Alex seemed to have assumed I'd read it. I guessed that it concerned crime, or possibly religion. I offered a few vague opinions, then finally offended him by saying without thinking, 'Eve is probably quite well informed about America's moral history.'

'I personally am not sure what Eve has to offer on the subject of morality.' Alex was abrupt.

'What do you mean?' I asked.

'Excuse me,' he said, frowning. 'I shouldn't have said anything.'

I wouldn't let it go. My hands were tight and I tried to stop myself glaring at him.

'But what made you say it at all? I've always thought Eve to be very moral – one of the most moral people I know.'

But Alex was thin-lipped and, I guessed, sorry he had spoken, because he wouldn't say anything else. I was tempted to inform him that his mother had sacrificed a lot for him to have the luxury of ingratitude, but I remembered that I'd already decided that Sam had jumped to conclusions concerning Freddie, and so Alex and I left each other excessively politely. He walked away down the street, his legs like the spindles of a bicycle wheel, flickering and hasty; his coat blew out like tatters. I pulled my own coat together and made my shoulders, which wanted to shiver, rigid.

When I got home, I called Maria to discuss Nick and Emily's wedding. This was only a few weeks away, but – as with Sebastian's return from India – Nick and Emily had called it off so many times that nobody seemed to quite believe in it any more; they discussed it with a raised eyebrow – as, indeed, did Nick. I wasn't interested in the nuptials but it seemed a good excuse to talk to Maria, have her voice in the apartment, even if it was only an imperfect transmission from another country. These days, without the prospect of Antonia turning up at short notice, my apartment seemed large and strange. My own company was too small for it; arriving home now, I suddenly didn't feel enough for the stare of the television, the two long sofas facing each other like icebergs on the vast floor.

'Are they really releasing doves?' I asked her.

'It's true,' Maria said. 'One of the bridesmaids has been put on dove duty. I get to carry the train. All ten feet of it.'

'Good lord.'

'Aren't weddings strange?' she continued. 'The idea that a big fat diamond or doves or a coach has anything to do with a relationship. I suppose it's just this obsession with the grand romantic gesture. But covering a bed in flower petals isn't love – proposing at sunset isn't love. People think the gesture is the feeling; they think the show is the truth. And how does it all end up? With me in a powder-blue satin dress, running for a bouquet I don't want.'

'I couldn't agree with you more,' I said enthusiastically. 'This whole idealised love thing annoys me – the insistence that there's this grand passion out there that's more important than everything else in life. But there's no such thing, and people find anything they can to fill that space – they get married based on lust or neediness and pretend it's fate. No wonder everyone ends up divorcing.'

'Better just to cohabit with someone rationally,' she said, sounding amused. 'Like good friends who have sex.'

'Well exactly,' I said. This hovered between us, in the suddenly quiet line.

'Really,' Maria said at last, 'your search for a friend to have sex with is almost more poignant – more romantic – than the search for grand passion, because it's less likely to succeed. There ought to be a film about it.'

She laughed, but there was an irritated clip in her voice – or I thought there was, before she carried on, 'Oh no! I refer you to the list: a monogrammed set of bedlinen. There's a specified thread count.'

Disappointed, I hid it and said, 'I've got a better one – crystal port glasses.'

'For the couple who has every other kind of glass,' Maria said, and we carried on in this way, until she said she had to go. After that I sat for a while unmoving, haunting the spot next to the telephone like a ghost, so I went out with Felix, and drank a lot, and ended up sleeping with a girl with red hair and a top that said 'Stop the war', though when I asked which war she wanted to stop, she said it was just a T-shirt, and in the morning I found I didn't feel very miserable any more, and could look back on the telephone call not as a signal ignored, but as one that wasn't noticed: just one of those things.

$\mathcal{e}$

Another unexpected consequence of not seeing Antonia any more was not *loneliness* – as I insisted to Felix – but an increasing sense of being on my own. Arriving home from work (as late as I could) was like rowing out into the middle of a stark lake: hours between myself and the next person. It was probably this that made me grateful for Theo's unannounced visits, so grateful that I didn't remind her of the lost contract, or try to force her to stick to times and dates, or even tell her off when she appeared at the office late in the afternoon ('I thought I would bring you lunch . . . but then I was so excited to see the office and I got lost on the way here, and I saw a homeless man, and he was hungry, so I gave him the lunch'), or at my apartment at night with one shoe missing, or in the morning while I was rushing to finish my coffee and get dressed for work ('Surprise!').

I didn't know exactly why she wasn't at her job, or who she was friends with now, or where she went at night, and I didn't ask. It wasn't hard to guess what she'd been doing with her evenings, stumbling in with large brilliant eyes like a lemur, her words tipping out in halts and rushes, hands quick with her cigarette; at other times silent, trembling and strange. I felt increasingly like a social worker, checking up on her with my form, ticking the symptoms of drug abuse; or a parent who has read an NHS 'Your child and drugs' pamphlet for the first time – hunting for the burnt tin foil, the empty plastic bags. And I was rewarded for my suspicion – being right, what a reward. Seeing her jump at nothing, skittish and incoherent, my rightness coiling in my stomach like an eel.

The worst time was when she came to my apartment at five in the morning, knocking on the door so loudly that I couldn't pretend to be asleep. I let her in and she clung to me, make-up all over her face. In between the dark stripes her face was white as wax, blurred with fright.

'It's him, Jonathan, it's him again,' she whispered, clutching my arm.

'Him? Has something happened?'

'The sign by the pool,' Theo said, not listening to me. She was shivering fiercely. 'Is that how he did it? Is it another secret? I've found it out now – they told me – they killed him, the ghost, our father . . . We're all in danger, Jonathan.' She gripped my arm harder, painfully now, and looked up at me with urgency.

'Theo.' I thought I was angry but my voice, when it appeared, was small and grieving. 'Theo, you're not making any sense. You promised you wouldn't do this again.'

The words appeared to wash her off me like a rush of water, carrying her down to the floor, where she put her face in her hands and cried: 'Why do they tell me these things? It's the truth and no one believes me! No one! You have to help me . . . I can't – can't . . .' She put her hands up as if to pull at her hair; they fluttered around her face ineffectively. I helped her up and made her come to the kitchen, where I gave her water that she drank obediently in between sobs, while I watched, helpless and frustrated, feeling an exhausting, bodiless nausea.

The next day I didn't say anything about the drugs, because the last time I had she'd lied to me, and I had decided then that I wouldn't ask her about it again.

Instead I suggested she go back to Evendon. 'London clearly isn't good for you, Theo. This can't go on. You should go back home until you can get yourself sorted out.'

Theo looked at me with alarm. 'No! I don't want to go back. I'm fine. I'm okay now. I don't need to be there. I can sort myself out here. I'm sorry I've been so much trouble. *Please* don't tell Eve.'

'Fine, I won't,' I was stern now, the fright of last night over. 'Not this time.'

Theo, responsive to disapproval, dropped her eyes. 'You don't love me any more,' she whispered.

'Of course I love you,' I said. But it was more complicated than that. My love for Theo had become a wary thing; watching her, I often felt as if I were crossing my fingers for an amateur aerialiste, swinging past lurid and frightened. It was a lot to ask to send love out to accompany her, where it could get hurt. So I loved her, but she was too risky – too uncontrolled – for me to do it without reservation, without holding my breath.

e

I didn't trust that Theo would sort herself out, but I didn't call Eve either. Then Theo lost the data-entry job ('Apparently they do notice what numbers I type in') and her housemate Lucy decided she couldn't live with her any more. She said Theo had given her bed to a prostitute who 'looked cold', and slept on the sofa herself. Then when Theo and Lucy woke up, the prostitute was gone and so was Lucy's television and my laptop, which Theo had borrowed without asking the day before. I called Eve after that.

'She obviously isn't equipped to live alone,' Eve said, business-like. 'I agree – she had better come back here.'

'I think that's best,' I said, with the uncomfortable feeling that

I was betraying Theo, a feeling that wasn't helped by Theo's reaction to the news that she was to go back to Evendon: she wept silently and profusely, as if someone had died. She stayed at my flat that night and fell asleep in a chair, her tipped, frowsy head protected by her crooked arm.

The next morning the driver came for Theo while I was at work, and I was relieved not to have to go through with saying goodbye. By the afternoon I was able to speculate pleasantly that after a week or two at Evendon she would feel more settled, more cheerful, and might be grateful for my intervention. With distance from drugs, parties and bad influences I hoped that she would be transformed, ready to return to the city sober and sensible, without the need for rehab clinics or anything so extreme. I avoided her calls in the meantime. 'She'll only want to come back to London if she talks to me now,' I said to Eve. I repeated, 'It's for the best,' but it tasted false in my mouth; like chewing on foam stuffing.

e

After the fortnight I had allotted for Theo to cheer up had passed, I went down to Evendon for the weekend. I had missed Nick's wedding because I was in Germany talking to the arrested restaurateur's lawyers, so I told him we'd meet him that Saturday.

When I arrived at the house, Mrs Wynne Jones let me in. 'Eve's in Dubai,' she said accusingly. 'Your sister went for a walk somewhere and then your guests arrived. Your mother is entertaining them.' I had a brief vision of Alicia being entertaining (juggling, riding a miniature bicycle?), but when I found her she was sitting in the morning room, straight-backed and bored as usual, with Nick and Maria.

'Maria?' I said, staring.

Maria laughed. 'Surprise! I hope it's a nice surprise . . . Oh Jonathan. You look disappointed.'

'Disappointed!' I repeated. My face felt stupid with sudden happiness. I noticed her hair was lighter, the colour of tanned pine.

'Congratulations, Nick,' said Nick, becoming impatient.

'Sorry. How was the wedding?'

'Horrific,' he said. 'A dove shat on Emily's dress – she was fuming. Then some child obliterated the cake. It was running for a ball apparently. I did say we shouldn't invite children, but Emily insisted on flower girls. So this fucking flower girl just smashed into the cake and it went everywhere.'

Maria started smiling. 'Sorry, Nick,' she said. 'It's not funny really.'

'Just don't laugh about it in front of Emily,' Nick warned her.

'Oh!' Theo said, wandering in through the French windows. 'Hello everyone.' There was a smear of mud on her cheek; she was wearing pyjamas tucked into wellington boots, holding some uprooted flowers from the garden.

'You look awful, Theo,' Alicia observed serenely.

'I think I lost track of time,' Theo said.

'For Christ's sake!' I said, more forcefully than I meant to, goaded by disappointment. 'You'd better get changed. We're meant to be going to the beach and you look like a mental patient.'

Llansteffan beach in late September was nearly empty, despite the unusual heat of the day, the unclouded bowl of blue above us. We bought chips to eat and sat on the pressed sand. In the distance I could see only a man walking with a small shape of a dog, leaping up beside him like a leaf in the wind. Maria rolled up her jeans and took off her jacket to sun her shoulders.

'I can't believe how long it's taken us to do this,' she said. 'It's ten years since we first came to this beach. Can we really be nearly thirty?'

She had won a research grant to work with an American psychologist at an autism centre. 'America's not ideal,' she said. 'But obviously Llansteffan doesn't offer the same opportunities.'

'Not many local autistic people.'

She smiled. 'Yes, no such luck.'

I asked Nick how his work was going, though I didn't really want to, and I saw he didn't really want to be asked.

'Oh, I'm working in the City,' he said. 'My, uh, father knew someone at Goldman Sachs . . . and as I was getting married, I thought I should . . .' He played with his cuff and looked uncomfortable, then concluded defensively, 'It's not easy to get into these firms.'

'I thought you didn't like your father?' Theo asked.

Nick murmured something about putting things behind him.

'Oh, how nice,' Theo said enthusiastically. 'Now you have a father.' She paused, and I waited tensely for her to continue, but all she said after that was 'I hope your job is fun. Eve finds me jobs too. When she comes back from Dubai she'll probably try to find me another one.'

'And how's Emily?' I asked Nick.

'Broody,' Nick said. 'She basically wants to give up work and look after children as soon as possible.'

'What if you wanted to look after the children?' enquired Maria.

'Oh, I don't want them at all. But it'll make her happy. Anyway, it has to happen sooner or later. Everyone – well, everyone who doesn't have much money, and that's me now – ends up in jobs that bore them, and children who scream in supermarkets. I may as well face my future. I sense a Renault Espace out there with my name on it.'

'Hard to see what could go wrong, when you've got a brilliant plan like that,' Maria said, throwing a chip at him.

I squinted at her eyes, lushly shadowed and aureate, and tried, as usual, not to want her. This longing should have eased up by now, surely – cooled down or burned out – in the years of friendship and disappointment, but here it was again, quick and sharp and reverberating in my throat: the perpetual renewal of wanting.

'How's Antonia?' Nick asked.

'Oh, we aren't together any more,' I said. As an announcement, this emerged rather small and flat, its importance lost in the wind.

'Well, I bet you recovered okay,' said Nick, and they all laughed. 'Are you with anyone else now?'

'No,' I said, glancing at Maria. She was smiling faintly, which was nothing more than the embers of her laugh, and her expression showed no change as I spoke. I changed the subject, annoyed with her, annoyed with myself.

After my break-up with Antonia I had thought I would be able to maintain a lifestyle of uncomplicated sex, stripped of the pink and white haze of intimacy; the hidden pains of intimacy. I chose women for their unavailability: tourists, strangers' wives or girl-friends. No head lasted too long on my pillow; there were no hairbrushes in my bathroom, no unknown music played when I turned on my car stereo. But I found that sex was rarely the simple thing it was when I was a student; it was less of a joke, it was in earnest now. More and more often, sex led to drunk female recordings on the answering machine – thin, high electronic voices, their resonance stolen and made threadbare – to arguments in bars, tears on the street. Being turned to in the morning with a hand searching for mine; sentimental eyes, running like water-colour. I decided to stay away from sex for a while.

Though I didn't like to admit it, that wasn't the only reason. There was also the fear. The small, specific fear of waking up in an unknown bed having had one of the dreams that came now to violently shake my good night's sleep, pick it up and hurl it like a roof in a hurricane. Twice, maybe three times a week. The ridiculous thing was that I woke up scared of nothing. My bedroom window at Evendon. Eve's voice, broken glass. Nothing, nothing at all.

I looked up at the beach, briskly shaking these thoughts out – returning to the idea of the four of us, sitting on Llansteffan beach again. I couldn't quite believe that we could all be here under the faint haze from the sea, the phosphorescent blue of the sky; it struck me as impossibly lucky somehow. Maria was lying on her back in the creamy sand, Nick was re-enacting the dive into the wedding cake, Theo was laughing, her eyes half hidden under the blown chrysanthemum of her hair, white in the light. Some of the long-held heaviness in my stomach eased, looking at her now. Then Maria glanced at me, and smiled, and I had the sense that I needed to remember this moment, to save it up like a nut, before the onset of winter.

℮

Before I went back to London I looked for Theo to say goodbye, but she wasn't in the house. One of the maids said she'd gone to Llansteffan – having forgotten that I was leaving that day – so I drove to the village to find her. I passed the beach, which was as bare as an Arctic plain, and drove slowly through the narrow high street with its row of small plain terraced houses and grey church, all silent in the evening sunlight that slanted steeply down. I peered into the windows of Mrs Edwards's shop and the post office, I circled the ruined castle with its winking eye, I slid through leafed tunnels and out into the green fields, and finally I had to come to a stop outside the pub, the Glas Dwr, where I had hoped not to have to look.

Outside the pub I saw Mrs Williams, coming out of a house. It had been a long time since I last saw her, but I recognised the sagging green coat, the unnatural fluff of yellow hair. My first thought was concern over my own escape, but it was too late. She had sensed my stare and her head began an inexorable turn towards me. Our eyes met, then she looked away, and continued walking. It wasn't Mrs Williams after all.

A glance around the dim interior of the pub, with its ghost of smoke, glass-ringed dark wood and unlit fire, was enough to ascertain that Theo was not among the five or so elderly locals who had taken up their usual placement at the tables or bar (a seating plan that I guessed had not changed for the last ten years), over whom a predictable and suspicious hush had fallen now that I had walked in.

The landlord looked up at me with a bright and sarcastic good humour from the thick dark of the bar and called over: 'You looking for your sister, Mr Anthony?'

'Jonathan,' I said. 'Yes, have you seen her?'

'She left just a few minutes ago to get cigarettes. Surprised you didn't pass her. She'll be back here in a couple of minutes, I'd say. Long enough for a drink.'

I hesitated, which he noticed, and his white-eyebrowed look of sarcasm deepened, which stung me into pulling up a bar stool.

'Thank you. I'll have a pint, please,' I muttered, looking arond long enough so that the gazes behind me fell away and conversation resumed. There was surprisingly little light in the pub given that it had four street-facing windows and all its chintzy little lamps were burning. I could barely make out anyone's expression, not even that of the landlord, who had moved back and was almost invisible in the gloom. I had no idea why Theo came here.

The landlord emerged once more, still smiling enigmatically, and put the pint down in front of me.

'This is a rare visit, Mr Anthony. Excuse me – *Jonathan*. Staying here for the weekend, is it?'

'Yes.' I was short with him, knowing that I amused him, and not wanting to give him any extra pleasure.

I pretended to look at my phone as I waited, but found myself thinking about Mrs Williams again. I worked my way idly through my memories of her, but they turned out to be erratic – fragmented, missing, springing out unpredictably, like elastic bands. Sitting at the table eating our way through a pack of biscuits while she blew smoke rings for us. Bandaging Theo's stung finger. Saying to Mrs Wynne Jones, 'Them two, with no father, and now no mother. It's shocking.' That had been a rainy summer day, I recalled; the water hissing and recoiling on the terrace, shivering warm like a monsoon. The way she said it with pity, but also enjoyment, a tone I didn't understand back then but knew very well now. Resentment – and why not? We weren't children to them; we were gold like the elephants in the morning room – teeth of pearls, jewel-eyed; when we spoke it was just the rustle of money. I could see how we were hatable.

But Theo still went to visit Mrs Williams, for months after she left. Theo never learned the unique buzz of sourness in a voice, a crimped lip, a dropped eyebrow. She didn't understand how she could be the subject of someone else's ill-feeling; she couldn't identify what might cause her harm. Theo came to this pub, where everyone would have heard Mrs Williams's stories – about how she was wrongly sacked, about how Alicia was crazy and tried to kill herself, about how our father had vanished then died and Eve was a bitch and I was up my own arse and Theo was good-natured but simple – and sat here anyway and felt that she was welcome.

'Got a lot on your mind?' I looked up, startled, to see the landlord leaning across the bar towards me, hands spread on the wood as if to say, 'Just your friendly local landlord.' Which, perhaps, he was. I recalled that he was the uncle of Maria's former boyfriend David, who I remembered with affection now that he was no longer her boyfriend.

'Not especially.' I made the effort to smile at him. He took this as an invitation and sat down just across from me. The odd lack of light fell over his face again, so it was hard to see much beyond the decaying glimmer of his eyes, the ironic mouth.

'Reminds me of when I had your father sitting across from me one night,' he said, speaking quietly. I looked up, startled.

'What?'

'He was drunk,' the man continued, ignoring my stare, looking up into the dirty corners of the pub as if my father hovered there, urging him on. 'And angry. Came in here silent at first, then after a few more drinks he had a lot to say. This was nearly thirty years ago. He was married to your mother but she'd moved back here. He came here after her.'

I felt a lurch of dread that kept me from getting up, made me still and quiet.

'Angry at Eve, he was. Said he had something on her and wasn't going to be kept quiet any longer. I've no idea what he was talking about.'

The man paused, shifted, and the light slipped back onto his narrow face, which looked both sympathetic and grim, with a vinegar dash of mockery. I couldn't understand what I saw, but seeing it allowed me to move again. Like an unhooded bird, I got up, pushing my stool back harshly, so that it clattered and all the old men looked up frowning.

'Why are you telling me this?' I asked.

'It's your family,' the man answered simply. 'Thought you'd like to know.'

'Well you're wrong,' I snapped.

He shrugged and moved away along the bar, sliding out of direct opposition to me, smiling to himself infuriatingly.

'So is this what you tell my sister?' I demanded.

'No,' he replied slowly, and he looked irritated now. 'Your sister's a sensitive soul. We try to cheer her up. She's not so tough as you.'

He made the word tough into an insult, so to insult him back I dropped several pound coins onto the bar, where they reeled and spun, and walked out into the cool dead light of the street.

'Jonathan!' Theo was walking back up the road, on the sunlit side, waving at me. 'How funny to see you! Why are you here? Were you in the pub?'

'I just put my head round the door to look for you,' I said, smiling at her. 'So, do you want a lift home, or would you rather walk back up the hill?'

'Lift! Lift!' cried Theo, laughing, and dived into the car as if I might change my mind.

FOURTEEN

Eve visited me a few days later in London when she got back from Dubai, arriving in an emerald suit and diamond earrings straight from another meeting. When she kissed me I could catch her perfume, which always reminded me of her study when I was young; lying on the sofa and listening to her speaking on the telephone and writing emails. Her steady voice and steady hand, her smile fixed and clear as a photograph, holding the measurable present. After my encounter with the landlord of the Glas Dwr, floating in his strange lightlessness like a pike, it was a relief to see her now. I had already decided I wouldn't mention what the landlord had said about my father, not wanting to allow his malicious story another undeserved repetition – or worse, make it look as if I believed it.

'I'm so sorry about Sam,' I said. For it seemed the trip Sam had wanted us all to make was to have been a deathbed visit, rather than a reunion. He died from cancer only a few months after I saw him.

'I know, it was very sad,' Eve said. 'I feel privileged to have shared at least some of my life with him. I'll always remember him fondly.'

I couldn't help but think of how Sam's absolute difference to

Eve had startled me in Los Angeles. Love, I supposed, was a strange and inexplicable thing.

'So . . . I have a proposal for you,' Eve said after a while, leaning forward. 'How would you like to design a new hotel? In Edinburgh. It would be very high-profile.'

'A new-build?' I asked. 'Is Charis doing that now?'

'Not Charis, Mensson,' Eve said. 'It's a boutique hotel chain. We bought them out six months ago; boutique hotels are growing incredibly fast right now, and it's a very interesting concept. The hotels themselves are so striking, very space-age. I thought instantly that it might be the kind of thing that would appeal to you.'

'It does,' I said with wonder. 'But I'm in legal wrangles with that bloody German restaurateur. The contract had no clauses to cover one of us being sentenced to prison.'

'Oh, you should have told me. We'll get a team on that,' Eve said cheerfully. 'How soon can you design something?'

'I'd start now,' I said. I already knew what I wanted to do.

'You'd have almost free rein,' Eve said. 'There are a few issues with the local heritage organisations, but we'll get them ironed out. Why don't you come to Scotland for some very early-stage discussions?'

We shook hands ironically and I opened a bottle of wine.

'You know, Jonathan, the idea of passing on anything more than money to my descendants really hadn't seemed a possibility to me before I met you,' she said. 'But even as a child you were so hard-working, already knowing what you wanted to do. And over the years I've been so proud of what you've achieved. I'll be even prouder to announce that we'll be working together.'

She put her hand on mine briefly, gave one of her smiles, so bright I felt the moment of its impact, pinned over my heart like an award.

'It means a lot to me,' I said. 'I hope I don't give you any cause for disappointment.'

'Never,' Eve said (though afterwards I wondered at the missing words: whether she had meant 'I never could be disappointed in you' or 'you could never disappoint me', or even a command: 'never disappoint me').

Later on I asked her: 'So how's Theo doing?'

Eve sighed and hesitated for a moment before speaking, as if unsure how to approach the subject.

'Well, I've been away most of the time she's been at Evendon – except for a couple of days – so I don't really know,' she said slowly. 'But she can be strange sometimes – the things she says. I think it's a form of attention-seeking. She sits up late at night, and is listless in the day. I don't understand what's wrong with her. She socialises with not only the maids, but the most undesirable sort of locals.'

'I heard about the Wendell thing,' I said. Wendell was a drunk farmer who owned a few weedy acres near Evendon. Recently some vandals had broken his windows, so Theo had given him all the money she had to replace them.

'Oh, it's just the tip of the iceberg – there are people lining up to take advantage of Theo's . . . good nature,' Eve said. 'I've had to stop giving her money because she either gives it to these parasitical new friends, or whatever charity manages to beard her on the street. Whales and beggars! I simply don't know what to do with her.'

She looked down, and with her eyes off me I noticed her age appear: a quick spectre over her lustrous face, a loosening of the skin under her eyes, a slide at the corners of her mouth. It was unsettling. But when she looked back up the effect was gone, and she was herself again. She saw my expression and said, 'Oh, I don't mean to worry you, Jonathan. It's nothing serious.'

I wondered then if I had done the right thing, sending Theo back to Evendon. I felt suddenly that she and Eve were too different to be pushed together, like an ice cube and a match. Or scissors, paper, stone – though that didn't quite work. Unless there was one for each of us: Theo the paper, Eve the scissors. I contemplated stone – the insensibility of it: solid, silent, achieving only the fact of its own stoniness. Jonathan the stone.

I realised that Eve was talking about Mensson again, and I hadn't been listening. I was frustrated at myself – the currents of thought that I couldn't help drifting down more and more these days. Eve thought I was the same as her – clean and quick and strong; she couldn't see this new fault in me, the wonderingness, the idea of wrongness. I wanted her certainty; I didn't want to be outside it with the rest of my family, wheeling unpredictable and fragile as moths, governed by their own winking neon, their mysterious signals. I wanted to go Eve's way – no doubt, no fright, just a trajectory, straight into the future.

e⌢

The day before I was due to fly to Edinburgh I got a letter from Theo. The envelope was wrapped in so much Sellotape it was almost unbendable. I had to cut it open with a knife. When I opened it I could barely make out the words, her writing scrawling and billowing over the paper like lightning.

Dear Jonathan,

Do you remember us ever having a camera, like normal people do? All we have in that album are photos by people who never knew us. There are ones of us all on the lawn and me and you sitting at the front. None of our father. It is hot outside and I can smell the roses. They smell of fakeness – I can't change the fakeness and it's all true now anyway.

Who cares what I do? If I go out or if I get lost or if I tell people about the ghost, even. We have a new housekeeper who I might tell. She likes to feed me, she's called Mrs North. She thinks I am looking thin. I suppose I am thin. But even if I was big, underneath I am just bird bones and mice ankles, all wrapped up to stop me coming to pieces. Eve says I am a burden on you and I shouldn't make you worry about me, but I had to write.

I want to shut my eyes and not hear things. I want to be with you. Please, please, please can I live with you? Please answer even if you just say no. I'm frightened you can't answer because you're not here any more. I'm frightened you've been taken away.

Theo

I read the letter through again, my hands tight on the paper. One of the new friends in Carmarthen must have given her some acid or something. I had read before that an addict could manage to get hold of drugs no matter where they were, but I had not thought that Theo was one of these people. I read the letter another time, and another. It did not seem to arrive from a real Wales, green and bright and simple, but from an eldritch, darkly forested country, cold, haunted with strange fires. I could only think of the German word – *unheimlich*, literally, unhomely – to describe it, the feeling of the known becoming foreign. Theo's letter, accidentally or on purpose, had taken the familiarities of Evendon – the roses, the photos of us on the lawn – and made them painful, frightening. It was oddly like a transcript of one of my own dreams.

I called Theo but her mobile was out of service, so I called Evendon and Eve answered.

'Hello, Jonathan,' she said. 'Is it about the hotel? I'm leaving in a moment so I can only talk for ten minutes.'

'Actually, I got a rather odd letter from Theo today and I just wanted to check if everything was okay at Evendon. She was . . . unlike herself.'

Eve sounded surprised. 'Everything's fine here. Theo's the same as usual, though you know what usual is for Theo. I certainly wouldn't have said there's anything wrong with her. She's probably being melodramatic.'

'Is she at home?' I asked.

'Yes, she's still in bed though. Shall I wake her?' Her voice, rich and cool and slightly impatient, steadied my unease, sobered it. I felt rapidly embarrassed that Theo's letter, which she had probably forgotten having sent, had bothered me so much.

I hesitated. 'No. No, don't worry. In fact, don't mention that I called.'

What was I meant to say to Theo anyway? Just the usual, and that wasn't ever going to fix her. I was tired of the way she refused to take any responsibility, any meaningful position. Even the things she cared about were absurd, unchangeable: homelessness, pandas, the death of our father. It was just more childishness: hiding in drugs and lost causes. I had always resisted calling Theo lazy, or aimless, but I thought now that both were true, and I'd probably made her worse by my fussing and nagging after her, like a dogged old nanny. Maybe if I left her alone for once she'd pull herself together.

What did the window say to the curtains? Theo had asked, at the Christmas table. *Pull yourself together. What did the curtains say to the window? Shut it.*

I hung up the telephone, threw her letter in the bin, and went to work on some ideas for the Mensson hotel.

℮⌒

Nick called me later that night to tell me he had lost his job.

'It's the fucking credit crunch,' he said, drunk. 'It crunched me. Fuckers. I might move to America, except it's worse there. Maybe I'll go and teach with Sebastian in India. That's how I feel at the moment. Like not telling anyone and just fucking off somewhere.'

'What about Emily?'

'Oh, we're having a "trial separation", as she calls it. I'm the one on trial, basically. Except I don't know what my crime is. I did shout at her the other day when she spent shitloads in Harvey Nicks. But she thinks our parents will just bail us out, and I can't go grovelling to them all the time. Fucking marriage. What a load of shit.'

'Why don't you come out tonight with me and Felix?' I suggested, alarmed.

'Why not,' Nick said, suddenly cheerful. 'Let's get drunk.'

We got drunk and Nick got drunker at a newly opened bar in Soho – called something like QP or MQ, initials nobody understood – roaming the mercenary white ballroom under the patterns of light and twinkles of darkness that made ghosts of everyone. The figures on the dance floor flickered, faded out, reappeared. I recognised a few people I knew, and who I had never really liked – the kind of people who would go to a bar like this in its first week, the consciously in-demand grandees of the guest list – but I didn't recognise them as being warning signs until I saw Antonia.

She was facing away from me, her hair shorter, showing the perfect slopes of her cheek and jaw. I travelled towards her unthinkingly, without any idea of what I would say, and found myself next to her ear.

'Antonia, how are you?' I asked it.

She turned around and looked at me silently for a moment and I felt the radius of her dislike, as if I'd walked into an abruptly cold room. 'I'm well,' she said at last.

'I'm sorry.' I stepped back. She nodded without expression, and I went back to rejoin the others. I sat heavily at the glass table, looking down through my green drink at my green-tinted feet, beginning to feel a little suspicious of myself. I wondered if I was the kind of man that women hate, one of those half-man, half-animal composites: a love rat, a dirty dog, a cold fish.

I *liked* women, I argued to myself tipsily. I wanted women to be happy; I just didn't want to have the responsibility of making them happy. I couldn't slow down enough to focus on them properly; they were like shapes outside a car window, still and highly defined for a moment, then streaking away. Maria was the only woman I could have done it for – always Maria – but she was too far away to catch hold of, a retreating smile hovering in the air like the Cheshire Cat's.

I tried to focus on the voices around me, but it was difficult. In my drunkenness I could hear only distantly the fierce chatter of the bar, rattling like coins in a moneybox.

'I'm telling him it's over for good unless he ends it with her. They aren't having sex – he told me so.'

'What the public don't know won't hurt them.'

'She looked like a whore.'

'What we need is to sell the whole lot off. The insurance alone is crippling.'

I couldn't tell where these conversations were coming from; I was slipping down, eight years old and under a table with a stolen canapé, watching the flash and flicker of shoes. I thought I heard Eve's voice just above me, but that was wrong, and I realised I had started to fall asleep, my head keeling down onto my shoulder like a bag of flour.

I left Felix and Nick talking to some women and went home, tripping as I got into the cab, and again on the threshold of my flat. I sat on the bench on my palm-barred balcony, high up and silent, looking out at the sky, which in London was always seen as if through frost. For the first time I missed the Welsh stars, so perfectly clear and white. I was too drunk already, I knew that, but I poured myself a large whisky, and another. The second spilled out of my shaking hand and onto my leg.

What had Theo said? The fakeness of the roses, was that it? Theo in her dark place, filled with possible things and lost things; everywhere she looked there could be a father, everything she turned over was untrue. MC and AA on every tree, broken glass on every flagstone, a curtain blowing out from a window and a steady voice. The ghost again, after all this time, the sad, ridiculous ghost. Last seen in a smashed-up jalopy south of Darwin, last seen on the terrace, the dark cut-out in a violent square of light, last seen on the busy street. I didn't know how to answer her – I didn't know what I was any more, on the inside or the outside, eyes open or closed, with Theo or without her. The thin edges of my skin were like the rim of a glass, holding me in. I tilted, but I righted myself; I didn't spill. My frustration with Theo and her letter returned, and I held onto it like a rope, to lead myself out of the dark.

℮

I flew to Edinburgh early the next day, though I was feeling increasingly uneasy about the hotel. When we visited the site, there were posters put up by local protesters, clamouring to save the defenceless nineteenth-century bricks and glass, deliberately neglected and slipping into damp and disrepair. The local press had remained neutral about the development, but *Private Eye* had called Mensson's proposals 'barbaric'.

I looked at the street with its tall Victorian structures and saw how the hotel would stand out against them, the shape of an armoured shell, plated in mirrored glass. I had thought this would be dramatic, but now – looking at it with flat, hung-over realism – the absurdity of it struck me: a crash-landed satellite in the dark, dignified stone of the neighbourhood.

I called Felix. 'What do you think about the protesters?'

'Not the sort of thing that bothers you, surely?' he said. 'To be honest, I don't care one way or another. It's down to you whether we take this on. I mean, we're pretty much going in different directions anyway. I'm quite keen on the whole sustainable thing personally. It's a growth industry. And it doesn't . . . you know, hurt one's conscience.'

'Yes,' I said, discomfited. 'Well, I'll think it over.'

By the time I got back to London that evening the squalid, swampy feeling of my hangover had given way to a clenching headache, and I still hadn't managed to have a nap. I got home, discarded my crushed suit and conveyor-scarred case on the floor of my apartment, and was just pulling the bed sheets over myself when Maria called.

'Jonathan, guess what – I'm in London tonight. There's a conference on and they said we could have the night off. Do you want to have dinner, if you're free?'

'Of course,' I said. 'I know a good place.'

I arrived at the restaurant first, moving within a paracetamol swaddling, in time to watch Maria walk in, wearing a black dress, smiling at the maitre d' who ushered her over. Her eyes when she saw me were darker than usual, sweltering gold in their blurred-black edges. I felt her gaze – the velvety weight of it – almost as something physical. But the contact didn't last long; she kissed me briefly then looked all round the restaurant, clearly amused at the pomposity of it, muffled up with drapes and napkins and heavy silver, patrolled by its multitude of waiters. We sat in the light of the same lamp and talked about all the things we usually talked about, and I saw despairingly how the night was going to go.

Finally, fiddling with my coffee cup, I asked, 'Have you ever been in love?'

She looked startled, then laughed. 'That's an interesting question. Yes, twice. Nearly three times.'

'What happened?'

'What do you want, the whole history?'

'Yes,' I said, 'That's exactly what I want.'

'Well,' she said, 'I'll try to tell it as a story, though really I didn't experience it that way. Love is more of a . . . mess, a heap of things. Then you try to put it in some sort of order, after it's over.

'So, once upon a time, when I was at sixth form in Bath, I got together with Guy. We were together for three years. We weren't suited at all; we had to fight our way away from each other when we went to university. It was painful. He was very wild afterwards; he liked drugs, sleeping around, the usual. I heard finally he met a girl and went the other way. She converted him – he's either a Mormon now or a Jehovah's Witness. Something strict, anyway.

'After that, while I was working in France, I was with Olivier. I loved him, though we were only together for about a year. Things started to go wrong when I brought home a backless dress. He made me promise I wouldn't wear it – not if he wasn't with me. I overlooked that, and I overlooked his moods when I mentioned my male friends. After a while I stopped overlooking things and was just unhappy all the time. I think part of the reason I was so unseeing at first was that I felt loose, unattached to anything in a country that wasn't my home. Like I might just blow away if I didn't have someone to hold onto me.

'Then in America I went on a few dates, just a kiss on the cheek – good night, nothing else. I had so little time I would actually just date people for months, without spending long enough with them to find out it wasn't going to work. In the end I started dating another psychologist at the clinic, Jack, and that turned into this strange relationship. It was like an endless period of "seeing each other", putting off making a decision. He was an extremely decent man, but not quite right. Do you know that feeling?'

'Sort of,' I said.

'I think I'm cautious, after what happened to my parents, and after those first two relationships didn't end very amicably. So when I met someone who – when I looked at him rationally – met all the ideal requirements for a partner, I convinced myself that I would be silly not to be with this man. Even though my heart wasn't in it.'

'Has it ever worked the other way round?' I asked her. 'You've convinced yourself *out* of something?'

She gave a startled laugh, then hesitated, for so long that I wondered if she was even going to answer. Then she looked up and her eyes, heavily framed, flamily lit, were impossible to interpret. 'All the time,' she said.

Before I could understand her, or reply, she continued fresh and bright, as if sweeping away the earlier moment, 'So what happened with you and Antonia?'

I remembered – unwillingly – the break-up with Antonia: the tarry atmosphere of conflict and failure like smoke, standing at the door feeling its pinch in my airways. Antonia staring at me with tears in her eyes, saying, 'How cold you are.' It was a thought I didn't like to spend much time on; an unsmoothed, wrong thing of the past. I had thought Antonia and I understood each other, but the longer I knew her the less I knew her, starting in bed and moving back and back, until she was just a dark shape in the doorway, angry and indistinct.

'Actually, I don't really know. We didn't have a very close relationship. We didn't talk much. I assumed we wanted the same things, from each other I mean, but it turned out we didn't.'

'I'm sorry,' she said.

'No – it's not like that. She was the one who ended it, but it was probably my fault that it ended.' I thought for a while. 'Yes . . . I'm fairly sure it was my fault.'

She laughed, then coughed, becoming serious, then started laughing again.

'Oh Jonathan . . . sorry. I don't mean to laugh at you.'

'It's fine,' I said. She was still smiling at me, without looking away, and I felt the sudden sickness of hope in my stomach. 'Shall we go to a bar?'

'Why not?' she said.

When we left I picked up her bag, which had spilled a book out onto the floor. 'What are you reading?' I asked.

'It's about an artist who became famous but used his influence for the wrong ends. He genuinely thought he was improving things though – making them better for his people.'

'Well, that was a mistake,' I said cheerfully, following her out into the evening. 'Trying to help the general public.'

'Don't you think achievement should be at least partly about improving things for other people?' she asked.

'No. One feels achievement after a game of tennis,' I said. 'But it doesn't help anyone. It's about the competition – about excelling. That's what life is like.'

'I see,' she said, lowering her eyes. The silence welled up. I paused, and saw myself – standing there under the awning of the restaurant – arms crossed, foot tilted up importantly. I saw the palely tasteful shirt, blazer over the arm, wrist weighted by leaden, expensive watch. The clipped fingernails and attended-to teeth, the chestnut flex of the handmade shoes, hair not too long, not too short. Back straight. Face shut up like a shop, mouth moving tensely, shortly; saying something ridiculous.

'Maria – that's wrong,' I said. 'I don't think that at all. Can we forget I said it?'

She looked back at me steadily, her hair unfurling from her collar like a flag in the wind, and smiled. She took my arm.

'Let's go to the bar at my hotel.'

After the bar closed we took the unfinished wine bottle and went to her room, which was luxurious and subtle: drifting low light, the window broken up with rain, the counterpane swallowing our edges when we half sat, half lay on the bed. The night was a drowsy boat, holding us both, tranquil and easy and slightly drunk. I held our glasses as she switched through the films on the television.

'They've divided them into categories,' she said. 'Love, sex, death. Which one do you want?'

'Love,' I said.

'I remember a conversation with you where you didn't think there was any such thing,' she said lightly, taking her glass back.

'Well, I've changed my mind. I do think a lot of relationships don't have much to do with love. But not all of them are that way.'

'Watch out, Jonathan . . . you're getting dangerously soft and squishy. Like a marshmallow. Or a teddy.' She dabbed me on the arm like a cat, teasingly.

'It's actually based on sound scientific principles of observation,' I said.

'Oh – you're researching the subject. So this was why you were asking me so many questions earlier? I'm a case study?'

'I asked because I didn't know anything about you,' I said. 'Like you said a long time ago.'

She stopped smiling and there was a pause. Her face was turned up to the ceiling, so that next to her I couldn't see her full expression.

'You said I had a favourable impression of you,' I told her.

'I remember what I said.'

I tried to make out some feeling in the parts of her face I could see: the sweep of her cheek, the side of her nose, lashes – an unreadable levee, an occlusion. In the absence of speak-response I felt suddenly unhappy. It was something I kept sliding into, that miserable feeling: the second time that night, the hundredth time that week. I was so familiar with it I could see its shape; it was my apartment at night, a stack of paperwork, the clamour of the phone, the coldness of the sheets. I imagined myself going back there and I didn't know if I could do it. Maria's face, still turned away, reminded me of Antonia, who had absolutely nothing left for me. No more effort, no more goodwill.

'I'm not sure what I'm doing any more,' I said to her. 'I'm tired – I'm tired of myself.'

She twisted on the bed, so that we were looking at each other, but didn't say anything.

'I'm meant to be building a brand-new hotel in the place of something old and beautiful. Is that what I do?' I said. 'But . . . I can't think of anything else I do. That's it. All I am is a man who builds new things.'

'No,' she said. 'That's not true.'

She put out her hand across the space between us and touched mine, and a silence developed. Maria's eyes did not move away from me; her mouth finally, unexpectedly serious. I lay still and surprised in the moment – the sudden luxury of it – the lightness of her fingers evaporating like vapour off my skin. I felt that to do anything now would be wrong; no movement or sound to disturb the heavy humidity between us, the gathering charge. Neither of us spoke; neither of us looked away: and then her phone started to ring, and it was over.

I wondered who would call her now, at one o'clock in the morning, until I saw her expression – startled, then abashed – and I realised who it was: someone she had promised to call later when she got home, someone who had waited for the call and had started to wonder if maybe she had forgotten him or fallen asleep, and in the end decided to call her himself, because he had been looking forward to a late-night conversation with her and it would be too disappointing to just give up and go to bed. I would have done the same in his place.

'You're seeing someone, aren't you?' I said.

'Yes.'

'That's him now.'

'Yes.'

She didn't move to answer the phone, which rang out, but it left us in nothing but the emptiness of its not ringing, having taken its insistent scissor swipes to the perfect silence of before, cut it up into pieces. I sat up and she lay back and put her arm over her eyes, almost defensively, then took it away.

'It's late – I'd better go,' I said. 'I'm sorry to complain about things to you. That's the problem with being a professional, I suppose . . . everyone wants a free consultation.'

She got up and followed me as I went around the room putting my jacket on, my shoes, reeling myself back in. She looked unsettled, and rightly so – how long had I been staring at her? I was drunk, that was the problem. I felt horribly close to crying.

'Jonathan,' she said, but then stopped, and by the time I got to the door, her old politeness had drawn back over her, hiding her expression. She murmured something about talking soon, and I said good night and left, hurrying down the hall, the blank noise of her door clicking shut behind me. Then I was out of the revolving hotel doors into the abruptness of the street, where I lifted the hand she had touched to my mouth, as if I might be able to bring it back, the complex smell of her skin: salt, caramel, the aftermath of perfume, the sun it had absorbed.

I knew I had to let her go, the idea of her. I counted up the years I had wanted her, to punish myself with the number. I wanted to stay out in the bare night and be scoured clean by the cold black air, the violent noise of the traffic. I wanted to be stripped of longing, the airless thirst of the body, the reaching of the feelings for something to rebound against. I went back to my apartment and made myself a drink I couldn't taste, holding my heart as if to stem a leak.

e⁓

At nearly four o'clock, hoping for a message from Maria, I turned my phone back on. I had missed fourteen calls from Theo – which wasn't unusual – and there was a voicemail waiting. I was relieved to listen to it instead of having to speak to her.

There was a long pause before she began to speak, during which I almost hung up. Her voice was frayed, slippery, as if she had been crying.

'Jonathan . . . I have to say this on the phone even though phones aren't safe, because I don't know how else to speak to you. But I have to tell you. I hid outside Eve's study when the solicitor came because I wanted to find out what she'd done to you. I heard them through the window. Eve said his name, she said "Michael Caplin". She said, "I don't see that as a problem." I remember every single word they said. The solicitor said, "He hasn't touched the money for a year now." Then she said, "Well we've had no sign of him here. If he doesn't access the fund it's up to him." Then I asked Eve later, "Where is our father?" and she was angry and said he was dead, and then I knew it was *her*, she must have killed him, because of the money, the money conspiracy with Tang Beijing and the gallery and the data entry, and I knew she'd done something to you too. I don't know if she's in the pictures now listening to me, in the television. You're gone . . .' She broke off, in tears. 'They told me you were coming back but I know they're lying. They've killed you. That's how they're going to keep me away from you. I don't have much time. I can't stay here; I'm going to escape. I worked it out finally, how to be with you and him again. I'll be a ghost too. They won't be able to find us, the three of us, and we'll be far away, Jonathan . . . we'll be so happy.'

She started to say something else but the end of the message cut her off, and when I called back there was no answer.

❧

I was shivering badly when I called Evendon. I sat on the edge of the bed in my apartment and watched my hands trembling on the phone as if they were made of paper.

After a long time the new housekeeper, Mrs North, answered, her voice muddy with sleep, then after another long time I heard Eve's voice, tiny, then real as she neared the telephone. 'It's who?' she was saying. Then she picked up the receiver: 'Jonathan, is everything okay?'

Her voice had the normal, substantial tone of someone sitting on a cream damask sofa wearing a silk dressing gown, looking out over an organised arrangement of lilies; the clipped sweep of the dark lawns in the light of the house. I could picture the way she always sat, like marble with a moving mouth, one leg folded over the other, toe pointing.

'I don't know,' I said. 'Has Theo been with you today?'

'She didn't come back last night so far as I know. She went out with a friend, I think.'

'Did she tell you when she'd be back?'

'She never does, darling. Is something wrong? Shall I tell her to call you back? Having said that, she has a thing about the telephone at the moment. She says she doesn't believe in it. It must be some new-age nonsense she's picked up.'

'I'm worried about her,' I said. 'About her state of mind. Can you tell her to call me when she comes home?'

'Of course. I suppose she has been moody recently. Sullen, almost. But I don't see that that's anything to worry about. You know Theo.'

'It seems I don't know much about anything,' I said. I hardly knew what I was saying. I had a growing dread of the conversation, but like a rolling car on a hill I could only watch it move, gathering speed.

'Jonathan?' Eve asked. 'Are you quite all right?'

'Did Theo ask you about our father?'

I could hear Eve's irritation now, twitching under the smooth, flat surface of her voice. 'She may have mentioned him. I can't quite remember.'

'Surely it wasn't that long ago. You can't remember what she asked you?'

'Jonathan, I don't understand why you're questioning me like this, at this time in the morning. This isn't like you at all. Are you drunk?'

'He's still alive,' I interrupted her. 'Isn't he?'

There was a silence.

'What did you do to him?'

'This is not rational,' Eve said, her voice colder and sharper than I'd ever heard it before, the clothes that her voice normally wore – the velvet and silk – all stripped away. I was broken up in many pieces; her voice whistled through the wreck, metallic and narrow. 'I think you'd better call me back when you're in a more reasonable mood.' So I hung up on her.

e⁓

I tried Theo's mobile several times but it just rang on, drilling its noise into empty space. The light from the window was a diluted black, like oil on water. I couldn't straighten or stand up; the centre of my body was all a cold hurt, a solid sharpness. I stayed crouched over myself, holding the telephone, which my fingers could not warm. I knew already that she was not going to answer it, but I came up with a scene in Wales, a lock-in at a pub, Theo's phone ringing in her bag next to her, the noise blotted up by their laughter. She would be smoking, wearing a torn pair of tights, one of my shirts, a silk scarf picked up on her way out, which would irritate Alicia. She had forgotten about leaving the voicemail because whatever she had taken earlier had dissolved now into harmless particles, easing its hold on her. Her friends were teasing her about it now that it was over. 'You were really freaking out,' one of them said. 'You were saying all kinds of crazy stuff.' Theo, embarrassed, winding her fingers through her hair, laughing.

After a while I was able to uncurl my spine, make my hands rigid enough to start my car. I drove towards Wales, nearly alone on the motorway as the night changed from charcoal to grey and the rain began, and even though I believed in the pub – gripping the idea of it so hard that its warmth and light began to waver, shiver like a flame – I could hear something else running above the pub's sounds, a list being counted down whether I listened to it or tried not to hear it, of all the things I should have said to Theo.

Then the telephone started ringing on the car seat next to me, and I saw her with her hair lifting like smoke all around her face, staring up at the clouds, which rolled on, marching across the sky.

2008

At the airport I watch my luggage slide away through long plastic teeth as the man at the desk looks at me suspiciously. With his slot-shaped mouth and unlit eyes, he resembles a switched-off DVD player. I consider smiling, to convince him that – despite my unshaven face and my slightly desperate appearance – I'm not a terrorist, but the disused corners of my mouth just won't do it.

As I wait on a nailed-down chair for the screens to tell me I can leave, I feel the light weight of eyes on me and look up to see a small child sitting in a pushchair opposite, watching me as it rotates a boiled sweet lolly in its bright green mouth. Children can enjoy the luxury of gazing; as we get older there are consequences for a stare, so we learn not to do it (or most of us do – Theo never did). I spend at least ten minutes under its unmoving, benign scrutiny, until it is wheeled away by its parents. Then I feel suddenly alone, and get up to wander the airport, looking for food I don't particularly want to eat.

In the end I join the nearest queue, which is at a fast-food chain. There are posters of American buildings on the walls with neon lights and Cadillacs outside. There are also mirrors, which reflect everything with a slightly yellowish tinge. I wonder if this is deliberate, a deflation of the ego: instilling a sense of self-hatred to encourage comfort eating.

'Would you like the meal deal?' the girl behind the counter asks, looking not quite at me.

'Yes please.' She is pretty; her hair is tied back and her pale ears and neck are exposed, the skin too young, too subtle for the cheap, bright uniform and stiff cap. But her face has a hard certainty, a lack of interest, sealing her over against her surroundings.

'What drink?' She doesn't look up from the little keypad.

'Excuse me? Oh, no drink, thank you.'

'The drink is part of the meal deal.' She looks up at me now, fingers hovering.

'Just cola, then.' As she keys it in I ask, 'What's it like working here?'

She pauses, not quite thrown off. People probably ask her this often, kindly mother-aged women, lonely or lecherous old men. 'It's a job, isn't it,' she says. 'Four pounds ninety-nine then, please.'

I hand her a note and get in return a dutiful smile, a flat-looking burger and some spindly chips.

'Are you happy?' I ask suddenly.

'What?'

'I said, thank you.'

When the flight is boarding I hand my pass over to three women, all in frosted blue eyeshadow, guarding their gateway casually, barely glancing at the paper. 'Have a nice flight,' one says, winking at me, so that the others giggle.

On the plane I sit next to a woman in a dark dull coat and glasses, who stares at the tiny film above our heads, uninterested in neighbourliness. Outside the window the sky looks like the Arctic; a blue sky over a tundra of clouds, pools of blue water. I read the in-flight shopping magazine to pass the time. Then I read the safety leaflet. I run through my escape route in my head before I realise that in a crash I wouldn't want to escape. I would shut my eyes and wait to see her. Over time, the details of what I have planned to say have fallen away; my offering condensed to its pure forms, its most simple elements. *I am sorry. I love you. Please forgive me.*

e

As the hours pass, the sky changes, becomes sci-fi, with suspended streaks of purple and white. Over this hangs a deep blue, fading to frozen white. It looks like glass, like the interior of a marble; a lifeless sky, not real.

I remember I have been given a free paper and take it out to read. It is my least favourite tabloid – far too outraged and moral for its own dirty stories, like a Victorian minister visiting fallen women. My family has a generous double-page spread today: 'The Curse of the Bennetts'. It reminds its readers that George Bennett excavated a few Mayan tombs in his time, some of which were said to be protected by curses. Therefore it would only be reasonable to expect his brother to die in debt, his wife to die young, and subsequent generations to be blighted by the ill-will of the ancient kings. Eve is featured in the largest photograph. Then there is Alicia, 'jilted' by her runaway husband; Alex, the embittered bachelor; Theo, the tragic granddaughter.

And finally me, cast as the estranged heir. My mother's previous comments on my absence are recycled, accompanied by a photograph of Alicia looking more glamorous than distraught, at a polo match. The picture of me does not resemble me particularly, which is a relief.

They got it wrong, the writers; it was not a curse. It was a spell of protection that finally dissolved, once the fairy godmother grew old and lost her powers, no longer able to stop time, to keep the palace asleep.

There were days back then when we would all sit outside, in summer, Alicia and Eve under the white umbrella like a sail, Theo lying on the grass. Happiness, of a sort, enclosed us, like a glass jar; everything outside was quieter than it should be. Theo would be smoking a cigarette, her eyes pale blue in the light. It was limbo, it was suspension; but all I want is to go back, lying with my eyes closed in the perfect, uncomplicated sun.

෴

I fall asleep without meaning to, only waking when the plane – screaming and shuddering like the heroine of a horror film – begins its landing. As people shuffle off the aircraft, the woman next to me fails to wake up. She sits with her head resting against the seat in front, almost in her lap, folded up. I have the weary feeling that she might be dead, but then her mouth moves faintly. Before I can tap her shoulder to wake her up, she looks up at the people moving, picks up her bag and joins them.

'Thank you,' the stewardess repeats over and over as we go past her, her smile becoming a little rigid at the edges, as I step blinking off the plane into the sudden and comprehensive heat.

PART FOUR

2007

She is gonn, she is lost, she is found, she is ever faire.

    Sir Walter Raleigh, *The Ocean to Scinthia*

FIFTEEN

I hung up the phone and stared at the scrubby trees of the lay-by, the green of the staring fields, the dull grey of the road sliding past like running water, the sky holding itself distant, as if nothing joined these flat, artificial things together any longer and their essential vacancy, their emptiness, was laid bare. I couldn't tell the emptiness apart from my own. I sat and waited for a thought – any thought – but I was hollowed out and weightless. I had no heart that I could feel, no stomach, no mind. I sat, blank-faced and rigid as an eggshell, breathing lunglessly, blinking eyelessly.

That was when the guilt began. I emptied myself out and it came to fill me up, and from then on I was just a shape around it.

Mindlessly I restarted the car and drove on. I reached the Severn Bridge and passed the tollbooths into Wales, which was colourless and cool, a shocked, suspended day hung with ghostly raindrops. As I drove past Cardiff I felt a rising aversion to the idea of going back to Evendon. I turned off the motorway instead and stopped in the nearest town, an unpronounceable and dingy place with one small bed and breakfast, which appeared to be closed. I went in anyway and got a room for the night.

'There are no sausages,' the owner told me sadly.

'What?'

She pointed to a board that advertised a full English breakfast: two eggs, two sausages, two slices of bacon, beans and fried bread or toast.

'No sausages,' she repeated. 'Sorry.'

'Oh,' I said, and we waited there while I searched for a response. 'That's fine.'

Once in the room I locked the door, closed the curtains and lay on top of the bed staring at the lilac walls, the embroidery of flowers that hung on the chimney breast opposite. I felt as if I was trapped in the air currents rising up from a furnace; I breathed a bitter smoke that excoriated my throat, burned like grit on my eyes. I tried to sleep, but the lids of my eyes were too red, too bright. Then I tried to remember her face, and was frightened when I couldn't. There was only a collection of shifting features, a blonde mass of hair. I tried repeatedly to gather these pieces up, but they were falling through night water; my fingers brushed them, but they eluded me. By the time the room became dark, I finally slept.

e~

The next morning I was weak, dried out, but lucid. Light welled through the thin chintz fabric at the window, the net curtains. I could hear the boom and rattle of lorries on the wide road just outside, voices travelling down the corridor. There was a man's voice, then a female shriek of a laugh, like a bird of prey.

I lay there confused in all my clothes, then got up and opened the curtains onto the sky, which was still wintry and heavy, billowing with brimming rain, silver with cold. I felt as if I had swallowed some of it; my stomach had that paralysed dread.

I stood without thinking for a moment. Then I remembered that my sister was dead, and the cold extended through me, settled and deep, snowing me in.

The drive to Evendon curved at the top of the hill, so rather than seeing the house grow steadily as the car approached, the road unrolled through a meshed corridor of trees, which finally dropped back like theatre curtains, revealing the tall frontage. The sight of it now – the rain slick on the grey stone, the closed doors – was too hard, too sudden. I sat blankly in the car until the new housekeeper, Mrs North, came hurriedly outside to meet me, forcing me to get out and greet her. She was only about forty, with a wide, unhappy face. She murmured how sorry she was. I had to go into the house with her then, where the familiar scent struck me, polished floors, lilies, perfume and air. It was the same as always. The red walls and Turkish carpets in the morning room, the parlour like a golden egg; the haughty, draughty hall, the ivory drawing room. My head hurt with the sameness of it.

'Did she leave a note?' I asked Mrs North.

'Not that any of us found,' she said. 'I'm sorry.'

'Who found her?' I asked. 'A gardener?'

'Actually it was a maid – a new girl – and her boyfriend. They were smoking I think, before they started work. Because it's secluded there. They heard her phone ringing.'

It was unbearable to me that the people to see Theo that way were not known by either of us. I think I must have winced, because Mrs North looked at me with concern.

'I'm sorry,' she said again.

Then Alicia came down the stairs, moving faster than usual. She clung to me briefly, uncharacteristically; a sharp, alcoholic smell came off her. Her fingers laced over my shoulders, weak and mindless, like seaweed.

'This is all very, very hard,' she said, plaintively. 'I'm not sure I can deal with it right now.'

⟡

I spent most of the morning speaking to police, doctors and reporters. I was aware of Eve not far from me, in my peripheral vision. We didn't talk to each other. I could hear her voice occasionally, saying things such as 'completely out of character', and 'a great tragedy', in the same way that she talked to the camera, and I wondered whether this death would become another of her turning points, another significant event in the story of Eve Anthony. Alicia wandered in and out, looking increasingly inebriated.

'Why didn't she swim? Surely you would automatically start swimming?' I asked the policeman.

'The pool is very deep in the middle,' he said. 'Your sister had stones in her pockets.'

'Oh.'

'I'm sorry, Mr Anthony. There are unlikely to be any complications with the verdict. It appears to be a straightforward suicide.'

'But what about the drugs?' I asked the doctor.

'Drugs?' he asked, startled.

'I don't know – LSD, something. She must have taken something?'

'There was no evidence of drug use,' he said. 'Though we can't be certain of anything until we receive the coroner's report.'

After that I'm not sure exactly what I felt or thought. When the crowds in the house had gone I lay on the sofa in the morning room with the doors closed. It seemed like the simplest thing to do. I floated in the damp, leaden light, static, eyes on the ceiling.

After an indeterminate amount of time I realised there was a figure in the room, blacked out by the window behind her, gradually turning into Eve. She stood very still, like always; no movement except the necessary movement, watching me.

'Jonathan?' she said now. 'Are you all right?'

'Did she say anything, before she left?' I asked. 'Did she say she was seeing a friend?'

'No. I barely spoke to her before she went. I had assumed she was with a friend.'

'What was the last thing she said to you?'

'I can't really remember. It was something odd. But then that wasn't out of the ordinary, for Theo.'

'You can't remember anything about what she said? Or aren't you telling me because it was to do with our father?'

Eve stepped closer to me, the shadow from the window sliding off her like an unveiled statue, suddenly white and hard.

'I know you're upset,' she said. 'We're all upset. But you're not being rational. Your father is dead. I don't know where this sudden interest in him has come from, or what it has to do with Theo, but it's not fair to accuse me of lying about him. Please be reasonable.'

I stood up then, hurriedly, and Eve stepped back just as quickly. If she were a different woman I would have thought in that moment she looked alarmed. But I was mistaken; there was nothing unusual about her expression, except for her eyes, which were lit brighter, the skin of her face tenser, colder than usual.

'Jonathan, listen. I don't deserve this treatment. I don't understand why you are angry with me.' I didn't say anything so she continued, more kindly, 'We are all grieving, darling. But this is the time to support each other, not turn on each other.'

'You'll never tell me the truth, will you?' I said wonderingly. 'Even now that I know it anyway. *The Secret Life of Eve Anthony*! Our father never died – you did something with him. You paid him off. But he came back for us; the burglar – that was him, wasn't it? And Theo saw him in London. She knew he wasn't dead. And I told her she was wrong,'

'You're not in control of yourself,' Eve said, but she was angry too, speaking forcefully, her eyes trying to get hold of me. 'You need to calm down.'

'Where's the death certificate? If I look, will there be a record of his death?'

She stared at me, silent.

'I suppose there won't be any record of you paying him, because you'd know how to hide something like that.'

'And is that the father you want back?' she asked, inkily quick. 'Someone who could be paid off?'

'You did pay him off!'

'I didn't say that.'

'No, of course you fucking didn't. And she saw him and I tried to pull her back. I told her she was wrong, because I trusted you. I admired you. I tried to be like you! I don't even know what you are. What does that make me? A bad copy of something fake. Worthless, worse than worthless. Theo was right but I told her she was wrong about you, wrong about our father. And who knows what you told her in the time that she was here. She would have been fine if everyone hadn't lied to her and fucked her up. She found out the truth because she heard you talking to your solicitor, and then she killed herself. It was your lie that killed her. And if I had been anybody other than the fake I made myself into, I would have helped her. Not sent her here to die, to drown in that fucking wasteland, that water, all alone.'

I was aware that Eve had turned and left the room, that I was shouting after her, but it didn't seem to matter whether she heard or not, whether my words were even coherent, smashed and blurred as they were, with anger, and tears that I hated myself for because for all the times I'd made Theo cry over something I said or did, she had never made me cry, not once.

℮↷

After that day Eve went to bed, and stayed there. I had only a tenuous sense of the days and nights, the lights going on or off, the curtains open or shut, but I was told it took a week to arrange Theo's funeral and in that time Eve was not seen outside her own rooms. Her food was brought to her but she ate very little of it.

The doctor had been called to determine if she was ill but she sent him away.

'She hasn't seen a GP in years,' he said petulantly. 'Your grandmother should be seriously encouraged to have some sort of check-up.'

I made the funeral arrangements for Theo myself. Alicia didn't offer to help, though she took an interest. After the shock of the first few days had passed there was something oddly energised about Alicia. She read the letters that began to arrive and took a lot of the phone calls. She was almost articulate when describing the minutiae of funeral arrangements, and once I heard the unusual sound of her laugh slip in from the hall. She had even started putting on more make-up than usual, sealing up fissures, plumping hollows, colouring herself in. Tragedy, and the displacement of Eve, seemed to have given her a new zest for living.

She came into the dining room one morning holding one of the black-edged funeral invitations, frowning. I wondered if that had finally done it; such a solid little piece of card, its hard, graceful lettering. *Dear Alicia. I would like to remind you that your daughter is dead. She drowned herself. The funeral will be on Friday; bring a bottle.* Her mouth was drawn up with disappointment.

'Jonathan, do you really want these invitations to look like this?'

'How do you mean?'

'They look . . . cheap.'

I revolved around on my chair with my mouth open. All I could think of to say was: 'Well, they weren't cheap.'

'The font . . . The card feels shiny.'

'They've been sent already. You can send more if you like. You could send apology notes, for the first set. Tell them I chose them, that I was deranged with grief. Hopefully people will still come.'

'There's no need to be unpleasant.'

There was a silence and then Alicia left, running her fingers over the card distractedly.

As a relation of Eve Anthony, Theo's death was reported by the papers and on the news. The female newsreader told the camera that Eve had been made very ill by the stress. She put on a grave face as she said it, looking down at her notes and then up again, sincerely. Her hair was stiff around her face, her eyes made up, but not too much. Then she said, *Now the weather*, and started joking with the weatherman about his humorous tie.

e

Theo was buried at the small church nearby, in the plot that contained the mossed entablatures of the Bennetts, under the shadow of the broken-nosed cherubs of Sir James's tomb. The funeral was closed casket, though the undertaker had told us that as Theo hadn't been in the water long we could have it open, if we preferred. I had refused, not wanting to see her bleached by death, the beginning of erasure. But as we stood around the grave I felt a sudden, agitated need to see her face. She was disappearing, slipping into a black gap, the disjunction between my memories of her and her burial. It was barbaric, that she could be put into the ground like this. The coffin, the sound of the soil and stones hitting it. The earth, the box, the bones and flesh. I stood in horror and repeated prayers.

Eve left her room for the funeral; Mrs North had kept her

informed of the arrangements. I was grateful for this. Mrs North didn't question why I hadn't spoken to Eve since my return, or why I took convoluted routes around Evendon to avoid Alicia. She just simply and quietly did her job. She was the only one in the house who hadn't stopped, seized like an old clock, a paralysed cuckoo halfway out of its door.

At the service Eve sat in a wheelchair in a thick veil, her back rigid, hands stiff. She had decided to get up and had found she couldn't. I could tell she was furious. She had accepted the wheelchair from the doctor with barely concealed anger. Alicia stood on my other side, making a delicate face at the cold air of the world, dabbing her eyes in the way she imagined other people might blot tears. In daylight, wearing black, the decline of her beauty could easily be tracked. The skin over her eyes draped in tiny delineated folds, like tissue paper, thinner and translucent over the rest of her face. Her hand on my arm was as light as dried flowers. Alex stood on the other side of me. He was cautious around me, though I tried to be welcoming. Alex, Alicia and I; we might have had some solidarity, but we were voiceless and divided, even now.

My friends stood behind me: Nick, Felix, Sebastian, with his hand over his eyes. I had waited outside for him to arrive so that I could speak to him alone. He stumbled as he got out of the taxi and again before he reached me, as if he had coordinated his limbs consciously before, and now that he wasn't concentrating they had all gone awry. His face, tanned by the months in India, was an intaglio of itself, a distraught negative.

'So it's true,' he said. 'This is real.'

I understood what he meant. 'Maybe only in a way?' I said. 'Right?'

He inclined his head in a weak acknowledgement, but apologised: 'I'm not feeling very metaphysical today.'

'No. Me neither.'

'I never knew anyone like her,' he said, his voice blurring. 'We wrote to each other – she forgot to write back half the time – she wanted to come and stay with me . . .'

'I talked her out of it,' I said. 'It would have been better if she had.'

'Not your fault,' Sebastian said, but I shook my head. There was a long silence, before we both turned towards the dark door of the church, a black cut-out arch. As I took his arm to steady him, I remembered him composing nonsense verse with Theo in the grass, consumed with his love; all that useless, redundant love.

$e^{\sim}$

Maria had not come, though her flowers had arrived. Her flight was cancelled because of a terrorist scare; she had been put down somewhere random in America, some patch of state, and was there waiting now. Nathalie Dumas was here. She had visited us a couple of times already to offer her help, and stayed to talk. She was one of the only people whose conversation I could stand.

I noticed several uninvited people, standing a little way back from the rest of the mourners, so I went over to speak to them afterwards. I had not known Theo's most recent friends, these left-out margin-people, though I recognised a couple of them from the village. A woman with black beads in her dreadlocks took my hand and sobbed. Her face was red from the cold and from crying, scrumpled up like a ball of paper. Dry-eyed, I envied her; I wanted to take those deep swallows of air, utter low, rolling sounds of misery. At nights my eyes groped blindly for their remembered sights, spilling tears; I had no more for public use. I touched her arm uncertainly, startled and moved.

Aside from the local undesirables there were a few younger people, one of them a girl I recognised, who worked in a bakery in Carmarthen. They stood in a group, excessively polite, conscious of not being known. While I was speaking to them I saw the landlord of the pub in Llansteffan, who had tried to give me a warning. Removed from the oppressive murk of his bar, he was small and old in the scarifying light and I was ashamed of how I'd insulted him. I went over to him to apologise but he waved it away. 'No need,' he said gently, patting my shoulder.

I stood with Theo's previously unknown friends as if I could immerse myself in them, recreate an entire version of her by gathering up everything she had previously loved, the other half of her life that I had not been part of. After a while I noticed Alicia looking nervously over, so I invited them all to the reception.

As we left the graveyard the farmer Wendell, of the broken windows, appeared at the gate. I had heard he was sober and working, though he was still poor. He stepped back when I went over.

'I just wanted to stop by; I thought it would be finished,' he said.

'You would have been welcome. You're welcome at Evendon.'

He frowned abruptly; his eyes were almost hidden behind sagging, stony lids, but I saw he was close to crying.

'I'll never forget what your sister did . . .'

'Theo was like that,' I said.

Silenced by the 'was', we shook hands. He went back down the road and I went back to my family and friends, standing indistinguishable in black, their faces white in the wind.

e~

It was difficult at the house to see the people I knew. Sebastian, who looked as if he might pass out, had been given one of Alicia's tranquillisers and sent upstairs to lie down. I wished I could do the same. Groups of my friends had drawn together and were talking mindlessly. Eve was a popular subject of discussion. She had not stayed downstairs for the reception on grounds of ill health and I couldn't speak to anyone without being asked about her. Present or absent, she was the biggest star, especially at Evendon, her own creation, her enchanted castle.

The next most popular subject for conversation was the weather.

'It looks like it might snow,' someone said next to me.

'It's a very clear day.'

'The garden looks beautiful; it would be lovely to have a walk down there.' There was a pause, and the girl who had said this, one of Theo's school friends, turned to me looking panicked. 'Sorry.'

'It's okay.'

We all trod, agonisingly obviously, through a conversation of blown glass, attempting not to break down its delicate structure. After a joke was made and guilty, surreptitious eyes were turned on me, I excused myself to go outside. Everyone nodded, being understanding. I could have done anything – hit somebody, smashed a window – and I would still be nodded at.

Nick came out after me. 'Sorry,' he said, 'I'm so sorry. I saw her a couple of weeks ago. I thought she was depressed or something, I just didn't realise. I should have looked after her.' His mouth as he said it moved strangely, upset, and I thought it was me speaking, and my mouth. The music was coming out through the open door, something sentimental, that Theo would have liked. I put my hand on his arm but couldn't speak. Then Nick went away and I found myself in the empty dining room, sitting at the head of the great cold table with a glass of whisky.

The coroner's report said that Theo hadn't used drugs, not for months. I was still floundering in this information, in how badly wrong I had been. I didn't understand what had happened, I was still retracing my mistakes. If Theo hadn't been taking drugs, then she was ill. I knew there were rules for healthy people and ill people. The healthy people look after the ill people. They protect them, and watch over them, and bring them the things they need. They don't ignore phone calls, throw letters in the bin; they don't lecture and complain and eventually get rid of the ill people, sending them as far away as possible. They don't turn their faces away and leave them to die.

Since Theo drowned, I had been unable to see her face, to recover a cohesive picture of her, in sound and colour. I had lost the ability to relive the past, got stopped somehow, only halfway back to Evendon, to how it used to be. I closed my eyes and for a moment I was almost there, half blinded in the sun, the scent of the jasmine over the door. Theo was under the tree in the garden, her hair alight, looking away from me. 'Theo,' I called, but she didn't hear me, and she didn't turn around. I opened my eyes and I was back in the dining room, just me, and the picture of Eve, alone in the long chill, in the open dark.

SIXTEEN

After Theo's funeral Eve stayed in her rooms. There were hundreds of condolence letters for her that went unopened, a tide washing up through the door and piling by her bed. Finally Mrs North tidied them optimistically into boxes, for when she might feel well enough to read them.

Eve wouldn't take calls, though I heard her speaking on the telephone. She received her solicitor once and her accountant twice. I knew something about what she was doing from the national press: she was retiring and selling Charis Hotels Group to its management. She was not keeping a seat on the board. The company's managing director made a speech about how hugely they were indebted to Eve, who had been not only an enormously successful businesswoman, but an inspiration. I saw his photo in the newspaper; his glasses reflecting sincerely in the camera flashes, talking shit.

Then there were no more visits and no more calls. Everything went silent. The knowledge I had about Eve came from Mrs North. It was hard to tell if she was eating any of the food she sent back to the kitchen. She sent another doctor away. The maids were to stay out of her rooms. Her light was to be left on, at all times.

'At night?' I asked.

'I don't know how she can sleep with all the lights blazing like that,' Mrs North said. 'I don't know if she does sleep.'

So she knew now, as Theo had, that darkness was not simply the absence of light. It had its own life, clinging on in the edges and crevices of the day, emerging at night, from the corners and the horizon, to eat everything up. I myself was not so fond of the dark, these days.

Eve only came down once after the funeral. She had walked all the way down the stairs and towards the hall before the exertion swept up to her head and she fainted. I was the one who found her there. When I saw the piled fabric on the stairs I thought for a moment that Theo was alive, and had dropped a coat on her way inside. Only Theo left that kind of casual mess.

Then I realised it was Eve, and thought at first she must have fallen down the stairs. It was not horror I felt then, but a rising, tentative relief. I hurried over to her and checked her unmoving face, then looked for her pulse. Before I had hold of her wrist, the thin voile skin there, her eyelids moved. Lying so clumsily, with the new central track of grey in her unpinned hair, without make-up, she looked like one of the women Theo used to befriend, the women propped in shop entrances with their ragged faces and swollen eyes. Her face had lost its lacquer, its lustre, the skin exposed like plaster.

I got her back upstairs myself and she leaned on my arm and sat down next to the bed. She looked at me speculatively, watchfully.

'I'll call you a doctor,' I said. She turned her face away.

The doctor came, pronounced her bones unbroken, tried to convince her to eat more, asked a few questions to establish if she was senile, then left.

I stayed in her room, and I came to sit with her the next day, and the day after. Mrs North was visibly relieved at this display of family feeling, but really it was a kind of punishment, for us both. I hated to do it but I couldn't stop myself. I needed to sit there and let the guilt hang between us like perfume, like the smoke from a roll-up, the faint hum of a vanished evening.

On the fifth day, lying in her bed, Eve said: 'Two funerals.' I thought she had spoken in her sleep at first, but then I saw her eyes were open. They were still unexpectedly sharp, with their distinct irises, their patina like black enamel, but they moved over me and the room without interest or expectation. Her voice was acrid, as if blown off the hot sand of a desert, choked by its own dryness.

'What did you say? Theo's funeral?'

'No, George's funeral. Freddie's funeral. Those . . . were my freedom.'

I had to lean close to make out what she was saying. No heat rose up from her, no scent. She could have been a dried leaf come to rest, a piece of balsa wood on the shore, her voice rustling and dry. I had to repeat what she said to myself to make sense of it, unsure I'd heard properly.

'What do you mean?' I remembered the visit to Sam. 'Did Freddie hit you?'

'Yes. Not just that,' she said. There was a long pause. 'I didn't . . . didn't want children.'

As I caught up with her meaning she began talking again,

more forcefully now. 'Freddie didn't drown. He was on the boat but he didn't fall in. Sam's friends took him away – Sam helped me. But Alicia must have overheard us, afterwards. She was young. She hid under tables . . . behind sofas. I never used to know where she was. But we only talked about what happened at night, when the children were in bed . . .' She paused, and I thought she would stop, but she was gathering up more power to propel the sound out of her throat, to stop it dipping and failing, and continued, 'I didn't know she knew. Not until her divorce. I wasn't going to let Michael have you two. Alicia was unfit. But he was . . . no good. Not as a father. Then he said Alicia had told him what happened to Freddie . . . she'd confided in him. He wanted money, he said, or he would go to the police. So I gave him money. He agreed to stay away.'

Her voice gave out and she coughed. The sound was like tissue paper being crumpled. She didn't say anything for a while but her eyelids drew down, almost closing.

'Eve, you should sleep.'

Her eyes opened again effortfully.

'Not finished,' she murmured.

'I'll come back and sit with you tomorrow.'

'Promise.'

The last person I made a promise to was Theo, age eight, tear-marked and crumpled, falling asleep in her elephant pyjamas. What became of that promise? Never mind. Eve's hand half rose towards me. I couldn't move to take it.

'I promise,' I said.

There was a silence and her eyes closed again. 'I'll see you tomorrow,' I said, though she didn't appear to hear me.

After I left her room I walked away quickly, as if she might call me back. It was only when I was lying in bed later that I tried to think about what she'd said. But I couldn't find a context for what she'd told me. I couldn't connect it to the Eve I thought I knew, because she hadn't existed for me since the day of the telephone call, and I couldn't assemble a new Eve, one that made sense.

I didn't know what Eve had expected from me either, a display of shock, curiosity, sympathy. I wondered if I should tell her that I just didn't have a full deck of feelings to hand, to apply to the appropriate situations. All I had when I shut my eyes and turned myself inward was my own shame. A wide plain of it, shimmering like water, dark and salt-tasting. I looked into this water and I saw nothing. But I knew that Theo was down there, just under the surface, her skin glowing pale, her lips blue and unmoving in the cold.

SEVENTEEN

The next morning I was going up the stairs to Eve and met Mrs North running down. When she saw me she stopped, her mouth open. 'Oh, Jonathan, quickly—'

'Call Alicia,' I said. 'She's in London. She might not be on her way back yet. Try the Montmorency Hotel – she was at a wedding there yesterday.' (Alicia's social life had apparently been entirely reinstated, as though it had been frozen in time thirty years ago, ready to be taken up where she left off. Her friendships were not governed by the usual rules of emotional connection; they were social alliances, historic edifices, standing grandly whether or not their human element was actually present. But now it appeared Alicia *was* present, wide awake and ready to join the party.)

I ran up the rest of the stairs, shouting back to Mrs North as I went: 'Call Alex. His number's in the book' – then, because I had almost forgotten that there was a chance of cure, of repair, 'Call a doctor.'

When I opened the door I saw the room was dark for the first time; only the strip of light running down the curtain gave Eve edges and a face where she lay in bed. She sighed when she saw me, a brittle noise, a crackle. Her hand lay folded and thin next to her. I sat down and was unsure whether to reach for it. I understood that this was a deathbed, and that I should take her hand, but I couldn't bring myself to do it. The hand lay there, reproaching us both.

She sighed again and half turned her head towards me, eyes closed.

'I have done very much . . .'

'There's no need . . .'

'. . . that is wrong.' Her eyelids were blank; it was a shock when she opened them and her eyes gave off their pained glitter. 'Should have done more . . .' There was another silence. Alicia won't make it, I thought. The doctor won't make it. There was a burning in my head, in my mouth.

'. . . for Theo.'

Snow was falling over her face; its animated lines were dissolving. They drifted, settled, gentler than they had been. I took her hand; her pulse was there, for less and less time. It ticked away; she was not conscious, and then there was the silence and the stillness, but more silent, and more still, than I had expected.

❧

Alicia took the news well.

'Oh,' she said. Then, after a while, 'I suppose we'll be having another funeral.'

I stood outside Eve's door while the doctor and ambulance drivers wrapped her up, to take her away. Alicia had stopped on the threshold, thoughtfully, then went downstairs murmuring something about having her coat on, as if this were not quite *comme il faut* when meeting dead people. Later I saw her in the gold back parlour, studying her address book.

Eve's death caused quite a stir in the media. She had been suffering from several small and hidden types of cancer, we were told by the coroner, any of which could have killed her, though the stress of dealing with Theo's sudden death could have played a part. Despite this, rumours began on the internet that she had been assassinated because she knew too much about JFK, or the Mafia, or both, and these made their way into the newspapers.

'It's a little late for all this, surely,' I said to Mrs North.

'It's disgraceful,' Mrs North said, glancing out of the window in the direction of the drive, where journalists had been turning up with regularity. 'I'm very sorry you have to go through this, Mr Anthony.'

It was Mrs North who had thought of an epitaph for Eve, after looking through some Renaissance poetry she had found in the library.

'*Truth and Beauty Buried Be*,' she read to us. 'It's from a Shakespeare poem.'

I looked at her when she said it, trying to find fraud, but it seemed she really believed in the same Eve everyone else believed in. She thought Eve had been a heroine for women and the oppressed; she was proud of finding the epitaph, and conscious of presumption. She was watching us with worry now.

'Eve would have wanted that,' I said, and Mrs North cried a little, and Alicia went back to reading a magazine, and everyone was agreed.

Theo had no epitaph: no last word, it seemed, had been able to enclose her, and so under her name I had left the stone blank.

℮

Eve's funeral in Wales was family only, but her memorial service at Westminster Abbey in March attracted crowds of people, standing outside under the cold clouds that plastered over the sky, stifling the light. Inside I stood with Alex and Alicia next to me. Alex was pale, and I was worried he might stumble or even pass out. He had given an angry laugh when he heard about Eve's death.

'Typical Eve, sidestepping the issue,' he said. Then he started to cry. I had invited him to stay at Evendon but he refused. 'I can't stand it there.'

I glanced at him, his flimsy hands, his profile a scrap of flesh above the solidity of the suit. I tried and failed to connect him with Eve, who in death had suddenly looked like herself again, lying like Snow White with her black hair restored, her serene face as hard and white as if it were all bone.

Some celebrities and politicians stood up to give readings at the service. In these Eve was benevolent and generous. She was courageous and hated injustice, she overturned prejudices, she fought like a lioness for the oppressed and vulnerable. She was warm-hearted and witty and a great conversationalist; a few quotations were attributed to her, some that she had genuinely said, others that she hadn't. Alicia nodded along to all of it next to me, eyes lowered, clasping her gloves like a suffering saint.

In the tears of the congregation – the words *good* and *perfect* and *kind* over and over – the features of Eve melted, swamped and softened, became more ideal. She was the newspaper article again, the printed speech on the side of a mug, a shining celluloid creature, a public possession. There was nothing else of her left.

e~

Nathalie and Nick Dumas came to the funeral but Maria hadn't been able to leave America; one of the autistic teenagers she worked with – Nick stumbled when he got to this bit – was on suicide watch. Maria was the only person who'd been able to do anything with the child. All this information I heard blankly. Maria had called and written to me, asking to come over, to help, but I couldn't answer her. With Theo's death a gulf had opened in me, grave-shaped; everything I saw or heard since vanished into that darkness, growing smaller and smaller. I lost track of who I spoke to that day, of whose hands I shook or cheeks I kissed. Flesh and wool and perfume and jewellery and hair; it revolved past senselessly, a collection of textures. And then it was night, and I went home and put my head down and dreamt not the bad dreams, but strange limping sequences of detail, half lit, oddly joined together. The gold elephants in the morning room, a green drink on a glass table, a tree with a heart carved into it, a fire blowing on a deserted beach.

e~

After Eve's funeral the house became silent, in a close, airless kind of way. Outside whatever room I was in I would hear whoever was speaking or walking outside. Sitting in the morning room now I could hear two maids talking.

'I'll scrub it. These old carpets are stronger than they look.'

'Are we meant to be staying out of Theo's room?'

'Keep out of there, Mrs North said.'

'Poor Theo.'

'Sssh. Keep your voice down. God, these pinch.'

'New, are they?'

'They pinch like bastards.'

'You know what, I think if I was Mr Anthony I'd sell.'

'Don't say that! He's gorgeous. I don't want him to leave.'

'You never saw him before. He looks tired now. He ought to get out of here. Go somewhere nice for a while. If I had all that money I'd go to the Bahamas.'

'The Bahamas won't bring his family back.'

'No,' the other maid agreed, and then they passed out of my hearing.

℮

'I thought a doctor should have been called for your sister. A psychiatrist,' Mrs North revealed suddenly, under cover of bringing me tea. 'I said it to your mother and grandmother.'

'What? Why did you think that?' I asked, my voice harsh with surprise. I could see Mrs North gathering up with fright, and I had to encourage her to sit down and talk.

'Well, Theo was shy with me,' she said. 'I never heard her say anything odd. But apparently she told one of the maids – Laura, the girl who found her – that she thought you'd been kidnapped, or killed, something like that. She thought there were ghosts here too. I thought it sounded like schizophrenia. People think that means having lots of personalities, but it doesn't. My friend had a cousin who was like that. He used to say the government was spying on him. Wouldn't have anything with a screen in the house.'

'What did Eve say to you when you told her?'

'She said "Thank you for your concern, Mrs North." I don't think she liked me saying it. They didn't call a doctor. I don't think Mrs Anthony realised how ill your sister was. She wasn't home very often. And she and Theo – they didn't seem close.'

'I'd like to speak to the maid who found her,' I said. 'Do you think she would meet me?'

'Laura? I could ask her,' Mrs North said. 'It might be a relief to her. I don't think she'd like to come back here, though.'

I looked around at the dimly lit room, the line of windows looking out onto the scrawny April garden, wet and wind-whipped, the cool light spilling over the floor like water, raising a bleak shine. Silence blanketed over us, hung from the heights of the ceilings, thick and unyielding. I agreed with Mrs North that perhaps it would be better to meet Laura in her own house.

*

Laura lived near the centre of town; to reach her house I had to walk through Carmarthen for the first time since Theo's death. People turned and looked at me as I passed the market but I barely saw them. The area had become a kind of doubled land-scape. My memories were attached to everything, past sounds echoed weirdly alongside present voices, new faces lay like tracing paper over old ones. I saw a dark, serious child and I thought it was me; I saw a large woman and thought it was Mrs Williams.

'Jonathan!'

It *was* Mrs Williams, approaching at speed, towing a young child with chocolate all round its mouth. She stopped, out of breath. 'Oh, that's done it,' she said, wheezing. 'Running like that.' She handed me a card. 'I was just going to post it.' Her face abruptly turned red; she wiped her eyes with her coat sleeve. 'Oh, Jonathan, she was a good girl. It's awful what happened. Terrible.'

Unsure what to say, I patted her arm, wondering how I could easily get away. But people who had been looking around at me cautiously now began to drift towards me. The woman who ran the cheese stall came over and started crying before she could say anything. Then a man told me a story about how Theo had left her wallet in his shop and been so sweet and charming when he contacted her to return it. 'She always used to pop in for a chat after that,' he said. 'I can't believe it – what happened.' A group of girls came shyly up to ask if they could have a photograph of her. In the end I had to tell them I was meeting someone. Mrs Williams decided she would show me the way, as it wasn't far from her own house.

'She was an angel,' she repeated before leaving, adding unwillingly, 'I'm sorry about Eve.'

Laura's house was small and hot; printed flowers around the walls, a pink carpet and a small pink mother who showed me in. Laura was a slightly plump and nervy seventeen-year-old sitting on the edge of the sofa; I noticed she wore a skirt suit, as if she were in a job interview. After I'd enquired politely about her A levels and so on, she was still looking at me with an uncertain frown, so I just asked her, 'Did Theo seem . . . unstable before her death?'

'She was unhappy. But she wasn't like a crazy person. She was just worried about weird things. She thought there were ghosts in the house. And she went to the graveyard looking for you, because she thought you might be . . . dead. She kept saying that at the end. I told her and told her you were only on a business trip. She said you'd been taken away and hidden. Then she said you'd been killed.' She looked up. Her eyes were a gingery, clear brown, slightly combative. 'Mrs Anthony wasn't sympathetic,' she said, her voice filling out. 'She wouldn't listen to her and she'd just walk out. She told Theo that if she didn't pull herself together you wouldn't come back, because you were tired of her acting so childishly.'

She started to cry.

'Theo was such a nice person, she really was. Mrs Anthony shouldn't have told her things like that. I don't think she knew how much it upset her. Theo didn't say strange things for attention. I think some people thought she did.'

'I'm so sorry you have had to deal with this,' I said. The room was crushingly warm; too pink, too dense. I stood up, with the sudden need to put as much distance as possible between myself and the healthy brown-haired girl, her tears dropping with energy; I would contaminate her somehow just by being near her, exposing her to the fumes from my nuclear heart, the dead river of my blood.

'Did you get severance money?' I asked before I left.

'Mrs Anthony gave me a lot of money. Too much money. I'm really grateful . . .'

'Of course, of course,' I was making for the door. 'I'm sorry. Good luck with your A levels. Thank you for letting me visit.'

'Oh, it's okay . . . goodbye,' she said, looking confused, and then I was out in the rain again, and safety.

℮

A week or so after my visit to Laura, I overheard Alicia on the telephone as I passed the morning room.

'Yes, it was,' she said. 'It's very sad that both of them died at the same time. Though Eve can't have expected to have an awful lot longer, at her age.' She managed to talk about it as if it had happened to another family.

As Alicia seemed in better spirits – the best spirits, in fact, that I'd ever seen her in – I waited outside the door until she had finished her conversation, then went in and asked her how my father was these days.

'What are you talking about?' she said, looking past me to the door as if she might be tempted to sidle around me and make a break for it.

'Eve told me,' I said. 'She and Sam had Freddie killed. You found out about it. You told my father. He tried to blackmail Eve. So she gave him the money but in exchange he had to go away, and then you all pretended he was dead.'

As the silence set in Alicia stood still, opposite me but turned away. No part of her moved, not her lowered eyelids, her grace-fully held fingers, her neatly placed feet. She looked as if she were at an official ceremony, standing decorous and quiet. I waited, uncertain of what might be gathering in her, moving under her motionless exterior. I was beginning to regret having spoken so harshly, to someone so frangible, only delicately held together. Her face was colourless above the intense black of her dress. I thought I saw her lip shudder. Then she said: 'What are you going to do?'

'What do you mean?'

'Are you going to tell everyone this? Ruin our family name?'

She stared at me for a while, and there, unsettlingly, was Eve: that impermeable surface of the eye, the face sharpening, coming into clearer focus. I stepped back, startled.

'Don't you think my life is difficult enough without you bringing all this back up now? If this is made public I'll say I don't know anything about it. I don't want to be involved. You'll embarrass us all.'

'Jesus Christ,' I marvelled. 'Your mother and stepfather murdered your father and you're worried about the embarrassment?'

'I barely knew my father. I barely knew any of them. And they're all dead. There is absolutely no point telling people this now. What would it achieve? Except to make us the family of a murderer.'

'I hadn't even considered that. I hadn't thought about making it public. My main concern was how you'd kept this secret so long and how you felt about it. Forgive me! I should have been thinking about what was really at stake – your place in the Royal Enclosure at Ascot. Not to mention the possibility of being snubbed at Henley Regatta.'

She ignored this. I felt the unfriendly light of her gaze moving over me like an MRI scan, analysing my soft tissues, trying to determine which of them might be likely to fail.

'I won't make it public,' I said with disgust. 'But for reasons other than how it might affect your social calendar.'

'Your architectural practice . . .' she began.

'I don't give a shit about that! I won't say anything simply because it's no one else's business.'

'Thank you,' Alicia said, with a long, distressed sigh, as if our conversation had been held solely in order to torment her. Her stare slid off mine and the resemblance to Eve vanished with it; she was Alicia again, turning away reproachfully. I watched the transformation with disbelief.

'And what if my father comes back, now that Eve's dead?' I asked.

She shook her head. 'I'm sure he'd rather keep his income.'

I moved away and sat down, baffled. I realised that Eve's death had given Alicia a type of freedom I hadn't initially recognised – not the freedom of truth, but the prospect of never having to be truthful, of living untroubled and thoughtless at the golden apex of society, our family's shame safe under the ground with the old queen, under the water with the sibyl.

No longer fixed in place by my attention, Alicia had begun to float slyly towards the door, like a child playing What's the Time, Mr Wolf?, so that I was tempted to jump up and chase her out of the room. Instead, I asked her, 'Don't you have any feelings about it?' not in the hope of a meaningful answer, but to be awkward.

'How I felt about it? Does that matter? Eve and Sam decided

everything between them. Then Eve and Michael decided everything between them. I was on the verge of collapse but nobody cared. Then I was simply abandoned, left alone to deal with two young children. Now you're questioning me and dragging these *things* back up. At a time like this. And now' – she delivered her trump card with oppressed nobility, slipping out of the door – 'I have a headache and I am going to lie down.'

The next day I called Alex and said I wanted to talk to him. He was surprised and uncertain on the telephone and I suspected he only agreed to meet me for a drink at a café near his university because he couldn't immediately think of a reason why not. But that was enough for me. The café was small and tired, its light coming from a cold fluorescent strip, colouring Alex with ill-health, picking out each depression in his face. His body appeared guarded against it, head tucked down defensively.

I took a sip of the coffee that had been brought over, which was bitter and lukewarm, but I didn't know what else to say just then, so I said: 'Good coffee.'

'It's horrible, I'm afraid,' Alex said. 'But I can only take an hour before my next lecture and this was the closest place to meet.'

There was a pause as we both inspected our coffees. Then I said, 'I wanted to talk to you about my father.'

'Ah,' Alex said. 'He didn't really die in Australia, did he? Do you know where he is?'

'I was hoping you might know that.'

'No, I never knew anything about what happened to him – I only had my own suspicions. Eve and Alicia have always insisted that he's dead.' He paused and looked at me with pity, the same look I remembered from childhood. 'I'm sorry. You were hoping for something more than that, weren't you?'

'Maybe you could tell me what he was like?' I said, after a while.

'Oh yes, I can do that,' Alex said, then started talking hurriedly. 'Well, he and your mother married young. Too young, without question. They met while Alicia was in sixth form, on a skiing holiday in Klosters, and then dated for all of three weeks before they decided they wanted to marry. I think partly Alicia was desperate to leave home and it was the quickest way to do it without having to do something intellectually demanding such as get a job or go to university. And of course she also must have had a longing to be "loved"' – he said the word uncertainly, as though it were foreign and he wasn't comfortable with its pronunciation – 'because that wasn't something we had much of, at home.

'After three weeks' acquaintance I can understand how Michael and Alicia thought they liked everything about each other. They were both sociable, fun-loving, that sort of thing. Your mother was quite different back then too. She didn't care that he wasn't "one of us". You didn't know that? Well, don't start picturing a cockney barrow boy or a Yorkshire miner or something. Alicia had her limits. But Michael was quite a vague person; his parents were dead and he had been in care when he was young. Went to a grammar school, I think. Eve was concerned about his history. She said he had come out of nowhere.

'Eve wasn't exactly pleased by the relationship but she never explicitly opposed it. I think she was relieved to get Alicia off her hands anyway. We were both of us a disappointment to her, in our different ways. It was you she saw as her heir. Which was probably harder, for you, than being another disappointment.

'Your mother and Michael's relationship got worse, as relationships do, though I didn't see much of them or hear the details. I had never been close to Eve or Alicia, and I think Michael correctly identified me as a bookish bore and went to great lengths to avoid my company.'

'Eve said he drank too much, he was depressed.'

'Well, I suppose both things could have been true. But none of that really defined him. I remember he was always very entertaining. Always full of ideas. I think he had periods of depression, but I'm not sure he would be diagnosed as depressed. And your mother certainly kept him company when it came to the drinking.

'I don't think Eve expected him to file for custody. God knows why he did. He was no match for her. I was at Evendon when she took a call from him about it. She didn't look so beautiful then. I know much has been made of her "radiance", but she actually lit up like that.' He pointed at the fluorescent light. 'It was unhealthy, disturbing to see. I'd never seen her so angry. The next time I saw her, Eve told me Michael had dropped the case. Then I heard he'd left the country. Then the next thing I heard, he was dead. Ah, the whole thing stank, as Sam would say. I didn't believe he was dead but I don't know why he never came back. I always suspected she threatened him.'

'He was paid off.'

Alex looked at me with concern, frowning. 'That's what Eve told you?'

'Yes, and Theo overheard a conversation between Eve and her solicitor to that effect. All he wanted was the money. Alicia said something similar.'

'It's true that he had no money of his own, no job. But for all his problems, I think he cared for you two. It wouldn't surprise me if there was some pressure put on him aside from money. Some offer he couldn't refuse. And Alicia – she would say that. She'll never forgive him for leaving her.'

I shook my head. 'You don't need to say that.'

'I'm not saying it out of tact. I've never been good at that.'

'Well, I suppose we'll never really know unless he turns up. Or I find him.'

'Are you thinking of doing that?' Alex said.

'More for Theo than myself,' I said. 'She wanted . . . she . . .'

There was a silence.

'You don't need to explain it,' Alex said, rearranging his hands with discomfort, until they sat more at odds than before.

'Anyway, there was something else I wanted to tell you,' I said after a moment. 'About your father's death—'

He interrupted me: 'My father was a cruel bastard. I used to dread coming home for the school holidays – and I was bullied at school. Sam was always good to me. I'm actually sorry I didn't make it over to visit him before he died. I know the circumstances of my father's death were somewhat dubious; I reached my own conclusions about it a long time ago. Similar to those concerning my grandfather's unfortunate fall down the stairs.'

'Do you think she . . . ?'

'I don't know. It's just a suspicion. I know she hated him, behind closed doors. I asked to see his picture once when I was a child and she said, "There he is, George Bennett. Clutching that ridiculous skull for all eternity." So who knows what *he* did to her. Not that it's any excuse. We all have our formative influences. But at some point we become adults and have to be responsible for our own behaviour. For example, I don't think I would be a terribly good father and so I've refrained from procreating. Someone else might take some sort of class to familiarise themselves with basic child-rearing skills. What I am saying is, there is nothing in Eve's history that could excuse, for me, her failure as a parent.'

Alex stopped speaking then, the way he always did: rushing his information out and then blinking off, like a computer printer. He made as if to drink his coffee, changed his mind as it got to his mouth, put it down again and folded his hands up rigidly.

'I understand,' I said. 'I'm angry too.'

Alex leaned forward for the first time, unfolding from his defensive position on the aluminium café chair. His eyes, far away behind strong lenses, were insistent.

'Jonathan, I can't help you with much, but I can give you some advice, when it comes to Eve. I couldn't forgive her when I was young and I'm not capable of forgiving her now I'm old. I am alone and all I've got is my resentment. Don't let that happen to you.'

I nodded, unsure what to say.

'I have to get back,' Alex said, standing. 'Good luck with finding your father.'

I stayed in the café for a while after Alex had left. After having driven from Evendon to London, I wasn't sure I could go back. I ordered another coffee and a pastry and left them on the table like a pay-and-display ticket, while I sat and thought.

I didn't know what I wanted from Michael, but finding him was the only thing I could think of to do. If I didn't search for him, I would be left with nothing. Only her, trying to see her face beneath the night water, diving to take hold of an ankle or a hem, reaching over and over again.

e~

After talking to Alex I quickly ran out of people to ask about my father. Eve had left no paperwork behind her, not even credit card statements or telephone bills. Her computers were wiped clean of anything that could be used by journalists or detectives. Her solicitors' faces were clean too, carefully empty, politely apologetic. Not at liberty to disclose. I searched the internet for Michael Caplins but found nothing except what Theo had found before me. So I looked up private investigators, and found Mr Crace.

'In a case such as this I'd say your chances of locating your father are good,' Mr Crace told me. 'Though you should also be aware that there is a possibility we may not find him.'

'How long might it take?' I asked him.

'Impossible to say,' Mr Crace said. 'When the person in question has been missing for over two decades, you can expect a certain number of blind alleys, red herrings, and so on. But, as I often tell my clients, this does not necessarily mean the overall exercise will be a wild-goose chase. I hope you appreciate my humorous point.'

This being delivered in the same affectless tone with which Mr Crace discussed payment schedules, it took me a moment to understand him. 'Metaphors. Very amusing,' I said.

'I'll call you as soon as I have new information,' Mr Crace said. He wished me a good day, and then I was out of his office and on the way back to Evendon, to begin my wait.

Even if Mr Crace is unable to find my father, I thought, if he is out there – floating in some dusk of the world, where news of Eve's death hasn't yet permeated – maybe one morning he might switch on the television and there will be some earnest biopic of her life, with an actress faking a smile on a podium, or he might buy an outdated international newspaper from a street vendor, as bicycles and children flit around him in the humid sunlight, calling out like birds, and then he'll see her name there, past tense, and he'll realise he can come back.

In the café in Oxford I had realised it was impossible for me to carry on living at Evendon. I was drinking too much, sleeping too little, feeling too angry. The estate had been left to me in Eve's will, so I told Alex and Alicia that I didn't want it.

'Would you like Evendon?' I asked Alicia.

'Oh, I don't know. Perhaps not . . .' Alicia said. 'Philippa Steele has been rather pressing about a vacant house next to hers, actually, in Chelsea.'

'Would you like Evendon?' I said to Alex.

'Oh, God, no. Thank you, but no. It has Eve written all over it. It's her house. And those pillars – no, thank you.'

I spoke to my solicitor and the estate agent and told them to organise the sale of the estate between them. Things moved quickly. A buyer was found – a Mr King – and the process of packaging antiques for auction began. Alicia wanted a lot of the furniture, jewellery, and paintings for her new house; Alex didn't want anything. I spoke to all the staff to tell them the new owner would keep them on. The faces in front of me were curious, belonging to people I hardly knew: the days of Mrs Williams and Mrs Wynne Jones were long gone.

Along with the house, Eve had left nearly all of her money to me. Alex and Alicia got five million each. Alex didn't seem to care, but Alicia frowned, and said, 'Well. That seems odd.'

'I don't want it,' I said. 'It's too much.'

I had never known how much money Eve had; I had never wondered about lack or surplus. All my life money had simply appeared to make the staff prompt and abundant, to feed the cars, to be turned into plane tickets and paintings, clothes, wine and food. Flowers and lights blazing all through the house, thriving on money. I never had to engage with the financial process of life, the cold, hurtful sale and exchange that drives people out of bed, lashes them into their suits, confronts them with a glimmering screen, sends them home late and tired, presents them with the paper and the plastic at the end, to spend. I did all that because I wanted to. Now I found I didn't want to any more.

The department-store developers I had been dealing with before Theo's death had already sent a stern letter about my contract, which had been making its laborious way through layers of lawyers over the last month. I went in to see them and the contract was dissolved. The partners of the firm looked intimidated when I sat in front of them. I was haggard from not eating or sleeping and I must have looked mean, slightly desperate; no longer the kind of person to address press conferences about cutting-edge design in the twenty-first century.

I bought a new phone and sent the number to Mr Crace. Then I locked up my own London flat with my laptop and mobile phone inside. The last call listed on the phone was from Maria. I didn't return it. I had nothing to say to her: the North Star of an abandoned course, the love of my old life.

In the weeks before the sale I was not as busy as I thought I might have been, so I went out walking. I avoided Llansteffan and Carmarthen; I felt a directionless fury at times and I didn't trust myself not to break the wing mirrors of cars, kick signposts, throw things at shop windows. Worse, I was afraid I might lose control of myself and attack somebody. The first person who mentioned Theo, or Eve, just for their casual daring in carrying on living, in rolling the names of the dead out of their warm red mouths.

So I walked all around the quietest roads, meeting only sheep or tractors, a few stray cars. Often I got lost. Sometimes I would sit down in an isolated place, until the sun faded and I would realise I'd been there for hours. Once, very early in the morning, I visited Theo's grave in Carmarthen, all the grass sparkling in the wet, pale light. There was no one there except me, and a few bouquets; cheap carnations, flowers picked from gardens.

I imagined her with her eyes closed, not far down. Her hair, that thick brightness surrounding her face like a sparkler; her

pale skin. I had said I didn't want to see her before the funeral;
now I couldn't picture her face. Mrs North said she was much
thinner, before I came back. Wasted away; all that living gone to
waste.

e⌐

A week before we were due to leave Evendon the rooms were
almost bare; their contents boxed up, ready to travel away in
different directions. There was something uncertain about the
house in its denuded state; it had lost its original power, when
before it had seemed the essence of what could be aspired to, the
blind, beautiful core of entitlement. Looking now around the
vastness of the sitting room, the white desertion of the hall, I felt
the sour pleasure of victory – a Bolshevik pleasure – watching as
the house's imperial finery was stripped and dismantled and taken
away.

But then – there was Theo's room. It hadn't been touched
since the funeral. As the final week ticked down, Mrs North asked
me tentatively what I was planning to do with her things. 'Oh,
I'm dealing with that tomorrow,' I said, as if it were just an orderly
item on the house-moving agenda, but I think we both understood
that it wasn't true. I had no plans for Theo's room. I hadn't even
planned how I was going to open her door. I went past it every
morning feeling a long cord of dread connecting me to it as I
walked away, stretching but never snapping.

When the next morning came I lay awake in bed wondering
how I would 'deal with' Theo's things. I had dreamt that I was
standing outside the room, not knowing if Theo or Eve was behind

the door, which had no handle, and no lock, and appeared to be drawn onto the wall. It was a strangely painful dream – pushing and shoving the not-door, half knowing that it was only a wall – and in the end it was worry that I might dream the same thing again, or something worse, that propelled me out of bed.

I crossed the hall, then stood outside her door for a while, coming to the conclusion that I couldn't go in after all. I looked at my watch. It was late in the morning, the time Theo would usually be getting up, leaving towels, cast-off cups of tea and half-eaten toast in a trail; the time I would be in my office, working. Here I was instead, staring at a door. In the end it was the sound of approaching footsteps on the stairs that startled me into opening it and going inside.

The curtains were open and the room was light, in a peculiarly still way. It smelt of emptiness; frozen breathing, old, cold perfume. I looked around and everything was familiar to me. I don't know why I thought it might have changed. The furniture was still plastered with a découpage of magazine pictures, carved with nail scissors a long time ago, to spell our names. A poster of an Indian temple was tacked over the bed, along with an article about the Humbug House, postcards, sketches. There was her bureau, with its tatty crowd of toys, a small dressing table piled with leaking cosmetics and jewellery. I picked up a brush, choked with long bright hairs.

It was in the drawers by Theo's bed that her treasure was kept. In one there was a heap of things that a child might hide away: an old pencil case, a blusher compact with no powder inside, a silver necklace, used-up pens and beer mats, a flattened origami swan, a small statue of Ganesh that Sebastian had sent her, an old Action Man discarded by me. In the next drawer down I recognised my own postcards and letters. There was a photograph of Sebastian, Nick and me, sitting in the kitchen at Charlie's party; I was raising my hand indulgently at the photo-taker. Then a few photographs she must have taken from the family album, of us as children. Another picture of me, this time as a two-year-old, glaring up at the camera, holding a red spade. The picture of my parents on their wedding day, a square of bright colour and light like a lit screen. My father's generous smile.

The third drawer down was filled with paper. I picked up the piece on the top, which said:

> *I've lost my brother, he's over the sea,*
> *Over where I want to be.*
> *He's the other half of me.*
> *. . . ~~Tree Bee~~ Happily?*

I held it as if a glimmer of life clung to it, a suggestion of her hand or her eye. I gathered up more pieces of paper to read, and then the unfairness of them struck me; that they should be here while she was not, this obstinate material, the signal of something that was gone.

I put it all into boxes along with the rest of her things, until the room was dark and everything was packed away. Then I sat in the quiet next to the pile of boxes. Sound rose vaguely up like heat through the floor. The thump and scrape of furniture below, the occasional word from one of the maids. Outside I could hear birds calling; an engine running. A depleted clock ticked slowly. Inside, my heart drumming, the interior noise of my breath.

When I stood up to leave I realised I had left the door open, and her scent had all blown away.

e⌐

I asked Alicia if Theo's boxes could be kept at her new London house, until I got back.

'Oh dear . . . well, there's not a great amount of space really. Not now all the furniture has gone in.'

'It has seven bedrooms. Put it in a guest room.'

She sat passively, eyes slipping off mine down to the floor. 'But,' she said after a pause, 'what if the other guest rooms are full and I need the—'

'Find somewhere. She was your f— your daughter!' Alicia looked alarmed and I lowered my voice. 'Remember?'

She murmured something about letting go of the past.

'Find somewhere,' I repeated, and went outside, where I crossed the terrace and walked away from the house and said, 'Your fucking daughter, you fucking bitch.'

e⌐

Once I had started walking I didn't turn back, travelling further away from the house, not realising the direction I had taken until there I was, standing in front of the trees at the start of the path.

I trod through the long grass and followed it: almost completely overgrown now with ferns and brambles. The dark green light splashed my clothes and face; there was that smell of water, of earth turned over in cold air. My feet rustled through layers of leaves, fallen bark, mulch. There were several sets of footprints in the bare, muddy patches of ground, crossing and overlaying the one-way set that Theo would have left.

I hadn't come here since I was a child, with Theo and Charlie Tremayne. The path was shorter than I remembered; the pool when I reached it was smaller. The water was still; whirls of tiny flies hovered above its empty glaze, patched with the chilly light. The overhanging branches of the willows sifted its surface into faint motion each time the wind penetrated through the trees, erasing and remaking my reflected face.

For almost a day Theo was here, they told me. I went over to the spot where I guessed she might have sat and saw the nymph still in place, almost completely green now, leaning down in dismay. Her face, dreamy and sad, was the same as Alicia's when she lay on the sofa that morning, a long time ago.

Then Theo had walked out, down this shallow slope. The water must have been as cold as this; curling up around her, climbing up her coat towards her neck, passive but greedy. She looked down into it, through the tense pewter of its surface, and saw our father. All I could see was darkness, greenness, the damp light broken on the surface. I couldn't see her.

I was knee deep in the water when I realised what I was doing. I waded awkwardly back, and then, the same as I had over twenty years ago, I turned around and ran.

2008

Every time I have been to New York I arrive at night, seeing it only as a dark, tall city out of the window of a taxi. I can't make out the buildings now: the windows of the bars and the street lights obscure the structures above them, blazing them out. Unwilling to go to the Charis hotel I usually stay at, I ask the cab driver to take me to the first hotel whose name occurs to me.

'Good choice,' the man tells me, eyes sectioned by the mirror. 'You've been to New York before?' He has a look of friendly determination. I try to smile.

'A couple of times.'

He is pleased. 'Yep. You get to learn a lot about people driving a cab. I could tell you'd been here before. Do you know how I know? You don't look out of the windows. The new tourists can't get enough of looking out of the window. You know, I got relatives in England, distant cousins. Where do you come from in England? Wales . . . I don't know Wales. My relatives live in Surrey. You know it? John and Linda Woods. No, I guess you wouldn't know them. So what do you do? Architecture! That figures. That's why you stay in nice hotels. I bet you've built some nice hotels. Is that why you're here – building something?'

I spend the journey defending myself against these

conversational shots until the cab finally pulls up to the side of the road. 'Well, here we are,' he says, sounding disappointed that our relationship must end so abruptly. 'Have a nice stay.'

As I get out I see the frontage of the flagship Charis hotel across the road, dimly grand in its brown stone, and almost turn back to the cab driver, startled. Then I wonder if, in my unreliable state, I actually said the name Charis to the driver without realising it. Finally I turn and see my own hotel behind me, situated opposite the Charis, facing off like two dowagers at a society ball.

'Of course,' I say, surprising the doorman. Of course it wouldn't be so easy. But then, Eve is with me whether or not my window faces the palace of the empire she has constructed, so I go inside anyway and take a room for the night.

In the end my room overlooks a different street. It is an extravagantly simple room: muted lighting, deep towels, prissily parcelled soaps. On the bed, a large square of glaring white, sits a box of chocolates, which I eat in lieu of a meal. I remember when Theo and I were ten and eleven, and we stole a bag of toffees each from Mrs Edwards's shop. I persuaded Theo into it, so that I wouldn't take the blame on my own if we were caught. On the way home in the car, before I could stop her, Theo put one in her mouth.

'What's that?' Miss Black asked. 'That smell?'

'It's my toffee,' said Theo, startled.

'It's not your day for sweets.'

Miss Black said this without actually paying Theo any real attention (she was almost at a roundabout, where she usually hushed us and occasionally swore quietly), but Theo went pale and cried out as if she were being tortured, 'I stole it!'

'Oh!' Miss Black was startled. 'Well, er . . . little girls who steal do not get any pocket money. Did you see her take it, Jonathan?'

'No,' I said, keeping my face expressionless. I was sensible enough to wait until I got home before I ate my own sweets.

eↄ

The next day I buy a map, hire a car and drive north-west. My journey takes a few hours, from the morning into the afternoon, and when I eventually get out of the car the temperature has risen to a lifeless heat, heavy and condensed, the sky cloudless and grey-blue. With the address Mr Crace gave me in my hand, I walk a few blocks, turn a few corners, and there it is: Ithaca City Cemetery.

The cemetery itself is large: the further in I go, the less the noise of the cars can be heard, dimmed by the pines that stand unmoving in the windless sun. My father's grave lies in the shade under a large tree, covered in a dry matting of needles, so that I have to sweep them away to see the stone. I run my fingers over the lettering. Michael Caplin. MC, cut deep. In the cool beneath the tree I might be back at Evendon, standing before the carved heart. In the dark beneath the tree I might be in my room at night, looking out onto the terrace at the splinters of crystal, a glass I recognise for the first time, fishing it out of my dream and bringing it into the light. *What happened to the sixth one?* Theo asked. *The sixth is . . . lost in history.*

Mr Crace told me that my father died here about a year ago, which meant Theo didn't see him in London after all. Michael died of a heart attack. He had lived in a rented flat in Ithaca for a year prior to his death. Before that his whereabouts were unknown. Mr Crace investigated further but it seemed Michael had no family here, and no friends that could be found.

'He appeared to have led a solitary life,' he told me.

'It's definitely him?' I asked.

'Without a doubt. He had identification.'

I sit on the grass now and try to feel something about my father's death. But I feel nothing. I was looking for someone I didn't know, who had as much meaning to me as anyone else lying here under their grass blanket, the other side of the boundary between earth and air. Less meaning, because I could probably go to the family of any of the other deceased and ask them what their husband or son or father was like and they would tell me and it would probably be true. I was not looking for Michael Caplin: I was looking for a half of Theo, a missing half, that she had wanted to see restored. I was looking for her, but she isn't here.

I leave the cemetery and walk to my car. Once out of the city I drive in the same direction as before, north-west, further into the land, waiting for the buildings to fall away and let me pass into somewhere relatively deserted, somewhere I can live until I decide what to do. From the air-conditioned car interior I watch the unfamiliar country move by, flickering in the heatwave. The vastness of America seems to be covered by a large grid of road, like a net over the land, staking and portioning it. I am never far from farms, motels, houses with a flag flying outside, gas stations, cafés, areas cleared for development. They peg out civilisation in the nothingness, punctuating the length of the road like fillips of sound over the fuzz of an untuned radio.

Finally I drive down a dusty white and straight track, lined with dry, rustling beech trees, abandoned except for two telephone wires stretching along its length, until I get to the edge of Lake Ontario, as wide and blue as a sea. I pull up at a small harbour. It is quiet; boats knock against each other in the water, a few men stand by a car. A white dog watches me from the back of a pickup truck. The scent of the tarmac rises in the heat.

I go into the fishing shop, where there are more men, standing and talking. It smells of old shade, the paprika odour of bait. No one pays any attention to me so I stand at the counter and wait until a man with a round beard and moustache joining up with his hair, like a bristly lion's mane, turns around.

'Need help?' As I open my mouth he asks, 'You fish?'

'No, I'm afraid not.' The brief opening in the conversation seals over; the other men turn away. 'I was actually stopping to ask if there's anywhere nearby that rents houses out.'

'Houses?' The man rubs at his beard.

'Bob's got a house,' someone else says suddenly.

They all look at a man who is presumably Bob. Bob has a tabby beard and a checked shirt; an unlit cigarette dangles from his hand like a uselesss finger. He looks uncomfortable.

'He's joking with you,' says Bob.

'Now, it's a prime location,' says the first man. 'Might need a little decorating.' There is laughter. I gather that the house is a wreck.

'It's a wreck,' Bob says.

'Could I see it?' I ask him. 'Please?'

He stares at me, then shrugs, and says, 'All right.'

❧

The house is at the end of another chalky white road through the trees, glaring in the sun, jolting our slow cars. When we get out, Bob simply shakes his head as if irritated with the house, for wrecking itself. (*You've embarrassed us both*, the head shake says.) The white paint is peeling away in strips from the faded timbers of its sides, the veranda droops, the pale grass is balding and scuffed. Thin, straight trees stripe the clear patch before the house with scattered shade. These jack pines, birches and poplars make the same hiss-shush as the cicadas, the rustling bracken. Everything is dry; the green is silvery up close, bleached out.

I notice the house has its own small white beach, breaking off into the water where a rusting boat is half floating, half sinking. The trees in the distance to either side reveal other houses, a luxury apartment block going up far across the water, but directly in front of me there is no other side of the lake; just an edge of water, turning into sky.

'So here it is,' Bob says shortly, obviously feeling that he has wasted a journey.

'May I see inside?'

Within the house there is a not-unpleasant sodium smell of age, dried-out wood. The floors are sagging; one window at the back is cracked and taped up. There is a card table in one room; an etiolated flowered sofa in another. As we walk around, the sun comes in at the back of the house, resting on the walls, suddenly soft, lighting up the empty floorboards.

'How much?' I ask.

Bob frowns, his face collecting up in bunches of wrinkles and cracks and beard. 'One thousand dollars a month.'

'Thank you. I'll take it. How long can you rent it out for?'

Bob stares at me. He lights his cigarette; it goes out. He doesn't bother relighting it.

'Ah . . . how long would you like it?' he says.

'I'm not sure at the moment. A few months. Maybe longer. I can give you the cash now.'

He rubs the back of his neck. 'It's got no furniture. You have your own furniture?'

'No. That's fine, though. I can get some.'

We stand there for a while.

'Have you stayed around here before?' he asks.

'No.'

'There's a hole, in the floor there.'

'Oh yes. I hadn't noticed.'

'Look,' he says. 'Just give me six hundred a month. That will be fine.'

Bob Heilman drives off eventually, shaking his head. I sit down on my new sofa, in my house, this house that, for me, exists only at the present moment in time.

$\backsim$

That night I lie on the sofa; I will have to buy a mattress tomorrow. The night here is densely black, combed by the sweeping sounds of the lake. It takes me a long time to attain a state near sleep; sleep itself is a challenge I will tackle another day. I listen to the flies doing their rounds of the ceiling. My mind wanders. The past flows out.

I remember teaching Theo her biology homework. She sat with her hands either side of her head, forcibly tunnelling her eyes at my diagram.

'These are crops,' I said, drawing them. 'And some flies.'

'They're dots, not flies.'

'Use your imagination. This is a bird. And . . . a cat,' I ignored her giggles. 'Now if the farmer puts pesticides on the crops, and the flies eat the crops, and the birds eat the dead flies, and the cat eats the birds, the pesticides accumulate up the food chain.'

'What happens to the cat?'

'It dies. Okay – no, no, it doesn't die. It just has a stomach ache.'

'Poor cat,' said Theo, drawing the diagram in her own book. She looked up and smiled; her sudden, uncertain smile. 'Thanks, Jonathan.'

In the morning, I investigate the house. The once-white kitchen is surprisingly functional. The refrigerator works; the oven heats up, and gives off a smell of stale fat. I find a mouse family in one of the cupboards. At first I have no idea what they are; the newborn mice in their nest made of scraps are squirming pink, like fingers. The mother looks up at me, nose whirling. I close the cupboard door again quietly.

All the rooms are bare, their wallpaper going yellow, peeling in corners. There are pink-flowered curtains in one room, a pink lampshade that has become a fairy castle for spiders. On the window frame someone has scratched *T loves J*. That's how life is now – these sudden pains waiting around corners, in hidden places. I leave the room, closing the door behind me. Later I find an old Easter card half under the sofa. It says *Dear Bob, Lois and Terri. We must meet soon! This is our new house number. Have a lovely Easter!* So it is Terri who loved J.

I wonder what I have got myself into, with Bob, who has presumably lived in this house, left, and failed to return. But I haven't got the energy to puzzle it out. I wander outside instead.

It is early but already the morning feels exhausted, faltering in the overbearing heat, the buzzing, still heat that rises from the trees and the cracked, baked white shore. The lake feels strange to me; it is tidal, edgeless, but it is not the sea. There is no hiss of water over sand, just a faint lapping sound. I am not on the edge of land; I am in the centre of land so vast it holds seas inside it. I think of Wales; its tiny convoluted roads, its dark green, the flickering light off leaves and water. My old country was a wild garden; America is an exposed plain, naked and indifferent under the blazing sky.

A large car, shiny and dark, appears at the end of the drive, surprising me. It bumps down until it stops in front of the house, black-windowed and confusing, and then a woman springs out.

'Hi!' She offers me her hand while remaining far enough away to give me a thorough look. 'You must be Jon Anthony. I'm Terri, Bob's daughter. Great to meet you! Thought I'd pop over and check everything was going okay for you here.' She is an attractive, tanned woman, wearing a pair of tight jeans and a tight top.

'It's fine, thank you.'

'I was kind of curious you decided to stay at all.' She pauses and looks behind me at the house. 'I mean . . . ! When my father told me he'd let this place for a few months, I just jumped in my car and drove right down.'

'Did you used to live here?' I ask when I realise she is here for conversation, and doesn't intend to leave without getting some.

'Oh yeah, right up until I was sixteen. But then my mom ran off and Dad and I moved, but he kept the house. I told him to sell it. I said, "Dad, you're just letting a whole lot of money go to waste having that house sitting there." He said he'd rent it out but I never heard of him renting it to someone till now. People used to ask – they thought it might be nice to lease it out for a couple of weeks in the summer. He always gave them a crazy price and of course they never paid it. Now no one even asks, it's such a dump. I heard he charged you less.'

I nod.

'So, what do you do?' she asks curiously.

'I . . . was an architect. I'm taking a break for a while.'

'Wow,' she says. The sun has moved and is in my eyes. I glance back at the house and shift on my feet, signalling retreat. Unfortunately I can't pretend I have something to do. I have nothing to do, and we both know it.

'So, do you know anyone around here?' she asks. 'I can show you around if you like. I could do with some company. Me and my husband are estranged – he had issues with his ex, she was very controlling. So whenever I ask him to do the dishes, it's like, I'm controlling him. Then he didn't want children either.' She sighs and gets out a cigarette. 'Do you smoke?'

'No.'

'Good for you. I'm actually down to two a day – I got a hypnotism tape to help me quit. I was on about twenty a day before.'

Go away, I think, trying to beam this thought at her. Go away, go away, go away. But she is still there, solid in the sun, lighting her cigarette and pulling her girlish top down over her midriff. In the end I say I have a headache and that I'm going to go and lie down. After she has reluctantly driven off, with a wave and a telephone number – 'Call me soon, okay' – I go back to sitting by the lake.

e

In the afternoon I go to the nearest town to buy food. The supermarket is in a broad grey park of other stores, their large signs and painted metal sides too bright, too cheaply done. The building is large – everything in it is large. Instead of a bag of corn on the cob I buy a sack, for only a few dollars. Cartons of orange juice are oversized, ice cream comes in buckets rather than tubs. Losing momentum, I abandon my list and buy a few random things instead, going back out to the car park, where a woman pauses from unloading her children and stares at me.

'Excuse me,' she says. 'I know you, don't I? Are you on television?'

'No. Sorry.' I get into my car as quickly as possible; she is still looking at me, frowning as I drive away.

This has happened to me before. *Are you somebody?* people ask – a question no one seems to think is odd. I know what it is; they recognise Eve in me. When I look back at myself I can see why. I unconsciously spoke the way she did, I sat up straight, I held my head up as if I were entitled to something, whether I believed it or not. I learned Eve's manner, without understanding that it was an act, or what it was an act of.

e

I spend the next few months doing very little. Some days I drive miles to the forests and go walking. Part of the appeal of this lies in the danger that I might lose my way back; get found years later, under layers of leaves and mulch. I see chipmunks, black squirrels, birds. I see bear droppings, but I never get anywhere near a bear. Perhaps they back off from my scent; they can smell that I am inedible, with my accumulation of pesticides.

In town I arrange for my post to be redirected from the London flat to the local post office, to leave some conduit of communication open. But having done this, I find myself avoiding the post office. Bob Heilman tells me, when he comes over to see how I am, that letters are gathering there for me. I wonder which of these letters are work-related – if I am wilfully destroying my career. I don't care whether I am or not. I look back and see that I was climbing the rope of an Indian magician; once I got to the top, I vanished.

Bob wanders around his former family home with evident discomfort. He asks what I have been up to with a wondering frown, the beginnings of suspicion. He often asks me what I will be doing when the summer is over, in accordance with our mutual pretence that I am a holidaymaker. He nods when I say I am waiting for a call, for family, for business. (I can't even remember the various lies I've told him.) 'No hurry,' he says.

e

After Bob leaves, I read a book bought at the supermarket about the Mayans (in which George Bennett makes a couple of dignified appearances), until it becomes dark. I've never read very much – not since I was young, when my favourite story was 'Little Red Riding Hood'. This wasn't the watered-down Ladybird version, but the one Eve gave me, by Charles Perrault. ('This is more like what goes on in the world.') In the original, no one is regurgitated, and there is no woodcutter. I thought it was a fair story and wasn't sorry for Little Red Riding Hood. I thought she was a pretty stupid girl if she was fooled by a wolf in a dress.

I'm not tired but I am bored of the book, and as I only bought one, this leaves me with nothing else to do except go to bed. I have put a new mattress on the whining, bowed bed frame – a space-technology mattress, which I bought because it promised a good night's sleep. It has yet to deliver on its promise, but it is very comfortable, a heavy, rubbery slab, firm like muscle. Lying on it I can feel my back lengthening minutely, uncurling into the hollows.

I wonder if there will be a time when everything that happens doesn't remind me of something vaguely connected from the past. I hear the frogs outside and I remember the night Theo stayed up in the toad-hatching season, going back and forwards with a bucket taxiing the tiny toads across the road they were trying to cross. I hear the shushing of the trees and I think of the walk down to Llansteffan beach, single file, drinking that undrinkable wine.

It takes nothing at all to bring back how Evendon used to be in the evenings. Alicia reading in the lamplight in the gold parlour, her silk legs always neatly folded around each other, tidied away.

Eve, in one of her rare moments of relaxation, reading letters. Theo lying on the floor, resting her elbows on a cushion, her legs waving absently like anemones.

'I heard this puzzle and I can't solve it,' she said to me. 'There are two doors – one leads to happiness and one to despair. The doors are guarded by two men. One always lies and the other always tells the truth. You have to ask one man one question to find out which is the right door.' She looked at me expectantly. 'I thought you'd be able to answer it.'

'Here's another puzzle: why can't Jonathan do his essay?'

'I don't know, why?'

'Because Theo's distracting him.'

How many times did I send her away like that? Now I am paying for it, empty and unsleeping, my memory of her like a light bulb I can't turn off, irradiating the bare cavity of my head.

℮

Terri 'pops over' again – hoping that I'm not feeling lonely out here by myself. She has realised it was silly of her to give me her number when the phone here has only just been reconnected. 'I guess I assumed you had a mobile,' she says, smiling at me. She has me down now for an old-fashioned English gent, I can tell.

She offers me the use of her pool in the hot weather; she lives only a short drive away. She has little barbecues, and she would be pleased if I could come; they don't have enough men. She yelps with surprise when I say I haven't been back to New York yet. I tell her I like the isolation of the lake, as politely as I can. 'Oh I completely understand – I'm a very solitary person,' she confides. 'I find it hard to trust people. But, you know, people like us, we need company sometimes . . .'

When Terri is gone I find myself thinking of Maria – her mouth turning up in its not-quite smile, her brown skin – and there it is. The return of love. I hadn't thought about it all winter, but I suppose it never completely goes away.

Did she really put her hand on mine, the last night I saw her? I didn't think she did it out of pity, but then I never did understand her very well. The half-real rainy light was shining over us both, lying on the bed. In that short time before the phone rang I felt happy – happier than perhaps I had ever felt in my life. Her little mistake and my greatest moment.

Maria is someone who still exists; she's working in Boston, in the Reiss-Carlow Centre for Autism and Spectrum Disorders. I know the telephone number of her office. It seems absurd that I could go into the house and within a few minutes I could be speaking to her. It is not Maria who is gone – it is the Jonathan who might do this. He is lost in a summer in Llansteffan, sitting on a beach with all the possibilities of the world in his head, complete and ignorant and heroic, like a medieval knight. He sits with the girl he loves, and thinks that he could have her, that it is all up to him.

∽

One night I pull a chair out to sit by the lake. The water is almost invisible in the darkness, close by my feet. The house creaks gently behind me with the slight disturbances of the air.

My grief over Theo is love, and guilt, the two of us on the lawn at night, the tears in her eyes, my voice like a flat hand, pushing away the dark. My grief over Eve is something toxic and complex. It is not only to do with disappointment, but with outrage, which makes it worse. I am angry with Eve, for not putting up a good enough show, one I could still believe in. She sits at the head of the dining table again, as the light in the windows sinks, telling a story. Her voice pulls me along, stringing misfortunes together like an out-takes reel, the actors falling off horses, tumbling downstairs, dropping through water. Her face by now almost lost, soft as ash, the words running on, uncoupled, no longer tied to a mouth.

I realise I have started to fall asleep, but I can't move, sitting there cold and heavy and upright. I dream I am on a plane. Out of the window, deep down, there is the water, where my sister waits. I could slip down there, and my life would come rushing back, and I would not be alone. I lean my face against the window, chilly with its closeness to the sky. The stars beyond it hang hazy and icy; they press down on me, pushing me into the morning.

I write on a piece of paper:

Maria

After a few hours I fold the paper up into halves, then quarters, and put it into a drawer in the kitchen.

I go to the supermarket under a flat, synthetic blue sky, thick around me, the heavy reek of a storm in the air. I take the same plastic bags I used last time; I seek out products that are traded fairly – organic corn, ethical meat. The origins of my dinner never used to bother me; these days I want to cause as little damage as possible to anybody, whether it is a Costa Rican banana grower or a pig in Denmark. I smile at the checkout staff, sitting up like a row of meerkats. They all smile back widely, and I can't help but miss Mrs Edwards, sullen and dense beneath her canopy of smoke.

I pay for my food and walk out into the beginning rain, where an enterprising tramp has set up near the trolley bay. I don't see him until he says, 'Any change?' He has bright green eyes, startling in his pocked face. I give him the rest of my notes.

'Thank you,' says the man, startled. 'Thank you very much.'

His hand retreats into his large blanket with the money, so that only his head and shoulders remain visible, hooded from the rain.

'You're welcome,' I say. He looks at me curiously; perhaps I have breached some kind of street etiquette, standing here too long. Or maybe other change-givers do this too; feeling that they should get a return for their money, hear a sad story of drugs or abandonment. I get in my car awkwardly.

Something about this man reminds me of Theo. Sitting there in full view, he has the same inside-out revealing of himself. I cannot work, they both say, I cannot be mended. Their dependency catches others like burrs, pulling out sympathy; they refuse to be separate, defined at the edges.

I, on the other hand, bowled through life like a marble, a rolling stone. I didn't gather any moss; but then I didn't gather much love either. Now I come to rest at the lowest point.

I go back to my empty house and listen to the clinking where the roof is leaking into buckets. Outside the rain hisses, like hundreds of pieces of paper being torn.

e-

I start again, sitting with my pen in my mouth staring at the square of white until it leaves its afterimage on my eyes. Then I write,

Maria, I

I consider the *I*, standing alone. As a letter, it doesn't seem appropriate for its subject. *I* is too simple – one line, straight up and down like a pillar or a flag pole. I can't identify with it. A spiral would be better, or just a scribble. I sit there for a while, but I can't get past the inexorability of the *I*, and finally I put the paper back in its drawer again and sit outside, watching the flickering cinema of the rain.

e-

It gets to the end of August quickly, and Bob asks me, 'You'll be moving before Christmas, won't you?' He explains that it will get very cold soon, and as the house doesn't have working heating, living by the lake will be out of the question.

Bob has taken to hanging around the veranda after I have given him his rent, making unpractised conversation, looking at me curiously all the time we are talking. I realise now that he is worried about me, so I don't tell him that I haven't planned so far ahead as winter. I give him a vague lie about moving to New York.

'I guess maybe you can design some buildings there?' is Bob's last attempt at drawing me out.

'Perhaps,' I say.

The rural American buildings I have seen, in this land of no ruins, are mostly a new, internationally familiar type; purposeful and hasty. They tend to be box-shaped, as if for storage – even the churches, storing worship. Where money has accumulated, the buildings are more lavish, such as the luxury apartments I see across the lake, those jaunty hybrids of Swiss chalets and Tudor mansions, Disneyland-style chateaux with pink roofs.

It strikes me now that what I would have built is worth nothing more than this kind of rubbish. I would have designed something large and demanding out of steel and glass; I would have hoped to win an award for it from somebody who would never live there. It didn't occur to me that buildings should be harmonious, much less beautiful; I thought the love of beauty was plebeian. I didn't want anyone to be uplifted by a building of mine – I wanted them to look at it and think of my name. Jonathan Anthony, Jonathan Anthony, a name without meaning, an empty waving placard.

Maria,

I've had a lot of wrong ideas about love in the past – ideas I am ashamed to remember. You probably wondered why I chased you and called you when I never had anything kind or worthwhile to say, but it was because when I was with you I had an idea of what love should be. I was just too cold and stupid to know that's what it was.

I understand love better now and it's still yours – it always will be – if you ever want it.

Jonathan

After a sudden week of bad weather, I wake up to see that the sun has rolled into the house. The stale rug and bleached-out floor have become an expanse of luminous polished oak, veiled with long squares of light from the terrace. Instead of old salt and decay, there is the scent of jasmine, of lilies. I can hear a woman's voice, in another room. I close my eyes again, but Evendon vanishes anyway. Outside the seagulls carp and squawk, harrying me back to America.

Later that morning I drive to the post office in town. I stand for an uneasy moment, hesitant, when the woman behind the counter asks, 'Is there anything else?' Before I can decide what to say, the woman smiles at me with recognition. 'Are *you* the Englishman staying at Bob's lake house?' she asks. 'I've got mail here for you.'

When I get home I put the stack of letters on the cardboard box I have been using as a table. A bound pile of paper, following me across the world. I eye it as I eat my breakfast. Then I take the pile and go outside to sit on the veranda, which is a well of sunlight. The week's rain has dried away already; the raspy hush of the trees sounds parched, the cornflowers are the palest of blues. Heat lies like a shiver over the water, blazes up again from the dusty white road.

I have two letters from Alicia. The first is almost energetic in its reproaches. Apparently some of her furniture was damaged in its journey from Evendon, which she stops coyly short of blaming me for. She complains that the optician has prescribed that she wear reading glasses, and manages to imply a fragile state of health. 'It is difficult when one is alone,' she writes. The second letter, which arrived last week, is shorter. 'How long are you going to stay away?' she asks. 'I have some news – I am getting married, to Sir Marcus Balfour. He is a close friend of Prince Charles. I hope you will return in time to come to the wedding. It is becoming very awkward answering questions about you, as if you are a recluse.'

It makes sense really; Alicia isn't the type to be left alone for long, she is a natural dependant. Of course she would get herself a husband. She signs off, 'Your mother, Alicia', as if she is reminding herself of our relationship.

Amongst the other letters there are a few from our lawyers concerning a book that's about to be published, a biography of George Bennett. It's a shocker, all right. Some of the details I had no idea of: apparently there was a high turnover of maids at his houses, one leaving after he slapped her for dropping his tea, one hit by a flying paperweight. He also ran a profitable sideline selling some of his more dubiously acquired artefacts on the black market. This George Bennett's veneer of gentility barely covers the primitive instincts of the bandit, the raider of not only foreign tombs and palaces but sickly American heiresses' fortunes; his spectacular, somersaulting death the natural culmination of a life of subterranean violence.

I know I ought to tell solicitors to challenge these claims, as Eve would have, but even if they are all untrue – which I doubt – I'm not sure I see the value in it. Eve had some power to prevent these things, but she has become copy herself for the journalists, and soon the biographers will move in, to write the 'real' story of Eve. Stories and stories and stories, appearing like rats poking their heads out of the cracks, after the last war is over.

e∽

Reading my letters disturbs me more than I expected; feeling the long reach of my family across the Atlantic. No reply from Maria, but then I hadn't really believed there would be one. As an apology letter it was too little, as a love letter, too late. I pour a glass of water and go out to the veranda again, where I sit thinking nothing much for hours, moving in and out of a doze, until the sun is almost gone and I am still leaning against the old, warmed wood of the house, wondering what to do next. I don't care, that's the problem. My heart could be meat packed in ice; I can't feel it, though I know it clenches and unclenches, it goes on, unreasonably and pointlessly. My life has stopped, but I am still here.

I need to go back and tell Theo she was right. I thought I was whole, but I was a blind eye. I thought I was unaffected, slick-sided, but I was afraid. I left Theo to take the weight of the lie herself, crowding in, getting into her breathing space. No wonder she never knew what was real.

I lie on the decayed veranda and the idea of never seeing her again swallows me. I am in the secret pool, immersed. My memories tangle around me like weed, clotted and slick. The sky is water, the air is unbreathable, looking up at the dark leaves through a weight of condensed green light. *We'll be far away . . . we'll be so happy*, she said. I could do it – go into the lake, reach the distant place and see her waiting there. I want to tell her I'm sorry. I want to reach out in some way, put my hand out, feel the blood extending through my cold fingers.

I breathe, I open my eyes. The night has started to slide over the lake, a purple like spilt watercolour graduating, merging into the horizon. I can hear the crickets; the birds have fallen silent. The pale cracked ground has turned a faint lavender colour in the light; the water is silverish. The sky above me is strange, lovely, like mother-of-pearl.

Then Maria is there. She stands there on the white ground, not far away, looking at me. There is a car behind her, its door left open. She is wearing a cream coat that glows like a moon in the dark, her legs dark and thin against the pale dust, her face a gathered radiance. It is the Maria of the last night in London, her eyes serious, her mouth sad. I don't say anything. I don't know whether I believe in her, appearing like this out of the shady corridor between awake and asleep, standing here by the dilapidated house like a projection, looking like my best memory of her, like something I've made up.

She walks over, and kneels next to me on the veranda, without speaking. She is so close that I can feel the air around me shift; resettling with her familiar perfume. She puts her hands out and they curl round mine, the surface of her palms like a small shock on my skin. Her eyes are dark topaz, amber; gold haloes out from her pupils like flares off the sun. Her hair falls down, a curtain descending; the heat from her flows into me, travelling towards my guttering heart.

EPILOGUE

2010

I am driving down to Carmarthen from our house in Berkshire, the car window slightly open, a thin stream of air knifing its way in, expanding into a rush of coolness. Maria holds her hair in one hand to prevent it licking across her face. It is a hot, blue day; we can see clearly all the way over the Severn as we cross the bridge.

'I dreamt last night we were on Llansteffan beach, making a sandcastle,' Maria says.

'Sandcastles . . . I haven't built one for years.'

'I'm not surprised. I would have thought you'd be completely against them. Mock-medieval, derivative: career suicide.' She laughs and then says, more thoughtfully, 'I often dream about us all, back in Wales.'

She touches my hand, because I know who she means by all of us. Maria, Jonathan, Nick, Theo.

'I don't have dreams any more,' I say.

'You still dream,' she tells me. 'You just don't remember them.'

'I'm happy with that. I like the night without them. It's peaceful.'

'Let's sit out tonight,' Maria says. 'We can just watch the sea from the garden.'

Maria: fan of the sea, of gardens. I know these things about her now. She likes horses, Bach, liberalism, whisky, ballet. She dislikes beards, religion, oysters, fur, hiking. I know that today, under her dove-coloured shirt, scarf and jeans, she is wearing cream silk lingerie, with lace straps, tiny pearls. I know that this morning when she woke up, her hair had wilfully sprung out over one ear, necessitating a flurry with the hairdryer. It still seems unbelievable to me sometimes that I am in a position to possess all this knowledge about someone who was once so far, so strange to me.

'How did you find the house?' I asked her on the plane home from America. 'It wasn't signposted from the road.'

'I asked at a fishing tackle shop. You'd been behaving oddly; people remembered you. They wondered why you would live in a shack alone.'

'It wasn't that bad.' I was protective of the house.

'I spoke to the owner, actually. He was relieved that I'd come. He said, "It's getting cold – take him home."'

'And so you did,' I said.

'So I did.' She widened her eyes with mock astonishment. 'And here we are.'

'Why *did* you come?' I asked.

'I would have come sooner. But you didn't answer any of my calls or letters, and in the end I flew to Wales anyway, but by then you'd left and nobody knew who you were. Then I got your letter.'

Maria said that when she first arrived at Evendon that summer and I came over from the garden to meet her, she saw a boy who had something bright about him, something interested. She felt excited, nervy and possible. He had a hopefulness like Theo's, but it was more protected; he cradled it like a wound. She realised he wouldn't let someone else get close to that. 'Then we saw the picture of Eve.'

'That picture . . .' I frowned.

'I understood you better when you talked about her. You had this future, just like her. It took up all your space.'

Maria said she was always half waiting for something to change in the Jonathan she knew, because she didn't forget him. She thought about him in France; she bought magazines if she saw his name in them. She was sad and pleased that he was getting what he wanted – solidifying, becoming more famous, building himself like a monument with no doors and windows.

Then she saw his uncertainty in London, hovering over him like incipient rain, but the timing was wrong – the phone call – and she let him leave, and then everything happened and after that he vanished. Then she got his letter and went to find him. He was not a man inside a monument any more. He was lying on the ground in the night, like something dead, something newly hatched, uncased and lost, bright again at last.

℮

After Maria and I left the lake house, we stayed in America for a few months while she finished her research term, then moved to England, where she opened her own clinic. She is becoming well known for her theories on autism and Asperger's syndrome, her avoidance of drug treatments. She spends hours with the youngest children, one who shaved off her eyebrows and hair, another, a musical prodigy, who has not spoken for two years. Like a parent she brings home the pictures one draws for her and puts them on the fridge, except these pictures are not of stick figures; they are fleshed out, they show light and shadow falling on the sides of a face, structured hands – the work of her genius child.

I am still an architect: a better architect than before. My first commission after I got back and rejoined Anthony & Crosse was a C-shaped Renaissance-influenced mansion for an internet billion-aire, with ornate mirrored glass, patterned brick, arches and domed ceilings. The *Architectural Review* called it a 'welcome volte-face from Jonathan Anthony'. Developers are phoning; they want office blocks, hotels, apartment buildings that won't annoy the locals. The words postmodern, neo-eclectic – even neoclassicist – are used. Of course, a lot of modernists won't speak to me now, and a piece appeared in one paper hinting that I was losing my nerve; seeking refuge from the demands of taut steel and concrete in the frilled parlour of period nostalgia. Another jour-nalist defended me, claiming I have brought a 'new coherence to architecture', which is not really true either.

What I like about buildings now is not just their own structure but the way they fit, the way they ease themselves into the landscape, wrap around their inhabitants. When I think of successful architec-ture I think of the row of small houses facing Llansteffan beach: vividly pastel, the ice-cream colours of the coastal sky. They are the idea of living by the sea, the small hope that comes from being at the borders of the land and the beginning of something else.

I told Maria I would build us a house by the sea, and she laughed, and said, 'Where else?'

$\backsim$

After I came home I realised I hadn't lost any of my friends, with the exception of Emily, who fell into the category of friendship only in the loosest possible sense. She and Nick divorced after a year or so, then Emily married a billionaire and became Emily Miloslavkaia – the dull ruler of her pricey corner of South Kensington. I hear she has struck up a friendship with Alicia; they meet for lunch to discuss their lives on the up and up.

After a while of pyjama-wearing introspection, Nick emerged from his divorce exactly the same man he had always been. He works in Dubai now as a sort of financial gardener, planting and trimming large sums of money for investors, so that more money can grow. I think he is happy.

After Theo's death Sebastian had gone back to India, and aside from the occasional, vaguely worded postcard of a monkey or a mango tree under a white-hot sky, no one had heard anything from him. Then he moved back, bringing a Keralan girl named Seema, who had lived near the school where he taught. She passed his window most days and winked at him, so he chased her and gave her a flower, and they started a secretive, cinematic affair. When her parents found out they shut Seema in a bedroom while prospective husbands were hastily surveyed. She escaped in the traditional manner – knotted bedsheets, the night-time drop into the garden – and now lives with Sebastian in Truro. When I met her I noticed her smile: wide, hopeful, the beautifu' white of a shoreline. It struck me with force – not painful, as it might have been, but strangely reasonable; as if a smile like that is greater than the sum of its parts, as eternal as a Platonic Form, constant and pure.

Not long after I got back I had to attend my mother's wedding, an autumn panoply of orange blossom, antique lace, sugared almonds and gold-leaf place settings, which set upon London society like a sparkling dragon, eating up the rich. A nightmare from start to finish, it did have the advantage of distracting Alicia from my recent absence. All peevishness was aimed at the wedding dress, the wedding planner, the wedding guests.

'It's such a *lot* of work,' Alicia said on the telephone, her voice an enervated near-whisper.

'Why don't you just elope,' I suggested. 'Go to Vegas. You could be married by Elvis.'

'You can be very strange sometimes, Jonathan.'

'May I bring a guest?' I asked her. 'Maria Dumas. You remember – from Llansteffan.'

'Oh, the daughter of Sir John Bankbridge. Of course you may bring her.'

Alicia's new husband Marcus reminds me of a background character from a novel or film: fundamentally one-dimensional, he fits neatly into a paragraph with room to spare. Every day he does battle with ramblers and the National Trust over his Surrey estate, and every evening he has a snifter of brandy and checks the racing results. He looks almost exactly like a Greek statue, with his hard blond hair and thin nose. He treats Alicia proprietorially, which she doesn't seem to notice.

At the wedding the bride and groom resembled the wax couple on top of their cake: elegantly made, pale eyes, pale skin. Alicia wore a strange constricted dress; high at the neck to hide the ribs bracketing her upper chest. The priest recited his parts theatrically, staring up at the ceiling like a tilted doll. The congregation sat in well-dressed rows, looking disinterested, as well they might. I was the only family member there, aside from a few distant cousins. Alex didn't come, which didn't seem to bother Alicia. I think she was pleased at not having to introduce a shabby, nervous man in a cheap tie – freshly unearthed and blinking from the depths of a library – as her brother.

I wondered if Alicia, whose Xanaxed gaze had an appearance of misty emotion, was in her vague state remembering her wedding to my father. I couldn't even imagine it. The reek of the church must have been the same; the pews and tapestry and vaporised wax and the velvety heaviness of the lilies pooling in my lungs. Time began to reel backwards as I stared at the two of them in front of the altar; their figures began to change. Alicia's dress ballooned, her hair curled down, age dropped off her. Next to her there was an indistinct man. Blond hair, dark suit, facing away from me, his shadow stretching back across the stone. My father, the missing person, lost and found and lost again.

I imagine sometimes that Eve meant to tell me more about him, right at the very end, and she didn't get the chance. I could almost see the sheen evaporating from her eyes as she spoke, her life rolling off her like steam. Just like a film, her head sinking back onto the pillow, eyelids dropping closed, like petals falling.

I'll never know what kind of man my father was. He and Eve stand at opposite ends of a long rope in a tug of war. Whichever one pulls on the rope, the other is dragged towards the mire in the middle. If my father was an innocent man, resorting to black-mail only to get custody of his beloved children, Eve was ruthless, making threats, half orphaning her grandchildren in order to protect herself. But if Eve was telling the truth, my father was a money-grabbing villain and she was protecting us too. It seems the truth, as usual, is somewhere in between the two ends of the rope.

Do I blame Eve for Theo's death? I don't know. Eve didn't hurt her on purpose; it was just bad luck that they ended up sitting down at the same card table, the innocent and the consummate cheat. And sometimes I think of the Eve in the photograph she showed us a long time ago, the girl with the tightly waved hair and the face like something newly shaped, not yet fired. In the interim between Eve Bennett and Eve Anthony I don't know what happened. I don't know everything about why funerals and deaths were her open doors, her escape routes. I don't know what was left out of her stories. I just saw a character, as incomplete as all her other characters, as powerless. She was a princess who fell asleep in a glass coffin and didn't wake up, a witch, a genie with all its power confined in a diamond, granting three wishes: George Bennett, Freddie Nicholson, Michael Caplin. She disappeared in the flash of a thousand cameras, she was sparkling and unreal, and when I remember the way she used to move across a room, sharp and pure and alien, I am not sure I can apply the usual standards of life to someone who never really took part in it.

Do I blame myself? Yes. More than anyone else, I should have understood what was happening. I was always between them: Eve and her structured fiction, her tropes and archetypes, Theo and her instincts, living in the flashes and dives of feeling, drawn to the lacunae, the blank spaces of the past. I stood at the boundary line, not listening, not looking, not speaking: Jonathan the stone, set like concrete. I look back and I long to shove my past self, punch his complacent mug, pull his hair – anything to shake him out of his sleepwalking state.

I told Maria that one night, trying to explain it, because in those early months the sleeplessness came and went like a dying neon light and she would find me awake at four or five in the morning, watching adverts, watching gardening programmes. She sat next to me and fitted her body against my side, touching my forehead with her own.

'She knew that what we had been told about our father wasn't true – she sensed it,' I said. 'She had these crazy delusions, I know, but it was because of that lie about our father. It was the beginning of her illness. Then in the end she spied on Eve and found out she was actually right, that we had been lied to, and so she thought all her delusions were true.'

'The lie couldn't have made her ill,' Maria said. 'I'm sure she did pick up on the tension surrounding the subject of your father – but you have to believe that if it wasn't that, she would have focused on something else.'

'I just wish I'd known. If I'd known what was going on I wouldn't have been so dismissive. I could have helped her.'

'What would you change?' she said. 'If you could have known everything?'

'I'd have looked after her. Taken her to a doctor.'

'So, you take her to a doctor and she gets a diagnosis,' Maria said. 'It's not good. So she goes to live in an institution, or she is given drugs that can't cure her, and she hates them because with the side effects she can't think properly, but you tell her she has to take them. So sometimes she takes them and sometimes she forgets, and her life is unhappy, and she might make the same decision in the end anyway. And whenever you see her you are either frightened, or resentful, or you pity her.'

I couldn't answer, so she carried on, her voice softer.

'The idea of that would horrify her. All Theo ever wanted was to be with you, with nothing else between you; no sadness, no guilt. You can give her that. Let her exist that way in your thoughts: just you and her.'

I nodded and took her hand, because I was grateful and I knew she was right. But I couldn't do it. I closed my eyes and tried to see Theo, but her expression was hidden by an umbrella, a straw hat, the light on the window, the high stalks of the grass where she lay, the layer of water. I didn't know how to get her back, without going back, to the place where she got lost.

⁓

Maria and I arrive at Castle Hill House to find Nathalie in the doorway holding a dog, which is almost strangling itself trying to get away and under the wheels of the car.

'What on earth is that?' Maria asks.

'Hello, you two – this is my new dog. Nick came over with Sebastian and Seema a week ago; they went to Carmarthen and found him there, in the town. He is a stray, I think; I have put up signs everywhere. Nick said I should call him Emily – poor Nick! – but it is a he. Sebastian says he should be called Bonzo.'

'Bonzo's about right,' I say. The dog looks up at us; it is white with ginger ears and mildly crazy blue eyes. It sticks out its tongue, which is a surprising pink.

Nathalie embraces Maria and kisses me, saying, 'I've been watching for your car, and I forgot to buy ingredients for dinner. I don't know what I'm going to give everyone.'

'We can have fish and chips later,' Maria says. 'But first Jonathan's going out for a while. Are you sure you don't want me to come?' she asks.

'I'm not even sure now if I want to go,' I say. But I get back into the car, waving at the two of them as I pull away, Maria with her hand raised to her eyes to watch me go. I remember standing at the edge of Evendon, looking out through the husk of the day for the wink of her window, thinking about what Eve told me about love. That it is changeable, but selfish. It has no permanence, but it demands to be the most important thing anyway. There is nothing reasonable about that. And Eve was right: Maria might die, she might leave me, she might decide she loves someone else. There are an almost infinite number of ways she could hurt me. But still, she is the most important thing, and if I can see that then I'm not standing at the border any more, looking out at the light.

Mrs King was surprised when I called her to ask if I could walk around Evendon's gardens. This is not an odd request, from tourists, but it is odd coming from me. 'I'll be out, I have a hair appointment,' she said. 'But Carmen can let you in . . . Such a shame to miss you, but make yourself at home. Well, it is your home – was . . .' She sounds embarrassed, and says goodbye rather hurriedly. I remember when I met her around the time of the sale she seemed unnerved, reaching out once to touch a table then retracting her hand, like a stricken snail's eye.

I drive up through Llansteffan: the small houses, grey and pastel, the tiny roads and their thick fringing of trees. I can feel the layers of memories accumulated over the land, the edges and surfaces of things wavering in time. There is Mrs Edwards's shop, the spot where I first saw Maria, the road Theo, Sebastian and I used to walk down. Then the beach rolls out below me; at the same time the cream half-moon where we made sandcastles, and the flickering dark flat, sweeping out beyond our fire. The sea is the blazing tide in the peak of the sun, grey and rainy, a black night sea, pale and periwinkle in the light of the morning. Finally I pass under the arched trees up the hill, the light darting through the branches and hitting the car window like arrows. I slow down slightly, delaying the turn in the road, but the trees are swinging out before me already, and then Evendon comes into view.

The house seems bigger, harder in its chequered grey and white; its windows blurs of reflective anonymity. The sun glances off the dark roof, having tracked its usual path over the house since morning, leaving the front in shadow. There are no cars in the drive except mine, which I realise I have just parked in its usual place, under a sycamore, pulling up there without even thinking about it.

I get out and stand by the car for a moment, looking up at the house and the large, square shape of shade it casts onto the gravel, the impermeable windows, the six stone steps up to the door, the clematis above the portico, dripping its heavy perfume. As I loiter, the door suddenly opens, and I have to hastily go over so that the housekeeper – Carmen, presumably – can show me in. She is shy, and is grateful when I tell her I can make my own way to the gardens.

When she leaves I stand by myself in the empty white hall, which gives no indication of being the scene of the dramatic death of George Bennett. The pillars seem thinner, stripped down, like two candles for a vigil. The small rosewood table with the telephone is gone, the bowls of lilies at the foot of the stairs. The rest of the hall is the same, the marble floor, the tall windows, filled again with silence, the glacial haze of desertion.

I don't take the opportunity to nose around; I pass through only a few rooms towards the terrace, same-shaped spaces that have become unfamiliar. The morning room is no longer red; there are no gold elephants, no Persian carpets. It is papered a chilly, dusty blue, with some pastel flowered rugs, an immense television on the wall, a couple of modern sofas like slabs of marshmallow. The dining room is presided over by a large photograph of the Kings, posing with two children and a boss-eyed cocker spaniel; a long reproduction mahogany table has been installed in place of the Georgian original. I see through a doorway the beginnings of the gold parlour, which now holds a pool table.

I have the feeling that the Kings, once they bought Evendon, realised they didn't know exactly what to do with it. The rooms are only half-heartedly furnished, their prosaic furniture scattered across the space like cargo after a shipwreck. In the time of Eve, the house was filled with collected light; it had an overt, watchful beauty. Now it is cool and gloomy, like a closed-down store. I thought that seeing it this way would have been satisfying, or painful, but it's neither, it's nothing. Evendon feels like what it is – someone else's house.

I step outside into the sun, its incandescence closing over me, forcing me to squint. Then the gardens slowly re-form in my vision, perfect and unchanged. The wide smooth stones of the terrace, where Alicia's roses are in flower, the neat herb garden. The lawn, banked with magnolias and beeches, bright rather than deep green, recently cut. The sky is fluorescent blue in between the leaves of the oaks that stand at the edge of the lawn nearest me, a cloudless, dreamlike colour. It is extremely quiet now that it is the end of the summer. There is a clarity to the heat, to the day, as if the fitful, humid fever of the last few months has collected and distilled.

In the still suspension the garden stops, becoming what it once was. There, a swan from the lake walking obstinately round the topiary patterns. The cook smoking a cigarette in the herb garden. The glass of gin and tonic sitting next to a large white umbrella on the terrace, the tennis balls scattering the well-kept court. The girl lying in the shade under a tree, her bright hair in her eyes, making daisy chains and drinking wine from the bottle. In the earth between the flagstones of the terrace, the wink of gold-leafed crystal. The woman's voice, like dark water, talking on the telephone.

The past isn't a story. It isn't Eve's story or my story. It is not linear, it is not fixed. The past is an unknown pool, its cool brim the border where memory begins. It ripples as the light changes; it is cohesive, a different substance to the present; it cannot be breathed. You can't tell it: whatever you repeat is not the truth, because it is not complete. All you can do is stare into the water, and try to see as much as you can.

I walk out onto the open slope, down towards the trees, until I reach the edge of the lawn, stopping where the path used to start, where the light shivers and breaks into pieces of shadow against the shifting lace of the tall brambles. It's a place no one knows about now, grown over, boarded up with long grass.

I know that if I walk to the water there will be no witch, no spell, no face appearing from the trees. It is not the ghost that holds me back; it is the absence of ghosts. I stand there a little longer, and then I turn back, and walk away across the grass, back through the hall and out of Evendon. As I pull away, the reflected house shimmers small in the car window like a television image, then blinks out.

I thought I had left something there, but I was wrong. Evendon is empty; it is windows and bricks, dust and fingerprints. She is not in the gold parlour on the cushions, not lying on the grass, not wreathed and still in the water. She is not part of a story. She is the other half; one awake, one dreaming in the young night. She is with me, just like always.